RABBIT

GHOST

RED RABBIT GHOST

JEN JULIAN

RUN FOR IT

Copyright © 2025 by Jennifer Nicole Julian
Excerpt from *The Black Hunger* copyright © 2024 by Nicholas Pullen

Cover design by Lisa Marie Pompilio
Cover images by Shutterstock
Cover copyright © 2025 by Hachette Book Group, Inc.
Author photograph by Phil Julian

Run For It
Hachette Book Group
1290 Avenue of the Americas
New York, NY 10104
hachettebookgroup.com

First Edition: July 2025

Run For It is an imprint of Orbit, a division of Hachette Book Group.
The Run For It name and logo are registered trademarks of Hachette Book Group, Inc.

The publisher is not responsible for websites (or their content) that are not owned by the publisher.

The Hachette Speakers Bureau provides a wide range of authors for speaking events. To find out more, go to hachettespeakersbureau.com or email HachetteSpeakers@hbgusa.com.

Run For It books may be purchased in bulk for business, educational, or promotional use. For information, please contact your local bookseller or the Hachette Book Group Special Markets Department at special.markets@hbgusa.com.

Library of Congress Cataloging-in-Publication Data
Names: Julian, Jen, author.
Title: Red rabbit ghost / Jen Julian.
Description: First edition. | New York, NY : Run For It, 2025.
Identifiers: LCCN 2024055067 | ISBN 9780316580564 (trade paperback) |
    ISBN 9780316580571 (ebook)
Subjects: LCGFT: Novels.
Classification: LCC PS3610.U53437 R43 2025 | DDC 813/.6—dc23/
    eng/20241121
LC record available at https://lccn.loc.gov/2024055067

ISBNs: 9780316580564 (trade paperback), 9780316580571 (ebook)

Printed in the United States of America

LSC-C

Printing 1, 2025

For Goldsboro and everyone I knew there

We're each of us alone, to be sure. What can you do but hold your hand out in the dark?

—Ursula K. Le Guin

1

Jesse keeps his dead mother's things in an old Tarbarrel tin. Pork jerky smell, black pepper and molasses, contained alongside photographs. His mother's senior yearbook picture—her sharp, toothy grin. A Polaroid of her and Aunt Nancy toilet-papering the Confederate Memorial in downtown Blacknot. Nancy was seventeen then, his mother nine, both dressed in bell sleeves and fringe like it was still the 60s, though the Polaroid was taken by Jesse's grandmother in 1982. On the back, an inscription: *Nancy Jane & Constance Louise, getting in trouble.*

Also inside the tin: twelve postcards addressed to Nancy while she was in graduate school, messages in his mother's affected teenage voice—*If you find a man in the Queen City, bring him home so that we might sacrifice him to the swamp gods and ensure the harvest.*

Also: one bracelet of black wooden beads, which he guesses his mother must have worn.

Also: a series of articles from the paper about how they

found her, dead, on the banks of the Miskwa River eighteen summers ago, and a small notebook of inscrutable thoughts, facts, and fantasies (Jesse couldn't remember his mother, so he resorted to inventing details), which he wrote when he was a kid. *River highest since 1980—average water temp 71°—she had black hair, pretty face, archy eyebrows—5 foot 1—shoe size 6 1/2, bad at singing—loved* Wizard of Oz, X-Files, *will-o'-the-wisp, animals—spoke French* and *Spanish—laughed at weird stuff like ghosts—smelled like cinnamon, fixed eggs better than Nancy, came home from work wearing costumes, played chess—*

And so on.

There are many things the tin does not include. According to Nancy, Connie burned a lot of keepsakes and photos in the years leading up to the final breakdown that killed her, including pictures of her and Jesse together. That is his least favorite detail about her, aside from being dead.

Remarkably, he didn't take the tin with him to college. When he packed last August, he decided to leave it right there on the upper shelf of his closet, its time-honored home. Now, after driving back the four hours from Greensboro, he finds that Nancy has used his monthslong absence as an excuse to pack up his bedroom to turn it into an office/meditation studio. All his posters and books and old school projects are stuffed away in boxes, the walls now hung with calming beach photographs, the closet clean of his baggy high school clothes and red Miskwa High sweatshirts.

And the tin, which is not where he left it.

"Where'd you put it?" he asks Nancy, trying not to panic.

His aunt stands in the doorway, looking sheepish. "I mean."

She gestures to the boxes. "I put away a lot of shit, hon. It's probably here."

"Probably?"

"I did throw some things out. Your old running shoes were biohazards. What did the tin look like?"

"Like a *tin*," he says. "It looked like a tin. Red. A red tin. It had the Tarbarrel logo on it. It had—all her stuff was in there."

"Her stuff?" Nancy says.

Jesse dives into the boxes. Some are open, some already taped shut. His aunt knows what he's talking about, of course, but in the face of his alarm, she stands calm. Or at least pretends to.

"I'm sure it's here somewhere."

On principle alone, he doesn't like that she's done this, just crunched down and packed away his entire childhood like a whole lot of junk. Trophies for cross-country crammed in with mix CDs, the complete films of Bogart and Bacall. In one box, he finds the many amusing pulp fiction book covers he hunted down in flea markets all over the county, then, digging deeper, a glass hand pipe containing the charred residue of some backwater ditch weed. He bristles at the thought of Nancy finding it. Sure, they used to sing along to Peter Tosh's *Legalize It* on car trips, but that doesn't mean he wants her to have a firsthand view of his indiscretions.

But then, maybe the invasiveness was the point. Maybe her whole meditation studio plan was just an excuse to go through his stuff, to try to understand him one last time, unravel his secrets, account for his high school misery.

"Oh, stop being so *frantic*," she says. "I'll help you."

"Don't!" he says. "Please, don't touch anything else. I'll find it myself."

"But you *know* I wouldn't have thrown that out."

"You just said maybe you did."

She laughs. Her expression is becoming strained.

"But I didn't trash anything *important*, sweetheart. Do you really think I'd just throw out—*that?*"

"Connie's things," he says. "My mother's things."

There's no official moratorium on mentioning his mother's name, though he realizes it's been a long time since it was uttered aloud in this house. Nancy steps back, no longer smiling. Her face flushes with indignation.

After a minute, she says, "You know, you've caught me off guard, Jesse, just being here. You insisted you were staying out in Greensboro for the summer. Since November, that's been your plan, right? Get a job, get an apartment. What happened?"

He can't even tell if she's happy to see him. Sure, when he first got in, she rushed out to the driveway to meet him, and when Dick, his red 1998 hatchback, let out its usual tricky sputter, she laughed and said, "Now, *there's* a sweet sound." All the neighbors must've heard it, too. Must've thought, *Oh, that's Jesse Calloway. Antsy Nancy's boy. He's back from college, finally.* Because he didn't come back for Thanksgiving, Christmas, or Easter. Nancy, who taught film and public speaking at the community college in Kneesville, had all the same breaks he did, so each time she'd drive out to see him, and they'd stay with Minerva, her old roommate from grad school, a silver-haired lesbian. And during every visit, Nancy praised the "culture" of the city (i.e., Greensboro) in comparison to the hick trashfire of Miskwa County, and then she drank too much wine and said she would be happy enough to see Jesse survive his freshman year without alcohol poisoning or gonorrhea, which he guessed was meant to take the pressure off or something. But in all that, there was never any talk of Jesse returning home. Nancy took him at his word.

"The plan," he says to her, "changed."

"It changed," she says. "What changed? You were *adamant* about not coming back here."

He rips up packing tape in snaky strips, one box after another.

"What *changed*?" she asks again.

He finds a plastic bin of photos: Jesse and Nancy at the carnivorous plant garden in Wilmington, another one of him and his grandfather at the Fort Fisher Aquarium, then a few with his former high school friends in their ninth-grade Halloween costumes, grins with retainer wires.

"I wanted to see friends," he says.

"Which friends?" asks Nancy.

"'Which friends?' Why does that matter?"

"Because. Some of your friends have a history of getting you in trouble."

He laughs. "Well, there you go. You got me. I drove four hours to get lit at some redneck barn party. Nothing like the *scene* in metropolitan Blacknot. Endless ragers. Orgies day and night."

Nancy's flush deepens.

"You had a plan," she says firmly. "You changed your mind so fast, that's all I'm saying."

"For all you know, I've been thinking about it for weeks. And anyway, that's got nothing to do with you culling out my shit without asking."

"Oh, Jesse, stop it. Just stop. I didn't—do you seriously think I'd do that on purpose, throw out those things, my *sister's* things...?"

She trails off, her voice breaking. Tears fog up her glasses.

Little fucker, says a voice in Jesse's head. First night home, and you have lied to Nancy and made her cry. Fine work.

"I didn't say you'd do it on purpose," he says, trying to be nicer. "It's fine. It's got to be here somewhere."

"I mean," she says tearfully, "you didn't even take it *with* you. How was I supposed to know?"

In hindsight, yes, maybe the tin would've been safer if he'd brought it with him to college. But he never missed it there. Until a month ago, he was hardly thinking about Connie Calloway at all. Back at school, he was an actual adult, savvy and queer and experienced. He got props for liking David Lynch and owning a discontinued car. It's 2015 and the 90s are cool again. Everything comes back around. Everything reincarnates.

That's what changing your life is like, he assumes: a reincarnation.

Nancy lifts her glasses, squeezes her fingers against her eyes. "I didn't throw it out, I didn't," she keeps saying. "At least, I don't think I did."

And he keeps saying, "It's okay, it's okay, I'm sure you didn't," though really, he just wants to find the damn thing so they can stop talking about it and she can stop crying.

Then, finally, hiding under a pile of Dashiell Hammett novels, there it is. The Tarbarrel mascot—a rosy-cheeked cartoon pig—beams goofily at him from the tin's candy-red lid. He takes a breath.

"It's there?" Nancy asks.

"It's here."

"Good." She leaves the room, swiping at her tears and muttering, "Came all the way back here to fucking worry me."

Sometimes, Nancy takes Jesse's bad decision-making personally, and that is not his fault.

What did she say back in August when she took his shoulders in the campus courtyard? She was crying then, too, their clothes damp with sweat from carrying his stuff upstairs in an elevator-less dorm. She hugged him like he belonged to her, a compact little yin-yang, light and dark. Nancy is honey haired and pink faced, and Jesse inherited his mother's wiry dark curls and brown eyes and sandy-brown skin. But they shared a cringey optimism there, in that courtyard.

"I knew you'd get out of there," she said. "You are going to kick the shit out of this place. You're smart. You bounce back. You always have." Something like that. He remembers looking around at everyone else squirming in the face of similar talks from parents, grandparents, siblings. Everyone is tough. Everyone is the most genius genius.

"I'm just lucky," he told Nancy.

"You're *not* just lucky," she said. "You'll show them. You're *resilient.*"

Then the fearsome Minerva swung back around in her SUV, driving without patience (she and her ex-wife had already seen their two children off to college), and she loaded up Nancy and the empty dolly and the bungee cords, and then, with a kiss and a blink, his aunt disappeared into the shaky summer heat.

Jesse was relieved to see her go. He carried his last box up to his room, a care package Nancy assembled: rolls of quarters, double-ply toilet paper, condoms (*I know you can get these at the health center*, she wrote in a mortifying note, *but still*). He met his roommate, a kid from Cary who introduced himself with a strong handshake, as if they were making a business deal: "Alex Khan. Poli-sci."

"Jesse Calloway," Jesse said. "Undeclared."

"You on Wipixx?"

Wipixx was a social media app Jesse had never heard of, so he didn't understand the question. At the time, he assumed Alex could discern immediately that he was a backwoods clown from a trashfire county.

"I'm sorry, man," he said. "Did you just ask me if I'm *on whippets*?"

Reincarnation indeed.

Jesse reclaims his room. He takes down Nancy's tranquil photos. Goodbye, sand dunes and softly waving seagrass. He tapes up all his pulp book covers in their place. There are at least forty of them, an impressive collection. However, when he steps back to admire them, he's disheartened to see that they don't look as cool or eclectic as he remembers. They look like a mess.

As he rearranges them, trying in vain to make them more aesthetically pleasing, Nancy sticks her head in the doorway.

"Did you even eat dinner?" she asks sharply. "You're like a rail."

He looks at her, startled. "I had something on the road."

"Well, if you get hungry, you know, there's a chess pie in the fridge. That's still your favorite, right?"

Jesse feels suddenly ashamed of himself.

Later, when he goes to the kitchen, he finds the pie in the fridge: a pristine golden disc of butter and sugar. He's not hungry, but he takes the pie out and stands in the kitchen doorway with it, fork in hand.

Nancy is grading finals in the den. The local news plays on mute. The windows are open to the night air of late spring, filling the room with an eggy smell. Nancy notices him standing there, sets aside her papers, and holds out an arm. He comes to sit by her.

"Sorry," he says.

"Same," she says. "I shouldn't have gone through your stuff without asking."

On the news, a young teacher leads a camera crew around his old elementary school. The hallway is lined with scribbly drawings of animals. Jesse experiences a wave of nostalgia. He pokes the chess pie with his fork.

"I know you can't help it," he says, "but you don't need to worry. I won't go anywhere near Pinewood. I promise."

"Hmm," Nancy says. "Thing is, sweetheart, it's Blacknot." She pronounces it the way the old locals do, like Black-*nut*. "If you're here, you're near everything."

Jesse shrugs and looks down at the pie in his lap. He begins to eat it, so sweet it feels like it's burning his tongue.

"You're not going to cut a piece?" says Nancy. "You're just going to eat it like that, like a monster?"

He licks the fork. "Uh-huh."

She digs in herself, and they sit like that for a while, trading the fork back and forth until there's a huge hole in the pie, as if an alien burst out of it. Jesse stares at the hole. Already, his stomach is telling him this was a mistake.

"Of course," Nancy says, "I'm happy you're here. Stay as long as you need."

"Thank you. I know."

"But you should know you won't find a job. Merle hired out your spot at the diner."

"I won't be here long enough to get a job. A couple days, tops."

She reaches out and brushes the hair off his forehead. "This new haircut...I don't know about this haircut. It's a little hipster-y."

He bats her hand away. "No, it isn't."

"What do you think they'll say about you when you're waltzing around downtown Blacknot looking like this?"

"They'll say, 'That kid has his shit together.' I mean, come on, I cleaned off the nail polish. What's the issue?"

She squeezes his cheek. "I just want you to be careful."

"I will, I will. Don't fuss."

He can see in her face that she doubts him; not that he's lying, but that he's making a promise he can't keep. This is often the soul of her doubt, and the soul of his deceit. He believes wholeheartedly any promise he makes to anyone, every time.

He goes to bed early that night. The drive wore him out, he says. By three AM, he's wide awake, listening to Nancy's snores on the other side of the house and staring once again at the collage of book covers on his wall. They're almost disturbing to him now; why is that? He lights a candle. His room is dark and hot. Most of these he didn't even find himself, actually. The best ones—*Alligator-Women from the Swamp Planet*, which features the tagline "They're here...and they're *horny!*" and *Attack of the Mutant Mushrooms*, in which the monsters resemble dildos—those were gifts from Harlan. Thrifting is one of few gay activities a closeted man can enjoy in this county.

If Jesse wanted to, he could find other pieces of Harlan all around the room. A pair of jeans, pierced in the crotch by a spring in Harlan's couch. A Union army coat button, which Harlan's uncle found at the battlefield over in Kinston. But only Jesse would know the significance of these things; Nancy wouldn't be able to pick them out.

God help him if she could.

But he's not here for this. He doesn't need this collection. He's not a fucking kid anymore. His aunt's impulse to cull, he feels it, too—though in a different, more volatile way. One by one, he tears the book covers away and takes them down the hall to the bathroom. There, he begins to burn them in the sink. The Alligator-Women curl up and turn black; the Mutant Mushrooms shrivel. The fire flares up unexpectedly and nearly catches the hand towel, and he is forced to open the bathroom window and let the smoke out into the night—

Whoosh. A flood of swamp stench hits him hard in the face. Low tide and hog farm. Confederate jasmine. Stale hot air. The assault seems personal, like this place has been waiting for him. Like it *sees* him. He never wanted to come back here. This stinking, suffocating place.

A rising wave of sugar burns the back of his throat. He leans over the toilet, and it comes up fast. A full-body retching. An exorcism.

That's a bad sign. A terrible idea all around, this trip. But then he returns to his room, drained and shaky, and he sees his phone lit up on the bedside table.

A Wipixx message from Cat:

> *Welcome home*
> *You want still pictures of your mother?*

His heart hammers. This. This is what he's here for.

> *Yes*
> *Please*

> *Tomorrow come town to bridge 9am*
> *Tell no one*

2

On Sunday, in church, Alice stands next to her stepmother, whose impressive lyric soprano rings in her ear like clover flowers. In all of Alice's eighteen years on this earth, this may be the only thing she has ever found impressive about Bobbie Swink.

Would you be free from the burden of sin? There's power in the blood, power in the blood. Would you o'er evil a victory win? There's wonderful power in the blood.

The congregation is especially sleepy this week, which lets Bobbie's voice rise to the rafters. Alice looks over her shoulder at a row of youth group kids who have been prodded to church by their parents, shadow-eyed faces dripping with hangover sweat. There was a party last night somewhere in town.

There is power, power, wonder-working power—in the precious blood of the Lamb.

Two verses later, Bobbie pokes Alice's arm. She takes a break between "sin stains are lost" and "life-giving flow" to hiss through her teeth—"Sing!"—but Alice shakes her hand away and stares straight ahead at the pipe organ and the strident bouquet of lilies on the altar. Bobbie wants Alice to take part in something, to blend in. Which Bobbie herself would like to do. Pastor Moseley once asked her why she didn't sing in the choir, and Bobbie, with an earnest modesty that made Alice cringe, insisted she couldn't carry a tune to save her life. "I would die of embarrassment," she said.

Eventually, Alice feels the gaze of her father, who's standing as an usher in the side aisle. She looks at him dead-on. Compared to the other patriarchs, Euel is scruffy in his wrinkled linen dress shirt, mustache untamed, hair loose and floppy on his forehead. He lowers his chin, raising his two salt-and-pepper eyebrows as if he knows exactly what's unfolding in her brain, as if he is asking her outright: *This is the hill you're gonna die on?*

Alice sucks in a breath, and as the congregation approaches the last refrain, she belts out the words, flat and heavy as a falling brick—"IN THE PRECIOUS BLOOD OF THE LAMB."

Bobbie grips her arm, digs her nails in.

"Beautiful, y'all," says Pastor Moseley. "Couldn't've sung it better myself. Praise be to God."

The congregation replies in dreary unison: "Praise be to God."

They sit. Alice looks at the indentations of Bobbie's nails on her arm, then at Euel. She sees his cryptic smile, the slow shake of his head. Eyes burn into her back; she can feel them. But when she turns to look, most of the congregation appears not to have noticed her outburst. In fact, there is only one pair of eyes staring from the far back corner of the sanctuary where the

Taylor family sits, Bill and Val and their pretty sixteen-year-old daughter, Morgan. The parents exhibit the stiff, bourgeois dryness typical of Alice's neighbors, but Morgan looks like many of the other youth group kids: slouched, sweaty, likely recovering from the Dixie bacchanal that's still in her bloodstream. She's glaring at Alice, mouth slightly open, an expression that hovers somewhere between puzzlement and scorn.

Alice turns away. For all she knows, Morgan is still drunk, agonized by the wail of the organ. Alice has been told she shouldn't drink at all because of the medications she's been taking, but even so, she knows if she ever went to a high school party—she would not; no one would invite her; no one would have the opportunity to—if such a thing ever happened, she would find it deeply unproductive. Without a doubt, an *ordinary* kind of rebellion.

She stays quiet until the end of the service, when the congregation parades out onto downtown Main Street, all quaint and sunny and lined with skinny, wire-bound oaks, new sidewalks filled with glittery mica. Pastor Moseley stands in the narthex, shaking hands. When Alice comes through the line, he bows his head to her.

"Mighty strong voice today, Alice Catherine," he says.

"Thank you," she says flatly. "I was moved."

Pastor Moseley laughs. Behind them, Alice can hear Bobbie thrumming with embarrassment.

"Nothing wrong with that," he says. "Always best to let the Spirit dictate your volume."

On the sidewalk, Bobbie whispers in her ear, "Why do you needle me so?"

"You told me to sing," Alice says.

"Oh, heavens, Alice. Be serious." She cranes her neck in search of Euel, but he's already gotten caught up in a conversation with Councilman Bale, his wife, Ouida, and chatty, doll-faced Mrs. Moseley. Bobbie watches the group nervously, gripping and un-gripping her fingers.

"I told him he couldn't go and chat forever like he usually does," she says. "You've got your appointment at one thirty."

"There's plenty of time," Alice says. But Bobbie is already trying to slide her way into Euel's conversation, laughing at someone's joke, tapping at Euel's arm. Alice stays where she is, lest she feel compelled to needle Bobbie more.

That's when Morgan Taylor pops out of nowhere.

"Hey, girl!" she chirps, leaning close into Alice's periphery. "Hi."

Alice steps back.

"Oh. Sorry. Didn't mean to scare you."

The girl is giving her a very odd, strained smile. In the glare of the sun, she seems even more wilted, eyes raccooned, pit stains spreading on her seersucker dress. She wipes her arm across her forehead.

"It's hot. You don't have a tissue or anything, do you? There's sweat in my eyes."

"I don't." Alice looks around. Where did the parents go? "Sorry."

Morgan fans herself with the church bulletin. "You're lucky. You look like you don't sweat at all."

"I guess."

"All graceful. All tall and stuff. How tall are you?"

Alice looks down at Morgan's sweaty ash-blond head. She is tall, it's true. But she has never been graceful. Before Euel took her out of grade school, the kids had called her Frankenberry because she walked with a forward lurch and hunched her shoulders. Spooky Alice with her strange, sallow complexion, and her huge eyes, so dark they look black, and her hair, kinked and coarse in a way that always stressed Bobbie—*Hair with personality*, she used to say. Her face, she's been told, is without personality, as blank as a glass of water.

No one would call Alice graceful unless they were flattering her. And now, going from what Alice knows about Morgan Taylor—an average, affluent, Southern American teen—and what she assumes Morgan Taylor has heard about her, she is right to suspect an ulterior motive to this conversation.

"Well, never mind," Morgan says. "Hey—you know you're only a couple houses down from me, right?"

"Yes. I know."

"Remember when you used to come over to our house to play with my sister and me? Lauren had a game where we all pretended we found a portal to this other world? And Lauren became a sorceress and I became a magic horse?"

Alice looks toward her father, chatting now with Pastor Moseley, who has slipped quite naturally into the conversation. They look like they're making plans.

"I don't know why I was thinking about that lately," says Morgan. "How've you been?"

"Sedated," says Alice.

Morgan's first response is to laugh, but then she seems to remember that two summers ago Alice *was* spending four months as an inpatient at Croatan Psychiatric Hospital. A silence passes. When Morgan speaks again, her voice is awkward and apologetic.

"It's—it's just like the song, you know. 'Twenty twenty twenty-four hours to go-oh…'"

"I think I should head on," Alice says, pointing nowhere.

"Oh. Sure, right. Catch up soon, maybe?"

Alice lurches her way over to Euel.

Her father extends his arm, drawing her in between him and Bobbie. "Alice Catherine," he says. "If we invite these rowdy folks over to the house tomorrow evening, will you play for them? I've been telling them how you're killing Debussy and you need a chance to show off." He pulls Alice deeper into the circle, letting the Bales and the Moseleys have a good look at her. "She's incredible, friends. She'll send you to a new plane of existence."

Alice would like to not be in this circle. She's starting to think she would rather take her chances with Morgan.

"I'm not any good with Debussy yet," she says.

"Like hell you're not any good. You're a demon on that harp. One thing, though—" Euel holds up his finger to the group. "They only get a performance if they behave."

"If *who* behaves?" says Pastor Moseley. "In front of my own church, you tell me to behave?"

"Just don't give him any rum," says Mrs. Moseley.

"And I'll drink whatever rum you don't give him," says Ouida Bale.

Their swell of laughter shakes Alice's brain. Over Ouida's shoulder, she can still see Morgan standing there on the sidewalk, looking at her. Then she slowly wanders off, and Alice wonders if she dodged that conversation too quickly. What was that about? What did that girl want? Girls like Morgan never had any interest in Alice, just as Alice had no interest in them.

So much has happened between now and those school days when Alice used to play with other kids, before her isolated homeschooling era. She barely remembers Morgan or her sister or their games. Recently, she overheard a conversation between Bobbie and Mrs. Taylor about how Morgan has "come out of her shell" in the past couple years, as if introverts were invertebrates. What they really mean is that Morgan is a girl who has figured out the rules regarding her volume: Don't be a drip, but don't be a loudmouth either.

Alice feels her stepmother beside her, an anxious, coiling spring. She reaches over Alice to pat her husband's arm.

"We should go if we want time to grab lunch."

Euel looks at his watch. "Ah. You're right." He waves broadly to his circle of folks. "Let's say six tomorrow? Six is good for everybody?"

Nods and affirmations. They all disperse cordially.

On the way to the car, Euel whispers to Alice:

"I thought we'd talked about going a little easy on Bobbie, hmm? Maybe give her some slack now and then?"

"I'm not any good with Debussy yet," Alice insists.

"You're not—aw, honey, they won't know the difference. Just do your best."

"I don't want to play."

He looks at her, their eyes level. She doesn't have his eyes, which are cheerful and blue, an unusual slate blue, the pupils surrounded by a ring of gold. Alice has wondered if that gold ring is why everyone finds her father so fucking charming.

"Yes, you do," he says. "You love playing more than anything."

Two hours later, she's sitting in her therapist's office at the New Bridges Counseling & Wellness Center in South Greene. Her therapist's name, for whatever reason, she can never remember. Kayla or Marla, or maybe Wendy. Alice turns a small black stone over and over in her hand. She stole the stone from the bowl-shaped fountain in the corner of the room and takes pleasure that the therapist doesn't notice.

It's not that she hates the therapist. The therapist tries. She lights her office with dim pink salt lamps and flameless candles, and the burbling fountain does put Alice in a calm state, as she assumes it's supposed to. The therapist is young and sweet-faced, and when she speaks, the confident positivity in her voice is so sincere it's genuinely affecting. Whenever Alice is in the room with her, she thinks, *Yes; maybe I* could *set reasonable goals for myself. Become less angry. More logical.*

"He told me to play for his friends again."

"Did that make you anxious?" asks the therapist.

Alice looks down at her hands and the stone hidden inside them. She shrugs.

"You've said you're uncomfortable playing for your father's friends. Why?"

Alice reflects on that a moment and says, "You know the story of the Pied Piper? Where he lures out the children? Playing for his friends makes me feel like the pipe."

"You feel like he's using you," the therapist observes.

"I do. Yeah."

"But in this scenario," the therapist goes on, "*you're* the one playing the instrument. Not your father."

She tilts her head, as if waiting for a reply, but Alice stays quiet.

"I remember a few sessions back," the therapist says, "you talked about how you sometimes frame your life as a fairy tale. Cinderella and her evil stepmother, Snow White, Sleeping Beauty. Now you're a pipe, an instrument. What links these? What did we talk about?"

The stone in her hand responds, a warm vibration.

"Agency," says Alice.

The therapist taps her pen, preparing to say something Alice knows she has said before. "Remember, if your father, or *anyone*, asks something of you, you're going to feel whatever you're going to feel about it, whether that's pressure or resentment or anger. The trick is to *choose* to deal with those feelings productively, to communicate them. Otherwise, they build up."

Sometimes, Alice can successfully convince herself that this is, in fact, her only problem. She is not good at managing her *feelings*.

It's a useful thought for today's session. Eventually, they move on from the issue of playing for her father's friends and dig back into Alice's past, when she ends up talking at length about the incident at Calvary Academy, third grade, when her teacher called her a liar, and she bit the woman's wrist so hard she damaged a ligament. Nine stitches. Alice can still remember the taste of blood in her mouth, how it felt like victory when Euel pulled her out of school. Just private tutors since then, and whatever Bobbie, a former middle school math teacher, could manage to stuff in her brain. Alice has an active mind, so she's been told. If she wants to learn something, she fixates on it until the learning is complete. But when it came to assimilating her with other kids, Euel posited that it was fine if Alice preferred being by herself—"All the great geniuses were mavericks," and so on—and Bobbie, though desperate for her to be "normal," was too ashamed to keep pushing all those ill-fated playdates with other homeschooled children. In fact, though she is now eighteen, playing pretend with Morgan and her sister was probably the last time Alice had what could be called friends.

"Nine stitches is an awful lot of anger," the therapist says. "You don't remember what you were accused of lying about?"

"No," Alice says, but that's not true. She remembers exactly. "It's all a haze. That was less than a month after my mother—after she left."

The therapist jumps on that, this easy explanation for the crippling of Alice's emotional and social state of being. She writes mysteriously and energetically on her legal pad, single words, Alice imagines, with a half dozen exclamation points. *Progress!!!!!! Coping!!!!!!* The therapist is a person who gets excited about moving past things.

Sometimes, she'll mention a goal: college, some big future career—Juilliard even! The possibilities!—as if all these things could be delivered at Alice's will. As if the psychiatrist at Croatan had not told her father that she wasn't stable enough for college, not anytime soon.

"Just keep in mind," the therapist tells her, "don't be down on yourself for being where you are. Don't worry about where other people are. You're in a safe space. You're talented. You're building boundaries between yourself and your parents. You have your library job. You are sorting things out, and that's exactly what you're meant to be doing."

This is exactly what I'm meant to be doing.

Then, as usual, she sets one foot outside the therapist's office, and her optimism dissolves.

Everything she left out of their discussion creeps back. She forgets to check the placard by the door to remind herself what the therapist's name is, and she begins to wonder again whose lucky tit her father pulled to schedule therapy appointments on Sundays. Now she's in the parking lot, fuming, and Tanisha Patton, Euel's beautiful, smartly dressed assistant, is already pulling up in her silver sedan. Agency. Alice weighs the word in her mind. What does anybody know about agency?

She gets in the car, still holding the stone she snatched from the fountain.

"How'd therapy go?" Mrs. Patton asks, and Alice answers automatically—"Fine"—while worrying the stone with her thumb.

Mrs. Patton side-eyes her. "What's that? A charm?"

"Just a stone."

"Onyx?"

"Could be." Alice looks at it, so shiny she can see a tiny reflection of herself. "I stole it from in there."

"Hmm," says Mrs. Patton. She turns west out of the parking lot and takes the long way back to Euel's house on Eden Circle, past the golf course, intermittent patches of swamp, a series of strip malls. They listen to Prince, an old CD Mrs. Patton has been playing in her car for months.

"So kleptomania's one of your things?" she asks.

"Not if I don't get caught," says Alice.

Mrs. Patton looks amused, but she doesn't say anything. Prince is partying like it's 1999.

"Tanisha," says Alice. "Are you free tomorrow night? Euel's having some people over for dinner. Pastor Moseley and his wife. The Bales."

"Tomorrow," Mrs. Patton says. "Tomorrow's my birthday."

"All the more reason for you to come. We can celebrate."

She laughs. "Baby, there are plenty of folks I'd like to hang out with on my birthday, and they ain't it. You have fun, though."

Alice looks out the passenger window at the trees blurring by, squirmy black power lines snaking overhead.

"It's going to be terrible," she says.

For a while, they don't say anything to each other. Mrs. Patton's only gesture is to glance down and brush a bit of lint off her blazer. Deep, vivid aubergine. Church clothes, probably—though Mrs. Patton is always immaculately styled, to the point where it sometimes makes her uncomfortable to look at. Chic jewelry, towering heels, glossy black nails. Her hair is always shiny and expertly relaxed. She's been Euel's assistant for over a year now. Confident. Flawless.

"So," says Alice. "Did you get them?"

"I did," says Mrs. Patton. "And you've got cash?"

Alice digs in her shoulder bag and produces a roll of about

three hundred dollars. Some of it is her own, earned from the small paycheck she gets from working at the library. Some of it she sifted out of Bobbie's pocketbook or her father's wallet. Fives and tens here or there.

Mrs. Patton unrolls the money and counts it quickly in her lap while sitting at a stop sign. Then she produces a brown paper bag from her purse and hands it to Alice.

Inside is a clear packet filled with tick-size black kernels. Witchfingers. They're so light in Alice's hand it's like holding nothing.

"There aren't many here," she says.

"You didn't say you needed a ton," says Mrs. Patton. "Plus, they're a challenge to find."

Alice opens the bag and taps one of the kernels into her hand. She holds it gently between thumb and forefinger, tests its puffy stiffness, smells it. Rot sweet, almost fruity. She tries to listen but detects no sound, like the thing is frozen.

Mrs. Patton watches her out of the corner of her eye.

"There are stories about how they used to eat them," Alice says. "Just like this."

"Who did?"

"The Angel Battalion, that spiritualist cult I told you about, hit their height in the 1890s. They thought witchfingers gave them visions of the future."

Mrs. Patton looks alarmed. "You said you were just burying them."

"I know, but I might like some visions. I could enjoy seeing the future."

"Alice, they're not for eating. You'll be throwing up all night."

Alice opens her mouth wide and holds the kernel over her tongue. Mrs. Patton stops the car in the middle of the road so she can turn and look at Alice as she speaks.

"Listen up," she says. "I got you those because I trust you. Okay? I had to find my way to some shady backwoods dens to get them and I've got a lot more to lose than you do."

Alice lowers her hand and contritely puts the kernel back with the others. "I know."

"I'd lose my job, my two boys. They would put me in jail. I'd have to watch footage of their high school graduations from prison."

"I was only kidding," says Alice.

"Just making sure you knew."

"I said I knew." Alice puts the witchfingers in her shoulder bag. "I'm not going to eat them. It's for a ritual."

"So you said," Mrs. Patton says.

"But if I ever did eat them, I'd report back to you all the visions I had."

"Mm-hmm. Can't wait."

When they reach the Swink property, Mrs. Patton takes the gravel drive to the guesthouse, which Euel once used as a music room. Now it belongs to Alice. A big boxwood hedge shields it from the gaze of the main house, which gives her some privacy. She has her own kitchenette, her own stone veranda. From there, she can see the Miskwa River through a drooping canopy of live oaks.

Mrs. Patton looks out on this pretty spread with raised eyebrows, then looks at Alice as if to say, *See? See what you're risking? This nice bit of independence you've managed to get for yourself?* And Alice returns a look that's supposed to say, *Fuck you*, though with her expressionless face, who knows if Mrs. Patton picks up on it. Plus, it does no good for her to lash out at someone who's been helping her. (*Transference!!!!!!*)

"You can handle that fool dinner by yourself," Mrs. Patton says. "That's what I think."

"But it'll help to have someone there who's on my side."

"And what will I *do* there exactly? Pick up people's empty drink glasses? Help Bobbie carry out the crackers and the cheese log?"

"No," Alice says. "Bobbie would never serve a cheese log in springtime. Cheese logs are for the holidays."

"Well, see. I didn't even know that. I never know these things. My husband will have something put together for me."

"Please. I'm asking you. Please come."

At the sincerity of the plea, Mrs. Patton's face softens into pity. "Not making any promises."

She lets Alice out at the door. No sign of life in the main house, which means that Euel and Bobbie are still out, running errands, visiting with folks, schmoozing. She never knows why their schedule is always so packed.

All the better. She waves goodbye to Mrs. Patton, her sedan disappearing down the drive. The witchfingers are in her bag, the black stone in her fist.

It is onyx. She can tell. When she holds it to her ear, its latticed molecules chant darkly.

Ai—ai—ai—ai—ai

FROM THE NOTEBOOKS OF
KATRINA MORROW, SPRING 1994

June 12

Yellow flowering saltweed, versatile and not hard to find. Grows at Hook Bend and sounds like kittens crying. Practical purposes—analgesic, improves skin, gets rid of eye floaters, smells earthy and eggy, opens the heart up.

Love incantation—My heart is open. Fill me up with dirt and water, breath and blood.

3

In Miskwa County, when you say "town," as in, "I'm going *into town* for the farmers market," it's assumed you mean Blacknot, though there's a whole constellation of other little boroughs nearby—Pinewood, Apple Hill, Shy Creek, Vernontown, South Greene—with their own character and disproportionate sense of pride. Blacknot sits on the north bank of the Miskwa River. The bridge—Jesse knows only one that Cat could be talking about—runs a mile across marsh and river into South Greene, which exists solely because rich people in the 80s wanted to escape the stench of hog farms. Since Jesse was a kid, there's been an emphatic downtown Blacknot revitalization effort, an insistence that the town is charming, despite the smell.

"The farmers market?" Nancy says. She turns from the stove, where she's frying sausage patties. "I need goat cheese. Let me get out of my sweatpants and we'll go together."

"Don't rush," Jesse says. "I'm meeting up with some folks there. Jaelah and her cousin. The usual crew."

"Isn't it weird for you to be out of bed before noon?"

Jesse steals a sausage barehanded from the skillet. Nancy slaps at him—"Tch! That grease will burn you!"—but he has told his lie so naturally that she sends him off with some money to bring back the goat cheese himself. Truthfully, Jesse has no idea whether his former friends are home from college and wouldn't want to see them anyway, and by the time he gets to the rendezvous spot—the bridge, where he will finally meet Cat—he's forgotten he even mentioned them.

Jesse is familiar with the rendezvous spot. A trail winds away to his left through the marsh and along the river, past the radio station and the Walmart and the movie theater, past soybean fields and stretches of pinewoods, all the way back to the high school. He ran that trail for cross-country many times. A weatherworn bench stands at the trailhead, looking out over the water, the black pluff mud, the bright green lawns and white plantation-style houses of South Greene.

He can't sit down. He paces.

The day's heat rises. The spot under the bridge becomes an odorous oven of fishy concrete and fry grease from the waterfront restaurants. Up the path behind him, in Spartina Square, the Saturday farmers market is at a boil. Sweating families claim picnic spots on the lawn, their unleashed dogs nosing their way into people's crotches and ice cream cups. White tents line the walkways, tables filled with produce, summer sausage, shells painted like Santa Clauses. A high school girl sells food truck biscuits with fancy toppings—Gouda cheese, candied bacon.

An hour goes by like that.

Music begins to play from the pavilion. Local cover bands

typically exhibit their mediocre skills at the farmers market every Saturday, though this—the discordant pairing of banjo and synthesizer, the hum of a theremin—is not a Carolina beach jam. The noise makes Jesse nauseous.

Why is Cat so late? Why are they not responding to his messages?

Another twenty minutes pass, and he leaves the rendezvous spot to circle the park, hoping to find that Cat is watching him from afar. Won't do him any good; he doesn't know what they look like. And this is an ordinary Blacknot crowd anyway, filled with the same old faces. There's that history teacher who once threw a chair against the whiteboard and still kept his job somehow; and that freckly girl who was in her parents' furniture store commercials; and the First Baptist pastor taking a selfie with his uncannily beautiful wife.

Under the pavilion, among the three bandmates who are retuning their equipment, Jesse recognizes Idgy Sawyer, who graduated two years before him, dropped out of college, and has now found his passion in writing strange, sad music. His current band is called the Undead Corpse of the Confederacy. They are selling CDs at a table next to the driftwood vivariums, ten dollars, cash, check, or Venmo. The bandmates behind Idgy appear nervous to be there, as if they're not sure what to do with their instruments, and the audience, too, judging from the array of faces, is regretting this.

Jesse edges closer. He hears someone shout his name:

"Calloway!"

He should not be as surprised as he is to run into someone he knows so quickly. Morgan Taylor, rising high school senior, is coming toward him across the grass. He spies her parents over by the courthouse garden, chatting with the Baptist pastor. South Greene people. Republicans in pastel.

"You're in big trouble, Calloway," Morgan calls to him.

"Why's that, M?" he calls back.

Upon reaching him, she immediately begins fiddling with his clothes, his hair, his partially grown-out undercut. She pokes at the cartilage piercing one of his friends gave him back in March.

"Hey, ow!" Jesse cries, brushing her away. "That's still tender."

"What is all this?" she says, laughing. "New clothes, new hair. Like you're in disguise."

"Maybe I am," he says. "I'm on a mission."

"Oh, a *mission*? Is that why you came back to town after practically a whole year and didn't even bother to tell me?"

"It's a secret."

"Well, buddy, you better share it. That's the only way I'm letting you off the hook."

Jesse glances over her shoulder at the trailhead. In truth, he would like to find someone to tell his story to, how he decided to come back and why. Still, he's not sure Morgan is the right person. She is what they call a "spring senior"—precocious, boosted to kindergarten at a young age and now on track to graduate at seventeen. She and Jesse hooked up in the fall semester of his senior year, then several times throughout the spring and summer, and she was always good at keeping her own secrets—quick, clandestine meetups at friends' houses, in his car, in the abandoned dugout at the middle school; they got pretty creative. But he's always questioned how well she keeps the secrets of others.

Morgan notices his hesitation. She looks across the lawn to her parents, still talking with the pastor. "How 'bout you tell me later. What are you doing tonight?"

"I don't know," Jesse says. "Nothing."

"There's a get-together at the Koonces'. Your buddy Red is back in town house-sitting for his parents. You should come."

"A party?"

"It's not a party." Her smile intensifies, almost hungry. "Come out! Why come back if you're not gonna see people?"

"I don't know if I want to see people." He stuffs his hands in his pockets. "*Who's* going to be there?"

"Who? I don't know. It's a little get-together. Red's friends. My friends." She shrugs and smiles. "And *I'll* be there. Looking to have a little fun."

Now that Jesse has spent a year in college, Morgan's flirting is greener than he remembers. Sweet, but a little embarrassing.

"Aren't you seeing someone?" he asks. "Back in February, you posted something—"

"Are you talking about Greg Stubbs?"

"Yeah, Greg Stubbs. How's he?"

She throws her head back and groans. "Oh my god, Jesse. That boy didn't know how to do *anything*. I'm serious." She whispers in his ear, "He thought the clitoris was in the butt."

Jesse laughs. "You're so mean."

"It's not mean! It's only mean if it's not true. I think he watches a lot of porn. He kept asking to put his thing on my face. Like, slap it against my face! It was weird."

"You shouldn't be telling me this."

"Why not? You don't know Greg. Who's it hurt to tell you?"

Behind them, the Undead Corpse of the Confederacy finishes one song, then another. A theremin warbles over the park. Jesse knows what would happen if he went out to meet Morgan. The question is whether he would benefit from the distraction.

"Why do you keep looking at the bridge?" she asks him.

"What?" he says, turning back to her. "I'm not."

She smiles. On the other side of the lawn, her parents laugh loudly at one of the pastor's jokes. "You should come out," she says. "You look like you need it. Plan smart, huh? Come at nine, leave by midnight. Avoid Peach Hill."

"Peach Hill?" he says. "Oh—that big sinkhole is still in the road?"

"Sure is, friend."

"You'd think they'd have filled it in by now. It's been, like, two years."

"Well," she says. "That's Fucknut for you."

Morgan leaves him, rejoining her parents across the lawn. They seem to pretend as though she never left, and she, too, laughs at the pastor's joke, though she wasn't there to hear it. Jesse has realized that you can always tell someone is from South Greene by the way they laugh, a kind of restrained, performative chuckle, but he's never told Morgan this.

He returns to the trailhead. Over the next half hour, he listens to Idgy's band. For a coda, they do a cover of the Pixies' "Wave of Mutilation," the most upbeat song they've played so far, followed by a spate of polite but unconvincing applause. All the while, Jesse wonders bleakly if Cat could string him along another month or so. They could, if they said the right thing, schedule another two or three secret rendezvous and convince him they'd be there for sure this time. Go to this abandoned warehouse, Jesse. Go out to the swamp and dig a shallow grave.

He's about ready to leave when they finally send word.

> *What is problem?*
> *Did you find is what given?*

Cat. With their frank, weird, idiosyncratic grammar. He looks to either side of him as if Cat might suddenly appear. A speedboat zips by under the bridge, sloshing its wake on the bank. Is Cat on that boat? A shirtless jogger comes up the trail. Is that them?

> *I thought you'd be here*

> *No*
> *I left for you under the bench this morning*

Sure enough, when Jesse drops to his knees and scrounges, he finds a brown envelope taped to the underside of the bench. His hands tremble as he pries it away. He is shocked at Cat's carelessness.

> *This was not well thought out*
> *Anyone could have found it*

> *Yes but you have it now?*

He doesn't reply. He runs to his car and speeds home.

*   *   *

Contents of Cat's envelope: photocopies of an autopsy report, a half dozen pictures of the scene, and an article from *The Horn*, Sunday, June 7, 1998. Jesse keeps the same article in the Tarbarrel tin, though Cat has highlighted this one and marked it up with marginalia.

PINEWOOD WOMAN FOUND DEAD

The remains of twenty-four-year-old Pinewood resident Constance Calloway have been found on the banks of the Miskwa River a mile from her home, according to the Miskwa County Sheriff's Department. Ms. Calloway and her fifteen-month-old son were reported missing Thursday evening by Nancy Calloway, Ms. Calloway's sister. The child was found on the banks near his mother's body, unharmed.

56 Redbug Rd, demolished in 03—walked from there??

lost time, 35 hrs between disappearance and discovery

On Saturday, June 6, at approximately six AM, fisherman Harry Bishop heard a cry while boating downriver and drew close enough to observe the scene, at which point he extracted the child from the riverbank and notified authorities.

"I thought I was hearing a ghost," Bishop said. "I wasn't six feet away when I realized what I was looking at."

(Bishop = obsessiv archivist, but nothing in his memoir notes??)

Ms. Calloway is believed to have died

sometime between three and five A.M. She was employed as a receptionist at the Tarbarrel processing plant, though she had not reported for work in the three weeks prior to her death. Her son is currently in the custody of Nancy Calloway. Ms. Nancy Calloway declined to comment for this article.

(demoted, work record missing)

Sheriff Martina Hupp states that the cause of Ms. Calloway's death was "at this time not determined to be suspicious," however, she is unwilling to release specific details at this time. The Miskwa County Sheriff's Department is handling the investigation.

(LIES—could not handle a suitcase w/ all ten fingers)

Jesse sits on the floor of his bedroom, the Tarbarrel tin open next to him. Cat's handwriting is fascinating—small, cramped, delicate. Girl handwriting. He's been wondering about their gender since they contacted him a month ago.

Not that this has been his most pressing question.

The pictures interest him the most. Here is the marshy bank where Harry Bishop found him. Two numbered placards mark some fragment of unseen evidence. In another photo, a large stick stands upright in the mud. Objects are piled around it: vines, a hammer, a candle, a bowl filled with stones, feathers, buckeyes, the skull of a small animal. Patchy shadows hang in the background, along with what looks like a soiled white sheet. Though he looks at it for a long time, he can't make sense of it.

Okay, Cat
What is this picture with the sheet?

They're quick to reply. They've been waiting.

What sheet?

Jesse looks on the back, where Cat has numbered each photo.

Number 5 with the dirty sheet

There is no sheet.

He looks at the picture again. His vision goes dim at the edges. Cat is right. It's not a sheet. It's a body.

Nancy calls his name from somewhere in the house. Jesse stuffs the contents of Cat's envelope into the Tarbarrel tin and shoves it under the bed. He fears that the panic will be there on his face and that Nancy will see it, but as she opens his bedroom door he sinks out of his body and into a state of calm, like he's watching himself from under the floor.

"Did you get goat cheese?" she asks. "You forgot, didn't you?"

"Yeah. Sorry."

"What are you up to?"

"Just going through old stuff."

Connie, pale gray and in a fetal position, wrapped mummy-like in mud-stained pajamas.

"You want to talk about it?" Nancy asks.

He laughs. "Talk about what?"

She looks at him awhile longer, then drifts away down the hall. He gets up and closes the door behind her.

Hours go by. Midday light shifts over his bedroom as he studies the photos, trying to see past the web of black hair that hangs in his mother's face. She looks drowned, only she didn't drown; the autopsy report says heart failure. Elsewhere, the report notes signs of stress and poor nutrition—brittle hair, yellow nail beds. She weighed only eighty pounds. Her teeth had become fragile, her molars fractured. *Possible drug abuse,* says the autopsy. *Unclear.*

What has she done with this stick?

Can you understand?
You do not know what it means?

Why would he know what it means, aside from the obvious? He could tell from the way the family talked about his mother that she lost her mind. Nancy would share childhood postcards, but she wouldn't speculate with him about how Connie ended up dead by that river, her young child exposed to snakes and alligators and deadly currents.

I don't know what any of this means

Well pay attention, nobody else cared to know
what it meant
Nobody asked questions
Your chance is now

Yes

So what next?

You have the answers?

Cat goes quiet for a while, but Jesse can see them in the reply, thinking. He grips his mother's wooden bracelet. He counts each bead.

First you must ask your friend Tooly how to get into Night House

Tooly? Can they really mean *Tooly*?

Tooly Quinn, Harry Bishop's grandson: a skinny, quiet, horsey-faced kid, kicker on the football team, notoriously stupid. By some miracle, he graduated in Jesse's year. Now he lives with his mother in a trailer west of Pinewood.

The Night House, which Jesse knows well, is up in Pinewood, too.

I already know how to get into the Night House

I've been there a hundred times

There is a secret way in

You must find it, Tooly knows

Tooly and I aren't exactly friends

Did Tooly's grandfather tell him something?

Can't I just speak to Bishop?

Cat pauses again, taking their time.

> *Are you saying*
> *that you are afraid of a person named Tooly?*

He laughs at that. He can't help it.

> *Cat, be honest*
> *Are you psycho?*

> *I don't think so*
> *This town is psycho*
> *Here everyone is fucked*

> *I want to find the truth like you do*

> *Then tell me who you are*

A silence passes as he sits there, hoping. Sometimes, Cat will withdraw when he asks too many questions. The next message he gets says *come out tonite mi amante!!*—which is not Cat, but Morgan. She sends it along with a gif of a girl sliding out of a chair onto the floor. *Imma be bored af . . .*

Jesse puts the phone on the floor, his palms damp with sweat. His fingertips look like he's been in the water, submerged in the river for hours.

Eight years ago, Nancy was banned from checking out books from the Miskwa County Public Library. Because of Jesse's investigating.

In the years after Mr. Bishop rescued Jesse on the riverbank, he shyly retreated to his old life. He did not respond to Jesse's emails, though it was possible that Mr. Bishop was not an email person. Still, Jesse knew that Mr. Bishop was an amateur genealogist, that he haunted the library archives on weekends, and when he found him there at one of the microfiche readers and asked him what he remembered, Mr. Bishop said, "I'll figure it out one day. But until then, let me be."

Beyond that, he wouldn't budge, so Jesse went to Miss Velda, the librarian. Her hair was already white back then. There's a saying in town that gossip ages you.

"Well," she said, "I always heard around town there was some man Connie was seeing up in Pinewood. A friend of mine said that girl courted pigs. A hog man, maybe, one of the white ones. 'Course they were mostly Mexican then and they're *all* Mexican now. Tarbarrel only hires immigrants. Swooped in, bought out the local folks, promised jobs, and they only hire immigrants. Now Pinewood's a trash heap, all those unemployed white fools with no education, drugs coming straight down the line from cartels through Wilmington—"

Jesse remembers a pause, a downward glance, as if Miss Velda suddenly remembered who she was talking to. Back then, his only understanding of cartels came from television; *Mexican* and *drugs* were words that snapped together. He didn't know then that the entire town suspected that he himself was part Mexican, that Mom Calloway had taken up with a man whose wife once babysat Nancy, a man from Oaxaca who spent his days shuttling pigs through chutes. This being the source of Connie's darker features in a family of pasty blonds.

Miss Velda then recanted and told him he had no business knowing about Mexican drug cartels. Still, Jesse pressed her about the pigs. What did she mean when she said his mother used to "court pigs"? And Miss Velda hedged awhile longer, as if trying to think of a child-friendly way to explain something else Jesse had no business knowing.

"There's a story in the Bible," she said finally, "where Jesus casts out a demon and sends it into a herd of pigs, and then sends the pigs over a cliff."

But this explained nothing, and he dreamed that night about pigs stampeding through his bedroom, and in the morning, he called his senile grandfather at the VA hospital. What was everyone keeping from him? What had folks been saying about his mother? That's when Nancy caught on. By the time Jesse showed up at the sheriff's station to ask for the case file, Sheriff Hupp had been instructed to turn him away, and when Nancy found out what Miss Velda told him, she descended on the library to rage that Miss Velda was an insufferable busybody shitwit who had no business interacting with children. Miss Velda told Nancy to please return her overdue copy of *Dreams from My Father* and never return.

All this to say, Jesse can't set foot in the library, can't smell its book glue and plastic and mold, without feeling vaguely mortified.

Snow-haired Miss Velda is still there when he visits that Saturday afternoon. She comes out from the back with a stack of books in her arms and looks astonished to see him.

"Hi, baby! Hi, hi! Oh, that haircut looks so smart on you. How's school?"

"Fantastic," he says, helping her with her books. He doesn't elaborate, which seems to disappoint her, and while he imagines it would be fun to spin tales to her about the hedonistic excesses of liberal campus life, he's on a mission here. He asks if Mr. Bishop is around.

"Oh." Miss Velda frowns, patting her bun. "I hate to be the one to tell you, but Harry passed back in December."

"Oh no! I'm sorry."

"Stroke. Sudden thing."

"That's awful."

"Just before Christmas, too, that poor family. First the grandson, now this."

She's referring to Tooly's older brother, Sam, who died a couple years back. Quinns are a type; they always know where to find meth and oxy and fentanyl. The younger ones bring their brothers and cousins to parties to help them sell it. Occasionally, they die. They OD, jump off roofs into swimming pools, wreck their ATVs. Miss Velda was right when she called Pinewood a trash heap.

Jesse was hoping he could avoid Tooly and deal with his granddad instead, but no. Whether Mr. Bishop ever "figured it out" or not, Jesse has missed his chance. Maybe Cat knew that already.

"You don't know where I'd find his grandson on a Saturday afternoon, do you?" he asks Miss Velda. "The younger one. Obviously. Does he ever come by?"

She laughs. "Little Tooly? At the library? You're kidding."

Jesse shrugs, smiling wryly.

"Last I heard, he was bussing tables at Fishingham's, but they let him go. Harry had his hopes up when that kid graduated, but you know Pinewood. Trees can't grow in salt mines, et cetera." She stands for a moment, hands on hips, then slides an incredulous eye to Jesse. "Are you friends with that boy?"

"No, not really. There's just something I want to ask him."

A pause settles between them. He can feel her antennae sparking.

"Maybe there's something else you can help me with," he says. "Can you tell me anything about the Night House? The old Simms place?"

"Oh!" Her eyes brighten. "Oh, yes, yes, *yes*." And she sweeps him off to the stacks.

In the nonfiction section, she points him toward several books that have been set aside on a display table. *Eastern Carolina Industry, 1865–1929*; *The 20s That Never Were: Exploring the Lost Generations of Blacknot*; *That Recent Unpleasantness: Despair and Decorum in Restoration Carolina*. The most surprising find is a book authored by none other than Harry Bishop himself: *Stars, Bars, and Gars: Fish Tales of the Miskwa River.*

"Self-published," Miss Velda says, like she needs to set the record straight. "Charles Mercer is the one who built that house. There's a biography about him somewhere…"

"I learned about him in school," Jesse says. "I'm more interested in the house itself."

"Ah well." Miss Velda finds a photo of the house in *East Carolina Industry* and shows it to him. "It weren't ever that impressive, far as plantation houses go. You can see here, where the original house is—it's not big. But then Mercer lost everything, and Simms moved his cotton mill down from Boston, and he bought the place for a steal, slapped all these additions on—see, the wing with all the dormers, and the widow's walk, and the wraparound porch in back. Victorian tackiness. There used to be oak hardwood in the front foyer, but Simms put in that hideous green tile, looks like a public bathroom. Nothing about the house makes sense anymore."

She checks in to see if Jesse's still listening.

"Green tile," he says. "Criminal."

Miss Velda laughs. "I'm sure that don't mean much to you."

Jesse scans the page in *East Carolina Industry*. In 1933, Virgil Simms's son hit the market crash, shot his wife and his two kids, and hanged himself in the attic. Then the house was purchased by a forty-something war widow named Clara Lewton, who turned it into a brothel.

"That's where 'Night House' comes from," Miss Velda says. "It's haunted, of course. Lewton's girls left in the early 50s and the place has been empty ever since."

Empty-ish, Jesse thinks.

"Miss Velda," he says. "Did you ever hear anything about a secret way into the house? Like a hidden room?"

"Never," whispers Miss Velda, captivated. "What're you looking for, the family silver?"

"I heard *Tooly* knows about a secret way in."

"Oh, wow. Well, I'll be."

Jesse waves his hand. "Just something I heard."

Miss Velda rubs her chin, eyes glittering. "I could look into that."

"Nah, just rumors. I wouldn't worry about it."

With this seed planted, Jesse then explores the nonfiction

section on his own. He returns to check out a copy of *Belles and BLOOD!: Strange and Unsolved Killings of the South*. Miss Velda looks at the book and then at him.

"Is your aunt Nancy gonna see this?"

"Miss Velda," he says, laughing. She continues to look at him, dead serious, until he shakes his head no. "Also—maybe don't tell her I was here."

Miss Velda slides the book over the counter. "Don't get me in trouble."

Nine ten PM. The lights of the Koonce farmhouse shine yellow on the lawn, shadows sliding across the porch, silhouettes in the downstairs windows. They're an old Blacknot family, the Koonces, not wealthy, but generous. Real people people. Robert Edward Lee Koonce III is now three years graduated from Miskwa High, and yet here he is, back in town to throw "the house-sitting party." And Jesse, standing tensely next to his car at the side of the road, knows that anybody could be here: bougie South Greene teens like Morgan, twentysomething townies, even Kneesville kids, whom he raced in regionals, or a random clique of girls from the Christian school in New Bern. Why those folks come all the way out here, he'll never know. Already, there are at least thirty cars parked all zigzaggy in the front yard, a bonfire flashing in the dark beside the barn, loud laughter, squealing girls, a boy's belch echoing into the crickety woods.

Jesse approaches the glow of the open doorway carefully, as if walking a balance beam.

Come early, leave early.

But he has a feeling he's walking headlong into chaos, like what happens at this party will echo through the lives of Miskwa County teens all summer long. These things are always like that here—all that school-year tension builds up and up, culminating in a desperate, messy, shit-faced event. On the porch, six recent graduates shout to one another, four girls saying over and over in a round how important their friendships are, two boys teetering on the verge of an explosive argument, Wolfpack versus Tar Heels. When Jesse enters the house there's another argument to his left, Tamera Dawes hissing into the face of her boyfriend, "It's not *about* what happened at cotillion, *Marcus*!" Jesse gives them a wide berth. He knows most of the faces—the kids sitting on the couch, cross-legged on the floor playing cards, blocking doorways. There are the Wyland brothers, edgelord assholes who succeeded Jesse on the cross-country team; valedictorian Emmalee Smallwood, who lost her mind after graduation and set her college acceptance letters on fire; and Idgy Sawyer, sitting mournfully at the bottom of the stairs picking at his banjo. Its twang clashes with the subdued hip-hop coming from a phone on the coffee table; someone has put it in a mason jar to amplify its sound.

He searches the room, face by face.

"Calloway!" Red Koonce thunders his name. "Is that Calloway?"

Jesse salutes to his host. "Red!"

Red is a big freckly guy, curly rust-colored hair stuck to his sweaty forehead. He pulls Jesse into a crushing bear hug. Over his shoulder, Jesse sees the beer crates piled fortress-high on the kitchen counter—piss beer, cheap.

"Goddamn, you little *shit!*" Red shouts, angry-happy, Jesse's friends used to call it. "I heard you were back in town, but I thought, naw, Calloway's too smart to come back just to hang out with the likes of *us.*"

"Give me enough to drink and I'll hang out with anybody," Jesse says. "Even you, Red."

He didn't intend to drink here, but the line comes easy—like riding a bike. Red grabs his shirt collar and yanks him toward the kitchen.

"Is Tooly here?" Jesse asks along the way.

"*Tooly?* Why?"

"I'm looking for him."

"I don't know who the hell is here. Come on! Let's get some drink in you, son!"

Jesse falls seamlessly into a conversation with a group of guys from Red's year. They talk about college and college ball and college drugs, and they talk about the high school (how shitty it still is) and the sinkhole (What town is so broke they can't fix a sinkhole?). Jesse finds an assortment of half-empty liquor bottles hiding behind the beer. People's voices circle his head, and he pours himself a shot.

A girl flies through the kitchen—"Hey! Calloway! Morgan is looking for you."—but he catches only a streamer of hair disappearing behind a doorway and doesn't know who it was.

"Okay," he says to no one. "I'll go find her."

Jesse finds Tooly on the deck with a few friends. Red has the back door open, people coming and going with the mosquitos. Jesse slaps one on his forearm. Bloodsplat.

As he approaches, drink in hand, Tooly looks up in surprise.

"Calluhwee." He slurs his words in a way that might be his accent or drunkenness or just a straight-up speech impediment. But his face isn't horsey; Jesse remembered it wrong. Tooly actually has delicate, vulnerable features, soft orange freckles on his nose and chin. His hair hangs over one side of his face like a blond eye patch.

"Whendju get in?"

"Yesterday," Jesse says. "I'm not here for long." His brain loops—*ask him about ask him about ask him about*. "Hey, I'm sorry to hear about your granddad. Miss Velda told me."

A beat. Tooly's three Pinewood friends glance at Jesse, then turn away and begin talking to one another. Tooly is jittery, his leg bouncing.

"'Kay, thanks."

Another awkward beat. There's supposed to be some casual conversation between condolences and the question Jesse wants to ask, but he's struggling to figure out what to say. At school, he and Tooly weren't anything close to friends. Though, when Jesse started sneaking up to Pinewood, to Bittern's Rest, to the Night House, Tooly was a regular fixture there. Were they friends then? Would either of them have ever called the other that sincerely?

Jesse says quickly, "I was wondering if—"

"Hey, man, I dunnonothin."

"You—you mean, about Connie?"

Tooly squints. "'Bout huh? Cannee what?"

Jesse stares, dumbfounded. "What?"

Are they that drunk already?

He tries again: "Your granddad—and Connie, my mother. He ever talk to you about it?"

Tooly begins to look irritated. "'Bout *what*?"

"About—" Jesse says. "About *finding* her."

Tooly lets out a noise, a grunt and a sigh at once. "Man—get out my face."

He shoulders Jesse aside and goes back into the house. Jesse tries to follow just as Red barrels his way onto the deck, bumping kids to the left and right, drinks sloshing. He zeroes in on Jesse, throws an arm over his shoulders, and stage-whispers warm, fermented breath into his ear.

"Hey there, skinny playa. There's some South Greene girls looking for you."

Jesse looks toward the door where Tooly disappeared. "Sounds promising."

"You be careful, son. Them girls over the bridge, they got little kitty cat claws."

"You actually say things like that, Red?"

Red hisses and pantomimes a cat scratch. Jesse ducks away into the kitchen. He can't find Tooly, but since he's already here next to the booze, he pours another drink.

Now he's crossing the yard through a skunky cloud of pot smoke and angst and emotional disasters. A girl whose name he can't remember is sitting in the dirt at the base of the porch steps, weeping; he worries she's alone until he spots a friend ferrying water to her from the kitchen—"You just need to hydrate, Lexi, come on!"—like Red's party is a team sport.

Morgan is over by the firepit with two other South Greene

girls, Brooke Barnes and Kayleigh Dowell, their cat-eye makeup stark in the glow of the flames. When Morgan sees him, she jumps up and squeals, throwing her arms around his neck.

"Where have you *been*?" Her hair smells like woodsmoke.

"Come late, leave late," he says. "Is Tooly out here?"

"Who?" Morgan hiccups. Jesse steadies her wobble and, to his surprise, feels concern. Why is that? He's seen Morgan drunk before; he's not her dad.

"What're you drinking?" he asks.

She shakes a metal flask at him. "Moscow mule. You want some? It's got vodka, cream soda, lemon vodka, strawberry bitters. And one other thing, I forget. Red made it for me."

"I don't think that's a Moscow mule."

"Maybe not to *you*, college boy. Here, you drink it."

He takes the flask and throws it back. Like a chess pie, the concoction is so sweet it's corrosive.

"*Shit*," he says. She laughs and pulls him down into the grass.

Morgan keeps him here. She won't let him leave. She points out Gregg Stubbs: a nondescriptly good-looking white kid over by the barn, whose stiff jaw gives the impression of someone who grinds his teeth. Occasionally, he'll glance in the direction of Morgan and Jesse sitting together by the bonfire and quickly look away.

"So that's the penis slapper," says Jesse.

"Shh!" Morgan claps her hand over his mouth. Her two friends flop over in hysterics.

"You *told* him about that?" says Brooke.

"Sure," says Morgan. "Jesse's one of the girls. You can tell him anything."

"I said Greg was trying to give her a wet willy," says Kayleigh.

"Shut *up*." Morgan throws grass at Kayleigh's face.

"No, I think they call that cockclocking," says Jesse. The girls shriek. Morgan yanks his hair.

"I'm serious, stop. He's standing right over there."

With one slow, conspicuous motion, all four of them turn to look at Greg. Greg ignores them, pretending to watch the drunken game of cornhole taking place on the lawn.

"He seems so sad," says Brooke.

"Well," says Kayleigh. "Now *he* knows what it feels like to get shafted."

They all lose it then.

"Y'all are the worst," says Morgan.

Morgan, Brooke, and Kayleigh's conversation spins so fast it's hard to keep up: Morgan feels bad about breaking things off with Greg, because Greg didn't do anything explicitly wrong. Kayleigh doesn't like Greg for watching so much porn, but Brooke says you can't shame people for liking porn, that's sex-shaming. And they're all sex-shamers for making fun of poor Greg's fetishes, shame on them. Morgan says it isn't even about the penis slapping. She says it's weird, because here she finally dated a guy her parents like, and she ended up not liking him. When Greg came to dinner, Mr. and Mrs. Taylor had only the most positive things to say about him—his strong handshake, his good manners. Mr. Taylor plays golf or something with Mr. Stubbs, so maybe that means Greg comes preapproved, like a car.

Jesse drinks. He enjoys sitting and listening. He likes how

girls let their conversations go off like a frenetic flying machine, how they talk as if he's not there, their daydreams and desires on display.

"So," says Brooke. "How's college life been for you? You seeing anybody?"

Jesse is still running checks on who comes and goes from the house, the circle of faces in the yard smudged in firelight. He turns back to the girls and realizes Brooke is speaking to him. "Like, dating?" he says. "Some folks here and there. Nothing serious."

"Girls?" Brooke asks coyly. "Boys?"

"Brooke!" shrieks Morgan, mortified.

Jesse stares at the three of them, their made-up faces sweaty and shadowed. He can tell Brooke's cheeks are flushed, that she's realized her mistake.

"Girls, boys," he says easily. "Everything in between."

Brooke is sheepish. Morgan glares at her. Jesse realizes he's still holding Morgan's flask. He tips it back until it's empty.

Where is Tooly? He doesn't care. He's no longer searching faces. The girls have caravanned to the bathroom, and he finds himself back in a conversation with Red, his gracious host. He's still in the grass near the firepit, sprawled on his back and gazing at the stars. Red is shirtless, slumped in a lawn chair.

"I worry about you, Calloway," he says. "Out there on your own."

"I'm not alone," says Jesse. "I've made plenty of friends."

"What kind of friends?"

"Nerdy friends. They're from all over. They're eclectic."

"Okay. I don't know what you mean by that, but nerds are good. You need to be around nerds, little dude, anybody who can chill you out. You were crazy. I mean—you were crazier than *me*, I think."

Jesse watches the blurred silhouettes of legs pass back and forth over the bonfire. *Crazy.* The word slides through his head like melted ice cream. When he closes his eyes, the earth tilts.

Red laughs. "Hey, remember that night you showed up at Jaelah Harrison's place? That was messed up, man."

"Nah, Red, that wasn't me," Jesse says.

"Yeah, it was," Red says, his voice floating along. "What do you mean that weren't you? You got stuck in the hedge. We had to pull your ass out."

"That was a different guy. A jillion years ago."

"Really, man?" Red laughs again. "Pretty sure that was your blood I had to scrub out of my sweatshirt. My mom thought somebody'd been stabbed."

Jesse doesn't say anything. Red shrugs, and then someone calls for him across the yard and he's gone. Jesse stays where he is. After a while, someone prods him in the ribs, hard enough to startle him. "Calloway!" Morgan says, leaning down to clap in his face. "Wake! Up!"

He rallies. The mason jar sound system whines out the refrains of Yeezy: *Everybody know I'm a motherfuckin' monster.* Morgan hugs Tamera Dawes, whose face is tearstained, and who says she's leaving and is never coming to another one of these fucking parties ever again. Jesse isn't sure where Brooke and Kayleigh have gone.

Tooly crosses the living room in front of him, following unsteadily on the heels of his friends.

"Hey," says Jesse, grabbing Tooly's arm.

Tooly stumbles and whips around, startled. "Spahder fangers," he says.

"Huh?"

Tooly's pupils are dilated. In the overhead glow of a string of Christmas lights, his face is sweaty and flushed. "Nothing," he says.

"Can I talk to you?" Jesse asks.

"Why? You lookinferHarlan?"

The room goes muffled, as if Jesse's skull has filled with cotton. Tooly's friends head outside without him.

"*Jim*," Tooly says combatively. "Jim Harlan."

"No," Jesse says, sparking awake again. "No, no, no, no. I'm *not* looking for him. It's not about him."

"Man, whatchuwan then?"

"Someone told me—they talk me to told you—" Oh hell, he's drunk. "Sorry. The Night House. There's something *in* the Night House."

Tooly blinks, dim-faced.

Jesse feels like the whole room is watching them. He whispers, "There's a *secret way* to get inside the—"

"Naw, naw," Tooly says. "Leave me alone. I don't owe you shit."

He hurries for the door.

Jesse stares after him, cheeks blazing, suddenly angry. *Owe* him? Jesse didn't say anything about anyone *owing* him, and even if he had, maybe Tooly *does* owe him. Because it isn't going to be Tooly who keeps this secret from him, not *Tooly*. For God's sake.

He pushes ahead through a knot of drunk senior girls, returning to the deck where Tooly has rejoined his friends. Tooly sees Jesse coming at him and stumbles back in surprise.

"Hey, what do you think this is about?" Jesse shouts. "I was only *asking*. I wasn't asking you to *do* anything. You don't owe me enough to answer a fucking question?"

Tooly, in reply, hauls back and punches him hard in the face. Jesse tumbles off the deck into the grass.

This happens so fast it feels more like a spell of vertigo than a punch. Then there's a wave of laughter, and the drunk senior girls are crowding around him, and a hot pain splits his cheekbone. Someone shouts, "Damn, boy, you took that one *full-on!*" By the time Jesse's sitting up, Tooly is sprinting off alone toward the tree line at the edge of Red's yard, and Morgan is poking her head out the back door, screaming: "Where's the fight? Did I miss it?"

He staggers down the hall, coming back from the bathroom. His cheeks are numb. Someone stares at him from the doorway, and he stops, squinting at a smeary backlit face. A familiar aura of concern and disapproval catches his heart. *Jim. Jim Harlan*. But no—it's just one of Red's friends.

"Hey, Punchy, want to learn to block?"

Jesse slides past. "Nah. I'm good."

Morgan meets him in the living room. "Why did he hit you? What happened?"

"I scared 'im," he says. "Don't worry about it."

Flash forward. They're outside on the front-porch steps. She grabs his shirt and kisses him hard, like she's trying to pin him in one place. He tastes the concoction they've been drinking all night, though now it isn't so bad. Like hot, melted Skittles.

Three thirty AM. Jesse and Morgan leave Red Koonce's place and head southeast toward downtown. It happens easily, like it was meant to. Morgan pats the dashboard of his car and says, "Hey, Dick, long time no see," and then she hooks up her phone to his cassette deck so that she can scream-sing pop songs. As usual, Blacknot is dead, the streetlights blinking, the river black and still. Jesse settles along the waterside east of Spartina Square and rolls down the windows. Warm swampy breeze. Undercurrent of hog farm.

Morgan finds *Belles and BLOOD!* in the passenger seat and skims through it. "Murder, murder, murder," she says. "Plotting to kill someone?"

"You bet," says Jesse.

"Can I help? Who's the mark?"

"Red. I want his party empire."

"Love it! Yes! And look—" She scrounges in her purse and presents a bottle of lemon vodka: "I stole this from his kitchen!"

Jesse's weird dad conscience comes back, making him wary. "You're gonna get me in trouble, M."

"Aw, hush, you like trouble." She takes a swig and hands the bottle to Jesse, but he caps it and sets it down in the floorboard.

Morgan watches him a moment. Then she reaches out to his aching cheek, brushing the spot where Tooly punched him.

"Does it hurt?"

"Nah," he says.

She leans forward and kisses him. He puts his hand on the back of her neck, fine, sweat-damp hair warm between his fingers. Morgan's face is a comfort: smudged mascara around big, bright eyes, a pillowy upper lip. Girl kisses are like that—soft and subtle. He kisses her back, first on the mouth, then on the throat, breathing in the smell of the firepit, the kitchen-cleaner sting of lemon vodka. He hears her breathing him in, too. He hopes his anxious day hasn't made him stink.

"Condom?" she whispers.

"I have one," he says, bunching her skirt around her thighs. "But we don't need it yet."

Morgan blushes, suddenly bashful. "Okay."

"What, Greg Stubbs never went down on you? Bet it would've been something to see him try."

"Oh, shut up!" She laughs, swatting at him.

He lets the seats back. The mechanics are tricky with Dick's console between them, but he's always enjoyed the challenge of sex in a car. The comfort of being tight and pretzeled. The thrill of being partly exposed. Morgan puts her feet against the door, and he slides her skirt up the rest of the way. He kisses the folds of her stomach, her pubis mound. "Oh," she says, and grabs a fistful of his hair.

He takes his time. He's in no hurry.

Then she screams, high-pitched, filled with terror.

Jesus, what did he do wrong? He pulls back, but Morgan, in her sudden panic, forces her skirt down and tents his head. He has to pry her hands off to free himself. When he finally gets a look at her, her face is white, eyes wide, and she's pointing, jabbing her finger over his shoulder through the driver's side window whispering, "There—there—there—!"

But there's nothing. The parking lot stretches empty up to Main Street, darkened in the lacy shadows of oak trees. Down the block, a red streetlight blinks.

"I don't see anything."

"It walked past the window. It looked in at us; I saw it!"

"Okay," he says, resting his hand on her arm. "It's okay. I believe you. What was it?"

"I don't know. I don't know. A ghost. A—a *creature*—Jesus." She presses the back of her hand against her mouth, eyes wet with tears. "No, wait—where are you going? Don't go out there!" She grabs for him. "Don't—!"

He carefully pulls himself away and steps out of the car, scanning first one side of the parking lot, then the other. On the asphalt, there's a smear of black mud, washed up from a recent rain. Also scat, little dark pellets the size of blueberries. He shines his phone out onto the park lawn. A dozen luminous eyes stare back at him. Over the rush of the breeze, he hears hooves treading in the grass.

"There's a bunch of deer." He leans into the window. "Is that what you saw?"

Morgan shakes her head.

"What did you see? What'd it look like?"

"I don't know. Not a deer. It walked by the fucking window."

"Look." He points toward the park. "You see them?"

The deer flee, skinny legs sweeping under a streetlamp on Desmond Street. But there's one among their herd that doesn't move. It remains beneath an oak tree, flat as a shadow, erect like a person, but leaching out a quivering, feral presence. Through a web of hair, it stares straight at him. He stares back. A ghost, like Morgan said? He can feel its gaze pulling at him. Seeing through him. He takes a step forward as Morgan cries out again from the car, "*Stop*, Jesse! Are you insane?"

He stops. The shadow is gone.

It doesn't take long for him to wonder whether he saw anything at all. He feels disappointed when he gets back in the car next to Morgan.

"I think we're . . . a little drunk," he says.

Morgan is still watching through the back window, but her face slowly trades its terror for embarrassment. She, too, is questioning whether she saw anything. When she turns back around, she avoids his eyes.

"Are you okay?" he asks.

Her face crumples.

"Morgan."

She begins to cry.

"But why—" she whispers shakily. "Why did Tooly *do* that to you? You couldn't have *scared* him. *Look* at you."

Jesse is surprised. He had assumed they were through talking about this.

"Maybe I should just take you home," he says.

"You hate me."

"Huh? Why would I hate you?"

"He's a homophobe. Tooly Quinn. Everyone knows it. That whole family's a trashfire."

"I wouldn't say that," Jesse says. "Look, I don't think that's why he hit me. Also, it's Fucknut. You expect folks to be woke?"

"I told you to come. And someone attacked you. I'm so stupid."

"Please, stop. It wasn't your fault."

"I'm sorry I told Brooke and Kayleigh you're bi. I'm sorry I invited Greg to my house and not you. You must hate me. I'm a fucking clown."

"M." He grips her hands.

She doesn't understand. He never wanted to go to her house. That was the point. When she first flirted with him at the diner that miserable summer and later hooked up with him at the live nativity in Spartina Square, he'd been looking for something that wasn't going to work. Maybe he had used Morgan, and maybe she had used him, too—as a fling, a personal rebellion. Jesse was not preapproved. But that didn't matter. Morgan was a rebound. They wouldn't have been anything to each other if Harlan hadn't ruined him first.

"I don't hate you," he says. "I'm not mad at you."

Morgan presses her face into his shoulder and sobs.

Later, he drives her back across the bridge to Brooke's place, where she'll sneak into the pool house and rejoin her friends. Jesse keeps the windows rolled down as he drives, allowing the mascara stains on his shirt to dry. Morgan laughs at herself in the side mirror.

"I'm a mess."

"Nah, you're all right, M," he says.

With their catching up unconsummated, he feels emptied out and stuffed up at the same time. It's as if two nights have taken place—a normal one, deeply familiar, and one where nothing was normal at all.

He needs to tell her. Set the record straight.

"What happened with Tooly was my fault," he confesses. "I was asking him some weird questions."

Morgan pauses from wiping the streaky eye makeup off her face. "What questions?"

"Did you know his granddad was the guy who found me? He died back in December. I didn't know that until yesterday."

Morgan has to think about this. When she remembers, her mouth falls open. "Oh."

"There's a special reason I came back. Someone has been contacting me about Connie Calloway's death. They have photos, case materials. I came here to try to link up with them."

"Photos," Morgan says. "Of your mother? Of the scene?" Her eyes press him with an expression of unwelcome pity. "That's awful."

"Yeah."

Morgan is quiet for a bit, as if waiting for him to offer details. When he doesn't, she says, "Who's this person you're linking up with?"

"Don't tell anyone about this, M, okay?"

"Swear to God."

So out it comes—Cat, who messaged him over Wipixx one morning after a bender, then the month of anonymous DMs, the promises, a wealth of secrets, the bridge rendezvous, the directive to talk to Tooly, to ask him about some secret entryway to the Night House. Morgan listens to his story. When he's finished, she squints at him.

"Why do you have a Wipixx account?"

"It wasn't my idea. My roommate suggested it."

Morgan glances into the backseat, where she tossed *Belles and BLOOD!* "Okay," she sighs. "How did this person convince you?"

"What?"

"*Convince* you. What did they do to make you think you could trust them?"

"Why wouldn't I trust them?"

"You never thought you should tell someone else? Sheriff Hupp? Nancy—?"

"No, no. Nancy will shut it down. That's what she does. And if I tell Hupp, she'll tell Nancy." He pauses, trying to remember which secrets he has and hasn't shared with Morgan—not his secrets, but Nancy's. Her and Hupp. Minerva, the proud sapphic roommate from grad school. "They're close, is all."

The worry in Morgan's face deepens.

"Look, you don't understand," he says. "They never told me the whole story about what happened to her. So if I go to them now, I'd lose my chance. Plus, I promised Cat I wouldn't tell."

"But you're telling me," Morgan says.

"I'm telling you because you're my friend."

He's well into South Greene—past the wrought iron security gate and the golf course, past vast front lawns, darkened facades, the extra wings that make the houses look like monsters with multiple backs. There someone's four-wheeler parked in a driveway. There someone's smooth, marshmallow-shaped hedges. A six-car garage faces the street, announcing priorities. He looks all around to avoid Morgan's skeptical stare.

"Jess," she says. "What if this person messaging you is out to hurt you somehow?"

He laughs. "Why would they want to do that?"

"Jesus, I don't know. There's some real kooky people out there. You don't know who you're dealing with."

"But I do know them," he says. "We talked for a month, I told you. We talked about Blacknot and what this place is like, what it's like to grow up here. They know it all. And they get the people here. They've been listening." He can tell from Morgan's look that she isn't convinced, but he goes on. "I *feel* like I know them, like I dreamed them. It's a connection."

Morgan shakes her head. "Sounds like a crush, my dude. Like you're into this person."

"No." He laughs again. "It's not like that."

"That's twisted." She points to the road. "Go on and pull over. Brooke's house is there."

Dick's engine sputters as he parks, loud enough to wake up the neighborhood. They both flinch, but no lights come on. All is quiet except for the usual summer riot of crickets and cicadas, the occasional croak of a bullfrog.

"Let me see these messages," Morgan says, holding out her hand. "I'm pretty good at picking up on subtext."

He doesn't want to show her. Saying all this aloud has him feeling embarrassed. While he believes the connection is there, he's afraid it'll go sour if he exposes it to scrutiny. Still, the longer Morgan holds out her hand, the longer he knows he must give her the phone, and he does, and she sits there for a minute, reading.

Eventually, she laughs.

"You're kidding with this," she says. "You're fucking with me. This was all a joke."

"No."

"Did Kayleigh put you up to this?"

"No?"

She reads from the phone, "Altar blood? Ivy tongue?"

"What?" Jesse says.

Her smile vanishes. She can see the earnest confusion on his face.

"It's just," she says slowly, "random words. It doesn't make any sense."

He takes the phone back from her. The Wipixx exchanges are as she says. Cat's messages, and his replies.

> **devilSage Arrow**
> **ember**
>
> **Smoke Needle Spindle grove**
> **Sage skull hemlock bone**
>
> **Smoke Needle palm Star sea arrow star**
> **Tar honey oyster**
>
> **Altar blood spade Arrow**
> **red Smoke ember**
> **laurel Honey Vessel**
>
>   **Palm root**
>   **Ivy tongue**
>   **tinArrow**
>   **Cross flesh Vessel**

"You wrote that," Morgan says.

"No, I didn't."

"It's right there."

"I didn't write it."

But he sees it for himself. **Iron feather spit Vessel / Crow vessel Dogwood briar Tooly / Cross knife wormMoss gate red Night House . . . Swallow thistle bone Hymn path.** This is his exchange with Cat from beginning to end.

"Honest," he pleads. "Just earlier today, I was reading these. Everything made sense."

Morgan's face is solemn, but her eyes show fear. "They must've gotten ahold of your phone somehow. They did something to it. Did you leave it anywhere while you were at Red's?"

"I don't know." His heart pounds. The light of the phone burns his eyes. "This is crazy."

Morgan unbuckles her seatbelt, but he doesn't want her to leave him. Cat has found him out. They know he's just shared their secret, and for the first time, he feels afraid.

"Cat," Morgan says. "Like the animal?"

"Like Catherine, I think," says Jesse. "What do I do about this?"

She gets out of the car, stumbling. At first, he thinks she'll wander off without a word, text him again when she's forgotten all this, but then she turns back and leans into the passenger side window. "Give me a day," she says. "I'm kinda shook right now." With that, she wobbles off down the sidewalk and disappears through a shadowed gate.

4

Alice has an ear. That's what her father calls it.

That sounds like he means musical talent, which Alice does have, and which her father has. But the truth is that Alice has the ear her *mother* had.

Her mother, who could not play an instrument or carry a tune, but who could hear frequencies in things that others could not.

Once, when she was six years old, her mother took her to the Tarbarrel holding pens outside Pinewood so she could see what her father did. She saw the pigs crammed together, their sagging pink faces, the sad crust around their eyes. The smell was shocking, but the sound was even worse—the roar of the fans that blasted out the stink and the boiling heat, the animals rooting and screaming, the sound their shit made when it dropped through the slats in the floor and slopped down the chute and was spewed into a lagoon with blood and stillbirths and disinfectant and insecticide, a foul pink morass. The hogs were not slaughtered here on the farm, but Alice could hear the drone of the trucks that transported them to the processing plant down the road, and the deep shriek of terror in their bodies, as if they knew what was coming.

"Did you hear them?" her mother asked. "Like *yeeeeeee, yeeeeeee, yeeeeeee.*"

"*Yeeeeeee, yeeeeeee,*" Alice repeated. Yes, she could hear them. She assumed, back then, that everybody could.

She remembers no other exchange during that outing, though she can see her mother standing on the rungs of the gate as she looked out over the enclosures, the giant fans blowing her bushy hair around her face. Pig smell clung to their clothes on the drive home. Alice can only assume this was all meant as a volley against her father in the war her mother was waging—for custody and for Alice's loyalty and affection. It's tough to align with a hog man after visiting a hog farm.

Euel has since confessed that he never wanted to be a hog man; he inherited the farm from his father; now he has delegated its day-to-day management to a corps of good ole boys who make their decisions hard and fast, which has made Alice wonder what it is her father *does* aside from have people over for dinner so they can eat Bobbie's food and listen to Alice play her harp.

Come over, come over, he says. *Let the talented Alice Catherine show off her ear.*

In her kitchenette, she puts three of Tanisha Patton's witch-fingers on a plate and listens to their sound. She powders them with a spoon. They squeak as they're crushed. That is when she hears them: *fimfimfimfim.* An ugly giggle. She taps the powder into a mason jar, pours in cooking oil and some red wine she stole from the main house. The oil is too quiet to hear, but the wine sighs—*wheylu-wheylu*—and the now-dissolved witch-fingers have a stifled tone, more like *fwomfwomfwomfwom*.

Then a mirror shard—*shink!* An oyster shell—*thung!* A strand of hair that belongs to Jesse Calloway.

She holds the hair up to her face. People have sounds, too, but they're complicated. Sometimes soft sounds, or music, or sometimes, with people like her father, a dark, meticulous grubbing, like roots expanding underground. Even in something as tiny as a hair, you can hear people: what they want, and what they need. To listen too hard is a breach of their privacy, but to listen a little is wisdom. Alice takes one of her own long, curly hairs and wraps both—hers and Jesse's—around a nail. Then she drops it in, seals the jar tight.

He is wandering.

He needs a star to guide him.

As she heads out onto the terrace, jar in hand, she feels its eager vibrations against her palm, the same eagerness she heard in Jesse's voice at the library yesterday, on the other side of the stacks. But she could not turn around then, not even to peek at him. Too soon, too soon. They don't meet yet. She could only listen to his voice, all quick and wily—*Nah, just rumors. I wouldn't worry about it*—how he plied pesky Miss Velda. Clever! And two minutes later he'd whisked away, and Velda was poking her white head around the stacks saying, "What you up to back there, Alice Catherine? Hmm?" because Alice always gives the impression of sneaking around, even when she's doing her work as she's supposed to.

But a star. Yes. A star jar. She takes a shovel from a hook on the wall and carries it out to the far northwest edge of the terrace. Here, she buries the jar in the flowerbed.

The vibration in the jar transfers to the earth. The ground under her feet changes. The grass changes. The river, swelled with rainwater and flowing east, changes. She crouches and listens.

Then nothing. The vibration stops, and she is left with the dull thumping of her heart and the dirt and the dead glass of the jar. She tilts her ear to the ground.

Minutes pass. She goes back inside and retrieves her stash from under the couch—the stolen bottle of wine, a set of lock-picking tools for doors, cabinets, safes, plus binders filled with research material, pictures and articles printed from microfiche, handwritten draft materials from Harry Bishop. He was working on his book for more than a year—a memoir project—and up to a week before he died, he was coming into the library almost every day, furtively occupying the niche in the archive room, where he would often leave his things unattended. It wasn't hard to steal them and make copies. The most important items in the stash, however, are five notebooks her mother left behind in Pinewood, which Euel gave to her when she was fourteen. They are filled with magic, so precious that Alice has copied them, too, over and over, and has stowed them in multiple hiding spots across the guest house.

She runs through the contents of the jar as dictated and knows she did it right. She did everything she was supposed to do.

She lays out a few of Mrs. Patton's witchfingers on the counter and crouches to look at them at eye level—a city of shriveled black kernels. Who did Mrs. Patton get them from? A cousin? A friend? Alice pinches one in her fingers, smelling it again. Sticky, cloying.

That's when she hears someone call her name from around the guesthouse.

"Alice Catherine? Are you here?"

She knows that voice, with its hangover rasp. When she hurries around the side of the house, sure enough, there is Morgan Taylor on the lawn. Morgan has traded out her white Sunday dress for denim shorts and a pink Miskwa High Volleyball T-shirt, but she still looks like some kind of infernal Southern pixie, stamping past the boxwood hedge.

"Alice Catherine," she says. "Queen of Cats."

"What?" Alice says. "What are you doing here?"

"That's what you called yourself." Morgan has a determined, wild-eyed expression. "When you played pretend with me and my sister, when we found the magic portal and transformed, you became the Queen of Cats."

Alice goes rigid.

"Cat," says Morgan. "You're Cat."

"I barely remember playing pretend with you and your sister," says Alice.

Morgan laughs. "Didn't I get it right, though? I think I did. You're the one messaging Jesse Calloway. I've been thinking about it all day—you've got all this spare time on your hands, you've got access to library archives in Blacknot, and you're a fucking weirdo."

"I don't even know Jesse Calloway."

"Yeah? Am I wrong? I don't think I am; I think it's you. I can see it in your face."

Alice almost reaches up to feel what Morgan is talking about. "No, you can't."

"Oh, no?" Morgan is practically breathless. "You were always creepy, but this is *cruel*. Jesse's mom is dead. What happened to her was awful. Why would you mess with him about that? What do you think you know about him?"

"You don't know what you're talking about."

"And how did you do that weird thing with his phone? Witchcraft? Are you a witch, Alice Catherine?"

"Go away," insists Alice.

"God, you're so weird it's disgusting."

"Get away from my house."

"Mr. Swink's house," Morgan says. "You just live here."

Alice's fingertips turn to ice.

At this point, Morgan seems to realize that Alice isn't going to answer her questions.

"I'll tell Mr. Swink about what you're doing if you don't stop," she says. "If you keep fucking with my boy, I'll tell my parents, your parents, Sheriff Hupp, and they'll send you right back to Croatan."

She stares intensely, perhaps waiting for the threat to have an impact. When Alice says nothing, Morgan seems disappointed. She points her finger and says feebly, "You just—you think about that. Okay?"

With that, she heads back up the lawn.

Alice goes around to the terrace and grabs the shovel.

Morgan barely has a chance to glance back before Alice is upon her. She cries out—"No?"—more like a question than a plea, as Alice strikes her.

The impact is a long, shivery chill, her skin and the shovel's blade, singing together.

FROM THE NOTEBOOKS OF
KATRINA MORROW, SUMMER 1994

June 25

No work at Leland's. Day off from the Stock-Hop. Went out to find periwinkles for a Love jar, came back sunburned. The neighbor kids make fun of me for burning, Almalita's oldest even said to my face that freckles make people look DIRTY. Sucio. But dirty is good, I like it.

Yesterday when the Golden Boy paddled up in his kayak to see me, he touched my arm and his fingertips left white marks and made the freckles dark. He's gone brown being out on the river. We sat on the porch and I got him drunk on peach wine, learned how to make it from a book I bought at a church yard sale. That man asked how long the recipe (!) had been in my family. I told him two hundred years. It helps to be a little mean to men, I think.

GB calls me "swamp bred." I thought he meant "swamp bread"—like bread with algae and crab bits and mud in it. Ha ha.

June 28

Fragrance jar
    1 rosemary branch, 2 lemongrass stalks, wad of cotton, 2 parts water to bleach

This used to be the nice part of the county, in the era before the pig farms. In the 1800s, the rich folks came up here from town, spun their estates and industry and lorded over the land like spiders. Slaves did all the hard work, picking cotton, tapping the trees for turpentine, but the way they told us about it in grade school, you'd have thought the slaves liked it, as if they were not people but rather cartoon dwarfs singing their hearts out.

I get why white folks in Pinewood want to imagine this rosy past. A hog lagoon is a horror—raw, raspberry-pink sewage. The fumes will kill you. I could step off my porch and walk three miles west and drown in a shitslurry.

July 3

GB played a mandolin for me. He's pretty good.

Water heater's still busted, but the rent keeps going up.

July 4

Birth Control jar

1 crushed witchfinger, 6 onion skins, 4 cricket legs, 2 parts stagnant water to wine (red, bitter, strong tannins), 1 spoonful lard, 1 robin's egg, crushed

August 17

Pennies and spartina grass, boiled to whimpering in salt water, for luck and money. Crackly rust dust from the car in the driveway to make it last. GB tells me to keep the job at Leland's but quit the job at Stock-Hop. Thinking it's cause he likes the thought of my hands on other women when I fit them for bras. Pervy pig man. Shift manager at Stock-Hop is handsy and GB does not like that at all.

Jar for Handsy Men

3 dead grubs—1 part salt water to vinegar (shrill as you can find)—a Stock-Hop manager name tag and the bands from his braces (he leaves them on the break room counter, disgusting)

I HOPE YOU GET WARTS, EDDIE. I hope your thing gets warts like a decorative gourd.

August 25

GB is going to get eaten by an alligator probably, he takes his kayak all up in those little tributaries and dead ends. Too curious for his own good. Yesterday he brought me back pitcher plants, wild onions, a snakeskin. For your witchcrafting, he said. Such a dumb boy, giving me stuff.

Last week he brought me stuff from the flea market—autoharp, fiddle, harmonica, great big bell jars, two broke on the trip. I don't like the flea market. I hate those old men in their lawn chairs, hawking all that old Confederate shit. They took advantage of him—he's too bright-eyed, smells like money, probably paid six times what this shit is worth. But he doesn't care, he has his daddy's money to burn, he just wants a nice conversation with some people. He said, Now you get to be serenaded by

HISTORY. I laughed at him for that. He deserves me to be mean to him for that.

August 26

Power's off again.

May need a side hustle to make rent. ████'s ideas are all crazy. She thinks we could pose as mediums and travel the state, exorcising ghosts from plantations.

5

The sun wakes him, knifing over the river and through his buggy windshield. Its heat is so intense it gives him goose bumps.

Jesse has spent the night in his car. His phone sits in the passenger seat, along with a half-empty bottle of lemon vodka. Lysol mouth. Sandpaper tongue. Face aching and hot. As his eyes adjust to the punitive light of day, he realizes he's back in the oyster shell lot by the marsh trail, the bridge to South Greene stretching out before him. Steam from the river sends up a luminescent haze.

He peels himself out of the car, joints popping, and wanders a little ways down the trail to relieve himself in the bushes. On the way back, a jogger wearing a trash bag passes by him.

"Looking worse for the wear," he says.

"Yeah," croaks Jesse, squinting behind his sunglasses.

He looks himself over in the reflection of the driver's side window and can see that the jogger is right. His right cheek is plum red and swollen, hot to the touch. He'll have to explain it to Nancy. At least Drunk-Jesse was wise enough to text her at eleven, saying he would crash at Red's place. *Who the f is red?* Nancy wants to know.

There are no follow-up instructions from Cat, and Jesse is both relieved and angered to see that the messages are back to normal.

I want to know the truth like you do

Tell me who you are then

Mostly, he's angry at himself. He probably should never have shown the messages to Morgan. Now he's warped whatever connection he had; his breach of Cat's trust has sent a little shock wave through the universe, and he's been warned. He entertains the idea that Cat is surveilling him, has infected his phone with spyware, can see and hear everything he's doing. This version of Cat is a maestro, wicked and professionally trained, which is not how he understands them.

He takes some time to clean up—hotel bar soap, a mini-bottle of Listerine. He's done this before. At the Chuckwagon, he orders black coffee and a Hangover Special, which is cheddar, egg, and sausage sandwiched between cinnamon rolls. The waitress, a veteran who's been working there since before Jesse came and went, says he looks like he's been run over twice and buried.

"Who'd you pick a fight with?" she asks.

"A bear," says Jesse, tearing sugar packets into his coffee. "I let him win."

"Psh. Bears remember. He might come back for you."

When the waitress comes back with his food, he's reading about the Michael Peterson case in *Belles and BLOOD!* She looks over his shoulder.

"That was an owl," she says.

He looks up. "What?"

"An owl did it. Killed that guy's wife."

Jesse stares incredulously at the crime scene photos, the sprawled and bloody corpse at the foot of the stairs. "If you say so."

By the time he heads for the Night House, Blacknot is awake and moving with church folk, the varied congregations of First Baptist on Main—Morgan's church, where he assumes she must be sweating last night's party out of her system—St. Paul's on North Desmond, Mt. Zion AME on the other side of the water tower. You could make a complete map of the county through its churches alone.

Now, though, Jesse is leaving Blacknot for a familiar place: a stretch of craggy road on the south edge of Pinewood, where the Night House stands abandoned. When Jesse was in high school, the house fostered a congregation of a different kind—teens and other young assholes with rituals of their own. Back in the 1950s, when Clara's girls packed up, they left behind a space where kids could sneak in and misbehave.

The house is off by itself down an overgrown drive, visible only from the houses in Bittern's Rest, which sit a football field distance away behind a grove of longleaf pines. Jesse parks his car around back, picking through the weedy lawn past charred spots where kids burned tires and couch cushions, scatterings of bullet casings from where others used the No TRESPASSING sign as target practice. The kitchen entrance has a lock you can outsmart with a credit card; as Jesse remembers, it's the easiest way of coming and going from the house. Now, however, it's boarded over with plywood. The first-floor windows have been boarded up, too, to keep out the riffraff. The riffraff have responded by spray-painting the boards with penises.

Jesse is undeterred. He knows this house's shortcuts and secrets. He circles around back and climbs the old wisteria vine, tendrils as thick as his arm, after which he makes his way over the roof and slips in through an upstairs window.

A familiar smell overcomes him: sickly sweet rot and heat. He treads carefully on warped floorboards. Many years' worth of graffiti layers the walls—*Mud Hogs 4ever; Madison French is a WHORE; joe's pecker wuz here, 2003.*

Using his phone as a flashlight, he makes his way into a coiling stairwell. Additions to the house have created odd shapes inside its rooms: narrow, dead-end hallways, doors that open onto walls, low ceilings that require crouching. He descends into the stuffy dark of the kitchen, where pricks of sun cut in through gaps in the boarded-up windows, little flecks of yellow on peeling wallpaper. None of the original furniture remains, though several lawn chairs have been abandoned here among beer bottles and cigarette butts and condom wrappers, along with an old Ping-Pong table, which is snapped clean in half. The living room is down another hall, through a series of lintel arches. A couple of couches have been deposited here, their sour fabric flowered with mold. To the left of the fireplace, there's a massive hole in the wall, which is roughly the size of a person. Another careless party casualty.

And the house is haunted, of course. He recalls Halloween freshman year, he and his friends following after big bad junior Red like ducklings: Jaelah and her boyfriend, Bash, and her cousin Spencer, all dressed as characters from *Adventure Time*. Jesse and his friends were shy in middle school, having mostly cohered over liking the same offbeat cartoons, and he thought it would be good for them, this rite of passage, which would help transform them into proper teens. He was Sam Spade that year, a cigarette behind his ear (borrowed from Red), a plastic Maltese falcon in his coat pocket.

He remembers Red stopping them in the candlelit foyer, pointing toward the thump of the partiers upstairs. "Hear that? That's Mr. Simms, dragging his wife across the floor." He laughed as he ushered them along toward the big entry hall stairway. "C'mon. There's a place in the old nursery where blood comes out the walls."

At first, the group clung together as they moved. Bash kept talking in kind of semi-ironic knight-speak—"Ruffians abound, friends! Look alive!"—while Jesse pressed so tight against Spence he could practically feel his pulse. They all let out bursts of crazy laughter, spurred by nothing, and they weren't even drunk; they did not drink; they still had that wild, kiddish energy that would let them get silly off Cheerwine. At some point, however, they grew brave and untangled themselves from one another, and in the murk of the house, Jesse lost sight of them. They were shouting his name through the walls, but he seemed to be stuck in some kind of eternal hallway and didn't know how to get back to them.

It was fantastic. Scary, but fantastic.

To his knowledge, those shy friends never went back the Night House. But Jesse did. Many times. He knows all its weird turns and dead ends, its hidden closets and creepy crawl space doorways. In fact, as he explores, he becomes more certain that he knows it room to room, that there's no secret to be found, no passage or entryway unfamiliar to him.

Still, he searches everything—the pantry, the closet under the stairs, the old dumbwaiter, filled perilously with paper wasps. Under a couch, he finds the skeletal remains of what looks like a possum. In the bathroom, a colorful array of fungi. Foot by foot, he inspects the floorboards for trapdoors, thumps his fist against the walls. He opens all the kitchen cabinets and shines his phone inside. Roaches scatter. His hair collects spiderwebs.

He searches until he hears voices on the lawn outside.

Then the too-close crack of a rifle.

"Fuck!" he cries, and hits the floor.

A man shouts at the house: "Get on out now. We know you're in there."

Jesse peers out the window through a gap in the plywood. Two men stand in the grass, their faces obscured by the rising sun at their backs. They carry rifles. One of them cocks his and points it at the sky.

"Get on out before we bust in after you," he says.

Jesse's stomach drops. His swollen cheek twinges like the tick of a bomb.

"Fuuuuuuuuck," he says.

Jimmy. Jimdog. James, named after his great-great-grandfather, patriarch of one of the oldest Pinewood families. Jim Harlan, who knows every story in the county.

He stands next to his uncle—the stout, scowling man who set the gun off. Harlan is twenty-six years old now, his body still slim and muscular in a graceful, dignified way you can appreciate even when he's standing still. He wears a tattered camo shirt Jesse remembers burying his face into. But the hollows of Harlan's cheeks are ragged with brown scruff, which Jesse does not remember.

Why aren't you shaved? he wonders.

Jesse can't stay in the house forever; they know he's in here. So he makes his way back to the second-story window, crosses the roof, and descends the porch trellis. Harlan's uncle, whose name is Laughton, shouts at him again as he makes his way to the ground:

"What you up there for?"

Jesse doesn't know how to answer him. He stands dumbly at the base of the trellis. Laughton steps closer, his rifle at his side, and Jesse sees up close his crumpled, moony face, perplexed and irritated, as if he's just been thrown into a conversation spoken in a language he can't understand.

"What you up there for?" he asks again.

Jesse looks to Harlan for some hint about what to do, but Harlan's doing that infuriating thing where his eyes are out of focus, where he looks at you but doesn't *see* you.

Laughton raises his gun and prods Jesse's ribs with the side of the barrel.

"Hey!" Jesse cries.

"Easy now," says Harlan, holding up a hand. "Let's not get physical."

"Step back, Jim, don't boss me," Laughton says. He asks his question again: "What you up there for, son?"

"Nothing," Jesse says. "You don't need to shoot me. Jesus."

"Mrs. Shatley called, said she saw a vagrant getting up in the house." Laughton gestures to the boarded windows. "You see all them boards up? What you think that means?"

Jesse considers the many spray-painted penises. "A phallic obsession?"

Harlan blinks slowly.

"Them boards mean they don't want you kids going in there no more," Laughton explains, as if speaking to a child.

"But there's nothing in there," says Jesse.

"What you after then?"

Again, Jesse doesn't reply. He glances between them, waiting for Harlan to intervene. Two pairs of eyes: Laughton's pale and tense, Harlan's dark and far-off. Then, after a long, awkward minute, a jeep from the Sheriff's Department rolls up the driveway, blocking Jesse's exit. The driver is Pete Sleight, a blond, affable former golden boy, not much older than Harlan, who spent all of high school being a mediocre wrestler and bullying goth kids. Now he carries a county-issued handgun. There are currently three guns to Jesse's one unarmed self.

Additionally, a squat, fat, beagle mix follows the deputy out of the jeep, its hackles raised. It surveys the scene with a low growl.

"That Jesse Calloway?" says Sleight. "Didn't think we'd ever see you back here. How's *college*?" He gives the word *college* a skeptical, sarcastic weight.

"Going as planned," Jesse says.

"Got a shiner there. You been getting in trouble?"

"No, sir. Stepped in the way of a cornhole game."

Sleight laughs. "Yowch. Nothing worse than getting cornholed. Hey, you sleep in them clothes, kiddo? You know Target's got a men's section, too."

Jesse smiles but says nothing. He does not like Deputy Sleight.

"Aw, hey, I'm just fooling," Sleight says. "What's the problem, anyhow?"

"This'n," says Laughton, pointing, "he climbed up in the house. Mrs. Shatley saw him get in through that window there."

Sleight arches his back and looks up, squinting. "Looks like that'd be the way to get in. What you doing up in that house, Calloway?"

"Nothing," says Jesse. "I just wanted to see what was in there."

"There's nothing in there," says Sleight.

"I know. I didn't know that before."

"He's giving you the runaround," says Laughton. "Smack him around a bit, he might change his tune."

"Ah man, Lot, much as I'd enjoy that, we can't smack folks around without a whole mess of paperwork," says Sleight. He squints at the house again. "This property belongs to the county. How'd them boards get up there in the first place?"

"We put 'em up there," says Laughton.

"You?"

"Me and Jim and some cousins from Apple Hill."

"Oh."

"Keep them damn kids out."

Sleight looks at Jesse, then back at Laughton. "So you, Jim, and them cousins, you defaced county-owned property?"

"Well, we weren't—"

"I mean." Sleight rests his arms akimbo and gazes at the house again. "Listen, Lot, here's my dilemma. If I write up a citation for Fancy McGee here, I'd have to write up a citation for all y'all."

For a moment, Laughton stands speechless. Jesse again tries to catch Harlan's eye and catches Sleight's instead.

"What'cha smirking 'bout, Calloway?" he asks. "You having fun? You want to get slung over the hood of that cruiser?"

Jesse straightens out his face. "No."

"No what?"

"No, sir."

Sleight smiles unpleasantly. The radio crackles in the cruiser behind him, and he heads back up the lawn, Laughton following stubbornly. Sleight's fat dog stays behind for a moment, watching Jesse and Harlan with dull, red-rimmed eyes. Then it yawns and trots off through the grass, leaving behind a brazen farty fug.

Jesse's face twinges. He looks up at Harlan, and Harlan, for the first time, looks back.

"'Let's not get *phy-si-cal*,'" Jesse says. "How do you say shit like that with a straight face?"

"Practice," Harlan says. "Why were you in there?"

"You want to know? That's why you and your uncle ran out here to give me the twenty-one-gun salute? Admit it—you saw my car and you got a little excited."

"I didn't know it was your car. I didn't remember what your car looked like."

Jesse laughs. "You're such a liar." He glares up the lawn, where Laughton gestures emphatically and Deputy Sleight nods smugly along, egos tripping over each other. Laughton makes frequent glances in Jesse's direction, rigid with suspicion.

"How 'bout this," Jesse says. "Tell me why you and Lot are spending so much effort to scare someone away from an empty house."

"Because it's condemned," says Harlan. "We don't want folks in it. They're tearing it down on Wednesday."

"No, they're not. What?"

"That orange sign there? That's a demolition notice."

"*This* Wednesday? Why would they do that?"

"Why would they not? Look at it."

"But—" Does Miss Velda know this? Surely, she would've mentioned it. "But there's history in that house. Real—history! It's been here forever."

"You don't care about history," Harlan says. "Why were you in there, really?"

A stone wells up in Jesse's throat. Once, he would've told Harlan everything, would not have been able to stop himself. Out it would come, like ticker tape. He bristles at the thought.

"Why does it look like a squirrel died on your face?" he asks.

"What?" Harlan laughs and scratches his cheek. "You mean the beard?"

"Beard is a strong word. Why did *you* think I was in that house, Jimmy? What were *you* thinking, siccing your uncle on me?"

"Come on, don't start."

Jesse laughs again. He feels lightheaded. Guns make him nervous. "Start *what?* You're the one with your dick out."

"I'm serious. Not while my uncle's here."

Jesse is ready to needle him further, but Sleight and his dog are coming back, Laughton close behind them. There doesn't appear to be any citation.

"Okay, Calloway," Sleight says with a sigh. "You've wasted my time long enough. Go on home to Nancy."

"I can go?" Jesse asks.

Laughton looks at him and shakes his head. Sleight's dog stares, likewise unconvinced.

"Yeah," Sleight says. "Get outa here."

This proves a challenge. Sleight has parked his cruiser so it blocks Jesse from backing out the way he came in, so he must drive around the house through a jumble of high weeds and shrubs and flooded grass. He gets stuck once, and Sleight and Harlan come over and slog into the mud to give his bumper a push. Sleight thumps on the back window and laughs at him— "Not the best vehicle for off-roading, huh, Calloway?"—and Jesse feels from the look on Harlan's face that his humiliation is complete.

When Jesse gets back on the road, he sees that Harlan and his uncle and Sleight and the dog have all reconvened next to the house where they were before. Harlan is explaining something. Sleight appears to listen. Jesse watches them, face flushed, heart still racing, and analyzes their movements, their posture, their faces, the rifles hanging stiffly on their backs. Laughton looks on edge, though he always does, but Harlan is on edge, too.

Cat, I'm worried

Tooly punched me in the face when I tried to talk to him
There are hick assholes guarding the night house
In three days it'll be demolished

What now?

What does it mean for this house to be demolished? Would all his memories go, too?

Back when he was fourteen, at that Halloween party, he'd let himself get lost, had followed that eternal hallway—like a secret passage in Clue—to end up in a shattered sunroom. This was where he met Harlan. While his friends wandered from one clutch of teens to the next, looking for him, Jesse and Harlan hung out on the porch alone together, talking. Just talking.

Later, Jaelah confronted him: "Who was that creep who kept bothering you?"

"What creep?" Jesse asked. He tried to explain that no one had been bothering him, but the boys took their cue from Jaelah and were also concerned. Red said that Harlan had dropped out of high school three years ago, and yet, in his twenties, he still skulked around this dumb teenage party scene. Who would do that? What could he want from Jesse? Funny enough, Jesse doesn't even remember what he and Harlan talked about that night, only that Harlan took the cigarette from behind his ear and lit it and said, "Play it once, Sam," as he blew smoke into the dark. Jesse said, "Wrong movie," delighted nonetheless that someone knew he was Bogart. All night, people had been calling him Inspector Gadget.

In the end, Jesse got a vibe from Harlan, same thing he'd picked up from middle school friends or summer campers who later decorated their social media pages with rainbow flags, who seemed, even as kids, to have a secret self. And it didn't stop Jesse from lurking on Grindr—not that he was *interested* in the tiny community of adult gays in Miskwa County; just curious—and searching in vain for the profile Harlan didn't have. And it didn't stop Jesse from changing his running route to take him up Peach Hill and into Pinewood and Bittern's Rest, to find Harlan fiddling with his truck in the driveway or drinking beer on his porch, asking Jesse if he wanted one— a lager—no, yeah, he remembered. Bogart. *Play it once, Sam.* And that, as they say, was history.

Now Jesse checks himself in the rearview mirror. Seeing Harlan again, he would've wanted to look clean and sophisticated, embodying his college era, but here he is with a dirty, busted-up mug, his hair filled with spiderwebs, his foppish clothes sweat-stained from the night before. He does not look sophisticated. He looks like someone who began his day pissing into a bush.

*   *   *

Bittern's Rest is not so much a neighborhood as a small curve of road, fifteen ranch-style houses with tin carports, single-wides, RVs, and a few sad army-green duplexes. Jim Harlan's duplex stands off by itself on the east end of the loop, partly hidden behind twisty oaks and holly hedges. Jim Harlan still lives there, Jesse assumes, in the same place he's lived since he was nineteen, sharing the duplex with no one. There was a story about why the landlord couldn't rent the other unit—crimes, smells, stained carpets—but Harlan changed the particulars every time he told it.

Jesse recalls other stories about Uncle Lot; Harlan made fun of him constantly. White-haired since he was thirty, humorless as dirt, Laughton once worked at the pig plant like Harlan but then ended up on disability, which exacerbated his neuroses. When Laughton wasn't cruising online conspiracy forums or hoarding dry goods in expectation of the nation's godless collapse, he helped around the neighborhood to a point bordering on obsession. It was understood in Pinewood that if you needed a tree hacked up, or a possum shot, or a wasp nest bombed, he was the man who'd bust out all manner of saw, trap, or poison and do it for free.

"He's a fixer," Harlan once explained to Jesse. "When he was in high school, some punks kept getting high and breaking in to vandalize the trophy case, and Lot took it on himself to rig bear traps for them. One kid got stuck there all night, dead of winter. Lost her foot."

"That's psychotic," Jesse said. "Didn't he get in trouble?"

Harlan just smirked and shrugged. "Nobody ever found out

it was him. They might've *suspected*, but you know—they didn't have to worry about that trophy case no more."

Once, Jesse asked if Harlan's uncle suspected what was going on between the two of them. Harlan burst out laughing.

"If he knew, he'd drag us into the woods and shoot us."

Jesse, who assumed this was a dark joke, laughed, too.

Among Harlan's people, there is no small honor in "sticking around," in "owning your roots." Harlan was—is—reasonably intelligent. He could've graduated high school, gone to college. But he followed the path of Uncle Lot, a man with the personality of a vigilante, fiercely loyal to his own, desperate to feel useful, lacking—Jesse thinks—moral imagination. It makes sense that Laughton would board up a house he didn't own and stand guard to ensure people he didn't like stayed out of it.

Doesn't matter that Harlan was—*is*—one of those people, those un-American degenerates Laughton complains about. Jim Fucking Harlan, twenty times more than his small uncle ever could be, deigning to be a *sidekick*.

This tragedy annoys Jesse, but he tries to ignore it the same way he ignores the pulse of the bruise on his face. He drives around Pinewood for a while, still looking for that idiot Tooly, trying to remember where he lives. There are several trailers that match the image he has in his mind—crooked blinds, a sun-bleached Confederate flag hung in the window—but when he chooses one and knocks on the door, a haggard-looking man answers, red-eyed, shirtless, a staticky yellow light pulsing in the dark room behind him.

"Yeah?" the man says, and Jesse's mouth goes dry.

"Sorry," he says. "Wrong house."

Pinewood knows Jesse is not Pinewood. He doesn't belong to the broken asphalt roads, the soybean and tobacco fields, the tiny churches and pro-life billboards, the scattered fruit stands and flea markets and the eclectic homes of folk artists, the kind who make sculptures out of bottles and car parts. Quirkiness and poverty, bundled like laundry. Just down the street from the haggard man's trailer is the spot on Redbug Road where Connie used to rent a house; years ago, many landlords sold their slums to Tarbarrel, who then razed them to build warehouses and hog confinements, expand their waste facilities. The smell here is awful.

He parks by the fence that marks off Tarbarrel property. Here, Jesse picks through the tall grass and milkweed, still damp with dew. He intertwines his fingers in the chain links, eyes the industrial pens across the field, their massive fans roaring. This is, he thinks, the emotional equivalent of the hobby historians who go out to old battlefields with metal detectors, but he soon begins to feel stupid, and the pig stench burns his eyes. The haggard man and a few of his neighbors have come down to the street to watch him, hands in pockets, heads tilted with a mix of amusement and derision. He wonders if they know who he is.

"Looking for something?" the man calls to him.

Jesse hesitates, his face flushing. "Do you know where I can find Tooly Quinn?"

"Not in that field, I bet. What you want with Tooly? You a friend of his?"

"Sort of. I'm trying to find him."

"Fishingham's," says one of the neighbors.

"He got fired from there," says another.

There's a brief contention about whether Tooly was fired or quit, but he definitely does not work there now. The haggard man then points out the Quinns' house down the way—a trailer nearly identical to his own, with marigolds growing in cinderblocks on the front deck. No car parked outside. No one home.

"What kind of car does he drive?" Jesse asks.

The man laughs. "Don't you know? Thought y'all were close."

Jesse didn't say they were close, he said they were friends, sort of. But he decides to take the hint and leave.

He searches a few more places for Tooly, both in Pinewood and downtown—the arcade, the bowling alley, that concrete lot beside the Stock-Hop where teenagers sometimes roll themselves down the loading ramp in grocery carts. No luck. In the afternoon, he buys a paper bag of hush puppies from Fishingham's and eats them in the Spartina Square gazebo, throwing crumbs at crows and flipping through the rest of *Belles and BLOOD!* Families mill about and shop, some still dressed in their Sunday clothes. He watches them, half hoping to see Morgan. It would be nice of her to text and check in, if she's not still shook.

But he doesn't see Morgan. Instead, through the crowd, at the intersection of Main and Desmond, he spies the dented front end of an old yellow pickup truck, its wheel wells speckled with mud and rust.

Jim Harlan's truck.

Jesse has an impulse to throw himself into the azalea bushes so he won't be seen, but in the time it takes to look there and back, the truck is already turning north, away from him.

He crushes the greasy hush puppy bag in his hands.

It's Sunday, he reminds himself. People run errands on Sunday. Harlan is probably out thrifting—old Nintendo games, vinyl, accessories for his Les Paul, boring stuff. But then, a few minutes later, when Jesse's getting into his car, the truck flashes in his side mirror, turning down the same street as before.

He whips around. The truck is gone. He tears out of his parking space and heads north up the street, but the Sunday crowd blocks his way at the intersection. By the time he's able to cross, there's no way to tell where the truck might've gone.

No, no. He was imagining it.

And why would Jim Harlan be following him anyway? Their thing ended, what, two years ago now? Harlan's not like Jesse. He doesn't linger. He doesn't scheme.

A crowd of kids and parents has descended on the library when Jesse arrives. There's a Children's Reading Corner every Sunday; this week, a library assistant is sharing Japanese folktales dressed up in a stunningly elaborate catfish costume, her headpiece complete with big wobbly eyes and blue sequin scales. Miss Velda, it's said, makes these costumes herself and requires that her assistants wear them. She is a dedicated librarian.

Jesse's here to return *Belles and BLOOD!* and to see if the ploy he set up for Miss Velda the day before paid off. If her curiosity led her into a conversation about the Night House, she might've learned something new by now.

However, as soon as she sees him coming toward her through the atrium, she becomes agitated.

"Oh—shit!" she says.

"Miss Velda?" says Jesse, taken aback. Across the room, the library assistant stumbles over her reading. A group of parents lift their heads at the swear, as if catching a bad smell.

"Honey," Miss Velda says, wide-eyed. "What've you gone and done to yourself?"

"This?" Jesse touches the feverish lump on his cheek. "It's nothing. I went up to the Night House this morning. Did you know it's getting torn down?"

"Torn down, mm-hmm," she says. "Honey, your aunt called not ten minutes ago. She's out looking for you."

"Nancy called here?"

"Didn't you put any ice on that? It looks awful. One of my cousins got a shiner like that when he was fifteen; it swelled up to the size of a tangerine and his eyeball *split open*. You need to tell Nancy, whatever you've been up to. I am not responsible for any of this."

"I don't understand," Jesse says. "Why did Nancy call *here*?"

"Pictures! She was all in a tizzy about some pictures." As she says this, something catches her eye past Jesse's shoulder. She whispers squeakily, "Lord in heaven, there she is now," and hurries behind the checkout desk.

Jesse turns to see Nancy coming toward him across the atrium, her sandals slapping the hardwood, her arms stiff at her sides. His bruised cheek throbs with sudden anger.

Pictures.

"I've been texting you," Nancy calls to him. "I've been driving all over looking for you; where—?" She stops a few feet away from him and already looks like she's about to cry. "What happened to your face?"

"Nothing," he says.

"Bullshit nothing. What is wrong with you?"

"Nothing!" he shouts, loud enough to interrupt the reading. Parents whip around, looking severe. The library assistant's catfish eyes wobble.

"Could y'all keep your voices down?" Miss Velda whispers. "This is a library."

"Shut up, Velda," says Nancy.

Jesse rushes for the exit, Nancy close on his heels. Outside, the afternoon heat has peaked, but the post-church crowd is still around. A restaurant patio bustles, its patrons sweating under umbrellas in the beer garden. A family sits at the Desmond Street fountain, eating melty fudge off wax paper. And off to Jesse's left, parked at the curb down the street, is the yellow truck. He can see Harlan plainly: Harlan's elbow hooked out the driver's side window, Harlan's scruffy face in the side mirror, cigarette hanging from his mouth like Robert Mitchum in *Thunder Road*. He spots Jesse, and the truck takes off, growling down a side street.

"Oh *god*," Jesse groans. The words force their way out of him, as if his insides had been squeezed. Then Nancy grabs his shoulder from behind. He wrenches away.

"I don't have time for this."

"You don't have *time*?" she says, bewildered. "What have you been doing all day?"

Jesse heads for his car, but Nancy grabs him again and yanks him back by the shirt, so hard he can hear the seams popping in his collar.

"Stop!" he cries.

"You need to talk to me," she says. "I hate when you're like this."

"I hate when you touch shit that's not yours. You're ripping my shirt; stop it!"

She lets him go, tears clinging to her eyelashes. They face each other on the sidewalk. Harlan's truck is long gone—Jesse has no chance of catching up to him now—so he might as well hash it out with Nancy.

"The pictures," he says.

Nancy nods and folds her arms. "How long have you had them? Who gave them to you?"

"Doesn't matter. Why did you think you could do that? You pack up all my stuff? You go through my things—my personal things?"

"You have been lying to me," she says. "You've been lying since you got here."

He hesitates, a lump of shame in his throat.

She goes on: "I don't care about the pictures. You have them. You obviously wanted to see them, and you found a way. Just talk to me. Tell me who did that to your face."

"It was an accident. At Red's party. We were playing cornhole."

"Red." Nancy's voice gets low and furious. "Was it a fight? Is Red—was Red that guy you were seeing?"

"No."

"Hon, help me out, will you? I don't want to see you fall into old patterns, not knowing what you're doing, who you're with. You were so *miserable* back then, I felt like I couldn't help you."

"You don't need to help me. I'm not asking for your help."

"So I just stand back? Wait until I get to find you black-and-blue in the goddamn ER again?"

He heads toward his car, too angry to speak.

"Don't turn around and walk away!" Nancy cries.

"I can't talk to you right now."

She runs alongside him. "You think I don't know what you're doing? You're *punishing* me for not letting you see those horrible pictures of her, as if you needed to see them, as if I'd be able to explain them to you somehow. I can't explain anything. She wasn't herself in the end and I told you that; I told you everything I could."

"It's not that," he says.

"Then what?"

"We can't even talk about her. We can't say the obvious thing."

"What obvious thing? That she lost her mind? That's what you want me to say? My baby sister lost her mind. You want me to say her name, too? Connie, Connie. Every morning like a Hail Mary or something, like penance? You can say her name, it's fine. I just don't want this sucking at the center of your life like a black hole, or for you to use it as some excuse to—"

She cuts herself off. Jesse stops at his car and turns to face her, daring her to finish the sentence. An excuse to act out? Binge drink? Blow off school? Do drugs in the woods and stay out all night? Lie to Nancy about whose house he was staying at? Get Jaelah and Bash and Spence to lie for him until they cut him out of their friend group? And there were also the lows—terrible lows—where he wouldn't leave his room and could not say what was wrong or who had hurt him or how he could be helped, and that made her helpless.

Overhead, a poplar is shedding fat green-and-orange petals onto the hood of Jesse's car. He imagines himself reaching up and tearing down the whole tree.

"Well," Nancy says timidly. "Maybe we should sit down and talk to Sheriff Hupp about the photos. What about that? She might want to know where you got them."

Jesse laughs.

Nancy continues, "What? She was there, wasn't she? She'd have more insight than me."

"I'm not going to sit and talk to you and Hupp," he says.

"Why not?"

"You *know* why."

Silence. Poplar flowers fall into Nancy's hair. She bats them away angrily.

"I deserve a private life, too, don't I?" she says. "Private thoughts and feelings."

"Yep," he says, getting in his car. "We both do."

"Christ, where are you headed now?"

"I'll be fine. Don't worry about me."

She bangs her hand on his windshield. "We're not done!"

He ignores her and speeds off down Desmond Street, blowing through one stop sign, slamming his brakes at the next. Two women in sun visors cross the street and give him a hawkish look. Morgan's stolen bottle of lemon vodka has rolled out from under the seat, a little more than half full. He looks at it. A tic pulses in his throat.

When Miskwa County gets dark, the whole sky seems to sink down. Jesse remembers that from childhood, like he could step

outside and find stars hanging in front of his face, close enough
to touch. Elsewhere, night skies are limitless, expansive, but
Miskwa's is heavy, slumping onto Jesse's old high school, the
library, the Chuckwagon, the fields and the hog farms, the
boggy pinewoods and trails he used to run until his shoes fell
apart, the grave in the Rosehaven Cemetery where his mother
is buried. Nancy is right about Connie being a black hole. Here
he is in her dark, empty orbit.

In the spring of his freshman year of high school, he met
up with Jim Harlan at Rosehaven to celebrate his birthday.
His own quinceañero. Harlan laughed at him for that. "You
mean quinceañera. Girls have quinceañeras." Jesse said they
have them for boys, too, but he was going off something told to
him by Luis and Matty, the Latino kids on the cross-country
team, and they tended to mess with him. Anyway, he and
Harlan had a bottle of whiskey to celebrate, which kept them
warm against the chilly March air, and they made their way
past the newer part of the cemetery, Connie's part, where the
tombstones are shiny granite and engraved with hearts and
teddy bears and Ford GTs, to the old part, where the graves
are raw and mossy, the names and dates scoured by time. In
the back near the fence is the Harlan family plot, a testament
to their former power. Harlan knew all the stories. Erasmus
Harlan, the cross-eyed Baptist reverend who could spellbind
a grown man with only his voice. His son James, the slave
catcher who sold his soul to the Devil for eyes that could see
through walls.

They sat side by side on Reverend Harlan's sarcophagus,
passing the whiskey back and forth while the stars hung within

arm's reach of their faces, and Jesse found himself telling Harlan about Connie Calloway. To throw a quinceañero, you had to have people, and Connie had shut everybody out, even her own family. Nancy said Connie might've dated some musician. How stupid is that? A *musician*. Soon as he found out she was knocked up, there he went. *Fwipp!* Gone. And Jesse is not even musical. Can't sing. Can't play an instrument. So this shithead gave him *nothing*. On and on Jesse went, relishing in his own fucked-upness in a way he would never do with his friends or Nancy. All the while, Harlan listened.

"Do you remember your mother?" he asked.

Questions from Harlan were always special. Jesse could feel his own heart glowing.

"I used to try," he said. "Don't tell anyone this. But I used to sit in my room holding her things—her postcards, this bracelet she used to wear—and I'd try to imagine how it happened. Like I could trick myself into remembering. I never did, but I'd always end up thinking of this story I heard. About this girl from Ohio. You heard it maybe. She was vacationing in the Amazon, and she came back with this bump on her leg. Didn't know what it was. Fourteen years later, it started moving, and a giant spider burst out of it."

"I believe I have heard that story," said Harlan. "Different version of it."

"Sometimes I think *I've* got a bump somewhere. From whatever horrible things happened back then. Fourteen years, so now would be the time."

He wonders now if he believed what he said back then. Or was he showing off? He'd felt proud to tell Harlan that story, as if he were proving himself worldly enough to be with him. It must've worked.

"Tough getting on without a mom," Harlan said. "Mine's been in prison since I was nine. Drugs. At least, that's what they got her on, in the end." He paused, reflective. "Actually, she might be out by now. Can't say. Haven't heard from her."

Jesse was eager to know more, but he tried to hide it. "And your dad?"

Harlan waved his hand, a gesture that seemed to illustrate a person vanishing into a mist.

"Probably not what old Erasmus would've wanted for his descendants," he said. "But oh well."

Was it weird that Jesse found this exchange of tragedies to be a turn-on? Afterward, Harlan threw the empty whiskey bottle against the obelisk of J. Wallace Kerrigan, where it smashed in the starlight. Then he grabbed Jesse's face with one hand and kissed him, while the other hand slid into his jeans. Jesse had been wanting this since October. He'd never gotten hard so fast in all his life. It was like Harlan could snap his fingers and there it was—*Atten-tion!*—and it was perfect, so perfect, getting each other off on the grave of a fire-and-brimstone preacher. Jesse hoped they'd made his cross-eyed head explode.

Now Jesse drives around remembering. Indulging. He does this until it's nearly dark, at which point he goes back to Red Koonce's place to return the lemon vodka, though not before he drinks enough of it to lose some feeling in his face. That's how he shows up on Red's porch, laughing, presenting the bottle with a flourish.

Red stares, puzzled and droopy-eyed. "What're you doing here?"

"I stole this from your kitchen last night when I was drunk. Thought you'd want it back."

"That? I don't want that."

"No?"

"I only got it for the girls. But I'll take it, seeing as you made the effort."

For a while, Red leans on the doorframe, like he expects Jesse to leave. When Jesse doesn't, Red says, "Oh—sure. Come on in, I guess," and steps back into the foyer. The porch and house are still trashed with party refuse, the air smelling of sweat and puke. There are even some leftover partygoers: Idgy, the Undead Corpse of the Confederacy front man, has traded out his banjo for a bong and is sharing it with his bandmate Dennis in the den. The third bandmate, an elusive bass player, is absent.

Then there's Tooly, sprawled face down on the couch, one skinny leg hanging off.

"Oh my god," Jesse says. Why did it not occur to him that Tooly never left Red's place? All that searching and the idiot's right here. "Is he okay?"

Red bends down and examines Tooly's face.

"Color's all right. Still breathing. We'll keep an eye on him."

"Jesus. What did he take?"

"Fuck if I know. Didn't he hit you? I heard last night y'all got into it."

"No. That wasn't Tooly."

"Oh, it weren't?"

"That was someone else."

Red looks at him curiously, then back at Tooly's slack face. "Well. He's not too bright. I do feel for him, though. The Quinns are an unlucky bunch." He claps his hands together. "Can I get you a drink, brother?"

He leads Jesse into the kitchen; the tower of alcohol seems much sadder and more excessive when the house isn't filled with people. Jesse wants to make a lame quip about letting his liver chill out, but he also wants a drink.

When he tells Red about the Night House, he nods with kingly wisdom. "Oh yeah, heard about that. Them tearing it down." He lifts his beer. "End of an era."

"Do you know *why* exactly?" Jesse asks. "That house has been falling apart for decades. Did somebody die in there?"

"A dude murdered his whole family in there."

"Well, yeah, but since then."

"Hmm. Maybe. Haven't heard nothing. You want a single? A double?"

"Double." What's wrong with him? This town. This town makes him drink. "I saw Jim Harlan and his uncle up there. It looked like they were guarding it."

"That guy!" Red busts out a heavy, deep-throated laugh. "Jim Harlan? Jesus, I thought he was dead."

"Dead? Why'd you think that? What's he been up to?"

"Haven't heard nothing about him. You're the one he was friends with; didn't y'all keep up?"

"No, we were more like acquaintances."

Red doesn't prod him about why he was up around the Night House in the first place. Maybe Red is perceptive enough to know about Harlan and him but chill enough not to care. In Blacknot, you're always wondering what people know and don't know about you, what they've heard and haven't heard, and whether they're chill about it.

Jesse decides to stay at Red's until Tooly wakes up. Red, Idgy, and Dennis want pizza. Jesse puts in money, even though he isn't hungry. He sips his drink slowly and is still nursing it when the pizza gets there. He can drink responsibly. He limits himself to one hit—two hits—off Idgy and Dennis's bong, then sits in the den and plays a few rounds of rummy with them. Dennis beats them all handily, at which point Idgy insists Dennis is cheating. He gives up on cards and retrieves his banjo.

"This is one I'm working on," he says. "It's called 'Fuck Carolina.'"

Jesse is the only person in the room excited to hear "Fuck Carolina." Dennis says he's not sure that one's ready, man, but Idgy, undeterred, plays his song about a tyrannical and sexually abusive father whose children murder him, cut him into pieces, and dump him in the marsh to be eaten by crabs. It's all obscenely bad. The hook is something like: *Mama says Spanish moss gonna soak up the blood, y'all. Daddy can't say prayers with a mouthful of crab claw.* The song ends with the children catching the crabs to be eaten in turn. Idgy says he wants to bring in an element of audience participation, having everyone scream the way crabs scream when boiled.

Jesse knows Idgy is thinking of lobsters, not crabs, but he doesn't want to interfere with the Undead Corpse of the Confederacy's artistic vision.

When the song is finished, Red looks confused.

"You're going to play this at the farmers market?"

"*Yes*," says Jesse, unable to hide his glee. "Please play it at the farmers market."

"Didn't they ask you to just do covers of Buffett and the Eagles and shit?"

"*No*," says Idgy. "Fuck those boomers."

"We got a gig tomorrow night at Willy's," says Dennis. "*And* Thursday. In Vernontown."

"Maybe," says Idgy. "If Robbie's cousin gets back to us."

Disagreement ensues about the dependability of Robbie's cousin. Red, who's sitting on the floor near Jesse, leans back on his elbows.

"I think the phone I'm sitting on is blowing up," he says blearily.

"Probably mine," says Jesse. "I'm super popular."

Red lifts his hip and hands Jesse's phone to him. He hopes it's Morgan. Or maybe even Cat, ready to explain everything. Wishful thinking. The message is from Nancy. She's apologizing angrily, first begging and then demanding that he come home. Jesse puts the phone away in his pocket.

"Just my aunt," he says to Red.

"Aw-haw. Came here to get away from Antsy Nancy."

"No, I didn't."

"Just like high school."

"Grow up, Red. Not everything's like it was in high school."

Red shrugs, taking this rebuke in stride. By now, Dennis has given up arguing with Idgy, and Idgy has moved on to play other songs from their album in progress: one about the Boston molasses flood of 1919; one about a ghost girl who burned in the Triangle Shirtwaist Factory fire; one that's a list of towns and schools where mass shootings have occurred. The album's trauma theme is relentless, and Jesse becomes less amused. His phone keeps buzzing.

Now he's hearing from the old high school crew as Nancy shoots off a string of inquiries to find him. *Does your aunt think we've been hanging out?* Spence asks, by which he means, *Does your aunt think we're still friends?* Because Jesse has not spoken to any of these kids since graduation. They've become strangers to him, less shy now, yes, but not by his doing. Spence is at Davidson, Jaelah at UNC. Bash is in Boston, maybe, pursuing an internship. They are all miles away and yet still hearing about his crap.

Not even the fearsome Minerva is spared. She sends him a message from Greensboro:

Go HOME. Stop torturing Nancy.

Jesse tosses back his drink and goes to the kitchen for a refill. He's been at Red's for hours. When he returns to the den, Tooly is sitting up on the couch looking pale and disoriented, the crease of the pillow engraved on his face. He blinks his puffy eyes against the overhead light.

Jesse stops in the kitchen doorway.

"Hey, bud," Red says to Tooly, speaking gently. "How you feeling?"

Tooly coughs and gags. That chalk mouth Jesse knows well. He gets a glass of water from the kitchen, and when he returns, Tooly is curled at the other end of the couch, shivering.

"Tooly?" says Jesse.

"Spahder fangers," he says.

"Spider fingers...?" Jesse whispers.

"Man, you were just dreaming," says Idgy.

Tooly grimaces and shakes his head. Jesse hands him the glass of water.

"Thanks," he mumbles. He locks eyes with Jesse. His pupils are large, floating in the gray rings of his irises. His blond eyelashes are so pale and delicate they're practically invisible. "Fuck, man," he says, laughing and pointing to his cheek. "I got you good."

"Yeah," Jesse says. "You remember that?"

"What, you gon get back at me? You gon hit me?"

The bruise on Jesse's face pulses hotly. "No, Tooly, I don't want to hit you."

"Why you here then?" Tooly sounds agitated, nearly frightened. "These arencher people."

Jesse glances at the boys, Dennis and Idgy watching blankly, Red looking uncharacteristically anxious.

"Hey," says Red, "it's all good. Calloway stopped in to say hi. He brought vodka."

"Yeah," says Jesse. He turns back to Tooly. "Do you think we could talk?"

For a moment, Tooly's face is blank. Then he scoffs, or maybe hiccups.

"Why?"

"Like, one on one?"

"Nah, man. I donwan no bitchass heart-to-heart with you. You wannask somn, ask."

Jesse takes a breath. He won't make the same mistake he did with Morgan, telling Tooly and everybody in the room about Cat. He won't mention his mother. He climbs onto the sofa and crouches in front of Tooly. Tooly frowns at this, pressing himself against the armrest.

"I want to know what you know about the Night House," Jesse whispers. "Someone told me there's a secret way inside."

"Who said that?"

"Doesn't matter. I can tell you know something."

Tooly shakes his head, flinging sweat off his shaggy hair.

"Tooly," Jesse says.

"Why you hassling me 'bout this? I hardly saw nothing; it spit me out."

"What spit you out?"

"The *house*, man."

Jesse looks toward the others questioningly, but they stare back at him in silence. What did he take to be riding on it this long? He leans in close to Tooly's face, decides to roll with it.

"Okay, it spit you out. That means you can get in. How do you get in?"

Tooly clenches his jaw. "Why? You affersomn?"

"Yes."

"What?"

"I'll know it when I see it."

Tooly scoffs, definitely a scoff this time. But after a moment, his face relaxes, and he looks at Jesse with—compassion? Remorse? Maybe nothing at all. Maybe whatever Tooly took emptied him out. "It's tricky. You gonget in the wall like, like you coming in from above. From up."

"Up, like from the roof?"

Tooly shakes his head. "Up—way up—like from the sky. You see the river."

"That doesn't make sense, Tooly. You can't see the river from that house."

Tooly scrunches one side of his face, as if thinking. Then his eyes lift, and his face goes slack again, and he stares at a space behind Jesse's head, toward the kitchen. He stares for so long that Jesse turns to look behind him. The shadow of the doorway blurs on the ceiling.

"What are you looking at?" he asks.

"Nothing," says Tooly. "I gotgetgoin." He uncoils himself and springs up from the couch, then doubles over as if experiencing a headrush. When that passes, he lurches across the room and grabs his keys from a glass bowl by the door.

"Wait a minute, man," says Red. "Don't drive like this."

"I'm meeting somebody."

"Meeting who?" asks Jesse.

"Don't you at least want a Red Bull?" asks Red.

Everyone follows Tooly to the door and onto the porch. Tooly picks up speed, jumping the porch steps, car keys jingling sharply. His car is parked on Red's lawn, a dented gray piece of shit with a flaked-off decal on the back window: GA$ OR A$$—NO FREE RIDES. Jesse shouts after him, "Meeting *who*?" but Tooly has already started the engine. He peels out, leaving fat muddy divots in the grass.

"That was weird," says Red as they watch Tooly's taillights recede.

"Yeah," says Jesse. "I wonder what's up with him."

"No, I meant *you*."

Red, Idgy, and Dennis all stand in a row behind Jesse, the moths and mosquitos circling the porch lights, landing in their hair.

"What?"

"The way you climbed up on the couch..." says Red.

"Yeah, why *were* you hassling him?" asks Idgy. "He's going through some shit."

"I wasn't *hassling* him." But the others are nodding, joining forces. A sticky tar feeling drips in Jesse's chest. "I wasn't. We were just having a conversation. It's just *Tooly*, for God's sake."

"Yeah, *just* Tooly," Idgy says. "Dead brother. Dead grand-dad. 'Nother Pinewood tragedy, just like that house. You think you're special, but you're the same as the rest of them kids who kept coming around, wanting in on some story that isn't yours."

Jesse stares irritably, his head in a haze. "That's not what I'm doing."

Idgy blows smoke over Jesse's head. "Why'd you jump Tooly at the party?"

"*Jump* him? Look at my face, man. Who laid into who here?"

Dennis speaks up, concerned: "But you did lie. You said that was someone else."

"Yeah," says Idgy. "Didn't he lie, Red? Didn't he tell you that was someone else?"

Crickets screech in the silence as their host looks embarrassed, like Jesse's deceit might be his own fault. He rubs the back of his head apologetically.

"Um," he says. "Hey, so, my parents get back tomorrow? We gotta get a head start in the morning, cleaning and whatnot."

"He means it's time to fuck off," says Idgy, as if Jesse might not get the hint.

Out on the road, the sky is so clear he can see the Milky Way, a sparkly blob reeling from one dark horizon to the other. He drives down Peach Hill, having drank and smoked just enough to fog his thoughts, sour taste on his tongue like a sausage skin. His mind turns over what Tooly said, what Idgy said. *Did* he jump Tooly last night? Was it hassling to pry him about what happened in the Night House? That punch had seemed defensive—all fear, no anger. Maybe Jesse has been insensitive to Tooly's plight. Though he finds it deeply hypocritical that someone like Idgy would accuse anybody of appropriating a tragic story.

Dark pines blur on the roadside, the occasional trailer tucked down a gloomy driveway. He has to go home eventually. He has to face Nancy. The night sky is getting closer and closer, and eventually he's going to have to crawl out from under it. In his pocket, his phone vibrates. More pleas? Another reprimand?

No. This time it's a message from Cat.

Sage skull Arrow
    marrow red Wound king clay
moon
Eye moss Vessel
    palm
gate Wing

He scrolls up. Cat's messages have retransformed into the

same type of mangled verses Morgan saw the night before. They parade across the screen like they're dancing, making fun of him. Cat is making fun of him. They're *doing* this somehow, changing the words.

"Asshole," he says to the phone, and returns his eyes to the road. A row of orange plastic barricades flares up in his headlights, blazing at him fast. He hits the brake, tires shrieking.

The *sinkhole*—!

His car rams the barricade. Crunching sounds. He clenches his eyes shut. In the next second, he'll tip forward, go vertical. The sinkhole will swallow him whole. But then the car shudders to a stop, and when he opens his eyes, he's still horizontal, and his headlights are beaming out over a wide, ink-black void.

The acrid smell of burnt rubber clouds the air. His fingertips spark with adrenaline.

He should've remembered the danger of the sinkhole. Pinewood boys die young every year. This is how it happened to Tooly's brother, Sam, at this very spot. Got wrecked and went out on Peach Hill in the middle of the night and whup—

Jesse cuts the engine, stumbles out to inspect the damage. Just a few new scuffs on the bumper, but the barricade is still under the car and he has no idea if he can get it out. He inspects the sinkhole, too: seven feet wide, unknowably deep, and spewing the stench of stagnant water. When he peers in, he fears irrationally that he might see Tooly's brother still down there, but poor Sam didn't die in the sinkhole. He died weeks later, at the hospital, attached to machines. It was in the paper.

Cat messages again:

Ivy hook rose
Jesse
Ivy mud
> **Crow vessel Hymn path**
> **moss gate**

Eye sage glass Vessel

Jesse lets out a cry and flings the phone into the ditch across the road. He hopes Cat feels it somehow, a stitch of voodoo pain, and for a while he stands there, glaring into the black mass of trees. A breeze picks up, blows over the sinkhole, whistles like breath over a bottle. It rustles the pines, trunks creaking against tilted trunks.

Once he has cooled himself, he trudges across the road and searches through the grass to find his phone. He picks it up again, cleans the mud from its screen—and he has an odd feeling, like an unwinding of threads in his brain.

Cat's messages haven't changed.

But he understands them.

I know about the demolition, but you'll get there in time

Sage skull Arrow, Sage skull Arrow—I know, I know. **Wound king**—destroy, demolish. He can see each thing. Their meaning weaves and spindles.

Promise, Jesse, make your way in, you'll see

Something moves in the trees. Jesse feels torn open, exposed. Since he arrived in this town, something has been watching him, he can see it now—some hunched, mud-matted figure, wide-eyed and quivering at the edge of the road. Quivering with fear? Fury? Is this really a ghost, like Morgan said? Sam Quinn's ghost?

Sam Quinn, come back to get him?

An engine revs down the road. Headlights burst into view like the grand cavalry. Jesse recognizes the rev of that engine, the sound of that truck as it screeches to a stop at the barricade. Jim Harlan gets out, his features obscured by the glare of headlights, but Jesse can pick out Harlan's shape from a mile away.

"What the hell are you doing?" Harlan shouts.

Jesse looks at him, trembling. When he turns back to the trees, the figure is gone.

"Hey." Harlan grabs his arm. "Hey!"

Jesse sways, his legs like jelly. He slumps to his knees in the road, clutching his phone to his chest so Harlan doesn't see.

Harlan crouches in front of him and takes hold of his shoulders. "Jesse, look at me."

Jesse homes in on Harlan's face, bristly as a sea urchin.

"Are you drunk?"

"Drunk?" he says. "No."

"Are you high?"

Jesse pulls away, irritation stirring him to his feet. *"No."*

"You smell skunky."

"Are you a cop now, Jimmy?"

"You're lucky you're not dead. Another few feet and you'd've gone right in that hole. What're you doing out here?"

Jesse heads angrily to his car. He doesn't intend to answer, but then his anger gives rise to a strange gratification. What is *Harlan* doing out here?

He turns back. "You *are* following me."

"What?" says Harlan. "No, I'm not."

"I saw your truck at the park, and at the library. Now you're here. Have you been stalking me all day?"

Harlan laughs. "Do you hear yourself?"

Jesse laughs, too. "You have, haven't you? You stalked me. *Stalker.*"

Harlan shakes his head wearily. He looks at the woods, then at Jesse's car.

"I guess you want help getting that thing out from under there," he says.

"No," says Jesse. The breeze picks up again. He can hear the trees creaking, the leaves in the underbrush shivering. Normal woodsy sounds. "Yes."

They end up in the parking lot of a twenty-four-hour gas station. Harlan goes in and comes out with two coffee cups and two packaged sticky buns. "Three sugars, right?" he says, handing a cup to Jesse. Jesse takes it, eats two bites of the sticky bun, and feels queasy. All the while, Harlan watches, leaning against the hood of his truck. Jesse eyes Harlan in turn. An ugly, half-moon scar stands out on his forearm like a knotted rope. Jesse's mouth goes dry.

"So." He is anxious for something to say. "Still working the killing floor at Tarbarrel?"

"Packer," says Harlan. "I've always been a packer."

"Right. Those pigs ain't gonna pack themselves."

"Mmm," says Harlan.

"I think I had in my head that you worked the killing floor because you used to hang up your company jacket by the door, and sometimes, whenever I walked by it, it smelled like blood. I don't know why I remember that."

A yawning silence.

"Any particular *reason* you've been following me?" Jesse asks.

Harlan gives him a cool look. "Any particular reason you were up in my neighborhood?"

Jesse hesitates, considering his options.

"I'm—investigating something."

"Aw, yeah?"

"Yeah. About Tooly."

Harlan says nothing.

"You know. Tooly? Skinny guy always coming around your place? I was just at Red's trying to ask him a couple questions and he took off like a maniac. I think there's something wrong with him."

Harlan inhales a sharp, irritated breath. "Sure. Got nothing to do with you, though."

"It doesn't? You sure?"

Silence. Jesse holds tight to his gas station coffee, sipping it slyly.

"I know something happened to him in the Night House," he says. "He told me."

"Look at you, little detective."

"He told me," Jesse says with intensity, "that something *happened* to him in there."

"And I'll bet that's why you were in there this morning."

Jesse's phone weighs heavy in his pocket, the messages from Cat sitting in it like a hex.

"Maybe. Maybe not."

Harlan laughs and shakes his head. "No, kid. I ain't playing this game with you. Not this 'Guess what I'm up to' shit. I don't need to know what you're up to. Not my business. I'm just telling you now that you're being stupid. You can't be nosing around like this in places you don't belong."

Jesse tenses at the familiar chiding in Harlan's voice. He imagines himself throwing his coffee in his bristly face.

"That's right," he says. "That's right, because you were never into games. You were always *so* up-front. No games with you."

Harlan sighs.

"You remember how I take coffee, but you don't recognize my *car*? I drove that car over to your place the day I got it, and *you* said—"

"Jesus."

"You said it'd be too small to fuck me in it."

Harlan stares with his dark, half-lidded eyes. "I never said that."

"Oh yes, you did, Jimmy, yes, you did. 'Little small for the long ride, chico,' that's what you said. And you were wrong, by the way. You can't imagine what that car has seen."

"I didn't remember the car was yours. I didn't stash away every little detail."

"Why were you and your stupid uncle guarding that house? Why were you following me? Were you worried? You think I'm here to make trouble?"

"Yes," Harlan snaps, raising his voice. "You show up in Pinewood, right near where I live. You won't tell me why. Yeah, I had a notion you might cause trouble."

Jesse's face burns. "My being here has nothing to do with you."

"Good."

"Don't you dare think I'm here because of you."

"Okay, kid. I mean—" He laughs again. "I'm glad to hear that. I'm just saying, maybe *you* don't remember all the texts and voicemails, but *I* do. And you coming over unannounced. And you sitting all hunkered in your car outside the plant—talk about *stalking*? Jesus Christ. When I heard you were seeing girls again, I was *relieved*, man, because that's what I told you to do. Find a woman to tamp down your crazy and *stop fucking with me*."

Jesse drop-kicks his coffee cup in a fit of fury. The lid pops off and coffee explodes everywhere, on his jeans and Harlan's. The empty cup goes skidding into the road.

For a moment, they stare at the rolling cup in silence. Jesse is mortified, not only for the outburst, but the fact that the emotion in Harlan's response has actually aroused him. He's humbled, subject to himself. When he speaks, his voice sounds like it's coming from inside a well.

"Sorry."

Harlan sighs again. He was always sighing.

"It's fine."

Jesse retrieves the cup and throws it away, the splatter cooling on his jeans. He's cooling, too. He turns to face Harlan across the length of parking lot.

"Listen, I'm not here for this," he says. "Honest. It was decent of you to help me with the car and everything. But, clearly, we need to stay out of each other's way."

"I think that's reasonable."

"Thank you."

"You should go home. You look like you ain't slept in days."

Jesse combs his fingers through his hair. "I sleep fine, thanks."

"Like you been teed up all week."

"I'm *fine*, Jimmy. Shave your own face, will you?"

He goes to his car, proud to have ended the conversation. Before he can leave, however, he looks over his shoulder and sees Harlan standing unnervingly still, gazing out past the gas station fluorescents into the black web of woods on the other side of the road. It hasn't occurred to Jesse to tell Harlan about the figure on the roadside, at the waterfront. Jesse has been drinking since he got here. He's a little high. He doesn't even know if he trusts his own senses.

"What," he says. "You see something?"

"No," says Harlan. His voice is theatrical, like the faraway persona he'd take on when he told ghost stories. "Just stay out of Pinewood, okay? It's not safe for you there."

"I'm not scared of Pinewood. I know the place as well as you do."

Harlan looks at him. His face is sad, disbelieving.

"You know what Uncle Lot used to tell me?" he says. "Better the devil you know, but the devil you know hits harder."

Another inky silence. One of the fluorescents flickers overhead. A gas station attendant cleans the windows—*squeak, squeak.*

Jesse glares at Harlan until he turns and heads back to his truck. "Good seeing you, kid."

Jesse doesn't know which of Harlan's stories were true. He recalls so many. In the cemetery. On his futon. In shabby lawn chairs on his back porch in summer, with the fireflies blinking, and Harlan with a sweating beer in hand, gesturing to the darkened trees.

"They say something's out there. In the swamp. Across the bridge in South Greene, they've forgotten. But here they remember."

"Like some kind of creature?" Jesse asked.

"Nah, bigger than that. Immersive. Like—the land has its own mind." He sipped his beer and squinted. "You know this county's known for cults? The Angel Battalion. New Psalms of the Lamb. You head north into the swamp and you get a little crazy. They've even sent the government out to investigate, couple suits from Raleigh. Didn't find nothing. Then this ethnography team come down from Massachusetts—they go upriver and find this church where the whole sermon's delivered in tongues. But the thing is, nobody in the congregation even *realized* it until the ethnographers showed up. They just spent so much time out there it warped them. And of course they picked up a few other—you know—unorthodox behaviors."

What behaviors, Jesse wanted to know. Orgies? His first thought was orgies. Harlan made a joke—"You little freak, why's it always orgies with you?"—and now, years later, Jesse can't remember if Harlan continued the story or if they had to follow the orgy line of thought to its physical conclusion. Either way, he's surprised he never connected any of this to his mother, who also headed north along the river and went a little crazy.

Now, as he pulls into his driveway on Dogwood Grove, he begins to shake. A new language comes to him, not in sounds, but in images bright with meaning: **Sage skull**—know—**Wound king clay**—destruction—**Hook rose**—promise. Morgan saw Cat's messages as inscrutable because they are and always were, but Jesse couldn't tell. As he examines them in his car, they remind him of one of those eye-tricking pictures. Lady or crone? Duck or rabbit? He can see and understand, but not at the same time.

Eye claw Arrow. Hook rose.

He writes:

> **Eye claw Arrow**
> **Hook rose**
>
> *(I'll try, I promise)*

How can you know a language you never learned? How can you write in that language without *realizing* it? Should he ask Cat, or would it break their connection? And was this why the connection felt so strong in the first place? He sensed—but he didn't *realize*—that when they wrote to each other the words came from behind a veil.

> **Stone owl**
> **Aster briar**
>
> *(Good night, dear friend)*

He's been sitting in his car in the driveway for who knows how long when Nancy startles him with a *rap rap* on the passenger window. Her anxious face hovers in the dark, one hand pressed flat against the glass, pleading with him. He expected her to be angrier.

He gets out of the car, shamefaced. "I'm so sorry."

"Do you know Morgan Taylor?" she asks, like she didn't hear him. "High school girl from South Greene?"

He hesitates. She has deflated his apology like a balloon.

"Morgan? Sure—I know her. Why?"

"Sheriff Hupp called me back. Some people told her they thought maybe Morgan was with you tonight."

Who told? Jesse glances fretfully from one neighbor's house to the next—he's not sure why; maybe he's worried they'll overhear?—but it's the middle of the night, and all up and down the street, every light is out but theirs.

"I saw her last night at Red's place. Why?"

Nancy has a stricken expression.

"Why?" he asks again.

FROM THE UNTITLED MEMOIR OF
HARRY M. BISHOP, C. 2013

This is a true tale. Heard it from neighbor Mr. W. and later from a boy in the schoolyard when I was twelve, maybe thirteen. First I ever heard the term *ill repute*. For some time, the widow Lewton's night women had talked of activity in their house, unexplained sounds and lights, strange objects appearing in closets, feelings of being watched, and so on. Maisie Kemp, twenty-one, was playing hide-and-seek with a client when the client went to Mrs. Lewton's dressing room and reported that he could not find Maisie and had been looking for nigh over an hour. "Well, that is the point of hide-and-seek," the widow said, but the client replied that, given the nature of services rendered at the widow's establishment, the seeking should have been more important than the hiding. Other women then aided in the search, but Maisie was nowhere to be found, and the client went home unserviced. Days went by. It was rumored that Maisie had met up with a beau from Jacksonville and skipped town altogether, and so the rest of the women carried on, business as usual. Months later, however, Maisie burst from the linen closet, dusty and screaming—"I'm found! I'm found! Jesus forgive me, I'm found!" But she could not account for where she had been. This incident is partially verified in an article in *The Horn*, noting a disturbance at an unspecified Pinewood home in September 1942. A neighbor woman claimed to have encountered a disturbed girl "stalking" through the cotton field behind her house, her skin red and peeling, "as if scalded with sunburn," her pupils "contracted to pinpoints." When interviewed, Mrs. Lewton and the other women of the house were unforthcoming.

6

Some state law has dictated that, due to Alice's illness, she can't take a driver's test until she's twenty-one, and so she has to be ferried around like a child from South Greene to the library where she works and back. At the end of the day, it's usually one of the library assistants who drives her, sometimes Miss Velda herself, even though she lives nowhere near South Greene and has to go out of her way to take her home. Today is a Velda day, and Velda—always eager to make small talk, even though Alice returns her enthusiasm with a long-suffering blank stare—wants to chat about Morgan Taylor.

Unsurprising. In less than twenty-four hours, Morgan's disappearance has become the county's star story. South Greene has sprung into action as if they were expecting it, as if this were *their moment*. Folks post updates to a hungry audience on the Find Morgan Taylor Facebook group. Right now, while Alice is riding home in Velda's car, half the town is following the directive of local law enforcement, sweeping the ground on foot, the tangly trails at the edge of the marsh, the Rosehaven

Cemetery—any devious spot where the body of a naive teen might turn up.

"It's awful strange," Velda says. "I mean, I hope they find her, of course, but to disappear like that, in the middle of the day?"

Alice shreds a knot in her hair and stares at the dashboard. Velda has a nice car for a librarian, one of those that starts with a button. Its insides whine like a spaceship.

"Y'all know the Taylors, don't you? They're only just around the block."

"I guess," Alice says.

Velda nods sagely. "Not exactly friends? Your daddy said you had some trouble with that, making friends. I get it. I might not look it, but when I was your age, I was a shy girl."

Shyness is not Alice's problem.

"Y'all got an alarm system at the house?"

"Yeah."

"That's good, that's good." She pauses. "Though, now that I'm thinking, I don't know if that would've helped the Taylor girl. These teens are not known for the best judgment when it comes to trusting folks. My urologist said that whatever happened to that girl, it probably involved somebody she thought she could trust." Velda flicks her eyes toward Alice. "Don't you think?"

Alice shrugs.

The librarian nods again. "It's rarely ever a stranger. Statistically."

The bridge to South Greene rises up over the river, swelling like the back of a sleeping animal. At the midpoint, you can see far and wide, the marsh with its thick black water to the west, the river with its singing green islands to the east. Alice wonders how far she could make it if she did a tuck and roll out of the car, jumped off the bridge, and just started swimming. Would she drown before they caught her?

"I'm sorry, sweetie," Velda says. "This whole mess can't be good for your anxiety."

Alice pries at the wad of hair she just extracted and nearly laughs. Anxiety? Is *that* what Euel tells people her problem is? It isn't *wrong*. Sometimes she's anxious. But she's not as anxious as Velda, sitting jittery in the driver's seat like a spark. Alice is pretty sure Velda only agreed to take her on at the library because she's desperate to know what Alice did to warrant institutionalization.

When Velda pulls up into the circle drive, Bobbie comes down the front steps to greet them. She and Velda smile tensely. Neither one of them cares for the other, but Velda performs the favor of ferrying Alice around, and Bobbie Swink's father-in-law has his name on the archive room.

"Thanks again, Miss Velda." Bobbie turns to Alice and clasps her hands together. "Just in time, too. You can help me prepare."

"Ooh, prepare for what?" asks Velda, unable to help herself. "Y'all having a shindig?"

The dinner. Alice forgot about the dinner.

Alice is a voracious reader, but only when it comes to her specific interests. She likes to read about Catherine the Great and Che Guevara, the Civil Rights Movement, and the IRA. She is fascinated by what happened to the Romanovs. She has an entire encyclopedia set about the lives of the saints. But the largest chunk of her library is comprised of folklore, Edith Hamilton's Greek myths and Andrew Lang's fairy books, Balkan tales, Russian tales, Gullah tales, Cherokee tales, many of which she bought from secondhand stores, or received as gifts from her father and Bobbie, who initially thought this was a good outlet for her.

The Queen of Cats comes from one of her childhood favorites, a Celtic collection. According to the tale, a farmer was once walking by a graveyard when he saw a procession of cats dancing on their hind legs and carrying a tiny coffin. They were chanting: "The Queen of Cats is dead, the Queen of Cats is dead." So the farmer, amazed by what he'd seen, went home to tell his wife about it. "There were these cats in the graveyard," he said, "dancing on their hind legs and carrying a tiny coffin. And they were chanting, 'The Queen of Cats is dead, the Queen of Cats is dead.'" Suddenly, the farmer's house cat, which had been lying on the hearth, sprang up and shouted aloud, "The Queen of Cats is dead? That means *I'm* the Queen." And then she vanished up the chimney in a twist of smoke.

Alice always enjoyed the timing of the story. The Queen of Cat's succession rested on what appeared to be ordinary cats. Or, she speculated, maybe there were no ordinary cats. They were all magic creatures in disguise, fooling the world until the right moment came. Strays used to come around her mother's house in Pinewood, skinny and long-faced, and Alice remembers feeding them lunch meat on the back porch. She would ask them what they were waiting for, but they never answered her. They sounded like soft velvet folding, like tiny shells dropping on glass. *What are you planning, kitty cat?* she'd wonder. *Would you rule us all? Would you destroy your enemy, the dog?*

There's this hair clip of her mother's—she always wears it when she knows she'll have to be around a lot of people. It's made from auger shells, arranged and hot glued into a spiral, and made at a time in the 90s when such DIY accessories were more of a thing. The hair clip looks good with nothing, but Bobbie, who spent years sighing despairingly about Alice's homely thrift store wardrobe, can forgive tackiness for sentimentality.

The augur shells—they don't sound anything like cats. They sound like the surf and the gluey animals that once inhabited them—but all together the hair clip sounds like a heartbeat. Alice can only guess it absorbed that sound from her mother as she was making it. When overwhelmed, Alice wraps her brain around the beat, that gentle *thup THUP, thup THUP.* Then, if she listens hard enough and deep enough, there's an extra sound, a powerful undercurrent, like a song that comes from the water—a rich, old, blue song. Nothing in her mother's notebooks explains what this sound is or where it comes from, but she knows that with it she is stronger. In control.

When ready, she crosses the lawn from the guesthouse to the kitchen patio. Twilight approaches. The grass, still warm from the heat of the day, whispers against her bare ankles. The river lets out a long, slow breath as the tide recedes. Through the kitchen window, Alice can see Bobbie already running in circles, can feel her helpless noise. Bobbie catches Alice watching her and glares back, giving a shrug like *What the hell are you doing?* Then, in a dissociative sweep, Alice is there, standing in the kitchen doorway. She sees Mrs. Moseley in a passionfruit-pink dress, sashaying toward the living room with a cheese tray in hand. Her husband is already sitting down with Euel, their laughter sparkling like soda. A blues record plays. Bobbie's at the counter cracking ice cubes into a punch bowl.

"Alice Catherine?"

Alice turns, her face flat as paper.

"What's wrong with you? Why are you standing there like that?"

"What, Bobbie? Standing like what?"

Bobbie cinches her mouth, fresh lipstick bright and pearly. "You knew I wanted you to help me prep dinner, and you went off and hid for an hour. Didn't you hear me on the intercom? What were you doing out there?"

Alice doesn't answer.

"Are you drunk?"

"No," says Alice. "You know I don't drink."

"Yes, you do drink. You stole a bottle out of the pantry last week, a pinot noir. I'd just brought it back from New Bern. I bet you've done that before."

"I didn't drink your wine."

Bobbie stares at her, angry, but also anxious. "Fine," she says. "I don't even need to hear it." She dumps rum and juice and grenadine into her punch bowl and places it in Alice's arms. "Go take this in there."

The ice cubes click and splinter, prickly all over. In the living room, Alice places the bowl on the table. From the record player, Bessie Smith sings soulfully about wanting to kill her cheating man.

Lord, I'm bound for Black Mountain, me and my razor and gun
I'm gonna shoot 'im if he stands still and cut 'im if he runs

"Are you guarding the punch, Alice Catherine?" asks Pastor Moseley, reaching past her to the ladle. "A futile effort, I'm afraid."

She almost smiles at him, then decides to stay in this spot by the punch as if posted there. Guests filter in, first Mr. Bale, then his wife, who's coming in separately from a County School Board meeting. Then, twenty minutes late: Tanisha Patton. One arm cradles a glass casserole dish; the other is hooked like a fish on Euel's elbow. Euel is thrilled that they all get to formally meet Mrs. Patton, he says, as they've probably seen her running around town doing everything under the sun for him. A real superwoman.

Mrs. Moseley says, as if fascinated by Mrs. Patton's presence: "Are you related to Nate Patton? The man who owns the bakery downtown?"

Mrs. Patton nods politely. "Yes, he's my husband. I take full credit."

"He makes those smart sugar sculptures."

"Spun sugar. He made me a bird in a nest for my birthday today." She holds up the glass dish, which contains a glazed golden sheet cake. "Also this. It's black currant and lemon."

"Oh my goodness!" cries Mrs. Moseley. "It's your birthday today? That's so *cute*!"

Mrs. Patton laughs. "Well, all right."

"How old are you? Is that rude? You look young enough that it's not rude to ask."

"The big three-six."

"No way. No *way*! You are not thirty-six."

"Euel, you dingbat," says Ouida Bale in her smoky voice. "You have this woman bringing her own birthday cake to this get-together? What's wrong with you?"

Euel smiles at Mrs. Patton. "Two steps ahead of me as usual."

Mrs. Patton responds with an enigmatic smile of her own, which bothers Alice. Then Bobbie comes in to greet the new-comers. She takes Mrs. Patton's cake with an "Oh no, you *shouldn't* have," and she means it. Bobbie has a three-course menu planned for the night, and Alice can sense that the presence of this additional dessert has her close to tears.

"We'll have to serenade you," Pastor Moseley says to Mrs. Patton. "I apologize in advance."

Mrs. Patton plays bashful. "There's no need to fuss."

"No! All the fuss, all the time," Mrs. Moseley says, waving her phone in the air. "Let's take a group selfie, document our coven. All y'all, come around here by the couch. You too, Alice Catherine, I see you hiding over there. Bobbie! Where'd Bobbie go?"

Bobbie returns from the kitchen, where she had taken Mrs. Patton's cake. Euel raises his eyebrows at Alice, and she lurches over to the couch and stands unsmiling in the back of the group. Mrs. Moseley takes a few pictures before she's satisfied with the angle of her chin. She cackles: "Tanisha, your skin looks amazing, I *will* need to know your routine. In. Detail."

Alice feels Mrs. Patton squeeze her arm.

"You owe me," she whispers.

Alice wants to squeeze her arm back, a silent thank-you, but Mrs. Patton moves away too quickly.

*   *   *

See how Euel arranges everyone at the table: Bobbie, tightly
wound, to his right, Alice to his left. Everyone else is seated
clockwise by how much he likes them, except for the person
at the end of the table, usually someone who has something
Euel wants. Alice assumes the target is Councilman Bale; he
arrived with a stubborn expression that seemed to say he wasn't
keen on coming in the first place. There's a tax ordinance up for
renewal; there's a contract underway that poses some interfer-
ence with Tarbarrel; or maybe it's more personal than that—an
argument or a grudge; Euel wants a concession. But then, to
Alice's surprise, Euel directs Mrs. Patton to this special seat—
it's her birthday, after all—and Alice can't tell if he's breaking
the pattern on purpose or if his plans have changed and he's
improvising. She only knows that when he looks at her and
winks, he can see her paying attention.

See, she wants to say to Mrs. Patton. See the room arranged
so that the corners of the furniture make a star, pinning the
guests in place. See the two beady-eyed hound dogs watching
from the painting over the minibar. See Euel make use of his
guests, letting them bounce off one another, hanging back from
the conversation but somehow quietly dominating it. There is
an energy baked into the room simultaneously relaxed and perfunctory. Euel grins and drinks and gets pink-faced. He has the
reputation of a lush, but he is in control. They don't even know it.

See, Alice wants to say. She doesn't think Mrs. Patton sees
at all. Despite what Mrs. Patton said earlier about Alice *owing*
her, she seems comfortable, sliding into the group like she
belongs. She comments on the records Euel is playing, how

much she likes them, laughing warmly (genuinely?) when the others make jokes. She seems to be getting used to Mrs. Moseley's constant talking. Meanwhile, Alice scours every interaction and eats only vegetables—no pork loin for her, no spiked punch. The room has become louder, so dense with conversation it's hard to hear anything else. The punch does its work. Tongues get loose.

"So I assume we've all heard about the poor Taylor girl," says Ouida Bale.

Alice's hands go numb. Her fork squeaks across the plate.

"Yes, dreadful," Bobbie says.

"I'm leading a vigil tomorrow, two PM," Pastor Moseley says.

"Unimaginable," Bobbie says. "Makes no sense at all."

"Doesn't it?" says Mrs. Moseley, who has been scrolling continuously through social media. "I mean, they've got a good chance of finding her, got the word out early, nearly three thousand shares. And I do hope they find her, I do. But let's be honest here..."

She leans forward, shirtsleeves flouncing.

"Are you reading the room, Selena?" asks Euel.

"I know that face," says the pastor. "She's about to say something she knows she shouldn't."

"I'm *not*. I'm just stating a fact, which is that it doesn't *not* make sense. In spite of *all* that church camp—everybody knows Morgan Taylor is a little quick for her britches."

"A little what?" says Councilman Bale.

"*Fast*," says his wife. "A wild child."

Alice clenches her teeth and glances at her father, but his eyes are on the ceiling, calm, pensive.

"Aren't all kids like that?" he says. "Eventually?"

Mrs. Patton laughs quietly. "Not *my* boys, I hope."

"Our two were all *sir* and *ma'am* right up until they left for college," adds Ouida, aggressive in her tipsiness. "None of this sneaking around."

"Right," says Mrs. Patton. "When you raise them right, they know better."

"She linked up with Nancy Calloway's nephew Saturday night," says Mrs. Moseley, ready to burst. "That's what her friends said. The two of them had a little *thing*."

Mrs. Patton looks taken aback, like the conversation has gone past her. The others scoff in disbelief until Pastor Moseley speaks up:

"No, friends, it's true. Our neighbor's son saw them leave a party together Saturday night. The sheriff has already been over to Nancy's house."

"Oh, I bet she has," says Ouida suggestively.

"Who is Nancy Calloway?" asks Mrs. Patton.

Ouida turns in surprise. "You don't know? You never heard that awful story about her sister? It happened up in Pinewood."

Mrs. Patton hasn't told the group that she's originally from Vernontown, not Pinewood. But Alice is sure that Mrs. Patton *must* know the story, because everyone remembers the child who was found on the riverbank, his mother dead nearby, the state of her so awful it brought the coroner back to church, or perhaps drove him away, depending on who's telling the story. It's hard to detach the Calloway boy from such a grotesquerie, to think of him as a budding adult who courts girls, goes on dates, has sex (with *whom?*). What an uncomfortable thought:

Those who see or experience such darkness surely carry it around with them, like a seed. They thought he was gone for good, but no, he's back. And a girl is missing.

"I was eighteen when that happened," says Mrs. Patton. "Stayed with my grandparents that summer, so I must've missed it."

"All Calloways are funny, but Constance was an occultist," says Ouida Bale. "No sane Christian woman buys that many candles."

"Carful, Ouida," says the pastor. "The same could be said of your essential oils."

"My oils are *useful*, thank you very much. They reinforce my sunny personality."

Mrs. Moseley says, "Did anyone look the kid up? He turned out to be quite the little weirdo," and begins pulling up pictures from Jesse Calloway's social media accounts.

Alice doesn't want to see this. She doesn't want Mrs. Moseley to circle Jesse around the table or to hear anyone theorizing about Morgan Taylor's rebellious ways. But she is more terrified about what they might say in her absence, what she might miss. The phone gets to her, and now she's looking at pictures she has seen before of a person she must pretend she has no feelings about. Jesse with his college friends, pretentious film kids, the campus running club, the LGBTQIA+ crowd. He has so many friends. In his profiles, he is coy about which team he plays for, but clearly something's up. On Halloween, he cross-dresses as Elizabeth Taylor's Cleopatra; he has taken the costume too seriously for it to be a joke.

Ouida Bale crows about this mark of apparent deviance: "The BTK Strangler did that. The one out in Wichita, remember?"

"I think the real crime is the eyeshadow," says Mrs. Moseley.

The two women laugh. Mrs. Patton appears uneasy, but she says nothing.

As for Euel—Alice expects no sensitivity from Euel. But when she turns to look at him, it still takes all her strength to keep the fury off her face. He's just sitting there. His expression is one of vague amusement.

This is how I know there's nothing in you, she thinks.

Councilman Bale clears his throat. "We don't need to be combing through the kid's social medias and whatnot. We already know the Internet is ruining them."

"Nancy will protect him, of course," Ouida goes on. "The trick here is getting the sheriff to be impartial, considering their special friendship."

"Conflict of interest," Mrs. Moseley practically cheers. "Conflict of interest!"

"What?" says the councilman.

Ouida turns to her husband and makes air quotes: "'Special friendship,' Eddie. Nancy Calloway and Sheriff Hupp have a 'special friendship.'"

"What are you talking about?"

She flicks her wrist at him. "I'll explain it to you later."

"Of course," says the pastor sagely, "you can never *really* control a teenage boy when there's no dad in the picture."

"Yes," booms the councilman, latching on to this point. "Nowadays, they'll tar and feather you for saying that, but it's true."

The conversation carries on like this for some time with Ouida and Mrs. Moseley speculating, and the pastor making dry remarks, and the councilman occasionally asserting spurious claims as if they were unquestionable. Bobbie contributes platitudes—"It really is something! So true! Strange as anything!"—when she isn't hopping up from her chair to grab a condiment or another sleeve of napkins from the kitchen. During one of these trips, Alice catches Euel and Mrs. Patton exchanging a look, an gentle eye roll that reads like *I told you so*, though it's not clear to Alice who told who what, or what the look might be referring to: the catty conversation, Bobbie hopping up from the table like a jack-in-the-box, a shocking secret between them.

Alice is starting to think she has no ally here at all. She grips the edge of the table and listens for the beat. That deep, deep song.

Thup THUP. Thup THUP. Thup THUP.

"May I be excused?" she asks.

Euel either ignores her or doesn't hear. He interrupts a disagreement between the pastor and his wife, saying, "Listen, listen. Slow down. I know y'all are having a good time speculating about this. But let's lay out the facts here before we get too crazy. What do we know?"

What *do* they know? What might come to the surface if they all keep drinking and talking?

"Morgan's parents," Euel says. "They went out to pick up a credenza from an antique mall in New Bern, leaving their daughter home alone. When they returned, they found her purse and her phone on the couch, which is where she threw them when they came home from church—but the girl herself had disappeared, in broad daylight, without a word to anyone."

"You think she was abducted?" says the pastor. "That's what you're saying?"

Is that what he's saying? Alice can't tell where Euel is going with this.

"It's that boy," says Mrs. Moseley. "I'm telling y'all. He came and picked her up."

"But she left her phone and purse behind?" says Ouida.

"I don't think it's the boy," says Euel. "His car is a lemon that can be heard for miles. That's what the girls said—a garbage can on wheels. And nobody saw any cars come or go from the house. Morgan was safe in her home, and then she *vanished*."

The guests look at one another. Alice feels sick. Any moment, her father will look straight at her. What do *you* think happened to Morgan, Alice Catherine? What's *your* theory?

"No one's disputing that she's missing, Euel," says the councilman, slightly irritable.

"Not missing," says Euel. "Vanished. From the Latin root *evanescere*—to slip away, like folks did in old fairy stories. Don't y'all know any stories?"

"There you go, then," says the pastor. "The fairies did it."

"Oh, I *dig* this theory," Mrs. Moseley says. "I *love* a dark fairy tale."

"I'm just saying," says Euel. "It wouldn't be the first time unexplained things happened around here."

He doesn't look at Alice as he says this, doesn't seem to be thinking of her at all. She breathes out slowly. At the other end of the table, Bobbie giggles.

"Y'all have got to forgive Euel. He can be a little—*woooooo*—" She holds her index fingers up to her head, wiggling them like antennae. "Of course, we wouldn't want to—not take this seriously."

The room goes quiet, as if everyone has been playing a game and Bobbie has just snatched up the ball and taken it off the court. Wrong game. Wrong rules. Euel looks at Bobbie, as if not sure what to do with her. Mrs. Patton presses her lips together with what seems like sympathetic embarrassment, but Alice spots the glance between her and Euel again, briefer this time, but still there.

Euel tosses his napkin on the table and breaks the silence. "Who's up for some music?"

In the living room, the instrument stands like a magnificent wing: a thirty-six-string folk harp with a walnut finish. She can hear the strings humming across the house.

"I haven't practiced," she whispers to Euel. "I'm too rusty; I told you—"

"One piece," he says, his hand guiding her arm. "Just one."

It's true that he doesn't force her. She chooses to sit herself down at the stool, the rest of the party around her in a semi-circle. She looks toward Mrs. Patton, who's standing next to Euel with a glass of sherry and a curious expression. She's never heard Alice play.

"Ready when you are," Euel says, lifting his glass.

She tunes the strings, thinking about what her therapist told her. Agency. Agent. I am an agent. I am a secret agent. I am the Queen of Cats. I know my father's game. *Thup THUP. Thup THUP.* And I can't arouse his suspicion by resisting too much, by being too difficult, because a difficult girl is a girl who's unwell, whose room will be searched, who will be sent to a place with only plastic cutlery and bathrooms with no doors. Or better yet, to jail. *Thup THUP. Thup THUP.* But what if I just play bad? He says one piece, so I will play one piece, and I'll play it bad. I'm a trickster. They won't know the difference. Debussy—what do they know about Debussy? "La Fille aux Cheveux de Lin." Who here knows any French?

So she plays. G-flat major, ad libitum. Her hands rise slow and fall heavy, the calluses on her thumbs and first three fingers pulsing numbly with each bright note, each humming arpeggio. Her performance is silted. The rhythm is off. She gets notes wrong. The music sinks like wet cotton. It stuffs her up.

She hasn't even made it through the second bar before Euel comes up and stands next to her, and she stops. She lifts her eyes to meet his. Charming dark blue eyes.

"Take a minute. You've got this."

"I told you," she says.

"Nonsense. Just get out of your own head."

Alice looks around at the guests—five pairs of expectant eyes.

"Okay," she says quietly, and starts again.

This gets to her: Her father is right that she loves to play, that it is one of her favorite things to do, that once the current of music swells from her, it feels good, powerful. Her music thickens the air, separate from the objects in the room but stuck in them, too, like a stitched thread. Stuck in each person by a needle so sharp they don't feel it. Her music twangs the web that hangs in the room—the Moseleys and the Bales, church and state, moldable people eager to be liked—and Bobbie, too, fretting about how the dinner went, about pleasing Euel and handling Alice. And Mrs. Patton. Mrs. Patton at the center of the group, a guest of honor. Her father stands next to her. Her father, whose fingers touch the edge of her skirt as she smirks and rolls her eyes. Her father, who grows like mycelium, a sinister fairy ring. It's you he wants. He sat you at the end of the table.

Alice sees the map of the county that hangs in her father's office, pink highlighter shading in the properties he owns. She sees her mother balanced on the gate of the pig enclosure, the big fans blowing her hair. *See. See. See.*

Mrs. Patton watches Alice play with her head tilted, the last drops of sherry swiveling in the bottom of her glass.

When Alice finishes the piece, she sits motionless and lets the notes die in the air.

The applause comes, restrained at first then gaining momentum, with Pastor Moseley putting two fingers in his mouth and whistling, and Ouida Bale shouting "Bravo!" Alice turns to her audience and takes a bow. When she rises again, she sees her father grinning. So pleased.

Sufficiently entertained, the guests gather in the parlor for dessert and conversation. Bobbie disappears into the kitchen again, insisting that she cut and serve the lemon cake Mrs. Patton brought. Alice makes a move for the door, but Mrs. Patton catches her arm.

"Stay!" she says. "Have some of Nate's cake."

"I can't have cake," Alice tells her. "My therapist doesn't want me eating processed sugar."

"Psh, sweetie, it ain't *sugar* that's messing you up. You can have a little cake."

The other guests have made their way back to average talk about neighborhood goings-on, whose kids got into which colleges and how the Mud Hogs did that year against the Kneesville Bees, et cetera. Euel is chatting with Councilman Bale in the dining room. Alice tries to back away, but Mrs. Patton is giggly and liquid, finishing up her second sherry. She pulls Alice down onto the love seat next to her.

"Your daddy told me you could play," she says. "But damn. He didn't tell me you could play like *that*. You're good. I mean, you're like a goddamn *pro*."

"Maybe it's the sherry," Alice says flatly.

Mrs. Patton laughs and lifts her glass. "Maybe. The sherry's pretty goddamn good, too."

Alice is disappointed in Mrs. Patton. She cranes her neck toward the dining room archway, where she can see her father working on Mr. Bale.

"You know," she says. "I wanted you to be here tonight because I thought you might be able to see what my father is doing. But I don't think you can. I think he's charmed you, too."

Mrs. Patton squints at Alice, then follows her line of sight through the dining room archway.

"What, *that*? Euel's a schmooze, always has been."

"I know he is. Every time he throws one of these, he gets something from the guests."

Mrs. Patton tsks. "Girl, come on. What you think your daddy is, a nun? He's doing business. He's a businessman."

Alice looks at Mrs. Patton and realizes that she's smiling toward the dining room. Her glossy hair and chic clothes. All put together. A beautiful woman, like all her father's assistants.

"Is it always business?" Alice asks. "For you?"

Mrs. Patton looks puzzled. "What are you saying?"

"Nothing. Never mind."

But her implication hangs between them. Mrs. Patton's eyes go cold. She throws back the last of the sherry and sets the glass firmly on the coffee table.

"What are you saying, Alice?"

Alice doesn't answer. She hears something.

Mrs. Patton shifts on the love seat, tugging down the hem of her skirt. "You had better *not* be saying what I think you're saying. You asked me to come, and I did. As a *favor*."

A sound in the air, familiar and distant.

Mrs. Patton goes on: "But that was my mistake, clearly. What was this to you, Alice? Some kind of test to suss out my loyalties? Maybe whatever's going on in this house doesn't need to be a war with two sides. God knows these folks aren't perfect, but I assure you, they are spending far less time worrying about you than you spend hating them."

What is that sound?

Bobbie's delivering slices of cake to the guests. Under the singsong cadence of her voice, the sound twitches. Alice strains her ears—

fimfimfimfim

"Courtesy of Mr. and Mrs. Patton," Bobbie is saying.

"Mr. Nathan Patton," Mrs. Patton announces to the room.

"That's all Nate." In the midst of a chorus of "Thank you, Nate!" from the other guests, she turns back to Alice. "Also, you are an adult," she whispers. "You've got legs. If you didn't want to dance for your father, if it tortures you so much, all you had to do was get up and walk out of the room."

"Shh," says Alice.

Bobbie hands two plates to Pastor Moseley and his wife, and the lemon makes a little hiss, like mist spraying *thusss thusssh*, and the cooked egg and flour fluff like fresh sheets, and there in the background, laughing like a sinister child—*fimfimfimfimfim*.

"Now what?" Mrs. Patton says irritably.

"There's something in the cake."

Bobbie did something to it. Revenge for Mrs. Patton messing up the menu. But no, Bobbie wouldn't drug guests—that would be indecorous. Mrs. Patton drugged the cake, as she is the one with access to witchfingers. But when Alice looks at Mrs. Patton, she seems bewildered.

"There's *what* in the cake?"

"You don't know. You didn't—"

Euel? It must've been Euel. He's onto her. This was a trap.

fimfimfimfimfimfimfimfimfimfimfim

Witchfingers. When consumed by the Angel Battalion, they gave rise to visions of an apocalypse. But no one could agree on what kind. Preacher Gannis saw a future in fire, while Marianne Duff, his young mistress, saw many miles of North Carolina marshland collapse into the sea. In the end, Gannis trapped his congregation in the church and set it ablaze. Marianne abandoned her bastard children and drowned herself in the river.

Alice watches the Moseleys dig in, the pastor licking icing off his fingers.

Bobbie comes back out with another slice of cake, this one lit with a birthday candle. The candle glows against her hostess smile. She doesn't even need to prompt anyone. They all turn and sing the birthday song to Mrs. Patton, whose face is a mix of surprise and pleasure and confusion—there's *what* in the cake? What the hell is happening right now? Alice looks at her father. He's singing along with the rest of them, though his gentle tenor is too quiet to hear. He sees her staring. Another wink. The song ends on shaky legs, with Pastor Moseley sinking into a false baritone—"And many moooore"—as Mrs. Patton blows out her candle.

Alice yanks the plate from Mrs. Patton's hands and flings it against the wall. The plate shatters. The square of cake sticks to the cream-colored brocade and, seconds later, unsticks with a plop.

Over the course of those short few seconds, the guests' eyes bore into her. Mrs. Patton sits with her hands outstretched, holding the empty space where the plate used to be. Her mouth forms an O, frozen in a candle-blowing motion.

Bobbie takes a backward step. She looks at Mrs. Patton as if to apologize, but her eyes swell with tears, and she ends up fleeing out the French doors to the patio. Alice flees, too—she can't bear to look at anyone, especially not Euel—but seeing as Bobbie picked her escape route of choice, she withdraws to the kitchen. There's that cake sitting on the counter, one third gone. The witchfingers are giggling away inside. Bobbie's out on the porch, sobbing, and Alice, watching her through the kitchen window, feels almost sorry for her. Bobbie is not an agent. Bobbie is in the dark.

Euel follows his wife outside and wraps her into a hug. Alice overhears them:

"She's been bullying me for days. She did this on purpose."

"Not on purpose, baby, she's just scared."

"*I'm* scared. There's something wrong with her."

Footsteps. The clack of heels headed for the kitchen. Alice wants to flee and return to the guesthouse, but she panics and ends up ducking into the pantry to hide. A door creaks.

"Alice?" Mrs. Patton's whisper is sharp and anxious. "Where'd you go?"

Through a sliver in the pantry door, Alice watches Mrs. Patton stop at the counter and stare at the cake. For a moment, she prods it with her fingernail. Then she leaves the kitchen the way she came in.

Alice takes a breath. The pantry is a warm, pleasant chorus of ingredients, though even from here, now that she knows what she's hearing, she can detect the sound of witchfingers in the cake. She should destroy it now, while she has the chance. But when she tiptoes out to do it, she realizes that it isn't a particularly sinister sound; it probably only seems sinister because she knows what it is. With all the other kitchen noises, it sounds perfectly innocent, like it belongs here.

She scoops a chunk of cake into her hand. The black currants shine at her like eyes. She hears Bobbie, calmer now and reentering the house with Euel. Alice returns to the pantry to hide.

The get-together is already breaking up—sincerest apologies, followed by embarrassed reassurances that no apology is needed. "We'll do it again soon." Someone enters the kitchen and leaves with Mrs. Patton's casserole dish, but Alice doesn't stop them. She remains on the floor of the pantry with the blob of cake in her hand. Then everyone leaves, their cars trundling away on the circle drive. Alice maintains her focus on the currants.

fimfimfimfimfim

Silence rules the house now. Bobbie is crying again somewhere. Eventually, Euel flings open the pantry door and finds her.

"What was that?" he asks. "Are you having a bad day?"

Alice looks up, clenching her hand to hide the cake.

"Yes," she says.

"What's that you have?"

"Nothing."

"Is that cake? Are you holding a piece of cake?"

Alice doesn't say anything.

"Do we need to call Dr. Lang?"

"No."

"Then explain what just happened."

"I'm sorry I humiliated you and Bobbie."

Euel shakes his head, a curl of salt-and-pepper hair hanging on his forehead. "Sweetheart, it's going to take a lot more than that to humiliate the likes of me. I don't care what people think about us. I'm just curious. We were doing good, I thought, you and me, all on the same page and having a nice time. Can you explain?"

She opens her hand, sticky with sugar glaze.

"I was jealous."

"Of Tanisha?" Euel lifts his shaggy eyebrows. "You were jealous because we were singing to Tanisha for her birthday?"

"Yes. I got angry."

He sighs, rubbing the side of his face. "I don't—honey, if that's true, I mean, if you threw a plate against a wall because you were jealous that somebody else was having a birthday—"

"That's bad."

"Well, it's not great," he says, laughing.

"I'm sorry. I'll go apologize to Bobbie."

Her father sighs again and drops his hands to his side. "Give her a day or so," he says, and closes the pantry door on her.

Alice flings the cake into the grass as she heads back to the guesthouse. The night insects scream at her. Overhead, she can see the light in Euel and Bobbie's bedroom, the two of them having their heart-to-heart about what happened at dinner. Alice doesn't care. She makes for the stash of witchfingers she has hidden under the couch, pinches out one of the little black kernels, and eats it whole.

For ten minutes, Alice sits in the dark on the floor of her kitchenette until the dull, raisin-y, freeze-dried taste has faded on her tongue. Then, slowly and deliberately, she retrieves her shovel, digs up the jar she buried the day before, and smashes it on the veranda. She screams, short, despairing. She storms down to the river's edge and screams at the water, storms back into the guesthouse and overturns the coffee table and accent chairs, flings a lamp across the room, smashes Mrs. Patton's remaining stash with her fist—*fimfimfimfimfim*. All the while, the rage hammers in her ears. It's something like

CURRANTSCURRANTSCURRANTSCURRANTS

CURRANTSCURRANTSCURRANTSCURRANTS

CURRANTSCURRANTSCURRANTSCURRANTS

CURRANTSCURRANTSCURRANTSCURRANTS

A sound upstairs brings her back. A whimper. The girl can hear her smashing around and Alice knows she's scared, and just like that, the anger dissolves, leaving behind only exhaustion. The events of the past two days bowl her over like a wave. It's almost too much to climb the stairs to her bedroom.

Morgan Taylor is where she left her, bound by a rope to a U-bend in her windowless bathroom. She looks up at Alice from the tile floor. A spot of blood has seeped through the bandage on her forehead, but she's alert. Watchful.

Alice sinks down on the side of the bed, staring at her prisoner through the bathroom doorway. She remembers that there's a saying around here: Worrying your plans will fail means there are demons in your neighborhood. Not worrying means they're in your house.

FROM THE NOTEBOOKS OF
KATRINA MORROW, FALL **1994**

October 3

Mourning jar
  Kneaded red candlewax, crushed cypress leaves, 1 T
sand, 1 tsp sugar water left in a clay bowl under the bed
overnight—should sound like way-off thunder

October 5

Mom Calloway is dead. Field pansies singing near the
gravesite.
  ▇▇ knows family lore—Calloway women have weak
hearts. They go fast and sudden. One minute her dad is glu-
ing a model plane on the porch, the next he hears a thump
inside the house and finds his wife at the foot of the stairs,
like some giant hand came down and flicked her soul right
out of her body. ▇▇'s dad and sister stood in shock at the
funeral. ▇▇ and me sobbed in the bathroom like we were
embarrassed, like it was greedy of us to feel so much grief.
  My own mother never liked me much, so ▇▇ let Mom
Calloway mother me, too. And what powerful mothering it
was! And how jealous it made me, how much ▇▇'s mother
loved her. I guess she loved her extra hard because of the
rumors. ▇▇ belonged to that man, the nanny's husband,
the pig worker from Oaxaca, who must be back in Oaxaca

by now after that spate of deportations in the 80s. No one buys the story about the great-grandmother with Lumbee heritage, how that is where she gets her coloring. Maybe only Mr. Calloway buys it. He dotes on ██ like a bird feeding a cuckoo. Everyone else is too polite to say anything.

Nasty to think about all this at a funeral—I know how much it would upset ██. But how could a woman as loving as Mom Calloway do something so low? Not just cheat but use someone. That man could not have been more than twenty. ██ doesn't even know his name.

GB sent her flowers. She took one of his yellow lilies and left it at the grave. Also a matchstick, a fishhook, apple seeds, and a tigereye stone. Nancy asked me what ██ was doing, but I thought she'd be annoyed if she found out we were still on our spellcasting, all the elaborate forms it's taken since high school. I said, Who knows, people grieve in weird ways. Nancy says she tries to talk to her sister and all ██ does is give her this sly, mean gator smile.

██ is not a cuckoo. If we're thinking animals, she's more reptile than bird. Sharp. Full of teeth.

October 19

Jar for ██'s grief

Glitter, 3 field pansies, 1 brass buckle, equal parts tea and mouthwash

She says her mom was the only thing that kept this place from being hell. A lonely hell. She calls me every day. She gets angry if I don't answer.

October 30

Almalita's landlord sold to Tarbarrel. She has three months to vacate. She's moving back in with her mom in Florida. One of the kids left a self-portrait for me in the mailbox saying "Bye-bye, naigher."

It's only a matter of time before my landlord sells, too. Talking to GB about this is always extra frustrating, he says it's just how his dad does business. These plans were in the works years ago—the neighborhood always knew about it. I knew about it. That row of Black families knew the hog lagoons were coming, but there's a difference between knowing and stepping out your door into a wall of stench.

I ask him what he'll do when I'm homeless and there's nowhere to live around here. He says, Easy. You'll move in with me.

But how can I live with a man I don't trust? He promises me a forest while holding an ax.

November 5

Pennies and dry crabgrass, boiled to silence in salt water, for money

November 10

Jar for ██'s new computer and fancy computer classes and fancy new job

1 scorched yellow lily, 1 T melted licorice, shrill cider vinegar

November 11

Jar for ████'s new place

2 scorched yellow lilies, her Tarbarrel lanyard, equal parts bleach and pig's blood. Tuneless frequency

November 13

Jar for Sniffing Pig Men

3 scorched yellow lilies, crushed rose hips, rue, and charcoal, black thread wrapped around a drill bit, tied tight, equal parts paste and ice water. Low beat in the ground at night—*BROMB BROMB BROMB*

November 29

GB's dad had a stroke Thanksgiving Day. Not a big one, but still. GB said he needs to take it easy. He's got this death grip on company operations. GB is trying to work his way in there and I don't know what that means for us, what it'll change. He says it changes nothing.

Laid out all his gifts on the bed yesterday. Always gifts with him. An amethyst ring. A silk dress, delivered in person by a man in tiny brown shorts. A cashmere scarf. Who the fuck needs a scarf in Miskwa? I laughed in his face when he gave me that. On the other

side of the bed, I laid out what I own—my shell collection, my fern Potty, a Sade cassette and Daddy's signed
Al Green LP, might be worth something nowadays. I
wanted to tie GB's things to mine and for the whole shitty
house to whisper us, we, us, we, us, we. Stupid. I could
just move in with him, lock him down. It might stop him
sniffing after other women, no, I'm not stupid. And the
new house in South Greene will be so big! It will have an
intercom, a jacuzzi.

He definitely sees me not trusting him. He acts dumb,
but he isn't.

December 16

Dream

███ and me were out in my yard together looking for
her mom's microwave, that one we set on fire when we tied
a shred of Brian Perry's underwear around a green army
man and put it in there to fry—voodoo magic, totally ███'s
idea. In real life, her mom came home from work and we
had to answer for the microwave, but in the dream I guess
we buried it so she never had to know. We started digging
somewhere around the pecan tree, and ███ unearthed a
bunch of skulls, and I got scared. I said, put those back,
we weren't supposed to dig those up. And ███ said, Don't
worry, Kat, they're just rabbits. If we find enough of them,
that's our ticket out of this nasty pig-slop town. But I don't
want to leave, I said, I'm in love with someone. And ███
laughed this awful, shrieking laugh. Him? HIM? That

PIG? If you're really that stupid, I'll be happy to leave without you.

When I woke up, my feelings were so hurt I started crying.

What are the rabbits supposed to mean? She used to call me Rabbit in high school. Used to peek around my locker door in the morning and say, Hello, Rabbit, grinning with all her teeth, and I always liked that she was the only one who ever used that name for me. Now I'm not so sure. What does it mean for us if she has all the teeth and all the power, and I'm just a little thing hopping along in the grass?

December 19

Heartbreak jar

Honey, cloves, orange rinds, 3 hairs from his mustache, his plastic comb, 2 drops of menstrual blood, one part salt water to a mellow red wine. Should sound easy. Keyboard and bass. Went all day like that, smooth and soft.

7

In January, his sophomore year of high school, Jesse began noticing things around the house: two coffee mugs in the sink, one with Nancy's lipstick, one without; an unfamiliar gray sock in the dryer. Nancy told him it was hers, but he'd never seen her wear socks like that. A boyfriend? He wanted to trade theories with his friends, but they were still side-eyeing him for flaking out over Spencer's birthday back in December.

Then one afternoon, a rare snow rolled in—just a dusting, really, but Jesse's chem class fell to anarchy. School let out early. The parking lot filled with the crunch of fender benders as hundreds of overexcited teens, some who had never seen snow in their lives, rushed to leave.

Jesse's house is only a couple miles from the high school, so he set out on foot. When he arrived, he heard scuffling and whispering, and he found Nancy and Sheriff Hupp sitting in the den together. Hupp's buttons were misaligned. She cleared her throat like a dad: "Aren't you supposed to be at practice?"

Nobody had noticed the snow. When Hupp left, Jesse assumed Nancy would confess, but Nancy said Hupp was there to talk about the thief who stole the Obama signs out of their front yard the other week, and when Jesse pressed, she said, Yes, what, did he think she was lying? Just drop it. It wasn't his business anyway.

That weekend, when he went up to Bittern's Rest, he was still thinking about Hupp and Nancy. At Harlan's duplex apartment, he sipped beer and shared a bowl, after which Harlan tossed him onto a futon mattress and flipped him on his back, a position that was okay at first but then became dizzying, as if Harlan were rearranging his organs. He tried to relax, but he couldn't. The pot made his head spin. Harlan said after a minute: "Are you not into this?" to which Jesse replied: "I think the sheriff is fucking Nancy."

They ended up sitting next to each other on the edge of the futon, Jesse divulging, Harlan listening.

"Your aunt?"

"Yeah. My aunt. And the sheriff. I walked in on them yesterday."

"Hupp?" Harlan's voice ticked up in disbelief, followed by thoughtful silence. "Marty Hupp...huh."

"I can't get it out of my head."

"So Marty Hupp is a queer. My uncle always said she had a funny step."

"You can't call someone 'a queer' anymore, Jimmy. It's just 'queer.'"

"Isn't she, like, sixty years old by now? What about the glass eye—you think she takes it out or leaves it in?"

Jesse covered his ears and flailed face-first on the mattress. Harlan-smell. Cigarette smoke and aftershave.

"Hupp is *married*," Jesse groaned. "She's been married since fucking Nixon was president!"

"What is is what is," Harlan said.

"I knew there were rumors about Nancy. I'm not stupid. I knew people talked. But I thought if she was seeing a woman, she'd tell me, not lie to my face like I'm an idiot."

Harlan fitted his chin into the crook of Jesse's shoulder. No scruff back then. "How come? She's got her own life. She don't got to tell you everything."

"She *should* tell me. She should *trust* me."

"Why? You don't trust her with all you get up to."

All you get up to. Harlan made it sound like a children's book, like he was out stealing from Mr. McGregor's vegetable patch. Jesse, too, had secrets, and while he wasn't expecting to make a coming-out rainbow connection with his aunt or anything, it certainly would've been easier to admit to her that he liked boys if she could admit that she liked women. His resentment permitted him to carry on deceiving her.

But she was not the only person he was lying to.

He thought about his school friends, the four of them outside behind the art trailer on Thursday afternoon, catching snowflakes on their tongues, how he and Spence raced to the far edge of the football field and flopped down breathless beside each other on the frozen ground, and suddenly it was like no one was upset with him about flaking on the party. They were back in middle school, when Jesse's feelings toward boys were just fleeting notions, when he could spend the night at Spence's house without this sense that he was dragging some dirty expectation across the threshold. Now he caught himself staring at Spence's mouth. The shadowy openings in the legs of his shorts. But their friendship was so wholesome it made him sad. Card games and frozen pizza. Anime and popcorn. When the crew made plans to hit up the thrift stores in Shy Creek over the weekend, Jesse said, Yeah, yeah, he was always looking for good pulp novels for his collection. He could help Bash find a costume for the Valentine's Day dance. He could comb through old records with Jaelah, though he didn't own a record player.

But the weekend was here, and Jesse surely wasn't thrifting.

Maybe, on some level, when he sent his apologies to the group text, they knew what he would be doing instead. They weren't that naive. Sometimes it did help him to think of them that way, to imagine himself as a depraved person they could never understand. Bash and Jaelah's relationship was basically asexual; they kept space for Jesus at dances. Spence was a rosy-cheeked virgin who had turned down an offer to feel up Madison French at a party in South Greene. "I didn't want to do it just to say I'd done it," he said. To which Jesse asked, "But did you *want* to do it?" And when Spence blushed and said, yes, he had, Jesse told him, without sympathy, "Then you should have done it, man."

Recalling all this on Harlan's futon, Jesse laughed. The sound of his own laughter was itself funny and wondrous, a bubbly elixir.

"What?" said Harlan. "What're you laughing at, you dope?"

"Nothing," he said. "Everything." He propped himself up on his elbows. "Hey, listen. What if we went official? I introduce you to Nancy, tell her to deal with it."

"Aw now, there's a fine plan."

"Did you know there's a law in North Carolina that if you're fourteen and pregnant, you can get married with your parents' consent? I looked it up."

"I don't mean to be insensitive here, champ, but you're liable to have a hard time getting pregnant."

"Auntie N," Jesse said, affecting his voice, "this ma boyfrand, Jimmy. He done knocked me up. We gon get married come June time."

"Oof, you are *high*."

"We gon have ten chillins. Git a big ole house in the swamp. He gon wrestle gators. I'm gon get fat, my tiddies gon git fat."

"This is not funny."

"Oh, *is it not*, Jimmy James? Don'tchu wan be my boyfrand?"

Harlan bowled him over into the mattress. Jesse laughed so hard he lost his breath. When Harlan kissed his throat he went elastic, leaning his head all the way back. He never called Harlan a boyfriend sincerely; the label felt stupid. Harlan was an experience. A *secret*. Jesse would study his spartan bedroom as if decoding ancient script—the outdated PC, the dusty guitar, the CD collection with a determinedly straight aesthetic, all Nelson and Cash and Skynyrd. The fruitiest music Harlan ever listened to was Pink Floyd and Dylan, though he owned two copies of *Highway 61 Revisited*. Why? Why did he have a painting of a white horse on his bedroom wall? Did someone give him that? Did he buy it himself? Jesse could've asked, but he was content to leave his thoughts unsaid: *If I wanted, I could undo you, crack you open. Me! Who'd have thought?*

* * *

Early Monday morning, Sheriff Hupp comes to the house to question Jesse about Morgan Taylor. She has always reminded him of a stick insect, an angular creature that looks at you with blank suspicion, cool and unconvinced. She's looking at him right now, just like that. One of her eyes is indeed glass; she lost the original to a melanoma some years ago. Here at Nancy's kitchen table, the glass eye is off-center, looking over Jesse's shoulder at the refrigerator.

Nancy stands in the doorway in her teaching clothes, voicing protests—"He didn't even see that girl yesterday. He saw her at that party Saturday night, but so what. How many other people were there?" But Hupp has proof that Jesse and Morgan are more than acquaintances. Texts. The testimony of Kayleigh Dowell and Brooke Barnes. Hupp proceeds to ask questions so flatly they never sound like questions at all.

When did he drop Morgan off at Brooke Barnes's place the night before.

(About four probably.)

How did he get that shiner.

(Stray beanbag. Cornhole.)

Could he account for his whereabouts yesterday afternoon. Who could corroborate that. And how *would* he describe this relationship with Morgan. Is he a boyfriend. A hookup.

"It's just chill," Jesse says, excruciated. "Not like a relationship relationship."

Hupp skritch-skritches onto a notepad with a golf pencil. He wonders what she's writing down: *Pretentious-ass player says not a "relationship relationship."*

"Did we not consider," Nancy says, almost frantic, "that this sixteen-year-old girl had a fight with her mom and ran off in a huff? You should go back to the girlfriends. One of them probably has her in her bedroom, watching TV. You should get them under the spotlight. They'll tell you."

At this point, Hupp turns in her seat and speaks coldly: "Ms. Calloway, your nephew is an adult. You don't need to be here while I ask him questions, is that not right."

"Marty," Nancy pleads, but there's no warmth there, no give. She sucks in her breath and leaves the room.

Hupp sits with Jesse in silence a minute, drumming her long fingers on the table.

"Jesse," she says, sighing his name.

"*What*," he says.

"Are you not worried about Morgan."

"Of course I'm worried. She's my friend."

"Then why are you lying to me."

liar, noun: **Foxglove briar**

"What makes you think I'm lying?" he asks.

Hupp rubs her temple, discreetly adjusting her eye. "I *know* you're lying. Half a dozen kids saw you jump Tooly Quinn at that party; they saw him bust your face. Then yesterday morning, Deputy Sleight finds you breaking into the old Simms place. That wouldn't be relevant to any of this, would it."

"I didn't—" he says. "I didn't *jump* Tooly. I don't know why they're saying that. I *approached* him, and he got freaked out and he hit me. I didn't want to make a thing out of it so, yeah, I lied. It's nothing to do with Morgan."

"And the Simms place."

"I went in there for the *nostalgia*," he says, laughing. "I spent like half of high school in there. And what does it matter? When was Morgan up in Pinewood?"

"Have you ever observed Morgan Taylor using drugs."

observe, verb: **Silver antler**

"No."

"But you have seen her consume alcohol."

"Yeah, everyone at Red's was a mess. What's your point?"

"And it's likely, maybe certain, that there were drugs at that party."

Jesse can see the icy gears of Hupp's brain turning. "It's likely."

"Have you ever given Morgan Taylor drugs."

"No."

"Do you know someone who might've given her drugs. Marijuana, prescription pills, anything."

"No. Why do you think I would know that?"

Hupp leans forward. "Because I know that you, at one time, had contact with someone in Pinewood who gets you in trouble. I want to find out if you're still in contact with that person, if in fact you came back here *in order* to contact that person. I know that Morgan Taylor was well and fine on Saturday; she spends a night with you, and she disappears on Sunday."

Jesse would like to turn things around somehow, would like to ask: Are you still in contact with your husband, Marty, you cheat? Does it make you feel better to call me a liar?

"I barely know Tooly," he says. "I never bought drugs from him; I never took drugs from him. If you think he's got something to do with this, why don't you ask *him*?"

"We will," she says. "We need to find him first."

find, verb: **Blood spade**

Jesse clenches his eyes shut. "He was at Red's last night. Then he took off somewhere."

He hears Hupp shift in her chair, but he can tell she's still looking at him, trying to pick out what he's not telling her. Sometimes, there's more than just you're-not-my-lesbian-dad dislike between them; sometimes, he imagines it's actual hatred, as if Hupp believes Connie's death destined him to be a problem child. That day he arrived at the station to ask her about Connie's death, she looked down over the counter and said to him in her cold, stick-insect voice, *I knew I'd see you here eventually. But I don't have a thing for you.*

When he opens his eyes, Hupp is holding her card in front of his face. "If there's anything new you come to remember," she says, "you can call me directly."

Jesse takes the card, as if Nancy didn't already have Hupp's number. He follows her into the den. Nancy rises from the couch, but Hupp ducks away and out the door as if yanked by a rope. Nancy, again, looks hurt. When she turns to Jesse, all that hurt beams right at him.

"Anything else you want to tell me?" she says sharply. "Heists? Off-shore bank accounts? Are you married?"

"You didn't tell Hupp about the photos," he says.

"She has enough on her mind. I'm serious, Jesse—why the hell did you go to a high school party? What are you up to?"

"Nothing," he says.

"Was it true what you said? You don't know anything about what happened to that girl?"

"I don't know anything, Nancy. Honest."

honest, adjective: **mirror ember**

She rakes him with her eyes. "I have to go to work. I'll be on campus until four. We're going to talk when I get back."

"It's fine," he says. "Take your time."

She picks up her bag from the reclining chair, moving slowly.

"Take your time," he says again.

"You need to be here when I get back," she says.

"I will. I'll be here."

But he's not fully there as it is. He watches her pull out of the driveway with his heart pounding. He hasn't slept much. All last night, strange images kept him up, threading through his mind—that secret language. **Tar swamp**, make dirty; **Bottle**, give; **Pearl**, take care; **Cross feather needle key**, what now. What now? The phenomenon he's experiencing is called xenoglossia. He looked it up. This is what the Pentecostals purport to do when they speak in tongues, but they don't use their divine language to communicate, not really. Jesse's brain is filled with *thousands* of translations. They won't leave him alone. He looks out the window and everything he sees contributes a living thought. **Oak**, stand; **Garden**, choose; **Cloud**, dream.

This makes him realize that the language, as he's been using it, feels incomplete, shallow, like it was never meant to be shared in texts, like it was never meant to be written at all. What's it for, then? What would it look like in its truest form?

The answer is nearly there, itching at him. Now that the house is empty, he goes to his room and takes Cat's photos out of the tin, laying them in a collage on the floor. River. Corpse. A stick in the bank, surrounded by a tangle of objects. His eyes, achy and sleepless, flicker over them. Ivy. Vessel. Candle. Ash. Stone. Skull. Water. **Claw hammer**, verb: reverse, revolve.

A sentence. Sentence as altar, expressed through things. He sees it now. He understands.

He writes to Cat:

Sage glass Arrow   *(I get it)*

     gate red seed Mirror sieve   *(in the pictures)*
Smoke Needle seed Briar   *(these objects are)*
     Splinter ink seed   *(words)*

star Ink thread   *(a message)*

The ground searches will take shape soon enough, people calling Morgan Taylor's name, appearing on country roads, prodding bushes with sticks as if the girl would spring out and cry, "Just kidding!" Everyone has seen the television specials and listened to the podcasts, and so they're vigilant, anxious about what they might find: a severed arm, a lock of blond hair sprouting from the ground. These are mostly Morgan's people, her church crowd, her teachers and neighbors, but there are others who don't know or care one whit about Morgan; they just want to be part of a story. Business owners shutter their stores so they can show up at search points. Mrs. Wilde, the middle school secretary, drives back from Mount Olive, where she was celebrating her son's college graduation. "I'll see his lazy behind all summer," she tells a friend. "And this is too big to miss."

Jesse is stunned at how quickly the Facebook page goes up, and how quickly someone from Red's party texts him a link to it (a girl he barely knows, whose number he has for reasons he can't remember). *Did you hear?* ☹ Yes. He heard. For a profile picture, the Taylors have chosen a church portrait of their daughter wearing a white pleated shirt buttoned all the way to her throat, practically Amish, not at all as Jesse knows her. It makes him mad. What if she *is* at a friend's house? Everybody in town is going to feel silly. Morgan will be mortified. All this stupid fuss.

For lunch, he heads to the Chuckwagon again, feeling the new tension in the air. He's wearing an outfit that he thought might help him be inconspicuous: sunglasses, raglan shirt, an NC State cap (high school holdover from when he used to pretend to care about college football). But when he walks in, he gets looks regardless. Full head turns. How quickly word gets around in this town! The veteran waitress who served him yesterday morning smiles tight-lipped when she brings his coffee to his booth. What's she saying to the staff in back? *Yep, he was in here yesterday reading a book about murder.*

But he can't worry about that right now. Cat has replied to his epiphany. He settles in for a conversation.

Stone

moon

Oil sage ink feather Vessel

    Dust seed

(right, but can you read them?)

He imagines Cat across from him in the booth. They have a new form, wiry and sharp, with an intense, dark-eyed face and features that shift as they speak. Their crown, if they have one, is not made of stars, but bristles.

devil Oil

(can't)

Fire rabbit claw arrow Dogwood briar

(my friend's missing)

The imaginary Cat leans back, arm draped across the booth. "You can't read them because your friend is missing?"

He didn't mean to imply these two statements were related, but maybe they are.

"I can't focus," he writes.

"Try," says Cat.

He's taken pictures of the photos with his phone so that he doesn't look freakish studying them in public. What makes so much sense to him in Cat's messages—predictable order, an obvious, reliable system of verb conjugations—is far messier in physical practice. Building an altar is a more complicated, intuitive process, and Jesse has no way to know his dead mother's mind.

"I don't know how to translate it," he says. "Pieces, maybe. Like the ivy."

"That is a command," says Cat.

"Right," he says. An auxiliary, a helper word. "But altogether, I can't see it."

"Why?"

Ivy claw hammer: (you) revolve, (you) reverse. Who was the command for?

"I can't read it if I don't know what everything is," he says. "Also, the words might have changed."

"How changed?"

"If anything was moved or broken, that could change the meaning. I don't know what she was trying to say."

"But is it correct," says Cat, "that this is a spell?"

The question chills him.

"I don't know," he says again. "Why did you think I would know what this means if you don't?"

Cat is surprisingly forthcoming. He imagines them sliding forward in the booth, the bristle crown shifting like the planes of their mysterious face.

"Because you knew how to do this without learning. I had to learn."

Cat shows their teeth. The crown is growing, creeping down their forehead like frost.

"How do you know that?" he asks.

"You told me," says Cat.

He shakes his head and says aloud, "I never told you," not shouting, but loud enough to get a look from the family at the table to his left. The Chuckwagon is nearly full, churning with fry smoke and patrons and hurried waitstaff. Burgers and grilled cheeses, shiny with grease, float by on trays. Jesse ignores all of it. He leaves his own coffee untouched.

Did he tell Cat? Have they had this conversation before?

No. He has to brush past it all: his mother knowing this language, him knowing it without learning it, and the idea that he and Cat apparently had a conversation about it sometime before now. Cat, a stranger, whom he's never met. And he has to imagine that Tooly, with his dilated pupils and dainty blond eyelashes, was telling him something important—*Up— way up—like from the sky*—and that Morgan—even though she spent a night with him on Saturday and disappeared on Sunday—is fine, will be fine, and it has nothing to do with Cat, who gave him strict instructions not to tell anybody about all this.

"If I really told you that," Jesse says, "I'm in trouble."

"No trouble," says Cat. "It is on our side; don't worry."

"It? What is it?"

Cat goes quiet for a while. Jesse crouches over his phone, waiting for an answer, the imaginary figure across from him dignified and calm. Their bristly crown shapes into spikes, two ears covered in fur.

red Rabbit ghost

The buried place. **Rabbit**, verb: buried, submerged, hidden. **Ghost**, noun: realm, domain.

"What are you talking about?" he asks. "What's the buried place?"

"Get inside the Night House," Cat says. "You will appear it."

Appear. **Mirror.** That doesn't sound right. Sometimes, Cat doesn't phrase things correctly. Jesse has always registered their occasional awkwardness with words, as if they weren't writing in their native tongue.

A congregation that speaks a secret language without realizing.

A piece of land with its own mind.

"Remember that man I told you about?" Jesse says. "The one from Pinewood? I saw him yesterday. I think he knows what happened with Tooly."

Cat pauses. He feels what he imagines is concern pulsing through the phone. "Him?"

"He knows a lot of stories."

"So do I," says Cat. "You think he is involved?"

"I have a feeling."

Another pause. "Be careful, dear friend. No time to get distracted."

They're right, of course. His feelings are small in light of all that's happening: the demolition of the Night House, Morgan's disappearance. Even so, he can't shake Harlan. Is this honest intuition? Or does he *want* Harlan to be involved because that means he gets to chase him? And all the while, his mother's mind is still unknowable, and the Night House gets closer to being destroyed, and Morgan remains missing.

Jesse feels Cat beginning to leave him, slinking to the door past families eating their oily lunches at Formica tables. He writes, fingers trembling:

Crow arrow Ash moth Dogwood
Sage feather Vessel
Smoke stag snake Flesh

(my vanished friend,
do you think she's in danger?)

Ivy heart moss Iris crown

(have faith)

Blood spade Stone
    Sea

(it's all good)

Cat stands outside on the sidewalk, their bristly crown merging with their head and neck. They shrink down and drop to all fours, four bony legs with white dewclaws, and spring across the road, a coarse tail disappearing under the shadow of a pickup.

The waitress prods Jesse's shoulder. He flinches. He was dreaming.

"You can take your check up front, hon."

He's been taking up a booth for too long.

"Thanks," he says. "Sorry."

At the register, the overhead TV displays Morgan Taylor's Amish photo on Channel 3 news. Kayleigh Dowell appears, seeming both sincerely worried and sincerely passionate about the opportunity to be on camera. Subtitles run haltingly: MORG   AN IS A STRONG WOMAN. SHE'S A FEMIN   IST WOMAN, AND A FIGHTER, AND AN IN   SPIRATION TO ME EVERY DAY

The diner patrons carry on talking, but Jesse can see them

taking in the news in glances. He wonders what Kayleigh has said about him to Sheriff Hupp, to Morgan's parents. *He had issues. She said he'd had sex with men, older men. He only ever wanted to sneak around. He made her lie to her parents. Drugs? Sure. With Pinewood boys, in the woods. One time, he crawled into Jaelah Harrison's backyard a bloody mess, out of his mind—*

Kayleigh talks into the camera, on and on. The lawns of South Greene shine behind her, vivid as Astroturf.

The afternoon slides along, its shadows slanting and bronzy. Morgan's searchers spread north into Pinewood until a whirl of activity circles the Night House. Women from the First Baptist Church set up tables to hand out water, sunscreen, bug spray; men distribute maps and plastic whistles. The Pinewood locals are curious and apprehensive. Some line up by the chain-link fence at the edge of the property: elderly winos, mothers with kids on their hips, restless-looking army vets. They know the assumptions being made here about Pinewood's criminal element.

Deputy Sleight is there to direct things, his fat dog close at his feet. They're all the way across the field and through the pine grove when Jesse pulls into Bittern's Rest, but he can still feel their eyes following his car, the deputy's suspicion, the dog's contempt.

Harlan's truck is not in his driveway, but Jesse, in the chaos, has forgotten that Harlan would be working on a Monday.

work, noun: **Pig bristle**

On he drives, taking Deer Church Road into Pinewood's town center: a fire station, a baseball field, an ABC store, an evangelical church that used to be a bank. On the west side of town, he passes two strip clubs—the Pink Gator and Sandy Mandy's—sources of anxious mystery for high school boys, who commonly referenced them to rag on one another. *Anything I should say to your mom at the Gator* and so on. Now hog stench fills the air. A few miles more, and the Tarbarrel processing plant stands across a muddy reservoir to Jesse's left, a twelve-foot-tall concrete statue of the grinning pig mascot leering at the parking lot entryway.

There was a dark span of time, after Harlan blocked his number, when Jesse would sit in the rancid air of the Tarbarrel parking lot waiting for him to get off work. Will he do the same now? He circles the lot, his hatchback sputtering, but he can't find Harlan's truck. Two men, workers in red shirts and white vinyl aprons, watch him from the loading dock, smoking cigarettes.

Jesse pulls up next to them and rolls down his window.

"Sorry," he says. "Do you know if Jim Harlan is here today?"

The two workers regard Jesse and look at each other.

"Harlan?" says one. "¿Te escuché bien?"

"Ya no trabaja aquí," says the other.

"Um," Jesse falters. He scours his memory for his two semesters of high school Spanish. "You said—no trabaja—he doesn't work here?"

"Sí. No longer. They let him go."

Why does that hurt to hear? Did he expect Harlan would've told him? For a moment, he sits with his hands on the steering wheel, thinking.

He calls out the window again: "Dónde—um—do you know where he might be?"

The first worker laughs quietly and tosses his cigarette off the loading dock. "La cantina racista."

"A bar," says the second, jabbing the first with his elbow. "He and his friends go for happy hour. They don't card lugareños."

"With Tooly?" Jesse asks.

A blank shake of the head. "I don't know what that is."

"What bar?"

"Willy's." The worker sweeps an arm toward the woods behind the plant. "If you take this road north a few miles, it's somewhere that way. But I wouldn't go there."

pursue, verb: **Hook wolf**

Jesse thanks the workers and heads on into the dim, woodsy north.

Was Tooly ever actually a friend of Harlan's? Mostly, he was just there in the background, tagging along after his older brother who *was* a friend, some grade school blood-bonded good ole boy. Jesse always had trouble telling those Pinewood boys apart. All deer-hunting camo and white trash sunburns and angry, ultraright politics, the outline of snuff tins in back pockets. If Harlan ever had friends of other races, they didn't keep in touch once he dropped out of high school. He never confronted the politics.

Of course, Jesse didn't either. It was only Tooly with whom he felt he could safely exchange insults. Tooly called Jesse pussy, homo, bitchass. Jesse rejoined with dildo, cousin fucker, short bus crypto-Nazi. A kind of rapport.

Once, Jesse got drunk off Hairy Crow whiskey at Harlan's place and threw up in the kitchen sink, and while Tooly at first mocked him and said he should go home if he couldn't handle the real shit, he later came in and sat patiently on the kitchen counter while Jesse lay sprawled and sweaty on the linoleum. "One time, I got so fucked-up, I ate a Twinkie with the wrapper on," he said. "One time, in church, I drunk a big-ass thinga Everclear and puked in my mom's purse." The anecdotes came one after another. Was he bragging? Trying to be kind? Harlan wasn't in the room then. He was on the back porch with the boys—their fat joints, their baggies and grams of things—thickening his accent, pretending he barely knew the insufferable teen pasted to his kitchen floor. That kid? That's just one of Tooly's little friends.

The bar in question doesn't show up on Jesse's phone; he's in virgin country now, untouched by the Internet. A few more miles north, and he loses his signal completely.

This is the part where he silences his fears, gives himself up to his intuition. He follows patched asphalt roads, then gravel roads, then dirt roads, his car bucking over potholes, and for a while, it feels like he's chasing something mythic, a place that may or may not exist, or that sprouts out of the woods like a fungus before melting away again into the ground. When he finds the bar—and he does eventually find it, tucked down a back road and partly hidden behind a stand of pines and kudzu—there's something bloated and fetid about it, like a mushroom. The porch beams are buckled, the windows dark. He deciphers with effort the hand-painted billboard in the parking lot: loopy words—WILLY RIVER'S BAR & POOL HALL—and below those, a waitress with a piss-colored beer in one hand, a bucket of oysters in the other. She's missing a face. It flaked off or was rubbed off, leaving behind a featureless blur.

anxiety, noun: **Cicada**

But it's only some dive, he thinks. Where folks hang out. Where Harlan hangs out.

He knows Harlan is here because his yellow truck is sitting in the lot, next to Tooly's car. GA$ OR A$$—NO FREE RIDES. Suddenly, Jesse remembers that this is not Tooly's car. He inherited it from his brother.

Pretend friends. Pretend distance. The night sky, sinking over Pinewood like a smoke screen.

Willy's is deceptively abundant with rooms. Every time Jesse steps past a doorway, he expects the place to end, but then he sees that there is another doorway, or a set of stairs, or a corridor to follow, and that leads into more rooms, sparsely populated with quiet patrons. The walls are home to what appear to be little altars for old movies or TV shows: *Old Yeller*, *The Andy Griffith Show*, *Forrest Gump*. The initial barroom is all *Dukes of Hazzard*. An enormous quilt hangs from the ceiling celebrating the Duke boys' fiery Dodge Charger on a background of Stars and Bars. An additional barroom is all *Gone with the Wind*, Scarlett and Rhett in bold sunset colors, but in this room there are also numerous Confederate flags, a cabinet of ceramic lawn jockeys, minstrel show tchotchkes, a dummy in a rebel uniform. The place is awash in racist flea market refuse.

As for the patrons, Jesse avoids eye contact until he gets a drink in him, which will improve his charisma. But he knows who they are. All white, mostly male, a mix of old and young, the sons of farmers and fishers whose polluted industries got edged out by Tarbarrel and who now have only the history of a name or a trade to give them clout. Harlan and Tooly—now, apparently, both unemployed—have washed up here like everyone else.

Jesse should feel sad about that, but when he spots the two of them at a corner table in the *Gone with the Wind* room, he can only find it in him to be angry and glare at them.

They stare back, their faces stretched and sleepless.

He takes a seat at the bar.

"Whiskey Coke, please," he says to the barman.

The barman grins. His glasses are small and round, like a jeweler's.

"You sure you in the right place?"

"Sure?" Jesse laughs. "Yeah, I'm sure. I'm in here, ain't I?"

"You got ID?"

His head buzzes. He sits with both hands flat on the bar top. "I don't have it on me."

"Well, I can't give you nothing. I'd get in trouble." He leans forward, beckoning with his fingers, and whispers: "You're too easy to clock."

A silence passes. The barman tosses a towel over his broad, stooped shoulder and disappears through a doorway. Jesse's mouth dries out like tinder. He sees himself in the mirror behind the liquor shelves, his battered face, his Wolfpack cap an obvious costume. He sees Harlan approaching the bar.

"What the hell are you doing here?"

Jesse looks up, relaxing his face. "Buy me a drink?"

"Are you serious?"

"One drink. C'mon."

Harlan shakes his head, horrified.

Jesse leans forward, scanning for the barman. He grabs a bottle of bourbon, pours it into an empty shot glass.

"*Stop*," Harlan whispers, grabbing his arm.

But Jesse has already tossed it back.

"You're fucking crazy."

"It's fine, man. I'll give you cash for it."

Harlan drags him off the barstool and into an adjacent room, where a drunken crowd of men is cheering rowdily over a pool table. Jesse finds himself pinned in a dusty nook behind the jukebox. The jukebox is playing "Mary Jane's Last Dance."

"What?" Harlan says. Jesse can smell the beer on his breath. "What do you want? If I give you what you want, will you go away?"

"I want to chat with you and Tooly."

Harlan sighs. "*Why?* Why you gotta bother Tooly about it? He doesn't need your bullshit. He's got it hard enough."

"Oh *wah*." Jesse feels brave, churlish. The bourbon is already doing its work. "I'm sick of hearing about how pitiful Tooly is. You think I don't remember how to read your dumb face, Jimmy, like I don't know when you're holding back? I'm not just fucking around here. I have—I have *seen* things, Jimmy. Strange, inexplicable things. A girl has gone *missing* and—"

"That South Greene girl?" Harlan interjects. "You're involved in that?"

Jesse's speech comes to a ragged halt. No Internet, no phone signal, but word of Morgan Taylor has still wormed its way through the backwater dregs of the county.

"I—" he says. "No."

"What kind of nuclear shit are you bringing to me?"

"I'm not *involved*. She's a friend. She's missing. You're getting me off track."

"Mmkay. Get back on track then, by all means."

A pulse stings Jesse's throat. He looks down and realizes he's still holding the stolen shot glass, a single drop of bourbon lolling about in the bottom. He tips it back onto his tongue.

"Okay. Okay. So this is going to sound way out of left field."

"Sure," says Harlan.

"Do you remember when you told me the story about that cult, the one that spoke a secret language without realizing?"

Harlan hesitates. Behind them, the men clatter their drinks together.

"No," he says. "You can't expect me to remember every story I ever told you."

"I'm not asking you to remember every story, Jimmy. I'm asking you to remember *one* story. And you're lying. I can tell from your stupid face."

A shadow appears around the corner behind them: Tooly, listening in. His face is puffy and tired, but his eyes are attentive, more focused than they were when Jesse saw him at Red's place. Harlan looks over his shoulder.

"Hey, man," he says.

Hey, man—gentle, like he's talking to a child. Jesse is irritated that Harlan has this paternal, protective thing going on with Tooly, irritated that he's jealous of it.

"What story?" Tooly asks. "I heared it?"

"I don't know," Harlan says. He appears to lose some of his resolve. "There's one—I don't know if you heard it before."

Tooly looks at Jesse, whose back is pressed against the wall. "You look scared, Calluhwee," he says. "You scared?"

Not scared. Nervous—which makes him hungry. A tanned, thin-armed waitress brings onion rings and Cheeto chili cheese fries and popcorn shrimp with plastic NyQuil cups of off-white tartar sauce. Also drinks: cheap beer, cheap liquor, two-for-one Monday happy hour. Jesse gives Harlan cash for a whiskey Coke. Before Harlan can begin his story, one of the drunk men crashes into their table, drains Harlan's glass, and takes off again yelling, "Too slow, Jimdog!" before slipping back into the knot of backs at the pool table. Jesse isn't surprised that Harlan knows these people. He tries to recall if he's seen any of their faces before at the duplex in Bittern's Rest, but again, in his memory the Pinewood boys are all one boy, a rangy creature simmering with machismo. Pinewood Boy's connection with Harlan is superficial. A wrestling match in second grade. A frigid hunting trip. Harlan dated Pinewood Boy's sister in high school (and must have inevitably disappointed her; since then, he has opted for a literal beard rather than a figurative one). Pinewood Boy simply doesn't know Harlan the way Jesse knows him.

Still, every interaction grates on him as it always did. Every nickname and inside joke and slap on the back. He's especially disturbed by the waitress, a ropy, threadbare woman in her late thirties, wearing a tiny dress of macramé fringe. She touches Harlan with a peculiar kind of affection, hooking her fingernails into his shoulder when she comes by.

"Who's Whiskey Coke?" she asks, nodding at Jesse.

"One of Tooly's friends from school," Harlan says.

Tooly says nothing. He has his arm wrapped around the basket of cheese fries and is slowly devouring them like he hasn't eaten in days.

The waitress taps her cheek. "You get in a fight, baby?"

"I was born like this," says Jesse.

"You look familiar. You got people in Pinewood? Wait, no." She prods her long-nailed finger at him. "I remember. You ran at Miskwa. You was always running up and down Peach Hill. In your little red hoodie."

He smiles at her. "Red Riding Hood, that's me."

"Lila," says Harlan, holding up his empty glass. "Can I trouble you?"

She gives his hair a tug. "For you, honey, always." Then she loads her tray and hustles off, fringe swishing.

"Ex-girlfriend?" Jesse asks. "Formative babysitter?"

"Don't," says Harlan.

"Don't what?" He grabs a handful of fries from the crook of Tooly's arm. "Tell the story already. You said you had it."

"These're mine," Tooly says gravely, tugging the fry basket toward the edge of the table. "No one else can have these."

Harlan sighs again, tracing his finger through a puddle of beer on the tabletop. But Jesse can feel him transitioning into storyteller mode. His shoulders loosen. His voice gathers heaviness, a bit of gravitas.

"All right," he says. "Uncle Lot told me this one a long time ago. He said it happened to a friend's cousin. This guy was driving around, north edge of the county, and saw this bar kinda sitting off by itself in the woods. Like this one. And he'd had a long day at work, so he thought, What the hell, drove up, went inside.

Now, he didn't know nobody there. Never seen these people before. And when he went up to the bar to get a beer, the barman said: Hog apple. And the cousin said, Huh? And the barman said again, Hog apple, hog apple. So he looked around like, Can anybody help me figure out what this dude's saying to me? And *everyone* in the place looked up and said, Hog apple. But the cousin brushed it off, bunch of weirdos, he figured, didn't matter to him. He could point and make it obvious to the barman that he wanted the home-brewed cider, and the barman got it for him, and it was the best cider he ever tasted."

"Wait," Jesse interrupts. "What does this have to do with the church, the ethnographers?"

"Let'm tell the story," says Tooly.

"This isn't the story I was asking for."

Tooly shrugged. "Well, maybe it's the one you should listen to."

Harlan carries on: "So this guy, this friend's cousin, he went to another friend, not Lot's friend, another friend, and said, I found this bar out on the north edge of the county and had the best cider I ever tasted in my life. And the friend said, Well, shit, let's go there. And the cousin said, Wait. The thing about this place, everybody in there, all they can say is 'hog apple.' And the friend said, You sure it weren't just some other language, like German? And the cousin's like, Nah. It weren't German. At least, he didn't think so. But anyway, they drove out there and found the place. And this time, when they went inside, the barman said, What can I do you for? The cousin was stunned. He turned to his friend like, Huh. Last time I was in here, all anybody could say was 'hog apple.' But then the friend was looking at him. Kinda squinting. Scared-like. And he said, What'd you just say? And the cousin said, Last time I was here, all anybody could say was 'hog apple.' The friend's eyes got real big, like, Are you fucking with me? What are you doing? And the cousin said, What are you talking about? The friend said, Fuck you, man. This ain't funny. Stormed out of the bar. So the cousin left, confused, but then when he got back to town, everybody gave him those same funny looks. He'd say, Hey, how you doing? And they'd say, What? Hog apple? What are you talking about? What's wrong with you? Are you crazy? At this point, the cousin was scared, and he tried to go back out and find the bar, but he couldn't find it. Like it disappeared. And then years went by, and he tried to talk to people, his family and his friends. Why can't you understand me? But all they could hear was 'hog apple, hog apple.' You're crazy, they said. Snap out of it. Why are you doing this to us? What's wrong with you? But he couldn't tell them. He lost his job, his girlfriend. His parents didn't know what to do with him. His friends didn't want to see him, because all he could do was say 'hog apple.'

"Then it happened, finally. Twenty long years later, he found the bar a third time, wandering drunk on the north edge of the county. So he staggered inside and raged at the barman, What did you do to me? Nobody's been able to understand a word I say for twenty fucking years. And the barman, cool as stone, said—"

"'We done warned you,'" says Tooly.

Harlan extends a hand, a gracious nod. "'But you drank it anyway.'"

Jesse leans forward, head in his hands. His palms feel funny against his temples, numb and hot. "I don't know what to say."

"He couldn't understand the warning," Harlan explains. "That's the whole thing."

"I get that, Jimmy. But that's not—it's not the one I was thinking about."

"Hey, cut me some slack, all right?" says Harlan. "Most of the time, when I was telling you stories, I was making 'em up off the cuff."

"So the whole thing about the cult, the ethnographers," says Jesse. "You just invented it?"

"I don't know. Probably."

Jesse sinks back into his chair. "No," he says loudly. "No, you're stonewalling. Why do you keep doing that?"

Harlan holds out his hands. "I don't know what you want."

"Answers, Jimmy. Jesus. You keep *lying*."

"You're shouting."

"No, I'm not; I'm just not ashamed of myself."

"I shouldn't've let you drink. You're underage."

"Aw, I'm *what*?" Jesse lets out a laugh like a shot. "Underage? Well, blow me down and fuck me sideways, I had no idea!"

The barroom has gone quiet. The drunk men pause in their drinking, staring as if someone had thrown a pall over their celebration. The waitress looks up from across the room, her face raptor-like in the blue neon of a beer sign. Harlan sits speechless.

"Sam," Tooly whispers.

Jesse turns in his chair. Tooly's angry white face stares back, his freckles brightening.

"What about him?"

"Sam was right about you," Tooly says, louder. "You're a manipulative little shit. A bloodsucker. S'what you came here to do, aren't it, suck someone dry? S'what you been after me and Jim for."

Jesse's cheek twinges, but he's not afraid. He's already gotten it from Tooly, and there are worse things.

"You gonna beat me up like Sam did?" he asks. "Is that all you can do?"

Tooly shrugs. "Maybe this time we'll kill you."

His threat slides off the table and sinks like a coin through the floorboards, slim, childish. Jesse feels it go and laughs.

"Sure," he says. "And maybe you can end up down a sink-hole, too."

Tooly stands. Jesse steels himself for another hit—he can take it, he was asking for it—but Tooly only shoves the table away and leaves the room, glasses toppling in his wake. Stares—from the drunks, the waitress, Harlan across the table, his face hard with contempt.

"Why'd you do that?"

"*He* was—" says Jesse, ready to defend himself. But Harlan's stare shames him. Jesse's eyes swell up with heat, the whiskey magnifying his sudden misery. He can see the face of the late Sam Quinn in his mind's eye—an older, squarer Tooly, wheat-gold hair, gray eyes, a cruel curve of a mouth. *You're really pushing it tonight*, the mouth is saying to him.

"Sorry," he says.

Harlan shakes his head. "I don't need to hear it."

Jesse nods, a stone in his throat. He gets up and chases after Tooly to apologize.

*   *   *

Harlan must also believe that Sam Quinn was right; this is why he cut Jesse off the way he did. Jesse is a bloodsucker. A curse. A changeling. He's the worst thing to ever happen to Harlan. Sam Quinn knew that. Sam Quinn—who came to the duplex with his fat joints, his baggies and grams of things, Harlan's dealer, but a good friend, too (with a history of grade school wrestling matches? Frigid hunting trips?). A good enough friend that Harlan now plays mentor to his brother. So the bond must've been there, but Jesse missed it. Didn't understand it. Didn't want to see it.

But Tooly has already disappeared, and now the bar's wood-paneled labyrinth threatens to swallow Jesse up, too. Cedar smell. Smoke haze. The patrons, sparse at first, are multiplying, and Jesse is stunned to see the bar fill up so fast. The whiskey is turning on him—what earlier made him loose and smooth now has him feeling helpless. And in the tenor of the conversations among the barfolk, what had felt like the washed-up despondency of losers is now angry, resentful. What are they talking about with such intensity? The town, the country, the world—how it all fell apart, how nothing's like it used to be back then (back when)? Modern life is a trap, a lie, a conspiracy. Jesse passes through rooms in search of Tooly, moving along the walls, keeping his head low. Blurry Pinewood faces turn and look at him with disgust, like he's spitting on the floor of their church.

Does the dim light make him look darker, Grandma Calloway's mystery lover exposed as if under a blacklight?

Or is it the Wolfpack hat? No one is wearing college colors here.

Whiskey Coke, a sorority girl drink. What was he thinking?

He searches out a bathroom up a set of narrow stairs. A place to hide and ease his panic. There, he leans against the sink. A dirty orange bulb flickers overhead. He takes off the Wolfpack hat and stuffs it in the trash. Underneath, his hair clings to his forehead.

They're people. Only people. Not demons in a story Harlan would tell, where misunderstanding some unsaid rule ruins your life. In Harlan's stories, otherworldly entities are always punishing humans for their ignorance and greed. Don't go in these woods, don't cross this river, don't pick these flowers or say that word aloud or shoot the deer that looks right at you. Nail horseshoes to the lintel of your doorway to keep out curses. This place is cursed.

Jesse reemerges from the bathroom to find Lila the waitress blocking his path in the stairway. She smiles up at him.

"Your friends went outside," she says, and gestures for him to follow her.

But she doesn't lead him outside. She leads him a long windy way back to the barroom with the *Gone with the Wind* posters and the minstrel figurines. Here, the barman is waiting for him on one of the barstools, tiny glasses flashing.

"Hey there," he says. "You steal from the bar?"

Jesse looks behind him to see the waitress standing with her tray over her chest. Her eyes glitter with delight.

"No, sir," he lies.

"No?" the barman says. "You sure? We was told otherwise."

"Who told you that?" Jesse asks.

"Don't matter."

"Well, I don't think you can trust—"

The barman's arm shoots out, snakelike, grabs a fistful of Jesse's hair, and yanks him across the room. "Wait, I have money!" Jesse cries. "I'll give you money!" He pries at the barman's hand, but the barman catches his arm and twists it behind his back. Jesse's shoulder spikes with pain, as if it might separate from its socket. He stops struggling. Now the barman is shoving him into a dim hallway cluttered with boxes. The waitress follows gleefully behind. The rest of the room is an audience, coldly attentive. No one intervenes.

"Are you going to call the cops?" Jesse whispers to the barman.

"We don't trifle with cops."

Jesse laughs at that.

"You think that's funny?"

"No. No, sir. I'm sorry."

"I bet you are."

A sharp turn in the hall. A dusty storage room lit with pulsing fluorescent light. The room is filled with liquor crates and kegs, massive coolers, thumb-size cockroaches, an open cabinet of short-range rifles, lengths of rusty chain. Jesse's blood roars in his ears. He holds his breath. The barman swats a mosquito away from his face, and in the wake of that small, careless movement, Jesse goes liquid, slides from the barman's grasp, and jets off. The barman, enraged, reaches for his arm, misses, stumbles. His glasses go askew. For a moment, the waitress readies herself in the doorway, as if she'll block him with her body. But when he blows past her, she shrieks like she's being murdered and covers her head with her arms. He sprints down the crooked hall, into the barroom, another room, another, through doorways marked with horseshoes. He smells them scorching the wood as he runs by.

Harlan is outside, as the waitress told him. Jesse finds him standing under live oak trees, just beyond a fleet of weathered picnic tables. The sky has gotten dark, the night air sticking to his lungs. He hears laughter, arguing, instruments tuning. Willy's drunkest patrons have spilled over here, their voices loose and wild, on the edge between inebriated joy and violence.

Pulse like: hog apple, hog apple, hog apple.

Harlan turns, blowing smoke from his cigarette. "What happened to you?"

Jesse folds over and puts his hands on his knees. "I think Tooly ratted on me about taking from the bar," he gasps. "That barman attacked me—they were dragging me into this back room with all these guns—"

The patio door flings open.

"Oh god, that's him."

Jesse crawls under a picnic table to hide. He worries for a moment that Harlan will rat him out, too, the way he stands there looking thoughtfully toward the door, but after a pause he comes over and sits, the crotch of his jeans at eye level. Jesse curls his knees under his chin, staring at Harlan's scuffed work boots.

Minutes go by. Harlan nudges Jesse with his foot.

"Coast is clear."

But Jesse doesn't move. A noisy crowd of men passes the table, a forest of legs and flickering light. He wants to reach out and wrap his arms around Harlan's leg and cling to it like a burr.

"I think they were about to kill me," he says.

"What?"

Jesse sticks his head out from under the table. "They were going to kill me in there."

Harlan looks down at him. The string lanterns overhead backlight his face. His cigarette smoke glows.

"I think you're exaggerating."

"Tooly said he was going to kill me."

"Tooly doesn't know what he's saying."

Jesse hears Harlan's unsaid accusation: Tooly doesn't know what he's saying, but *you* do.

"Jimmy," Jesse whispers. "Listen."

"Why don't you get out from under the table. I can't hear you, and it don't look no better if I'm sitting here talking to myself."

Jesse crawls out. The whiskey has laid a weariness on him—his limbs are heavy, his head overstuffed. He can tell that Harlan is also weary, the way he smokes his cigarette in slow motion. He doesn't look at Jesse. He watches the crowd. At the edge of the woods, on a little stage, a band tests their equipment. Idgy and Dennis, the sole standing members of the Undead Corpse of the Confederacy.

Jesse is stunned. "No, they're not playing *here*," he says. "They'll get destroyed."

Harlan shrugs. "They played here before."

"You're sure it was this band? These guys?"

"They play old shit, Pete Seeger, Willie Nelson—old murder ballads and folk songs. 'Sweet Caroline' sometimes. Folks eat it up."

"'Sweet Caroline'?" Jesse says, incredulous.

"You never seen a crowd of rednecks sing 'Sweet Caroline'?" Harlan offers a sly look. Jesse laughs nervously.

"No. I guess not."

But Harlan is right; both Undead Confederates seem unbothered, comfortable even, among Pinewood folk. Jesse wonders if their band name is less ironic than he assumed it was. He wonders if there are latent politics in Idgy's discordant ballads about child sexual abuse and labor rights tragedies, things Jesse missed when he believed they were silly and one-note and overearnest. Idgy is dressed like the Willy's crowd—jeans and plaid. Maybe that isn't ironic either. He crouches at the edge of the stage, summoned by a member of the crowd. Jesse recognizes the pale neck, the shock of blond hair. Tooly. Idgy nods as they speak. His expression is understanding.

Then he moves center stage and begins to play. Dennis buzzes a snare drum; the hissing effect is strange, but not wrong. Idgy sings: *Delia, oh, Delia / Delia all my life.* Someone in the audience wolf-whistles, but this is the only bit of rowdiness. Otherwise, folks listen. Tooly sits at a picnic table, enfolded in a clutch of his people, and listens, too.

That sticky feeling drips in Jesse's chest again. He remembers. Sam Quinn played this song. Not a half hour into that terrible night, he snatched up Harlan's Les Paul from its stand

in the den and played this song—*She was low down and trifling /
And she was cold and mean / Kind of evil make me want to / Grab
my sub machine*—and Jesse recalls being shocked, because he
hadn't known that Sam could play or sing or could do anything
artistic, brutish as he was. That was the night Sam went off, the
night Jesse showed up bloody and tripping, crawling through
the hedge into Jaelah Harrison's backyard prom after-party.
Harlan ended things three days later. *It's too much*, he wrote.
And that was it.

Delia's gone, one more round, Delia's gone.

Jesse realizes that Tooly must have asked Idgy to play this.
Tooly, who looks over his shoulder and sees Jesse. Who sits,
still as an owl, and stares with a contorted mix of rage and
dread as Jesse thinks his apology across the crowd. *Sorry about
your brother, okay? He was awful, but he didn't deserve* that.

At the end of the song, Tooly gets up and heads inside the bar.

Jesse's hands begin to shake. He straddles the bench to face
Harlan.

"Listen. Listen, Jimmy."

"I'm listening," says Harlan.

Jesse struggles to organize his thoughts. What does he want
to say? What's the magic sequence of words to get Harlan to
help him? On stage, Idgy begins a new song: *Virgil Cane is the
name / And I served on the Danville train.*

"Okay," Jesse says. "You're right. You're right, Jimmy. I
shouldn't've said that thing about Sam. About the sinkhole. All
my shit with Sam aside—I didn't need to say it. And—and the
underage thing. I was just—I didn't mean it. I just wanted a
response, any response."

Harlan lights another cigarette and says nothing.

"But I'm not here to cause you trouble, Jimmy. I swear. I don't regret anything. I don't want to do anything to hurt you. Look—" He holds up his phone. "Check for yourself. I deleted everything, texts, pictures—"

Harlan waves the phone away. "I'm not worried about that."

"What then? What? Why won't you talk to me?"

"It's your *being* here. That alone. You think these people don't see what you are?"

Jesse hesitates, breathless. Pulse like: hog apple.

"What I am?" he says. "What am I, Jimmy? What am I to you?"

"Come on, kid. You can't ask me that here."

"No, Jimmy, I need to ask. Because I still don't know what I owe you, or what you owe me, and I have a feeling—and I'm not trying to manipulate you or threaten you—but I have this feeling like you owe me more than what you're giving me. And any second now, Tooly's going to find that barman again, and they're going to come back out here, and if they catch me they'll beat the shit out of me or shut me up in that back room and kill me, and I still won't be able to make any sense of anything, and I still won't know what happened to my mother."

Harlan narrows his eyes. "What the hell has your mother got to do with it?"

Jesse laughs. Out it comes. Like ticker tape. "That's what I mean, Jimmy. This isn't even about you. I told you that from the beginning, but you didn't believe me. And maybe I should've been honest and told you it was about my mother, but I couldn't. I just—"

"You couldn't," Harlan says.

"I couldn't."

Hog apple, hog apple. There's no hog apple in his secret language, Jesse realizes. Only **Pig fruit**, verb: to play pretend, as a child. Is that something? A mistranslation? Are he and Harlan speaking different versions of the same language? Either way, they're starting to understand each other now; he can see it in Harlan's face—a dawning recognition. A breeze picks up, carrying on it the smell of his cigarette smoke and aftershave. Jesse's forehead burns.

"Are you trying to see your mother?" Harlan asks quietly.

See. See? Yes, he said see.

"You heard—somebody told you that Tooly saw Sam in the Night House."

Jesse picks this up fast and clings to it. "Yes. Yes, Jimmy. Yes."

Beyond Harlan's shoulder, the barman has reappeared at the door. This time, he has friends with him: two long-legged men, chewing toothpicks.

Jesse ducks back under the table.

"They saw you," Harlan says. "They're headed this way."

"I'm going to run for it," Jesse whispers.

"Go left, behind the stage. There's a path; it'll take you back to the parking lot."

"Come meet me there?"

But Harlan is already getting to his feet. He intercepts the barman and his posse: "Hey, Dodd, I just remembered to ask you— did Uncle Lot ever get up with you about that vintage rototiller?"

Jesse doesn't hear the barman's response. He springs out from under the table, skirting the edge of the crowd, moving fast and low. Someone behind him shouts, "There he is, there he is!" and he hears a clamor, as if one of his pursuers had crashed into a row of beer glasses. He passes the stage. The amp thunders in his ear. When he reaches the path at the edge of the woods, he looks over his shoulder and is astonished to see the chaos he's left behind: The barman's henchmen are on the ground and half the crowd is in an uproar, all while Harlan stands there looking stunned. At first, Jesse thinks Harlan must have punched someone, though it's such an out-of-character move he nearly laughs. Then he sees it: a round black animal clambering thunderously atop a crowded picnic table, shouldering aside patrons, pinning Jesse down with its small red eyes. The creature barks at him, its teeth roped with slime and foam.

"Betty!" Deputy Sleight shouts from the edge of the crowd. He's still in uniform. He calls to the dog like he's amused at the commotion it caused. "Down. Dooown. Come."

The dog listens but takes its time, resuming its place at Sleight's side with apparent resentment.

Jesse, meanwhile, hides behind the downswept branches of a cypress tree. The dog has seen him, but Sleight has not. Sleight, in fact, speaks to the bartender and Harlan as if he has no idea he interrupted anything, and the Undead Corpse of the Confederacy, true professionals, carry on without so much as a misplayed note. *The night they drove old Dixie down!*

"Shit in hell, what a day," Sleight says. "Either of y'all seen a kid around named Tooly Quinn?"

"No," says the barman.

"Nope," says Harlan.

Jesse hurries away down the path.

*   *   *

ghost, noun: **Moss thorn hemlock**

Literally, memory sickness.

Tooly saw Sam in the Night House. But Sam is dead. Sam has been dead for two years.

Jesse crouches against his car in Willy's parking lot and wonders about this. Police presence has some folks making a run for it, including Tooly, whose car Jesse spies escaping into the night. Jesse doesn't leave yet. He stays and waits.

His longing for Harlan used to trigger fantasy memories— which is to say, things he wishes they'd done together but never did. A day trip to Kure Beach, Jesse riding shotgun in Harlan's truck, rows of ice cream–colored houses on stilts. It's cold. They have the beach to themselves. They hop reckless and barefoot on the rocks above the tide pools. In another memory, they have a loft in a city, and Jesse is going to college, and Harlan is getting his GED. Sometimes he has a lucrative trade job, an electrician, a pipe fitter. When that gets dull, they smuggle drugs or exotic pets, but in a screwball way; their dealers are harmless characters. Sometimes the loft is a lighthouse, the city a remote island in the Florida Keys.

All this to say, when Harlan appears in the parking lot and sinks down beside him on the ground, it feels like one of those fantasy memories, like something he wishes had happened but didn't. It stirs up a green, stupid, fourteen-year-old's hope.

Harlan leans his head back and sighs.

"It happened last August. Tooly hasn't been the same since."

"So you believe him?" Jesse asks. "When he says he saw Sam?"

Harlan laughs grimly. "I don't know, man. Uncle Lot always

said that house was cursed. More than just haunted. That's what Mr. Bishop told him."

"Tooly's granddad."

Harlan nods. "Weird guy. Tooly says when he died, he was writing a book about, like, the county. His crazy life story. Something."

"Was my mother in it?"

"I don't know, kid." He gives Jesse a sad look. "You've got to—forgive me. I forget sometimes, what went down with your mom."

Jesse doesn't reply. He's thinking. Tooly's brother went out on Peach Hill in the middle of the night and fell into a sinkhole and died. But in the Night House, maybe he's a ghost. Maybe that's where all ghosts go, and Sam Quinn has been hanging out with his granddad and the Simms family and Connie Calloway.

Jesse springs up. The secret language fills his head. The dead are alive. You can see them.

"I have to go. I'm going back to that house."

"By yourself?" Harlan gets up, too, swaying with weariness. "No. You can't go in that house alone at night, fucking *drunk*."

"I'm not drunk," Jesse retorts. He pauses and takes account of himself. "Okay, I'm getting there. I'm sobering up. But if you're that worried about it, Jimmy, then *come with me*. And we can put this shit to rest once and for all."

He gets a high saying that. What a small tug it would take now to unearth Harlan's secrets. He can't go home. Not now. Tomorrow, Harlan could be sealed up again, Nancy might hog-tie him and deliver him back to Greensboro. The dead could go invisible. *You owe me.* Does Harlan feel that, Jesse like an oyster knife, cracking him open? *You owe me this.*

FROM THE UNTITLED MEMOIR OF
HARRY M. BISHOP, C. 2013

In real life, the rabbit is prey, but in folktales, he is the quickest and wiliest of animals. This I learned reading the Br'er Rabbit tales my third-grade teacher gave me. Daddy did not want me reading these tales because he knew them as "slave stories," and my teacher only convinced him to let me keep them by explaining that the book was written by a white man. Still, Br'er Rabbit the character was not invented by a white man, and Daddy never warmed to him because he was vermin, something for us boys to shoot in the garden, and because he stole and lied and otherwise got away with insolent, unchristian-like behavior. Were it not for the threat of getting whupped, it would have been funny, how mad Daddy got over a make-believe critter.

Rereading those tales years later, as a father and grandfather, I can see from his point of view. Br'er Rabbit is wily, but he is also without mercy. In one story, he traps Br'er Wolf in a box and slowly boils him alive, because it does not pay to be a predator in a folktale. Nowadays, I think of Daddy's rules and warnings all the time, his lectures and whuppings when we misbehaved. I figure now his anger was just fear of all those things he couldn't tell us. I felt that fear, too, watching the grandkids grow up, and I never read them any Br'er Rabbit tales. Those boys were not interested much in stories anyhow.

8

By Tuesday morning, Alice regrets her outburst the night before. In the early mist, long before her shift at the library, she goes out to the veranda to retrieve the items from the shattered jar—the mirror, the needle and thread, the oyster shell, and the nail wrapped in hair. Then she sweeps up, rights her living space, throws Mrs. Patton's fake witchfingers in the trash, and fixes herself breakfast. When she's finished, she takes a plate up for Morgan.

"Egg whites?" Morgan says hoarsely.

"All I've got," says Alice. She sits on the edge of the bed with one of Euel's antique revolvers, which hisses and crackles. Morgan looks at the revolver. After a few minutes eating in silence, she laughs.

"You got me good," she says, gesturing to the bathroom walls.

Alice doesn't reply.

"I guess it was shitty of me," Morgan says. "I shouldn't have threatened to turn you in. We girls need to stick together.

When you let me go, I'll tell everyone it was a man. He blind-folded me and kept me in a shed. I never saw his face. People will believe me..." She trails off, tugging balefully on the rope that connects her to the pipe. Another moment goes by in silence as she examines what remains of her breakfast. "Do you have any sugar for this grapefruit?"

Alice stands and places the revolver in her skirt pocket. She's at the bottom of the stairs when the screams begin. Morgan doesn't scream when the revolver is visible, so to make her stop screaming Alice has to go back upstairs and stand in the bathroom doorway with it. She doesn't have to point it at Morgan; having it in her hand is enough.

Morgan crouches and emits high-pitched sobs, her red cheek pressed against a blanket. Alice has filled the bathroom with blankets to muffle the sound.

"I told you," she says. "No one can hear you up at the house."

Crack-sss-inkink-crack. The gun's crackly metal power fills the room. Morgan cries awhile longer before she finally sits up and wipes her nose on her forearm.

"So no sugar?"

"I'll get you sugar," says Alice. "I need witchfingers."

Sniff-snort. "I don't have any on me."

"You know what they are?"

"No."

"Drugs." Alice sits on the edge of the bed. "Do you know how to get drugs?"

"I know people who know people," says Morgan. "It's a small town."

"Who would know?"

Morgan blinks her big wet eyes. "Red Koonce. Pretty much anybody in 4-H. I've never heard of witchfingers—is it a Pinewood thing? Is this whole mess really about drugs?"

Alice folds her legs on the bed. "Would Jesse Calloway know where to find witchfingers?"

Morgan laughs and shakes her head. "No. Why would he?" After a pause, she seems to resent the question. "You know, when me and Jesse first started hanging out, I got told he was this hard-edge kid. Like, freshman year, he was quiet, kinda offbeat, and then, boom, this hidden delinquent just burst out of him, and he got crazy, and he got in with a bad crowd, and whatever. But when I got to know him—you know, he just wanted to have a good time. My boy doesn't have a network, or like, a system. For anything. He just flaps his way along, like one of those blow-up men outside car dealerships."

She goes quiet, noticing how attentively Alice listens. Crouched, with the gun at her side. "Why are you obsessed with Jesse?"

"I'm not."

"Are you going to kill him?"

"No."

"Please, don't. Don't hurt him. People don't understand him."

"But you do?" Alice asks.

Morgan curls inward. "I don't know. I don't think I should tell you any more."

Alice takes a deep breath, rises, and begins gathering dishes. Morgan grabs the grapefruit and holds it to her chest.

"I want this."

"Fine," Alice says. She takes the dishes downstairs. Morgan begins screaming again.

In the process of serving Morgan food, bringing her extra bedding for her comfort, and ensuring the free flow of her circulation, Alice has come to realize that she was not prepared to have a body and all its humanly needs shackled to a pipe in her bathroom. Morgan's rope is just long enough that she can sit askance on the toilet, which is good. But bodies are complicated. Morgan says she has cramps, that she's due for her period, that she's constipated, has heartburn, needs her medicated face wash, is getting a rash on her forehead. The head wound makes her dizzy, causes mood swings. This morning it had scabbed over and begun to bleed again. Alice didn't have any antibacterial ointment, so she smeared it with sage honey. "It's antiseptic," she said, when Morgan flinched away. Since then, Alice has been afraid to see what's under the bandage.

Maybe she could've just confronted Jesse rather than attack Morgan. *I told you not to tell anyone. Keep your mouth shut.* But then she would have come off as threatening, and if he had reported that to Morgan, maybe Morgan then would've given her up. Overall, Alice believes she's making progress with Jesse. They had a productive back-and-forth yesterday. True, she didn't know what to say when he told her he was worried about his missing friend. She wanted to comfort him but could only offer a platitude, fully formed, from her glossary. *It's all good.* Literally—"Good finds all."

But that was before she knew that the jar didn't work, could not have worked. And so she sent along an anxious query this morning:

Any progress?

No reply.

"Murderer!" Morgan wails down the stairs. "It's been two days; I *smell*; I need to *shower*! God, please help me. *Murderer!*"

Alice climbs the stairs again and stands in the bathroom doorway. Morgan sobs into her knees on the floor.

"I am not a murderer," Alice says. "I'm not going to kill Jesse Calloway."

Morgan doesn't look up.

"I know him. We met each other, up in Pinewood, in the Night House. I snuck out and went up there the night I got sent away."

"You're evil," Morgan moans.

Alice doesn't contradict her. She's entitled to her opinion.

"This is a nightmare," she goes on. "This isn't real."

"Listen to me. Jesse is my *brother*."

That reaches her. She lifts her head, wet-faced and puffy-eyed. "Literally your brother?"

Alice is pleased that Morgan is curious, a surprising feeling. She will explain, but first she runs a bath for her. Bath salts, nice ones with French names. Citron. Brise de Lavande. The bathroom fills with fragrant steam. As Morgan bathes, Alice keeps the gun nearby, watching but not staring. She hasn't seen another person naked since Croatan; two of the girls on her floor were exhibitionists of a kind, one plainly vindictive about it, the other enlightened, raised in a mountain commune. Morgan is neither vindictive nor enlightened. She hunches to hide her body, looking over her shoulder with wounded eyes. She takes her time.

When she's finished, she towels off, wraps her hair, and dresses in the clothes Alice laid out for her, a yoga outfit; the therapist once suggested yoga to help with Alice's neuroses. All Alice wants now is for Morgan to be comfortable. Upon seeing that her wrists are beginning to blister, Alice wraps them in gauze before reaffixing her to the pipe, at which point the girl sits down, pink and fresh-faced in a fragrant cloud.

She seems in better spirits.

"All right," she says. "I won't make any more noise."

Alice sits cross-legged on the floor so they're eye to eye. *Crink-crink-ssss-crack*, says the revolver.

"Jesse is my brother," she says again. "My half brother."

"So Mr. Swink is his dad," says Morgan.

Deductive genius, thinks Alice. *Hercule Poirot over here.* But she does not mock Morgan. It's unfair to mock someone who's chained to a pipe in your bathroom.

"Does Mr. Swink…?" Morgan goes on. "Does he *know*?"

"There's no way he couldn't," says Alice. "When Connie Calloway was nineteen, she got a job as a receptionist at the processing plant. My father met her and took her on as a personal assistant. They had a fling. It ended. Then she found out she was pregnant."

"Oh," says Morgan. She unwraps her hair and begins to comb it with her fingers. "And Jesse doesn't know either, I guess."

"Not yet."

"But they don't look alike. How do you know for sure?"

"I suspected it," Alice says. "Based on some things my mother wrote. As soon as I met Jesse, I knew for sure. When I came back from Croatan, I got that job at the library. I started digging around about the Calloways."

Morgan frowns. She continues to comb her hair. "And you didn't tell him then?"

"I wasn't sure then. Now I am."

Morgan appears unconvinced, almost irritated. "So you met him. But he doesn't know you're the one who's messaging him."

"That's right."

"Why not just *tell him*? Tell him you're his sister. Tell him what you want."

Alice feels defensive. She doesn't know why she feels compelled to tell Morgan anything. In her head, all of this makes sense, but if, for instance, she were to try to explain it to her therapist, who assumes Alice's main issues are failures of communication, any understanding between them would dissolve like smoke.

Still, Alice does want to be understood.

"Because," she says, "he hasn't met me yet."

"You just *said* you'd met him."

"Yes."

"So you were lying? Y'all have never met."

Alice has hit a block.

"I don't know how else to explain it," she admits. "I need witchfingers so I can draw him to me. So he can *see* me. He's *supposed* to see me."

Morgan stares, not understanding. She begins trying to braid her hair and finds she can't do it with her hands tied. "Could you blow-dry my hair for a minute?"

Alice is taken aback by how confidently she requests the favor, how quickly she changes the subject. "I don't have one."

"You don't?" Morgan looks at her pleadingly. By now, the sun is creeping over the north side of the guesthouse, spearing in through a gap in the curtains. "Could you get one for me?"

Moments later, Alice is heading barefooted up the slope to the main house. The mist has cleared; yellow sunlight cuts across the bridge with a buzz saw shriek. Euel's car is gone, but Bobbie is in the kitchen, dressed and ready for the day and cleaning up after the dinner party. Alice steals past her, up the stairs and into the master bath. When she comes back down, she sneaks through the living room, where the harp glows in the morning light, its strings humming. Bobbie catches sight of her as she's sneaking past the kitchen doorway.

"Oh, Jesus Christ, Alice!" she cries. "You scared me."

Alice freezes and turns. Bobbie stands there at the sink, dish rag clutched tensely in her hand.

"You're still in your pajamas?"

"I'm what?" Alice says.

"I'm driving you over to the library. Selena expects me at Youth Outreach in twenty minutes."

"But you don't need to drive me now; it's Tuesday. I do afternoon shifts on Tuesday."

"Right, but—you've got—it's therapy at three—"

"I just had therapy."

Bobbie looks stricken. "Alice, we talked about this. Your therapist can't do it Thursday this week. She had to move you to *Tuesday*. Today."

Alice can't remember. Every day prior to Monday is formless and vague.

"I can't."

"Therapy is a priority, Alice."

"Then I can't do my shift at the library. I need the morning for self-care."

"Why do you have my hair dryer?"

Alice looks down at the hair dryer, its plastic buzz grinding. "One of my books fell in the tub." She gives Bobbie a long, steady look. "I can't go to the library today."

Bobbie is eyeing the hair dryer, as if Alice might do something awful with it.

After a pause, she says "Fine" very quietly. "That's fine."

She turns away. Alice slinks to the door.

Outside, she can tell that Morgan is screaming in the guesthouse. She can hear the ragged spirit of Morgan's screams before she ever hears the screams themselves. When she crosses the lawn and goes inside, the screams stop abruptly. Upstairs, Morgan is red-faced and sweaty again, the gauze on her wrists unraveled. She sees the hair dryer in Alice's hands and smiles brightly. "Oh good!"

Alice sits on her knees behind her and gently brushes and dries her hair until it fluffs. It's tempting not to listen to the sounds of Morgan over the drone of the hair dryer. Birdsong. The hiss of hallway gossip. The squeak of tennis shoes on a gym floor. When she finishes, Morgan stares straight ahead at the wall.

Morgan couldn't have been more than six when Alice played pretend with her and her sister. The sister, Lauren, was about nine. Alice remembers now that Morgan was dead set on being a horse, even though her sister told her she couldn't, she *had* to be a human if she wanted to play. No. For Morgan, it was a horse or nothing. Fast. A wild child. She would tear through the dandelions and set them on fire with her flaming tail. Alice liked that. Of course Morgan could be a horse. She could be a horse and burn up the whole lawn if she wanted. Even back then, in Alice's mind, being a human was a point against you. Maybe, if things had gone differently, Alice and Morgan could've rubbed off on each other. Found common ground. Been friends.

She turns to her mother's notebooks for help.

There is no clear recipe in here on how to make a friend, no jar to build trust with someone you have hurt and whose dignity you have denigrated, and who is tied clumsily to a pipe in your bathroom.

So Alice has to improvise. She takes two dried dogwood blooms, a shred of Morgan's cotton bandage, dips them in wine, and drinks from the glass. *Whey-whey.* Upstairs, she lights two beeswax candles on the dresser. Morgan watches her from the bathroom, eating the grapefruit from earlier and tearing its rind into confetti.

"What are you doing?" she asks.

Alice settles on the floor with her wine. In her pocket, the pistol's shiny barrel says, *Sssssssstt.*

"Why are you drinking wine?" Morgan asks. "It's morning."

In fact, it's just past noon, but Alice says, "I know," wets her finger with the wine, and runs it along the rim of the glass. The glass rings clear and soft. Morgan listens warily, a piece of grapefruit in her mouth.

After a moment, she says, "You're not trying to cast a spell, are you?"

"No," says Alice.

Morgan flinches, her hair wispy in her face. Baby hair. Fairy-folk hair. "Could you stop making that noise? Please?"

Alice stops what she's doing with the wineglass and lets the sound hang in the room.

"Are you afraid of spells?" she asks.

"No," says Morgan, tucking her knees under her chin. "If you want to do spells, that's fine. I'm not some raving Bible thumper. I just don't want any spells done on *me*."

"I didn't think you were a Bible thumper," Alice says. She sips the wine, considering. "Did you ever hear anything about my mother? She used to live in Pinewood. Her name was Katrina Morrow."

Morgan shakes her head.

"It's all right to say if you heard she was crazy white trash. I've heard that."

"I haven't heard anything," Morgan says softly. "I don't remember."

"My father used to cheat on her. With Connie Calloway first, like I said. They were friends, my mother and Connie. He ruined their friendship. But my mother—she chose him, and they had me, and then he cheated again. And he kept cheating. And then she left him and was in this custody battle, and when I was little, she took a bunch of stuff from his house—his guitar, some jewelry, some old watches. She sold it all to pay a lawyer, who was not legit, in the end. He cheated her, too. And my father—he pressed charges and used it against her."

She sips again. The ring of the wineglass keeps going, sliding down her throat. Morgan looks thoughtful.

"Man," she says after a pause. "What a fuckboy."

Alice laughs, and the sound surprises her. Morgan laughs, too.

"I didn't know Mr. Swink had that side to him."

"Yeah," says Alice. "He did take it back. Dropped the charges and all, said he felt bad. But it's not the worst thing he's ever done. The worst thing was teaching me how to play. That's what killed her."

Morgan's breath quickens, her fairy hair fluttering. "Killed who?"

"My mother. She's dead."

"Oh—I'm sorry."

"It happened a long time ago. Jesse and I have that in common."

Another silence. When Morgan speaks again, her voice is high and pliant: "You said—teaching you to play? Mr. Swink, he plays music?"

"Right," Alice says. "*Did* play music. After college, he was in a band. Several bands. He played the folk harp in a gospel band in Boone, then in a Celtic music group in Wilmington. They sold CDs to tourists. Swink is an Irish name. It means 'pleasant'—or 'peasant'—something like that. My father used to say that music was in his blood. He loved seeing an audience come alive. That's love, he said. When you play it perfect, they can't help but love you. When he first started teaching me, he told me that music is like a spell. He knew something about spells because he'd seen them, back when all he did was float around, up and down the river in his kayak, looking for new places to claim."

Alice pauses. Her tongue feels heavy. She can't remember the last time she talked aloud for so long with someone listening, and Morgan *is* listening, her face tense and bright.

"*He's* the one who told me about all this, though he won't admit it now. One of my first lessons—we were practicing mandolin on the back porch. And it was a summer evening, and I hit this sequence of chords, I swear, it lit up every lightning bug in the yard, all at once. As soon as it happened, I knew the music had done it. Or rather, that *he* had done it *through* the music. He knew it, too. But he didn't admit it. He winked at me like it was a game. Like we were pretending. Still, it kept happening. With bugs. But also birds. The neighbor's Maltese. The fish, they'd jump right up on the dock. And then, of course—people. The housekeeper. That nervous woman from the DEQ. His new father-in-law, Frank Calhoun. By then, he had me experimenting with other instruments. He wanted to find out which one was the strongest. That's how we came to his old folk harp. Trial and error. And I loved it. I did. All his winks and spells. Back then, it didn't feel like he was using me. It felt special."

Alice frowns, tapping her finger on the stem of her wineglass.

"When my mother disappeared, I tried to tell everyone that she was dead, but no one believed me. Now I'm convinced he killed her. More than ever. Because she would not have given up. My mother had been cheated and discarded and evicted from her home, but she would not have given up on this place. She was too invested in it. There's—I don't know if you've sensed this; I think a lot of people sense it and won't admit it—but there's something buried here. In the swamp, in the river. And in the *history* of this place, these ghosts, these knots of time that double back and loop around, they give a kind of speech to things. A kind of meaning. What was happening back then between my mother and Euel—it was bigger than just some quarrel about cheating; it was a long cycle of these same kinds of battles, over and over. On the one hand, you have something pure and wild and real, and on the other, you have the fuckboys and the pig men, these entitled, empty men and their blind, vain women, thinking they own this place, flushing blood and shit into the river, poisoning everything. My father thinks he can put it all behind him, pretend it never happened. He thinks he's tamed this place and all its ghosts and shadows with a map and a smug look. But I'm not going to let him forget. Through flood or fire, whatever it takes, I won't let him forget what he did. What he destroyed."

Alice pauses. Morgan has been listening, but her face has a closed-off quality. She says nothing in reply.

That's when Alice realizes that the room is in complete disharmony. The latent ringing of the wineglass, the hiss and crack of the revolver in her pocket—it's all at odds with the sound of Morgan herself. Birdsong and tennis shoes, a giggly laugh, all her scoffs, moans, and sobs, backtalk muttered behind parents' backs, the smack of chewing gum to disguise alcohol on the breath, a tired, raspy voice singing church hymns. An ordinary girl with ordinary rebellions. Alice is disappointed, though not surprised, to find no understanding between them.

It won't be like that with Jesse. Jesse will believe her, because by the time she sees him again, he'll have found the buried place and seen it for himself, and he'll know that what she has to tell him is true.

But why has he not messaged her back?

Morgan opens her mouth, her face straining toward what might be an empathetic expression. Before she can say anything, Alice hears the click of footsteps on the walkway outside. Someone is approaching the guesthouse.

A knock. Morgan's face goes blank. Before she can scream, Alice lunges at her and stuffs a gag into her mouth. Her wineglass flings its contents over the carpet.

Morgan fights hard. She knees Alice in the ribs and knocks the wind out of her. Alice pins back her arms, but she slams the two of them against the sink cupboard with such force she breaks the door from its hinges. She wails with rage under her gag.

"Shh!" Alice wrestles her to the floor and, pushing against her head with her elbow, reties the gag tight.

Morgan's wailing tapers off into a whimper.

"Stay quiet," Alice whispers.

"Mmm," she says, quivering in compliance.

The visitor knocks again.

Alice's therapist likes to emphasize how important it is for Euel and Bobbie to at least make nods toward her privacy and independence. Usually, if they want to see her or ask her for a favor, they signal on the intercom before making their way down from the main house. Alice figures Bobbie may have returned from her volunteer gig and has eschewed this protocol so she can give Alice a piece of her mind. But it isn't Bobbie at the door. It's Mrs. Patton. She's elegantly dressed as always, standing stiffly on the front steps in spring-yellow heels and a matching blouse, two large earrings framing her cheeks like silver shields. Alice opens the door.

"Catch you at a bad time?"

Alice has been too preoccupied to mourn her loss of trust in Mrs. Patton.

"Yes," Alice says, smoothing down her hair. "You caught me at a bad time."

"I stopped by the library earlier, but they said you were taking a personal day. Thought I might come see you at home."

The spirit of Morgan's rage and fear shrieks its way through the upstairs bedroom. Mrs. Patton doesn't hear, as if her great big earrings shield her from the sound.

"Your mouth is bleeding," Mrs. Patton says.

"Yeah."

She looks concerned. "Do you have a minute?"

"Not really."

"This is important. I want to talk to you about what happened last night. Make sure you're okay."

Mrs. Patton's concern seems sincere, but this only stokes Alice's anger.

"You didn't need to come check on me. I'm not a child."

"You seemed fine for most of the night, and suddenly..."

"We don't need to talk about it."

Mrs. Patton's frown deepens. "Your father told me why you did what you did. That you were—that you were jealous of the birthday song? That didn't sound right to me. I wondered if there was another reason."

Can she be this stupid? Either Mrs. Patton herself was duped or the currants were some half-baked con. Alice is furious at her regardless.

"I don't like birthdays," she says.

"But you—"

"What do you want? That was the reason. I wanted to ruin your birthday."

"Alice—"

"I'm busy right now. I'm doing self-care. You're interrupting my self-care."

She moves to close the door, but Mrs. Patton wedges her foot in, winces, struggles to pry the door back open.

"You owe me an explanation!"

"I *did* explain; you just didn't like what I said."

"You're acting like a freak, Alice. Is this the way you treat your friends?"

Alice shoves against the door, forcing Mrs. Patton back. She cries out as the door catches on her shoe, snaps the heel right off, and slams in her face. This was an accident, but Alice likes it. It sends a clear message. They stare each other down through the glass, Mrs. Patton looking first stunned, then almost frightened, as if she's had a jarring realization. *She knows what she's done*, Alice thinks.

Mrs. Patton gathers both of her shoes in her hand and waves them furiously at the door. "This isn't over. We *will* talk about this."

"Talk about *what*," Alice says. She watches Mrs. Patton storm back to her car, barefooted.

Upstairs, Morgan lies sprawled on the bathroom floor, her red face wet with tears. Alice checks her phone.

"Currants," she says bitterly, still raging. "I didn't even know for sure if that jar would work. But it certainly didn't work with currants, that *idiot*—"

She hurls the phone on the bed.

"Twenty-four hours. I haven't heard from him in twenty-four hours. So I don't know where the hell he is. If he's gotten to where he needs to be, or what'll happen if he doesn't. I don't know."

She looks at Morgan, who is breathing heavily. The rash on her forehead stands out like a wine stain.

"But why am I telling you? You'll be happy, I bet, when all this falls apart. And I'm back at Croatan. Won't you, Morgan?"

Morgan springs up. She grabs up the broken cabinet door in her bound hands and throws it at Alice, hits her forearm. Alice then picks up the door and smashes it to pieces against her dresser, and when Morgan curls up tight with fear, she feels, to her astonishment, a wave of shame.

Minutes later, a check mark bruise forms on Alice's skin. Scraped flesh and little specks of blood going *ichichichich*.

About six miles out from Willy's to Bittern's Rest, Jesse's phone picks up a signal again, and all of Nancy's messages come through, increasingly frantic, one after another. He turns off the phone. His car—Harlan would not let him drive—is back at Willy's. Though Harlan is not exactly sober either; he just holds it better.

Harlan parks in his driveway. In the dark, on the other side of the pine grove, the shadow shape of the Night House crouches, the wrought iron widow's walk crowning the roof like a cage. If the house could make a sound, it would be howling.

"So," Jesse says, "did Tooly *speak* to his brother? Or just see him in there? What level of contact are we talking about?"

"Don't know," Harlan says. "Didn't make much sense, the way he explained it. Hey—are you sure you want to do this? It's pitch-black in there with the windows boarded up; there's broken glass and shit…"

"We can't come back in the daytime. That nosy neighbor Whatshername will see us. Why, Jimmy, you scared of ghosts?"

"I'm scared of tetanus," Harlan says, opening the driver's side door. "Let's just make it quick, all right?"

They gather two big flashlights out of the back of the truck and cross through the pines. The front door was open earlier in the day for Morgan's searchers. Now it's sealed up again with fresh plywood. Harlan says he'll go back and get his crowbar, but Jesse leads him around to the back of the house, to the wisteria vine and the open window over the porch roof. Harlan hesitates. Tetanus minefield. But Jesse scoots his way up and Harlan follows at a slower pace, winded by the climb.

Jesse almost laughs—*That's what you get for smoking*—but he's losing his breath, too. The house is pitch-black, just like Harlan said. The air is dead as a tomb. In the green-tiled foyer, a parade of footprints lights up under the beams of their flashlights— police from earlier in the day, Jesse from the day before.

"You said it was last August when this happened?" Jesse says.

"Mmm," says Harlan. "He was buying from a cousin or something, meeting him here, I think. He'd been using more."

Jesse swings his flashlight from one ceiling corner to the other. He takes in a slow, dusty breath.

"He was upstairs? Downstairs?"

"Downstairs when I found him."

Jesse looks over his shoulder. "When *you* found him?"

"Yeah." Harlan rubs sweat off his forehead. The house is a hotbox. "Kid, I feel obligated to tell you, what Tooly saw in here, it didn't *help* him. He weren't any better afterward. I mean, you've seen him. If anything, it made him worse."

"It won't be that way with me," Jesse says flatly.

"What do you mean?"

"Show me where you found him, Jimmy."

Harlan looks at Jesse a moment, then carefully makes his way around the stairs to the sweltering dark of the living room. Jesse has been wondering if Tooly was high when he saw his brother, an easy and admittedly disappointing explanation for Sam's presence in the Night House. But he trusts Harlan's fear as a gauge. There's more to this than a bad trip.

Harlan leads Jesse to the fireplace and stops at the hole in the wall.

"Here. I hadn't seen him in a few days. Then I'm out washing the truck, and I hear someone screaming. It was him."

"Screaming what? What was he saying?"

"Just—I don't know, man. Not words. He was *screaming*."

Jesse leans into the hole and shines the flashlight around. Its inner walls are blackened with mold.

"He was in this hole?"

"He was"—Harlan puts up a hand as if touching an invisible barrier—"inside."

"In the wall. *Inside* the wall."

"Had to break him out with an ax. He was a mess. Incoherent. My uncle came over to make sure we were all right after, and it freaked him out, seeing the kid like that. He said, *That's it. The Devil's in that house.* So he and some friends, they took it on themselves to board it up."

"Your uncle," Jesse says. "The fixer."

"Right," says Harlan.

Jesse imagines it: disembodied shrieking, Harlan hacking away to get inside, and Tooly tumbling into his arms. He imagines Laughton, scowling with determination as he hammers the boards in place. They, the forgotten blue-collar men of Pinewood, took it upon themselves to end the reign of the Night House.

"Who all knows this happened?" he asks. "Besides you and your uncle."

"Don't know. We wanted to keep it quiet, but you know what this town is like."

Jesse lifts a leg into the hole and steps inside. The floor gives slightly, softened by rot. To the right, his flashlight shines on a wall with exposed lath; to the left, the bricks of the fireplace. Jesse puts himself all the way in. A tight squeeze. He shines his flashlight upward.

Spiders. Thousands of fat black spiders hanging in the darkness. In the beam of the flashlight, they shine like stars, like a galaxy, vibrating against their webs.

"Spider fingers..." Jesse says.

"Huh?" says Harlan. "Hey—get out of there, would you? There could be nails, snakes..."

Jesse steps out, shivering excitedly. He walks the length of the wall and comes back. "But how did he get *in*? And how long was he in there for?"

"I—" Harlan shakes a centipede off his wrist, wincing. "I don't know. He was meeting the cousin the night before, he said, but—it was almost noon when I heard him screaming. And that was in August. You feel how stuffy it is right now—he'd've been cooking if he spent more than fifteen minutes in there."

"Weird," Jesse says, circling the hole with his flashlight. "'It spit me out…'"

"What do you keep whispering about? You're giving me the creeps."

"He said the house *spit him out*." He turns the flashlight to the ceiling. "I asked him how to get in. He said you have to get up in the wall, like you're going in from above."

"Like from upstairs?" Harlan asks.

"A crawl space," says Jesse.

"Wait a minute, kid…"

Jesse is already headed for the stairs. "You up for getting inside a crawl space?"

"*Wait.* What'd you mean? It won't be that way with you, like it was with Tooly. What'd you mean by that?"

"It's not obvious?" Jesse feels his way along the stairwell, pea-green wallpaper crumbling under his touch. "He knew his brother. So seeing him again hurt. It fucked him up. But I don't know my mother. So it won't hurt me like it did Tooly."

Harlan moves slowly behind him, unconvinced.

"Are you—how, how do you know that?"

"I know because I was *told* to do it. I was led to this."

"Led by *who*?" Harlan walks behind, breathing heavily. He's *so* not as fit as he used to be. He, who liked to pretend he wasn't vain about his appearance but would turn toward the sunlight in his bedroom when he took off his shirt, so that Jesse could see the definition in his abs. Jesse used to like that about him—his vanity.

Now, partway up the stairs, Jesse's foot sets off a crack from the step, improbably loud, and behind him Harlan clutches the banister, ducking down like he's been shot at. Jesse shines the flashlight on him, his face sweaty, eyes wide. He seems diminished, curled and thin like a wood shaving. Something metal glints on his belt.

"Is that a *gun*, Jimmy?" Jesse asks.

Harlan sucks in his breath.

"What are you fixing to do? Shoot all the ghosts?"

Harlan's eyes aren't looking directly at Jesse, but at a spot on the stairs just past him. Jesse shines the flashlight there.

"Did you see something?"

"See something?" Harlan says. "No. Go on up, will you?"

He pauses, studying Harlan's face. Back at Willy's, their old rapport seemed within reach, but the atmosphere between them has become suspicious again. Jesse is more annoyed than nervous. Harlan's knuckles cling to the banister, bone white.

Jesse reaches his hand out behind him, feeling the air.

"Christ, Jesus, kid, will you stop that?" says Harlan.

Jesse's face pulses at the impatience in his voice.

"I didn't see anything," Harlan insists.

"If you say so," says Jesse, continuing on.

The sounds of the house swarm them, its creaking and moaning, its skittering vermin, its boggy breath whispering through the twisty, second-floor hall. The house isn't dead. It isn't a tomb. It's alive and breathing. Why didn't he recognize that before?

They investigate the upstairs crawl spaces and find only dead ends. One, which Jesse thinks is right above Tooly's hole in the wall, opens up only to the brick flue of the chimney. Then they go up to the third floor—the attic room. Here, the space is bare, caked with dust and dried leaves. A dim square of light filters in through the fractured window, its glass filmy, the color of seaweed. Jesse rubs it with his shirtsleeve and peers out. A half-moon hangs in the sky, bright and silver. When he steps back, its glow strikes the opposite wall.

Way up—like from the sky. You see the river.

Here, the wallpaper has been scraped off, leaving behind a landscape of spotty mold. A large crack snakes from floor to ceiling. Jesse touches it, tracing his fingers along its curves. It's as thick as his finger in places. He can hear Harlan's fretful breathing behind him.

"This looks familiar," says Jesse.

"Nothing up here," Harlan says, pretending to be calm. "Dead end."

"No." Jesse's mind is waiting for him to see it, and when he does, his heart springs up like a flame. "I know what this is."

"Water damage."

"Jimmy, don't you recognize it?"

"Recognize what?"

Jesse steps back. Undeniably, he is looking at an aerial view of the Miskwa River. He can trace his fingers along each familiar spot. "Here's Hook Bend. The bridge is here—downtown here, and South Greene across the way. And up there is where it widens in the swamp, all the tributaries. Do you see it?"

He looks over his shoulder at Harlan, who is frozen in the middle of the room.

"Jimmy?"

Harlan's mouth twists, his face contorting, shaking.

"Why are you so scared?"

"I'm not," he says. "I just think you shouldn't—*huuh!*"

He recoils, making a sound as if someone had pressed the air out of him. Jesse turns back around.

The river has widened. Or rather, it is now a craggy six inches wide, as if it always was. A warm, swampy smell rolls out of it, carrying a sharp, metallic undercurrent, like heat lightning. Jesse shines the flashlight into the dark, but the beam goes on and on in all directions. He sticks his hand in. It feels like nothing. He turns the flashlight off and now sees that the darkness is filled with starry blue specks. A galaxy of spiders and indigo light.

"Don't," says Harlan, so quiet Jesse almost doesn't hear him.

"Do you see this?" He laughs and looks over his shoulder. "Look!"

"Kid, don't."

Jesse looks back. The rift is now wide enough to step through.

"No," says Harlan. "This was a mistake."

"I'm not afraid."

"No, no—"

"It's all good, Jimmy." **Blood spade Stone Sea**

Harlan doesn't listen. He lunges at Jesse and grabs his arm. Jesse's body jolts as if subjected to electric shock. Harlan's cowardice infuriates him. All around them, the sounds of the house grow louder, until it's not just groans and creaks, but squawks and yowls and cracks in the dark. The smell from the rift becomes lurid, dizzying.

"Let go of me!"

"Shut up," says Harlan. "Just *shut up*."

He has Jesse around the waist now, so tight it shunts his organs into his ribs. Jesse claws at Harlan's arm. As he's dragged to the doorway at the top of the stairs, he pushes Harlan back into the jamb. A snowfall of dust sticks to their skin. In the struggle, their flashlights fall to the floor; they fight against each other in total darkness.

"Let *go*!"

He shoves again. The hilt of Harlan's gun jams into his back. Jesse has a thought, a bit of delirium—*That a pistol in your belt, buddy, or are you just happy to see me.* He doesn't say it aloud, but he wants to mock Harlan. Make light of his terror. Instead, he flings an elbow, which catches Harlan off guard, smack in the jaw; then he pulls free, grabs up a fallen flashlight, and races for the opening, so fast he doesn't know if he's running or falling.

Harlan shouts after him—"It's a mistake!"—but he's already through.

Alice is at the main house when Bobbie comes back to retrieve her. Her shame has only grown more acute. It leaks through her, tinges everything. She tries to be apologetic as Bobbie drives her in silence to New Bridges.

"Did it go well?" she asks quietly. "At Youth Outreach?"

But Bobbie gives her a cold, distrustful look, which does not allow for conversation.

Despite her best efforts, Alice is beginning to wonder if she's made a wrong turn somewhere. It was never necessary that she be so hostile toward the other people in her neighborhood, toward Bobbie. In fact, Alice might have had a natural ally in her stepmother; Euel has manipulated her, too. But there's been so much petty push and pull between them, so much grasping for control over things that, in the end, don't matter at all. Alice's posture. Her manners. Her ugly thrift store clothes. Singing or not singing in church. Bobbie couldn't have children of her own; she always wanted to be a mother. But she was simply too trivial, too timid, too ordinary to be *Alice's* mother, just as Alice assumed that Morgan would be too ordinary to be her friend.

Still—what if it never needed to be that way? What if Alice has been going about her plans all wrong? And if she could be wrong about one thing, she could be wrong about Jesse, too. She could be sending him out to nothing. Or into harm's way.

Alice is not ignorant to the violence that simmers in Pinewood, its dark hollows.

All throughout her session at New Bridges, she thinks under her therapist's blank, searching look, the glow of the salt lamp reflecting on her glasses. The onyx stones in her fountain chant gently—*ai-ai-ai-ai*—but Alice's head is such an orchestra of angry noise she can barely hear them. She's been sitting in silence for a while now.

Thup thup, thup thup, says her mother's hair clip. *Ichichich*, says the bruise on her arm.

Kayla or Marla or Wendy says softly, "I'm sorry we had to rearrange the schedule. I know you're not used to meeting today."

Alice sits at the edge of her chair, intense, alert.

"Do you think this may have thrown you off?" the therapist asks.

"No," says Alice. "I don't mind the schedule change."

"You seem different than when I saw you on Sunday. Quieter."

Alice touches her forehead, which is hot under her fingertips. "I had some plans recently. They haven't been turning out the way I want."

The therapist perks up. "How so?"

A sickly sweet smell leaks from a hot stone lantern in the corner, some incense contraption. Alice scowls at it, wants to spit on it, see if she can make it hiss.

"All right," says the therapist. "You know you don't have to tell me everything. Tell me one thing—a small specific thing that happened since I last saw you."

Alice's eyes drift from the stone lantern to the therapist's bookshelf—all the mindfulness manuals, books on gardening, yoga, Eastern wisdom. What does this obtuse white lady know about *Eastern wisdom*? And there, in the middle of that thought, is when Alice notices the nameplate, sitting between a pink quartz sphere and a photo of the therapist and her husband somewhere in the Southwest.

"Alice Catherine?" says the therapist.

Her name. The therapist's name. It's been sitting on the bookshelf the whole time. Her name is *Katrina*.

And all of Alice's shame turns to fury once again.

She expects Bobbie to stick around until after her session is over, but it is, in fact, Mrs. Patton who's waiting in the parking lot for her. The glint of her silver sedan stokes Alice's rage.

"Bobbie sent for me," Mrs. Patton calls through the passenger window. "Said she had a few more errands to run."

Alice resents this change. Short of walking home, she has no choice but to accept Mrs. Patton's ride. So she does, wordlessly, and Mrs. Patton takes the long way down the wooded road like usual, fiddling with the air-conditioning, playing that same Prince CD. She vibrates with nerves like a tea kettle, her eyes tense. Alice stares out at the looping power lines in silence, wanting Mrs. Patton to feel unnerved.

"What is going on with you?" asks Mrs. Patton finally. "Aren't you going to say anything?"

"I don't have anything to say. If you have something to ask me, then ask."

At first, Mrs. Patton says nothing. Alice continues watching the power lines.

"I worry about you," Mrs. Patton says.

"No, you don't."

"I'm not saying that as an argument—"

"You don't worry about me," says Alice. "Who am I to you? Crazy Alice Catherine, in her big house, with her rich daddy. You're not worried about me."

Mrs. Patton frowns. Her kettle squeal gets louder. "Well. You said it."

Alice leans forward. "What did you just say?"

"*You said it*, Alice." Mrs. Patton's voice bites, so different from the sly smoothness she put on at dinner. "With your house and your rich daddy, and all your self-pity. You said it. It's enough to make someone wonder why you're sabotaging yourself. Boredom maybe, I don't know."

"I am not sabotaging myself," says Alice. "*You* sabotaged me."

"Oh, did I? How exactly."

"You *know* how. The witchfingers were currants. Freeze-dried currants."

A cold silence settles between them. On Mrs. Patton's stereo, Prince keeps singing: *dance, music, sex, romance.*

"Well, I didn't know that," Mrs. Patton says.

"I'm pretty sure you did."

"The man I bought them from, that's what he said they were."

"Yeah? And they just happened to be an ingredient in one of Nate's cakes?"

"You leave my husband out of this," Mrs. Patton says sharply, but her voice shakes. She's reconsidering her approach. "Look, I don't know a thing about drugs. I don't use drugs. I never did."

"You knew you were giving me currants, though. And not drugs."

"You said you just needed them for rituals."

"You didn't think it mattered?"

"Jesus—Alice, do you not know what *symbolism* is? Besides—" Mrs. Patton's face twitches. She speaks fast: "Besides, you can't buy witchfingers. People don't use them. That's a myth."

Alice laughs. "A myth? Are you serious?"

"Claviceps carolina," says Mrs. Patton. "A species of ergot. It grows on the marsh grass here, but it doesn't—it doesn't *do* anything. They don't sell it up in Pinewood. And I didn't know that, because *I don't use drugs,* Alice. When you asked me about it, I thought, 'Witchfingers? Maybe that's a thing,' and I looked it up and guess what. *Nothing.*"

"Witchfingers are real," Alice insists. "The Angel Battalion—"

"It's make-believe."

"Those stories are real."

"No, they're not. If you heard them from your mother, go ahead and assume they're not real. All that about the swamp and the river, that witchy nonsense. It was a *game*. Into her twenties she was still pretending with that shit, like a teenager."

A dark, sizzly heat cuts Alice through, throat to navel.

"Did Euel tell you that?" she asks. "My mother was playing a game?"

Mrs. Patton tch-es, flips her hand. "Euel didn't tell me nothing. I figured that out on my own. I knew your mother. We lived on the same street. When she moved out and they built that warehouse, the contractors found those foolish little jars buried everywhere..."

"She didn't move out," says Alice.

"Moved out, was evicted, whatever." Mrs. Patton shakes her head. "This was all just foolish. You ask me—the only Black woman you know—to buy you drugs, and I think, *Yeah, it must help her, believing in all this.* I didn't think you were crazy for that. I thought you were sheltered. And sad."

"She *didn't* move out."

"Listen, I'll get you your money back; it just might take a few days."

"I need witchfingers."

"There's no such thing."

Thup THUP, thup THUP—the rhythm shakes Alice's skull. She is in control. She is an agent. "I put my trust in you, Tanisha. You shouldn't have done this. You picked the wrong side."

"Yeah, maybe," she says, laughing. "I don't feel good about it, if that makes you feel any better. But—I know you won't risk saying anything."

Alice eyes her. Mrs. Patton is not so sure about that.

"Have you gotten to see the little scar on my father's stomach? Has he told you how he got it?"

"Okay, enough," Mrs. Patton snaps. "You had better quit implying things about me and your father."

"We were having an argument at dinner. He said things to me about my mother, not all that different from what you're saying to me now. It wasn't real; it was all pretend. I told him he was a liar. Back and forth we went. But I got the last word in that time. Stabbed him with a kitchen knife."

For a while, Mrs. Patton says nothing, calmly puzzled.

"That's why they sent you away?"

"Why did you think?"

Mrs. Patton tightens her grip on the steering wheel. "I don't know. I thought maybe you tried to kill yourself. That's what girls like you do."

Alice just laughs.

Another silence: Mrs. Patton, contemplating. "But people would've said. They'd know about it—"

"I was a minor. Record sealed, kept under wraps. Euel got treated at the hospital in Kneesville. Bobbie told everyone I had a 'breakdown.' She wouldn't dare say the truth."

Mrs. Patton is starting to believe it. Her face falls.

"If that's true..." she says. "If that's true, Alice, then it makes me sad. If I stabbed my father when I was sixteen, they'd've charged me as an adult, thrown me in jail for a decade. You got four little months in Croatan."

Alice is still laughing. "You took advantage of a suicidal girl."

"And you? You heard—what—about my 'people'? Thug cousins in Vernontown, connections in Wilmington? What about me said 'I'll sell you drugs,' huh? My style? My taste in music? Or was it something about the color of my skin? We were marks to each other. Period. Let's leave it at that."

She clears her throat, a brittle sound. Alice hears the fear in it.

They pull into the gravel driveway on the west side of the house, past the tennis court, which Euel put in for Bobbie, back when she still played. The net has fallen and is rotting apart. The court is covered in leaves. The house would feel more like itself if it was all like this. Decrepit, sun-aged, every surface dimmed by mold and moss.

"You didn't stab Euel," Mrs. Patton says. "Did you?"

"Is that what you want to know?" asks Alice. "Or are you more curious about the cake. That's why you came by earlier today, isn't it?"

"Cake?" Mrs. Patton seems to have forgotten. "I don't give a fuck about that cake. You're crazy."

"You'll never know the truth," Alice tells her. "You're a fool."

Mrs. Patton parks the car with a jolt and stares furiously ahead. Alice hears her. Each breath the woman exhales is packed with whispers, the click of schemes. Maybe she thinks she's been scheming Euel, too, same as she was scheming Alice. But both sides is still a wrong side. Betrayal is betrayal.

She gets out, her pulse thumping in her ears. Then Mrs. Patton gets out, too, and shouts at her, shrill and desperate: "Alice, wait!" She'll beg her not to tell Euel, or she'll demand to know the truth, or she'll insist she's not a fool, Alice is the fool, Alice is the one who was fooled. But whatever Mrs. Patton intends to say, she doesn't get the chance.

A great crash comes from inside the guesthouse.

Mrs. Patton looks up, squinting through the sun to Alice's bedroom window. Alice squints, too. The world around her curls and discolors like a burning film strip. "What the hell was that?" Mrs. Patton makes her way around the side of the house and Alice follows with a hand inside her bag, fingers curled around the grip of Euel's revolver.

Thup THUP—sss-crick—thup THUP—criss-crack—

Sneaky Morgan Taylor. Fiber by fiber, she has unknotted the rope. The bathroom door has failed to contain her, or else in her desperation she has manifested some superpower, like mothers who lift cars off their children.

Mrs. Patton reaches the veranda and looks in through the sliding glass door, just in time to see Morgan Taylor crash down the stairs, sweat soaked, bound by the hands and trailing the rope that, in her panic, tripped her. She hits her head on the banister as she falls, then lies still on the carpet.

Mrs. Patton stares through the glass. She turns to Alice.

"Oh," she says, with the quiet wonder of someone seeing clearly.

The house splits open. Jesse hangs in this space in the wall, gasping for breath but not sure if he's even breathing at all. The indigo points of light swell around his head, brighter and heavier, until the air burns hot and is filled with vivid blue. The electric smell intensifies; he imagines his body wired with incandescence. He steps without being sure there is any space to step and ends up back in the attic room where he started. Only now there's light pouring in through the window. Jesse approaches it, but the brightness is so intense he can't see out. He puts Harlan's flashlight on the floor.

Harlan himself is gone, but Jesse is not alone in the room; some feet away, there's a man with his back to him. He is hanging from the rafters by a rope. He turns slowly, and Jesse sees his swollen face in profile, pale blue in the brightness. One bulging white eye pins Jesse. Seems to see him. The rope creaks.

Jesse stares, frozen. He tries to believe he's not seeing what he's seeing. But then, the dead man is also in the room alive, preparing the rope with which to hang himself. He's standing next to Jesse with a flushed face, blood on shirtsleeves. In fact, the attic room is filled with people, with multiple versions of the same person. Teenage boys come in through the hall and tag the rafters with spray paint. They sit cross-legged in a circle and share booze and look at porn, and sometimes they have their cocks out, careful not to touch one another. They do all these things in a sequence, but also at the same time, their bodies occupying several places at once. They don't notice the dead man. They don't notice Jesse. And behind the boys, layered and faded in a way Jesse can't see clearly, there are more. A crowd of young men and women, sometimes talking, sometimes fucking on rickety brass beds that have long since disappeared. Sometimes it's just girls alone, conspiring with one another, drawing symbols on the floor in chalk. There is Tooly, coming up the stairs, his eyes wide with terror. He inspects the wall. He disappears inside it.

Jesse stumbles to the stairs. To move anywhere against this crush of ghosts is like fighting a current, and when he makes it back to the second floor, it's the same thing. Ghosts crowd the hallway. They come and go. Women drag their long dresses along the floor. They carry children. They chase children. They run, laughing, chased by men. Two teenagers sit on the stairs and snort white powder off the blades of their keys. Alongside them, Jesse sees himself coming up the kitchen stairs, sleuthing, dressed in the clothes he wore to Red's on Saturday night. He hears a gunshot.

Downstairs in the living room, the light is brighter, the noise louder. Jesse searches for the face of Connie Calloway, but the room is all chaos. Deafening parties, fiddle players, pianists, folk singers, hooting crowds with bad teeth, a gramophone blaring a Dixieland jazz band, young women fucking men, one another, young women playing light as a feather, stiff as a board, servants and house slaves ducking along the edge of each room. A naked woman demonstrates crops and cat-o'-nine-tails. A man carries a coiled whip through the kitchen. It drips blood on his leather shoes. A woman slaps a young Black girl's face so hard she spins around like a girl possessed. Another gunshot. Something upstairs thuds to the floor. There are teenagers rolling in barrels of moonshine, kegs, and coolers. Animals make their nests in the walls and produce generations of offspring. They crawl across the floor, every rat and raccoon and cockroach and stray cat that has ever made its way through here. A possum scurries out of the fireplace and dies and turns to bones. An alligator slinks through the foyer, its primitive green eye sideways blinking at Jesse, as if it could see him.

He can't see his mother, and no one can see him. He's a ghost.

"Hear that?" says Red Koonce, standing in the foyer.

Jesse hears a woman shrieking. Another gunshot.

"That's Mr. Simms, dragging his wife across the floor."

Red is a luminous Julius Caesar in a blue-striped bedsheet. He orates to four anxious-looking freshmen, *Adventure Time* fans dressed as characters from the show, all except for Jesse, with his savvy Sam Spade costume, his thrift store trench coat so big on him it dusts the floor.

Did they all really look like that? So dopey and baby-faced?

Through the bright window of the kitchen, he sees himself and Harlan backlit on the porch. Harlan is also storming toward the fireplace with an ax. Inside the wall, Tooly is screaming, screaming, like he's boiling alive.

"Jimmy?" Jesse shouts at the ceiling, in case Harlan is still here. "Jimmy, help!"

But what could Harlan possibly do?

On the porch, Jesse offers Harlan the cigarette that was behind his ear. The first move. Harlan touches his wrist as he takes it. "Play it once, Sam"—and fourteen-year-old Jesse grins and grins. He loves every second of Harlan's attention. In the kitchen, his friends sweep by looking for him. Jaelah is close to tears, her pink wig off-center. "Where *is* he?" she whispers to the boys. "I want to go *home*." Spence's baby face is creased with worry.

A shriek. A gunshot. Blood drips from the ceiling onto Jesse's arm. A dark stain, spreading.

He flees through the dining room, past the tinny shriek of

silverware and radio chatter, smells of bloody roasts and burnt garlic. Too much. Too much. He can't breathe. His mother isn't here, or if she is, she's as buried as she always was, swallowed up. He runs to the foyer, throws open the front door, stumbles onto the porch. The air outside crackles.

Relief at first.

Then he's everywhere.

In every place and every time, scattered across the county. In his high school, in the public library, at home on the couch, in his bed, in the kitchen, on the porch. Smell of glue and apple juice of his kindergarten classroom, and the patchouli oil Nancy once spilled inside her purse, his eighth-grade girlfriend's waxy lip balm and Morgan's citrus perfume. Smell of dirt, mushrooms, pot, semen, whiskey, puke, cigarettes, a cherry ice from the waterfront. He's running every route he ever ran, feeling every blister, every itch of poison oak, every wet slap of mud on his legs. He runs along the river, under the bridge, in a loop around the track at the high school where there are eyes on him, where Harlan watches and smokes and feigns disinterest. He runs on Peach Hill, where Harlan's truck pulls up beside him. He sits on the kitchen counter in Harlan's duplex. *Did you watch* The Maltese Falcon *like I told you? Did you watch* The Night of the Hunter? It's him and his friends, Harlan, Morgan, and they're all making out, telling one another secrets, having sex, crying, and in between there are boggy dark spots on the land, and Sam Quinn is smashing Jesse's face with his fist, and Sam Quinn is dying at the bottom of a sinkhole, and Jesse is crawling through the hedge in Jaelah Harrison's backyard.

And at the center of all this, as far as he can see from the porch of the Night House, is a monstrous rift in the sky. It snakes from one edge of the horizon to the other and is stuffed with bright blue stars so close it's as if he could reach out and pick them like oranges. The rift X-rays him. Sees him. An open eye, a mind, conscious of his mistakes, his ill thoughts, his stupid hopes. The rift sees him so intensely he feels he's being picked apart, sucked toward a space where he would lose his whole being. His own mind. So he throws himself down on the porch, crawls back inside, and slams the door.

Some time passes, or whatever it is time does here. Jesse lies still on the tile in the foyer. When he's caught his breath, the house is quieter. He hears frogs, and the slow creak of the walls settling. He can still see the ghosts of all the parties, but they're faded—all but one: a sallow-faced teenage girl sitting on the floor of the dining room. She looks like she's staring right at him, her dark eyes wide, her mouth pinched shut.

Jesse stands shakily. The girl's eyes follow him. She has a ghoulish appearance, though she couldn't be more than seventeen. Her hair and clothes are damp-looking, clotted with dust and spiderwebs. In fact, she's shivering in the cool air. She has a backpack, which she hugs to her chest.

"Can you see me?" he asks her, though it's obvious she can.

Laughter carries from the living room. The girl looks anxiously toward it. There are at least three people in there. One of those laughs is Jesse's own.

He returns to the foyer and peers around the doorway. Just shadows at first, playing on the wall. Then he sees the camping lantern on the floor, the shining faces of Tooly and his brother,

Sam, both blond and skinny; Harlan stands closer to the wall near the stairs, smoking and looking miserable; Jesse himself lies on his back near the fireplace.

When is this? He's wearing his red hoodie, a pair of holey jeans that are too short for him. His hair is longish, in his face. He looks like the kid in the Sam Spade costume, but stretched on a rack and subjected to sleeplessness.

Oh yeah. This is that night.

He looks over his shoulder and sees that the girl has also approached the foyer, though she keeps a few steps behind him.

"Are you trapped in here?" he asks her.

She stares, her face unreadable. In the living room, Sam grabs a bottle of Hairy Crow whiskey and drags it closer to him. The girl scurries away at the sound, disappearing from view.

"Feelinnit yet, Calluhwee?" Sam asks. His thick, reedy accent is just like his brother's.

On the floor near the fireplace, Past-Jesse stares at his hands. "Don't think so."

"Give it time."

Tooly laughs—a boyish giggle.

"Steve says they set that truck on fire," says Harlan, looking at his phone. "The one out by the cemetery."

"He told me he annis cousin would blow it up," says Sam.

"Just telling you what he wrote. 'This shit is on fire.'" He shows the phone to Sam.

Past-Jesse sighs from the floor.

"We could go out there and see," Harlan says through his cigarette.

"Yeah, let's head out there," says Past-Jesse. "Get the whole hillbilly gang together."

"Rednecks," says Harlan, poking at his phone. "If you're gonna insult us, get it right. There's no hills here."

Past-Jesse props up on his elbows and speaks with acid in his voice: "Oh, *fuck you*, Jimmy."

Harlan's eyes flicker from Jesse by the fireplace to Sam by the camping lantern. He drinks the whiskey. Out of the four of them, Harlan is the only one standing, which makes him seem like he might spring away at any moment.

"Ignore him," he mutters to Sam. "He's just drunk."

"Yeah, your boy's really pushing it tonight," replies Sam.

Tooly giggles again. "I been drunk since like noon."

"We can stay here if y'all want," Harlan says, taking the whiskey bottle from Sam. "Whatever blows your skirt up."

Past-Jesse laughs. "Jimmy, you've never blown a skirt up in your whole dumb life."

Tooly snorts and covers his mouth.

Harlan carries on like he doesn't hear them: "Rusty got a bunch of bottle rockets last time they went to South of the Border. Seem like duds."

"Bottle rockets?" says Sam. "Shee-it. That won't do nothing."

Past-Jesse and Tooly continue laughing. They feed off each other. Their laughter is pointless and mean, growing louder, shaking the dust off the ceiling.

"Will y'all shut the fuck up?" Sam says, knocking his brother over with his foot.

"Hey," says Jesse. "Don't you be kicking my frand now. We go waaay back."

Tooly curls into a ball on the floor. "Homedawgs! Blood brothers!"

"Golly dern, I'd take a bullet fer 'im," says Jesse. "Mah bestest frand, Tooly."

Harlan looks at Sam with pleading eyes, like he wants Sam to do something, or not do something. In his desperate silence, Past-Jesse and Tooly ease up on their stupid laughter, and the dust settles, and the room goes quiet. Harlan slips his phone into his pocket and hands the whiskey bottle back to Sam.

In the foyer, Now-Jesse watches this scene with a pit in his stomach. Sam and Harlan trade more back-and-forth about where they're going to go; it doesn't make sense to hang around here, though it doesn't make sense to go anywhere else either. Meanwhile, the girl is still hiding in the dining room, her eyes wide.

Jesse whispers at her: "What's your name?" But she doesn't answer.

Then Sam and Tooly get up and approach the foyer. They don't see Jesse. They carry the camping lantern out, leaving Harlan in the living room doorway. For a while, Harlan stands there, quietly smoking. Now-Jesse comes up behind him. His past self is still lying on the floor by the fireplace.

Harlan drops his cigarette on the floor and stamps it out. "You coming or not?"

Past-Jesse glares over his shoulder.

"You don't gotta come. You could go home any time."

No reply.

"What do you want from me? I *asked* you if you wanted to come out. I don't get why you're acting this way." He gestures to the front lawn. "This about them? You expect me to just blow 'em off? I can't have friends no more?"

Past-Jesse hauls himself to his feet and lurches over. Miles away, the junior prom is in full swing. The theme is "heaven," all tinfoil stars and cotton ball clouds, a priggish reminder for teens to protect their virtue. But Jesse is depraved, and therefore above it. In the living room doorway, he clenches his fists and shoves Harlan, an action that from afar looks both vicious and pitiful, like the snarling of a tiny dog.

"*Cunt*," he says through his teeth.

When Past-Jesse leaves, Harlan follows like a man being led to the gallows, extracting a last cigarette.

Now-Jesse tries to watch them, but he can't see out the windows because of the brightness, and he's afraid to go out on the porch again. But through the door, he can hear the rev of a truck engine, Tooly hooting with laughter, and Past-Jesse hooting along with him. They're going to wake up the neighborhood. Then the engine fades, and all he can hear is frogs and crickets.

"Was that you?" asks the girl. She stands close enough behind him to make him jump, close enough that he can smell her. Her tangled hair has the swampy scent of someone who's been swimming in the river.

"Yeah," he says. "But I—"

What does he want to say? Part of him would like to somehow account for and contextualize his jealous fury over two years late, but that wouldn't mean a thing to this girl.

"I don't know what's happening," he says.

"Follow yourself," the girl suggests. "See what happens then."

"No, no. I can't leave this house." He gestures toward the

door. "There's a gigantic rift out there, this void, like this huge eye opening up. I know how that sounds, but I swear, it just about sucked me into it."

The girl stares at him blankly. "Oh."

Jesse slides down against the door and puts his head in his hands. The girl has made all of this more real and, in that same sense, has given him permission to despair. She approaches and touches his wrist. He can feel her touch. The hair on his forearms stands up.

"What happened to you?" she asks.

"I don't know. I don't know what to do."

She tilts her head, studying his face. Her eyes shine in the brightness from the windows, but her pupils are large. To her, the inside of the house is dark.

"I know you," she says. "Was your mother Connie Calloway?"

Jesse looks at her, stunned.

"Is your name Jesse?" she asks.

"Yes," he says. "Are you Cat?" He jumps up, pointing down at her in triumph: "You're Cat. You have to be."

The girl stares up at him from the floor. When she stands, she's taller than he is, but she hunches. "My mother was Katrina. I'm Alice."

"Alice," he says breathlessly. "Maybe it was your mother, then. She's been contacting me through Wipixx. She told me she knew things about Connie Calloway. She asked me to come here. I thought I might *see* her."

"See your mother or my mother?" Alice says.

"*My* mother. Cat, it's Cat, like the animal. Is that your mother?"

Alice shakes her head. "My mother is dead. Like yours. What's Wipixx?"

As quickly as it swept through him, his elation fades, and he despairs again. He goes into the living room but isn't sure what to do once he gets there. He begins to pace.

"Don't panic," says Alice.

"Panic!" he cries. "What do I do? What if I can't get out of here? What if this is—what if I'm in *hell*?"

She doesn't do what he wishes she would do, which is to reassure him that he's not in hell. Instead, she appears to be thinking.

"Are you from the future?" she asks.

Jesse looks around the room. The ghosts are still there, coming in and out of focus. The partying teens. The brothel women. The bloody stain spreading on the ceiling. Harlan, chopping away at the wall with his ax.

"I'm from Blacknot," he says.

"You are from the future, aren't you," says Alice. "I think there's something I should show you."

She retrieves her backpack from the dining room and sets it on the floor in front of him. The backpack is stuffed with objects—glass jars clinking together, plastic bags of shells and stones, papers, journals, various herbs and flowers, half crushed. A sharp medicinal smell.

Jesse leans over her shoulder. "What are you doing here?"

"Hiding," says Alice. "I thought this place might keep me safe, but you and your friends were already here. Look—" From deep in the bag, she produces a pocket-size black notebook, which she hands to Jesse. "This belonged to Connie. My mother had it."

Jesse takes the notebook, half expecting his hand to pass through it. But the book is solid. Real. There on the inside cover is his mother's handwriting, recognizable from the postcards she sent to Nancy:

cloud Ash blood spade
Ivy wheel worm red Rabbit ghost

"'If found, return to the buried place,'" he reads.

"What?" Alice cranes her neck over his shoulder. "Where do you see that?"

"I don't understand," he says. "She *wrote* all this? She just— *came up with it*?"

"I think so. It belonged to her."

"But what was your mother doing with it?"

Alice shrugs. "They were friends once. Close friends."

He sits on the living room floor, the book open in his lap. Alice crouches behind him as he thumbs through the pages. The book is part primer, part glossary, containing within it a vocabulary composed entirely of concrete nouns—combinations of objects, materials, colors, animals, components of the landscape. Here, he can see the verb declensions as his mother devised them. Want. Wanted. Does want. Might want. **Altar. Ash altar. Honey altar. Sky altar.** And so on. He can see her in the words, playing around. An alligator is an **Iron tooth pistol.** A tree is an **Air saint.** A weeping willow, an **Onion air saint.**

"What do you make of it?" Alice asks. "What did you mean 'buried place'?"

He smiles at her, trying not to appear as sad as he feels. "I don't know what it means. I was just reading it." He points to the inscription on the inside cover again. "Here."

Alice's face hovers over him, her eyes bright and hungry. "You can read it?"

"Apparently. You—the person who's contacting me, they've been writing with it. I've been writing back."

"So then you *know* this language."

"Yeah," he says. "I know it."

"But how? How'd you learn it? You have a notebook just like this?"

"No. I didn't learn it. I just know it."

Alice leans toward him, hair hanging in her face. Suddenly, she clasps her hands over his.

"But why are you upset?"

"I'm not upset," he says, taken aback. "I'm—I don't know what to feel. Maybe I just don't get it. She made this. I can see where she crossed stuff out. She was fixing things, making it up as she went along. She made it all up."

Gently, Alice takes the notebook from his lap, flips through the pages, and closes it.

"I don't have the answers," she says.

"There are no answers," says Jesse. "I thought—I thought I would find my way into this place and *see her*. Instead it's like every bad thing that ever happened in this county is coming in and out of this house. I feel like I'm going crazy."

Alice nods slowly, her pale face attuned to him like a moon.

"And the whole time—" Jesse goes on. "The whole time, it's like she just gets harder to understand. I just have these pieces, these things people say about her. I found my way in here, and still…"

"But what do people say?" Alice asks.

He laughs and shakes his head. "That she was crazy. Difficult. Promiscuous. Everything I am, not super-fucking enlightening, right? Miss Velda, you know, the librarian, she told me a long time ago that my mother *courted pigs*."

"Pigs?" says Alice. "Did you say 'courted pigs'?"

The ghosts in the room grow bolder, but Jesse tries not to notice them. A grinding noise churns somewhere outside the house. Maybe the big rift in the sky is eating something, a mouth and an eye all in one.

"Pigs," he says. "She had a reputation. My mother."

"No, no," says Alice. "'Courted pigs.' That was about my father. There was a saying in Pinewood about him."

Jesse blinks at her, confused. "*Your* father?"

"My father. Euel Swink."

"The Tarbarrel guy?"

"Yes. He liked Pinewood girls. He liked them young and poor and dependent on him. *He* was the one with the reputation. If Euel pursued a girl, she was 'courting pigs,' 'running with pigs'..." She trails off. A sudden misery crosses her face. "My father was a pig."

Jesse presses her: "So Euel Swink pursued my mother? That's what that means?"

"I don't know," Alice says quietly. "I guess it doesn't matter now."

"What? No, *of course*, it matters. Alice, please, tell me what you know. Is Euel Swink my father?"

Outside, the grinding sound grows louder. Alice looks out the window and becomes alert.

"Probably," she says. "Maybe. Jesse, the sheriff just pulled up."

"The sheriff? Where?" A prying neighbor must've heard Jesse and Tooly's commotion, called the cops. But Jesse can't see the sheriff, and what he hears sounds like something else. Off in the brightness: a mechanical *bleep-bleep-bleep.*

"She's headed for the house. We need to run." Alice stuffs Connie's notebook into her bag. It pains Jesse to see her take away the notebook. He wants to beg her for it, keep it awhile, but a violent splintering sound shakes the house. Thick gray dust cascades from the ceiling. Alice grabs his arm and pulls him into the kitchen, where she shoves her bag out through an open window. The outside's screeching brightness pours in.

"I can't go out there," Jesse says.

"But I can't stay," she whispers. "If I'm caught, I'll go to jail."

He brushes past that. "Alice, you told me to come here. What do we do?"

The house is crashing, shaking. Maybe the big void in the sky has come too close and is devouring it, will devour everything—first the Night House, then Bittern's Rest, then all of Pinewood, all of Miskwa County, the river sucked up like a giant noodle. But then he hears the mechanical bleeping again, the crunch of the front porch coming down, the shatter of the dining room windows.

It's an excavator.

He realizes that he can't stay here either. He has no idea what will happen if the house is demolished with him in it.

Alice seems to recognize their impasse. Her expression is conflicted. She pulls him into an embrace, which surprises him, but he hugs her back. Her hair smells like the swamp, and a longing springs up in him, newly sharp. He's been looking for this and he didn't know it. Not a mother, but a sister. Lost like him.

"I'll come back and help you," she says. "I'll make contact. Something good has happened; I can feel it."

"I have to leave *now*, Alice."

"When you do, come find me."

Then she pulls away and hoists herself to the windowsill. He practically shouts at her, "But *how*? How do I get out?" and she whispers back, like it's obvious:

"The way you came in. Always the way you came in."

Then she's gone. He's astonished, and sad, that their encounter is over.

A moment later, Sheriff Hupp's stick-thin figure steps into the kitchen. Hupp, with her familiar scowl and narrow eyes, shining a flashlight through the room. She doesn't see him.

Smash. The excavator's steel claw bursts through the front wall of the dining room. The ghosts of a thousand dinner parties die again.

The way you came in...

He runs to the second floor. The house's occupants crowd him. The two teens are still doing coke on the stairs. Jesse from Sunday morning is still sleuthing around. In the attic room, Mr. Simms turns slowly on his rope. Harlan shouts, "Shut up. Just *shut up*," as he drags Jesse away. Their struggle shakes the doorframe as the excavator shakes the house. "Let *go*!" Yes. The opening is there. Tooly Quinn enters it, wide-eyed, trembling. Jesse sprints toward it after he's broken free of Harlan's grasp. The rift is black and glittery, the only place in the house untouched by light. Harlan shouts, "It's a mistake!" and Jesse realizes that might be true. There is no guarantee he'll be back where he was. He could get stuck in a wall like Tooly. He could end up somewhere even more split apart than this. Or on the other side of that void.

But he runs through anyway.

This time, the light in the attic is faded and dusty. Morning daylight, syrupy yellow. There is no one in the room but Jesse. He flees to the second floor for his escape window, the porch roof. Down the stairs, the excavator gnaws its way deeper. Half the facade is gone. A rafter comes loose in the hallway, collapsing behind him in a shower of debris.

He emerges, so covered in sweat and dust he probably looks like a monster worming its way out of the house. He hears shouts. Some Pinewood folks have gathered at the edge of the lot to see the neighborhood giant go down. They point at him and take pictures with their phones.

Then the real show. He squirms his way free of the window, too rushed, too panicked, and loses his footing. Inside, the excavator smashes into the stairs. The whole house convulses as if stabbed in the heart. He reaches to grab something for balance but finds nothing.

The sky tilts; pine trees go sideways; someone in the crowd shouts, "Ohhh!" as Jesse tumbles off the roof and crashes onto the lawn.

Alice gets into Mrs. Patton's car, the driver's side door wide open, keys swinging in the ignition. Backpack. Hair clip. No, the hair clip is missing. Where has it gone? She looks back at herself from the rearview mirror—a sheen of sweat on her face, a spray of blood across her nose. Her skin stings. She rubs the blood with the back of her hand and smears it.

If she closes her eyes, she's back in the room with Mrs. Patton and Morgan. Mrs. Patton is saying, "Wait, Alice. Wait, wait, wait," because there's a gun pointed at her. Morgan lies motionless at the foot of the stairs. Mrs. Patton looks between Alice and Morgan with her hands up. Improbably, she begins to laugh.

"This has gone too far. You need to call the police."

Alice turns the key and reverses the car, overcompensates with the wheel and the brake. She has always been afraid of driving, has only driven a few times before—lessons with Euel in empty Sunday parking lots. Once she gets on the road, though, it's easier. Watching is not the same as doing, but it helps to be observant.

She can't say that she has never wanted to hurt anybody. To do what she's done, she would have to hate both Morgan Taylor and Tanisha Patton. She would have to be evil like Morgan said. *Ichichich.*

Alice drives slowly through South Greene, but her mind is still back at the guesthouse. She is tiptoeing across the living room, crouching to touch the side of Morgan's face. The girl's eyelids are purplish and swollen, her blond hair dark with sweat. Her hands rest gently on her chest, bound, as if in prayer. Mrs. Patton is saying, "Alice, do you hear me? Call the police!" but Alice doesn't answer. She leans her ear toward the floor.

Thup, thup. Thup, thup. Is that the hair clip, or Morgan's heartbeat?

No, no, this is not what she wanted to happen. She doesn't

hate Morgan Taylor. She doesn't hate Mrs. Patton. She doesn't even really hate the neighborhood. These dopey people. She doesn't hate the gate, or the bed of daylilies, or the stop signs, or the telephone poles. She crosses the bridge, and she certainly doesn't hate the river, bright and stunning in the sun. When she gets to downtown Blacknot, she begins to cry. She has never seen the town like this, blurry and unstable. She doesn't hate the traffic lights, or Spartina Square, or the library. She wishes, for a moment, that she could stop and get out of the car and be embraced by passersby, tourists, local shopkeepers, but that probably wouldn't help her. They wouldn't understand.

The back of her head hurts from where Mrs. Patton hit her with the table lamp. Red scratches crisscross her fingers—Mrs. Patton's long nails, trying to pry away the gun. What happened? Obviously, Mrs. Patton didn't think Alice would have the guts to shoot her, but that's what Alice has done. The gunshot shattered the sliding glass door and left Mrs. Patton lying against the sofa with a pillow pressed against her stomach, her yellow blouse gathering blood.

"Alice. Alice, wait…"

Alice must have shot her. How else would that have happened?

Sirens. Alice called the police. As she was leaving the house, she called and then threw her phone into the river, convinced they'd be able to track her. She realizes she has Mrs. Patton's phone, too, and tosses it onto the side road just north of Blacknot. Nobody notices her. Nobody even glances through the windshield.

On the road north, she catches the foul smell of her father's hog lagoons. The cords on the power lines get thinner and thinner, and the woods grow dense. It crosses her mind now that she could keep going. She could go until the car runs out of gas, or she could go until she's caught. But the inside of the car sounds like machinery, and the blood on her face sounds like chewing, a wet, relentless grinding so loud it makes her nauseous. On a stretch of highway a few miles past Pinewood, she pulls onto a dirt road and follows it. To her right runs a wire fence and a ditch filled with shrubs, honeysuckle, wisteria, and beyond that is a sandy field of young tobacco plants. To her left are skinny pines, hurricane-stripped, cloaked in a tangle of underbrush. The edge of the Miskwa Swamp. Alice goes until she is beyond view from the highway, at which point she pulls off into a ditch and gets out. No one around. Just that fence, the field. Mrs. Patton's car glints in the sun, like the shell of an enormous silver bug.

For a moment, she stands in the dusty road in her big sunglasses, her head stuffed up, her eyes hot with tears. The bag in the passenger seat—what the hell did she even bring? The contents of Jesse's jar, his mother's lexicon, her mother's spells, her father's revolver—*crkkk ssst*—a bottle of wine, a random assortment of things from her kitchen and pantry, water, a little food. Haphazard.

She turns and faces the underbrush, holding in her head the map of the county her father keeps in his office. If she heads east, she'll find the river. Shouldering her backpack, she leaves Mrs. Patton's car behind and enters the woods, the thorns, the mud, the sagging heat, the whining mosquitos, the voices of all those living things sparkling and humming and twanging.

As she makes her way, she imagines what she might've said if she'd told her therapist the truth, if she'd split herself open, right there in the soft pink light of the office.

She would say: I made a mistake. I attacked that girl.

And the therapist would say: Tell me what you mean by *attacked*, Alice.

Sunday, with a shovel. She's still alive. I'm keeping her in my bathroom.

You're what?

I panicked. She was threatening me. She was going to tell my father about my plan.

What plan?

To look for the buried place. My mother could use its power. Jesse's mother, too. And my father, but he used it for harm.

What do you mean?

I mean my father is a monster. Why else would he give me a therapist who has my mother's name? What kind of a mind-fuck is that?

Alice, your mother's name was Katrina.

Yes. Right, it was Katrina.

My name is Kaitlyn.

No—no, I saw your nameplate—

Here, Alice reconsiders. Maybe she read the nameplate wrong. In fact, now that she thinks about it, the more she can clearly see the name KAITLYN.

Maybe I did read it wrong.

And the therapist would say: Well, if you're wrong about one thing...

But it doesn't change what my father did.

Alice, I need you to be more specific. What did your father *do*?

He had me play for my mother.

Your mother, who left.

But she didn't *leave*. She wouldn't. I remember—the last time I played the harp for her, I was eight years old. It was raining. These fat drops kept hitting the window, hard, like bullets. We were in the living room. My father stood in the doorway. He was drinking whiskey and wearing corduroy loafers. It says something that he didn't even put on real shoes when Mom came over. He hung back in the doorway and didn't sit down with her. She didn't love him anymore. She was trying to get custody of me.

Alice, your mother *did* leave. She couldn't pay her rent. She left town.

Then why didn't she say goodbye? Why would she leave behind her notebooks? No. Listen, I'm trying to tell you what happened. I played Satie, *Gymnopédie No. 1*. I was perfect. When I was done, Mom told me I was so talented, and the music was so beautiful. But she was crying. She sounded as if she had been filled with rocks and tar. She looked like she was seeing the end of the world.

She left town to live somewhere else.

That's not what happened. You know the story of the Pied Piper, right? He leads out all the kids. He drowns the rats and the kids.

Yes. That's a fairy tale.

But a fairy tale can still mean something. My mother drowned herself in the river. Like the cultist Marianne Duff. Like Connie Calloway, who went out into the swamp and died on the riverbank. I didn't see it, but I felt my mother drown. I felt this place take her. He told me to play the harp for her. I played it perfect. That was what he wanted.

Is there really a girl in your bathroom, Alice?

I was eight years old. Mom came over, and he told me to play for her. She sounded as if she had been filled with rocks and tar. He wanted her to disappear, because she wanted me. He used me to win. I played perfectly for her, and she saw the end of the world.

Alice wonders if that's where she's headed now, wading through swamp water and brambles, her skin scratched and bug-bitten. Her sandals are gone, sucked away by the mud.

Who would've thought that the end of the world would be here, in Miskwa, just a few miles north of where she lives? Maybe it's not such a frightening thing. Maybe the end of the world is a way to get somewhere else, somewhere strange and dangerous, but better, more wondrous. She continues east, her bag teetering on her back, while the afternoon light sinks around her, first orange, then pink, then violet. The heat eases, but the humidity stays, hanging on the woods like a fleece. River sounds meet her from the north, the steady inhale as the tide rises. She pictures her father's lazy face, the map in his office and the river winding through it.

This is a place of endless sounds: pinesap, cypress knees, pitcher plants, sphagnum moss. What should she listen for? Ah, there: spartina grass, winking like wind chimes. She approaches the river and can see it growing from the water by the bank. And she can hear what she knows is witchfingers, their arcane whispers, their kept secrets.

She gets a jar from her bag. The pods grow in the stalks, fat and purple-black. When she wades into the water and plucks them off, they cackle, like they know what she's going to do.

Jesse Calloway in College

It was meant to be a reincarnation.

New friends, new habits, new intellectual ways to think about the films he loves and a new visual language to translate them. In Film Appreciation, he can write an entire paper about the tattoos on Reverend Powell's fingers, or Phyllis Dietrichson's sunglasses, or Joel Cairo fellating his cane. And he does! With enthusiasm, if not control. The composition of each black-and-white shot opens a maze of possibility.

That's what it's like here at every turn, every person he meets like a series of doorways to explore. People in college are easy to talk to. There are always new subjects to discuss. He doesn't think at all about what they know or don't know about him. He becomes close with some friends of his roommate—Alex Khan, poli-sci—three of whom are in the film class, too. There's Soledad, her girlfriend, Mia, and Mia's more-than-friend Olivier, who was in her polycule in high school. There's Olivier's brother, Hugo, a senior, and his partner, Annika, a gorgeous twenty-three-year-old whom middle-class couples pay to come to their homes and teach classes on rope play. Alex isn't a wild kid himself—when Jesse first met him, he seemed almost rigid—but he associates with a liberated crew, so un-fucked-up about their sexuality that they assume queerness until proven otherwise. At a Labor Day party in Hugo's apartment, they play Never Have I Ever; Jesse reveals his experience, bashfully drinking his whiskey Coke while the others laugh and cheer him on, this little ingénue from Pig Country. Jesse has spat, swallowed, smoked, sucked. In a graveyard, in the rain, in the bed of a pickup. "Sleeper Hit," they call him.

He shares with them card games and old movies. He makes Olivier watch Fritz Lang's *M*, despite his aversion to subtitles. He introduces Mia and Soledad to *Key Largo* and enjoys their analysis of the costumes and forgives them when they make fun of Johnny Rocco's line deliveries. In October, he follows the crew to the Woods of Terror, where Annika works as an actor; he laughs himself hoarse when she jumps out from the cornstalks in a bloody bridal gown, shrieking at them in Russian: "Moy muzh! Gde moy muzh?" At the end of the semester, he takes a trip with everyone to see a band in Asheville and, as they get closer, presses his hands against the passenger window like a kid—"Mountains! Look, mountains!" And everyone says, yes, those are mountains. That's what mountains look like.

As for his romantic life, he's comfortable, if not careless. He sleeper hits Olivier after a Halloween party, then Mia when Soledad goes home for Thanksgiving. For a little while, he sees Kai (physics), who knows how to get fake IDs. Then Hollis (studio art), who can ferret out pot and X. Then, for a second, Laurencia (international studies), who frequently shows up at the gay bar smeared in glitter. Whoever Jesse's with, he feels sincere gratitude and affection for them, though he wants to explore his options. He makes that clear. And if his friends begin to tell him about their messed-up childhoods and their complicated relationships with their parents and their toxic exes, this is not meant to pressure Jesse to share his own stories. His mom died. His aunt raised him. So what. He has split his life in half. It's true that when you share a story it becomes something other than yours, an item for interpretation and misunderstanding; nobody tells you that, but it's true. So Jesse takes his friends' fun and joy and pretentious wisdom. He takes their film nights and mountain road trips and glitter body paint and the two AM IHOP runs deep in the urban sprawl of West Market, that time of the night when he's both starving and sick to his stomach.

But such good times come with an inevitable weariness. His grades drop in the spring. What was once funny—going to Trader Joe's and bumping into the exhausted adjuncts buying three-dollar wine in their sweatpants—is now sad. And he's beginning to wonder if all this taking has a price, as it often does. Once, on a Saturday night bender at a sticky-floored dance club, he finds himself arguing with Soledad about Mia and some dumb thing that was said or not said; their relationship was open, but Jesse was not open *enough*, and Jesse, not knowing what that means, snaps at Soledad and snaps at Alex for not backing him up, and later, still irritated with all of them, snaps at Olivier about an opinion on *Chinatown*, a film that no one in the crew but Jesse has seen because everybody knows that Roman Polanski is *problematic*. It becomes clear that everyone is mad at Jesse, that he has not been paying the proper dues for their friendship, and that liking *Chinatown* is also *problematic*, a red flag signaling corruption in his heart. So he abandons them in the club, dances for hours, accidentally spills a drink down a girl's shirt, misplaces his wallet. The bar-tender loses their patience with him. "Time to go, friend," they say, flapping their arms to usher him away from the bar. When they say "friend," they mean "asshole," and so Jesse wanders alone downtown until his feet ache, struggling to remember where he left his car.

He decides to go stay with Nancy's friend Minerva in Friendly Acres; he would rather spend the night there than face Alex back at the dorm. But then, on second thought, it's nearly sunup, and it might be even worse to subject Minerva to his nonsense, this woman who doesn't even know him that well, and who's never seen him on a bender before. She might be appalled, turn him away, call the cops, or worse, *call Nancy*. So he pulls over on the side of the road by the airport, gets out, and sits in the grass.

The sky brightens and floods the tarmac with a pinkish-gray glow, dewy air making way for the mugginess of morning. When the sun's first rays spike over the trees, Jesse's skin lights up with glitter (did he run into Laurencia?) and the stamp on his hand has smeared into some unrecognizable shape. He can't remember what it was before.

That was his night. And this is his morning: a long sit in the grass, the expectation that any moment an airport official will show up and tell him he's trespassing. But before that can happen, a familiar car pulls up on the side of the road. Alex and Olivier appear, frowning with what Jesse can only assume is reproach. Olivier is covered in glitter, too, his hair a puffy disco ball, his eyeliner smeared from one side of his face to the other, like Daryl Hannah's android character in *Blade Runner*. Alex, in his typical fashion, is wearing a Hawaiian shirt tucked into boot-cut jeans, his hair as neat and flat as it was when he left the dorm with Jesse the night before. Alex says, "We got your wallet," waving it over his head. Jesse stares at him, shamefaced.

"How did you find me?"

Olivier shows Jesse a social media post from a couple hours before, an abstract blur of what might have been grass or dark sky. Location: Piedmont Triad International Airport. Ten likes. A kid from the LGBTQIA+ Student Alliance responded with a laugh emoji and a question mark.

On the tarmac, a plane screams by and takes off, growing smaller and smaller. The three of them watch it for a while before anyone speaks again.

"We thought you were about to get on a flight," says Olivier.

"Maybe," says Jesse. "The thought might've crossed my mind."

"Wouldn't get far without your ID," says Alex. He looks at his watch. "So you want breakfast? Or do you—I don't know, are we interrupting? It's fine if you want to watch the planes some more. We'll just wait over there by the car."

Jesse's head pounds. He squints up at his friends. Still new friends. "I'm sorry," he says, "for getting mad about *Chinatown*."

The two of them look at each other. Olivier shakes his head and laughs. "It's all good," he says. "Don't even worry about it."

So dumb. Jesse thinks later about just how dumb it is, sitting with Alex in a booth at a twenty-four-hour diner while Olivier drives his car back to campus. Why did he do it? Why apologize for *Chinatown* and not for showing his ass the whole goddamn night? He drinks coffee and sobers up, and he and Alex stare silently through the diner's smudgy plate glass window—at the used auto lot across the street, at the chicken trucks and old Dodge pickups, the empty Vietnamese restaurant, the bail bonds place, its LED lights blinking. Not that it matters, but Jesse believes he's right about *Chinatown*. It's a great fucking movie.

He sighs, his breath fogging the window. "This is the part of town where the mob meets up."

"Ah yes," says Alex. "The famous Greensboro crime syndicate."

Jesse draws an X in the patch of fog. "This will tell them we're ready for the drop-off."

They order a monstrous breakfast; Alex doesn't eat pork, so it's all eggs and carbs—French toast, bowls of grits with butter and grated cheddar, biscuits the size of their faces. Hangover appetite. The waitress is friendly, but pointed: "Y'all had a long night, I'll bet." Jesse smiles at her, feels a little judged.

When she walks away, he says to Alex, "This diner looks just like the one I worked at in high school. Same layout almost." He points to the jukebox. "Same albums even. Steely Dan. James Taylor. Over there—see?"

Alex turns around and looks. "You want to play Steely Dan? I don't have any quarters."

"Nah. That's okay."

"What's your hometown again?"

"Blacknot."

"*Blayuk*-nut," Alex says, exaggerating Jesse's Southern diphthongs. "What was it like in *Blayuk*-nut?"

Jesse responds in his typical way: "Fine. Small." Alex has even asked him a variation of this question before, but with the disinterested tone of someone who expects a simple answer.

"Can't be any worse than Cary," says Alex.

"It's definitely worse," says Jesse. "We had one coffee shop. It was called Jesus Christ Is King at Debbie's Coffee Shop."

"But that's a different kind of worse," explains Alex. "That's at least quirky. Cary is like—it's like a suburb designed by Starbucks. All this creepy sameness. It's ironic because they called us clones in high school—the Khan clones—because I had four siblings, and at one point we were all there together. We don't even look alike. But it's a sci-fi horror movie when five brown kids from the same family attend the same school."

For a while, they eat in silence, cleaning their plates. The waitress swings by to top off their coffee. More diner patrons come in, and the morning traffic outside gets loud, filling the air with the smell of diesel.

"I can't imagine having four siblings," Jesse says. "My aunt would've exploded."

"Yeah, it got fucking wild," Alex says. "The house was never quiet. Nobody respected anybody's space. And I didn't have anything in common with them. It's like four roommates I've got nothing in common with."

Jesse sips his coffee. "*We* don't have much in common."

"What are you talking about? Of course we do. According to the algorithm we're, like, the same person."

"So," Jesse reasons, "I guess, you're *me* if I grew up in Cary and had four older siblings. And I'm *you* if you were an only child from a shitty small town."

"Yes," says Alex. "You would now be a stylish Pakistani majoring in poli-sci."

Jesse laughs. On the table, Alex's phone lights up with a text.

Alex looks at it and quickly replies, then tucks the phone away in his pocket.

"Sol," he explains. "She wanted to make sure you weren't dead."

"Oh," Jesse says. He checks his own phone. "She didn't message me."

"Well—" Alex sops a piece of French toast in his egg grease. "She said she was annoyed with you. But I think it's more like she's worried."

Jesse begins to feel queasy. A paranoid thought: Is Alex doing reconnaissance, having breakfast with him so he can report back to the others? Maybe he's expecting a more thorough apology, an explanation, which the others can pick apart. *What do you expect? He likes* Chinatown. But, no, no—Jesse should be *moved* that a friend is worried. He should be *glad* she notices that something is wrong with him. *(Is something wrong with him?)*

Alex sees the hurt and conflict in Jesse's face, which means it must be obvious. He looks stunned, unsure what to do.

"Are you okay?"

"Yeah," Jesse says, laughing. He rubs the back of his head, the undercut fresh enough that it's still strange to the touch. "I'm fine."

Alex, too, looks worried. "Well, you know yourself," he says shortly. "You know your limits. If you want to party, consensus seems to be that's what college is for, and we can always get you back safe to the dorm at the end of the night—if you want to do that. You don't have to yeet off like you did."

They sit in silence for a while, Alex eating the last of his French toast, Jesse staring at the chipped blue polish on his fingernails. A stone forms in his throat, the remains of a drunken weepiness that sometimes gets ahold of him when he's coming down. Alex is right, of course. He's used to Alex being the sensible one. Jesse tries to imagine him at fourteen, at the high school in Cary with all his siblings—and one by one, he imagines all his new friends like that, with their teen angst and vulnerability and dumb decisions, before they progressed into the confident, worldly people he knows and loves.

He wonders if you can be a complete person without a history.

After breakfast, Alex drives them back to campus. He blasts hip-hop and rolls down the windows, and the air beats at Jesse's face. The downtown skyline rises to meet them, yellow in the hazy morning.

"I know what I need to do," Jesse says. "I just need to keep my shit together until the end of the semester."

"What?" Alex shouts.

"*My shit*," Jesse shouts back. "I just need to keep it together."

Alex nods and gives him a thumbs-up.

Jesse doesn't know what to make of that glib response. Did he miss his opportunity at the diner to tell his story?

By the end of the morning, Alice will contact him.

Hello Jesse. You are from Blacknot
I am too

And right now, he knows it would be a huge relief to tell *some*body *some*thing, but the longer he goes holding back, the tighter the story coils inside him, and the less it seems possible to tell it. And if he *were* to tell it, he wouldn't be able to explain what it meant. Someone *else* would tell him what it meant.

Someone would say, *You're traumatized*, or, *That grown man was a predator*, or, *This explains everything*. Why he fucks carelessly, why he goes on benders, why he stormed off in a snit at the club last night, as if you could take every shitty thing that ever happened to a person and plug it into a formula that explains how they might act or think.

You don't know me, but I trapped here

But that's the rub: How much of it *is* trauma? What he saw on the riverbank when he was a baby must have imprinted on his brain somehow, even if he doesn't remember it. If somebody told him this is what seeded the insidious loneliness that led him to Harlan, he would believe them, though maybe that loneliness simply came from growing up in Blacknot, or being weird, or liking boys, or wanting big, wild, dangerous things to happen to him in a place where the happenings seemed so small. And he knew it—yes—he knew that what happened with Harlan was dangerous, not a little fucked-up. But how much? If you could measure it, what would that piece of his life look like? And how could you distinguish it from *you*, your own free, ridiculous self, who might be fucked-up for countless other reasons?

What is the outside like?

Alice's messages will hit hard. His friends have not used Wipixx for months since a swarm of edgelords and alt-right assholes descended on the LGBTQIA+ Student Alliance account. Alex has told Jesse he never wants to hear about Wipixx again.

But Jesse will have no reason to think Alice is trolling him, or that she's posing as anyone other than herself. Her words will evoke in him not a longing for Blacknot, per se, but sparks of memory so pure and vivid they make his whole college life seem fake. This isn't who he is. He's the one who runs trails through fields and pine trees and down Peach Hill, where there is no hill. He's the depraved kid getting fucked on Harlan's couch, the wretched creature Harry Bishop found by the river.

The outside is lonely, like the inside

This response will require context. Otherwise, it seems like he's telling this trapped person that there's no hope, and he doesn't feel that way. So, late at night, while Alex is asleep, he'll stay up explaining things to her. And sometimes their chats will be light (*Did you ever vandalize the Confederate Memorial downtown? / Ha, no, but my aunt used to do that*). And sometimes, he will let his secrets slip, and it feels good.

When I was 14, I was with a man from Pinewood
A sexual relationship
He was 21

That must have been strange

It was strange, but not all bad
It destroyed me when he ended it

Do you hate him?

Yes, no

He was lonely too

Everyone here is

Freaks like us

Freak, **Rust witch hazel**. See also: curse, changeling.

Not to say that every message from Alice will be perfect, that she won't frustrate or confuse him, that she won't sometimes take a seemingly cruel length of time to reply. But he strives to be patient, and when the replies do come, they wrap tight around his heart like wire, and he can see her star crown taking shape in his dorm room. He skips classes waiting on her. He texts excuses to his friends' group chat when they make plans to hang out. They don't insist. They're tired of him.

There is another way hidden in Blacknot

Not inside, not outside

A place for us maybe

What does that mean?

I have kept secrets, I meant to tell you sooner

Swallow thistle, secret.

I can't go back there

That place will mess me up

It is not messing you up now?

And on it will go like that, until all he thinks about is Alice, what he will say to Alice, how she might reply, what she knows or doesn't know. And all the while his mother's witch language works on him without his knowing. It wraps his heart up tighter, seals his mouth like a spell, and draws him toward home.

9

He can't breathe. Alice has assumed the place of the amorphous stranger he always spoke to in his dorm room, the shifting face crowned with stars and bristles. Alice, with her big eyes and schemes, her monotone voice, the smell of river water on her hair. She said she'd make contact, and she did.

His eyes are closed. He's lying face down in a bed of crushed thistle and Virginia creeper. A crowd gathers, a ring of muffled shouts and curses, as if he'd fallen from the sky and not the roof of the Night House. Then he hears Harlan—"Back up, back up, give 'im space"—directing everyone in that steady Harlan way.

Sunlight flickers over his eyelids.

"Kid," Harlan says. "Say something."

Jesse moans. Harlan touches his shoulder and he barely feels it. "Don't *move* him," snaps a woman in the crowd. Oh god, he's paralyzed. He's maimed for life. But then, after a moment, he gets his breath back, and with that comes the feeling in his extremities, including a deep, sharp pain in his wrist, the left wrist, which caught him as he fell.

Harlan gets him sitting up. His wrist is broken, already swelling. Somebody else flags down the driver of the excavator. The driver comes around to the side lawn, livid and terrified.

"There weren't nobody in there," he says to Harlan. "We *looked*." He appeals to the crowd. They stare blankly at him. "*Fuck*," he says, stamping the ground. "*Fuck* me."

Jesse sits cradling his wrist while Harlan tries to calm the driver and two other baffled crewmen. They checked, they say. They checked *twice*. They had all agreed the house was empty. Harlan doesn't argue with them. He loads Jesse into his truck to take him to the hospital. Jesse's head rings. His wrist aches so sharply that his eyes water. As they ride away, he notices the clock on the dashboard through a blur of tears.

"Noon?" he says. "How long was I in there?"

Harlan doesn't answer him. He stares at the road for what feels like a harrowing length of time. Then, finally:

"Did you see her?"

Jesse's heart freezes. Alice? How could Harlan know about Alice?

"See who?"

"Stonewall Jackson," Harlan says sharply. "Your *mother*. Who do you think?"

Oh. His mother. Jesse breathes through his teeth and tries not to cry. His mind lurches, and in its chaos, he can feel Harlan losing his patience.

"I didn't—no. I didn't see her."

"Yeah." Harlan nods angrily. "Of course not. Was it even about her? Was that true?"

Jesse shivers. "What?"

"Your mother. Right. 'Cause you knew that'd work on me."

"What are you talking about? I wasn't tricking you—"

"You had *no reason* to come back here. None. You could've grown up and got your college education and flown your little Pride flag and moved on with your life, but instead you show up in *my* town, and stir shit up, and force me to fucking rescue you. It's deranged."

"No, that's not what I was doing, Jimmy!" Jesse cries, panicking.

"Enough," Harlan says. "I've had enough."

The Harlan Jesse saw in Willy's parking lot is gone. He doesn't even ask Jesse what he *did* see, doesn't seem curious at all about where he went for all those hours, doesn't want to know what happened to his flashlight, which Jesse left on the floor in the attic. It's lost, stuck like a splinter in that crazy house.

Harlan's temper has abated by the time he pulls up at the hospital, but Jesse is crying in earnest, his tears gumming up the dust on his face.

"The cops are gonna show up soon," Harlan says. "They'll want to know where you were."

"Christ, Jimmy." Jesse wipes at his face. "You called the cops?"

"I didn't. But I bet your aunt did. It's Wednesday."

Jesse stares, bewildered. What's significant about Wednesday? Then he gets it: He's been inside the Night House for a day and half. He wriggles his phone out of his pocket, its battery almost drained, its screen frantic with another slew of texts and calls from Nancy, from the sheriff's office.

"Come on," says Harlan. "You gotta get out of the truck."

"But what do I tell them?"

"I don't know. Just leave my name out of it, okay? Don't tell them I drove you over to the house."

"But *how*, Jimmy? My car's still at the bar. How did I—?"

"Jesus, kid, I don't know. Make something up. Say you don't remember. You're a mess. You got wrecked and blacked out. Won't be hard to convince them it's true."

Jesse's face burns. The ringing in his head takes on color: an orange iris pulsing behind his eyeballs.

"All right, come on now." Harlan reaches over him and opens the passenger side door. "You can't sit in my truck and cry. Pull yourself together and go inside. Hurry!"

Jesse gets out. Harlan closes the door behind him. He offers an apologetic look through the window, and Jesse wishes he'd just pick a lane and stay in it—soft or hard, but not both, it's infuriating. When the truck drives off, Jesse imagines that part of him leaves his body and goes with it, following Harlan back to the duplex. It witnesses as Harlan tells his uncle what happened in the Night House. It screams in Harlan's ear.

Meanwhile, at the hospital, Jesse gets X-rays and pain meds and is fitted for a brace. He hears his aunt arrive, her distinctive sandals slapping down the hall. She hugs him, too relieved and exhausted to be angry at him. When he breathes her in, she smells like sleeplessness and underarm sweat.

Somehow, Nancy has beaten the cops there, but he can hear them coming, too, the stoic *clomp-clomp* of sheriff boots. Hupp won't go easy on him simply because he broke his radius. She's ready to catch him in a lie.

Nancy doesn't want him caught off guard. She updates him:

"Jesse, they found that girl. They found your girl, Morgan."

"Morgan?" he says druggily. Of course, he didn't forget; it's just that there's been a lot to process lately.

Nancy adds: "She's *alive*."

Forty-three pigs escape from the Tarbarrel farm, nineteen boars and twenty-four sows. An alligator fleet swarms in the river to the north; it's not clear where they came from, and it would be too difficult to count them.

Morgan Taylor was unconscious when they brought her in yesterday afternoon. She stabilized last night, and her family arranged her transfer that morning to Bryce-Nova in Kneesville, a much nicer hospital. Jesse wishes he could see Morgan, but he knows that would be impossible. He imagines the flowers and stuffed animals that will be sent to her, a pile of them growing next to her parents, her sister coming in from out of town to hold their hands.

Mr. Swink's assistant, Tanisha Patton, is still at the shit hospital in critical condition. Two witnesses, unable to witness. The sheriff's office, upon determining that Alice must've taken off in Mrs. Patton's car, put out an APB. No luck yet.

Hupp grills Jesse in the conference room. She lays out every suspicious thing they found in the guesthouse at 403 Eden Circle: the black-and-white police photos, Connie's autopsy report, newspaper articles printed from microfiche about her death and what followed, a picture of Jesse's first-grade class, a picture of his high school cross-country team in the paper, his senior yearbook photo, social media photos, printouts from an embarrassing film review blog he wrote in middle school, his searing take on *The Imaginarium of Doctor Parnassus*. Why Alice Catherine thought this a worthy addition to her stash he has no idea, which is exactly what he tells Hupp. He didn't know why this girl was interested in him. He didn't know that she stabbed her father in the stomach with a paring knife when she was sixteen. No, he has never met her or spoken to her before. No, he is not aware of any attempt she's made to contact him. Hupp isn't convinced. His explanation is full of holes, but he can tell she doesn't know how to disprove it or connect it to what happened in South Greene.

"'Can't remember, can't remember,'" she sneers. "You lost a whole entire day, is that what you're saying? You must think I'm a fool."

"No, ma'am," he says calmly, fidgeting with the brace on his wrist. The pain is subdued, stuffed as he is with painkillers, but he still hears that ringing in his head and even suggested to the physician that he might have a concussion. "Maybe," the physician said dryly, shining a light into his eyes. "You could also just be hungover." Like Harlan said they would, the medical staffers take one look at Jesse and buy his explanation wholesale.

Forty-three sows and boars. The Tarbarrel insurance assessors will blame it on an earthquake, unfelt and undetected, but still somehow violent enough to damage the enclosures on the north end of the grounds. Now the pigs are on the move, their herd loud, nervous, and fast. They uproot shrubs and set off car alarms and shit indiscriminately. They move like they want to be somewhere. Only when they get past the high school do they slow down, and when they make it to the service road behind the Walmart, they meander and block both lanes.

Their little eyes stare at Jesse through Nancy's windshield, their bodies a fluid pinkish wall in the road. He never realized how obscenely naked pigs look.

"God," says Nancy. "What now?"

Jesse has been quiet and contrite on the ride home, cradling his broken wrist, and Nancy has not raged at him nor demanded answers. She has told him that they're going home to pack up and leave. The physician advised Jesse not to drive with the brace, so she's going to deliver him back to Greensboro herself. There, he'll stay with Minerva until they can make other arrangements.

"Where did these assholes come from?" Nancy asks, of the pigs.

"I don't know," he says. The pigs' assholes are, in fact, a prominent feature of their blockade.

Nancy lays on the horn and rolls down the window. "Get out of the way, pigs! Move!"

The pigs turn to the car with their fat, defiant faces, but they don't budge, and the noise of the horn is only making the whine in Jesse's head louder. After a minute, Nancy stops, but she grips the steering wheel, as if she were about to plow through the pigs head-on.

"You sure it's a good idea for me to leave town?" Jesse asks. "I think it'd set Marty off."

"Marty's got no reason to suspect you of anything," Nancy says. "You haven't set foot in South Greene since you dropped off that girl. She knows that."

"Are y'all fighting about this?"

She doesn't look at him. "You could say that."

For a moment, she's reflective, and he thinks maybe she'll admit to something substantial between herself and

Hupp—what exactly it is they have in common aside from being in a small town and possessing similar proclivities. But Nancy only clutches the wheel tighter and shouts at the road:

"There's no way she can suspect you of anything! Marty said that poor girl had been tied up in the bathroom. Absolute insanity. This lunatic should've been in jail years ago."

A pause.

"We don't even know the Swinks. I told Marty that. When would you have even had the chance to meet this psychopath? She was homeschooled, for Christ's sake."

Jesse says nothing and looks away from her, back to the wicked beady stare of the pigs.

"You don't know her. You've never talked to her. It's ridiculous."

She waits, glancing at him out of the corner of her eye. Still, he doesn't respond, and in his silence, he can feel some of the will leave her. He can almost see it sift up from her body and out the open window, where it mixes with the yellow pine pollen and the pig stink. She breathes out a tired sigh. He feels an apology in his throat, but he's tired, too—tired of carrying his secret life, tired of apologizing for himself.

"Goddamn it, Jesse," Nancy says.

The gators are another thing, seemingly unrelated, unless the escaped livestock let off a meat cloud to attract them, a many-legged buffet. They swim in from upriver, agitated as hornets. Are they in heat? Is that why they're so aggressive? By the end of the day, the sheriff's office and the town council and the department of recreation will issue their advisory. No fishing.

No kayaks. Keep your pets inside, don't let them wander—
seven have been snatched already.

Something inexplicable is happening to Jesse's sense of space.
If he turns down his thoughts, he can feel the pigs. He can feel
the gators. They move through the water like little green stars.
When Nancy pulls into their driveway, he gets out and looks up.
It's evening. Lightning bugs flash in the hedge. A memory surfaces: Nancy in the middle of the night, standing tensely on the
back patio in her bathrobe. She cranes her neck toward the shadows, as if she saw something out there in the yard. He crouches
down, spying on her through the kitchen window. How old was
he then? Six? Seven? Nancy was his whole world for a long time.

"What are you looking at?" Nancy asks him. She's holding
the key to his hatchback, the car itself parked on the curb in
front of the house. A neighbor retrieved it for them and left the
key in the mailbox; any longer in the parking lot of Willy's and
it might've been towed.

"Nothing," Jesse says. "Can I have my keys back?"

Nancy stares at him. He must have a wild look on his face.

"How about I hold on to them for now," she says, putting
them away in her purse.

She follows him inside, then to his room, watching as he
retrieves the Tarbarrel tin from its hiding spot in his bedroom.
He sits on the floor, opens it, and shows Nancy the photos
and their envelope. She's seen everything already, but now she
knows where it came from.

"How long have you been talking to her?" she asks.

"About a month," he says. "But I didn't know who she was."

"And she told you she knew all these secrets about Connie? How did she convince you?"

"I don't know. She didn't *convince* me. She told me there was more to know, and I believed her." This answer doesn't satisfy Nancy. He tries another approach: "She said her mother and my mother were friends. Is that true? Did you know Alice's mother?"

Nancy sucks in a breath. "Katrina? Yes. She and Con were friends."

"Close friends?"

"I don't know. I was away at school." She's lying here. He can tell. He pushes the silence between them, lets it sit there. "Yes. All right," she says. "They were close. But they had a falling out. She wasn't even there at the funeral. Some years later, she left town."

"Alice said her mother was dead," says Jesse.

"Well—that's a shame. We didn't keep in touch."

"What was the falling out about?"

"Oh, I don't know, hon. What does any of this have to do with you?"

"My father," he says. "I think Euel Swink is my father."

At first, Nancy looks confused, as if she'd never considered that Jesse could even have a father. Then her face becomes heavy, and Jesse is almost certain he's observing the realization in real time, the unpacking of a thought she never considered, and he himself realizes that he has no idea how Nancy ever processed what happened to her sister, or what that meant to her, to *have processed* it, if in fact she ever did.

"Did this girl tell you that?" Nancy asks.

"No," says Jesse. "She said Mr. Swink and Connie had a relationship."

"They had a working relationship. She worked for him."

"She said he had a reputation."

Nancy doesn't say anything, but he can see her searching her memory. Has she heard of this reputation? She sits on her knees in front of him.

"Listen. You have to realize, just because this girl told you something that's possible, that doesn't mean it's true."

"I know," he says.

"Is this what you've been after? You wanted to know who your father is?"

"Maybe," he says. "I mean—no, that wasn't what brought me back, but—"

"What then?"

"What then *what*?" he says, annoyed. "I'm here to figure out my shit. What other reason do I need?"

"Honey—" Nancy says. She takes hold of his face with both hands, but he leans back, pulling away. "Honey. Do you not see what this person is?"

"I see what she is. I think she's been telling me the truth."

Nancy nods. A silence passes, and she smiles sadly. "Listen to me. I know that there are some things I haven't been—forthright about—with you. I can see now, looking back, that maybe I should've made different choices in that regard."

"You and Marty."

Her face is pained. "Yeah. Me and Marty. It's not a good—it's complicated, sweetheart, because I knew you were—different. Long before you told me. And I couldn't—relationship-wise, it just wasn't a good example for you."

"You made things lonelier than they needed to be," Jesse says.

She grabs his shoulder. "And I never intended that! I'm happy and proud that you're who you are. But I wanted your life here to be as safe and normal as possible, because I love you so much, and because your mother loved you. Connie loved you."

"Did she?"

"Yes!" Nancy grips him tighter. "Of course. I know that her actions—didn't always make sense. But she worried about you constantly. Your safety, your future. She would call me in the middle of the night, crying, *worried* about it, that she couldn't do enough for you, that she wasn't good enough for you. She was like that to the end. The night she died—whatever she was doing on that river, that—thing—that she built—wherever she was in her mind, she kept you with her because she thought it was right."

Nancy's speech is hurried. This can't be the first time she's told Jesse that his mother loved him, but it feels unreal.

"We can talk about that later," she goes on. "I'll set things right—or at least I'll try. I owe you that. But right now, please, please, please, put these things away and go get a shower and pack your bag."

"We're really leaving?" Jesse holds his mother's postcards to his chest. "Marty said—"

"I don't care. You did nothing wrong. Whatever the Swink girl did has no bearing on you. So yes. We're leaving. Promise you won't fight me on this?"

"I promise," he says. She needs this promise, so he sends it out to her, empty air. **Foxglove briar.** Liar.

Moments later, he hears her in the kitchen, taking down Tupperware from the cabinets. He charges his phone and checks for messages. Nothing from Alice, just a few jokey exchanges among his college friends in their group text. He would reply, but the texts go back so far he's not sure what they're talking about. In the bathroom, he runs the shower, and in the mirror, he can see the swipes on his cheeks where Nancy rubbed off the dirt with her hands, and the fading bruise on his right cheek where Tooly hit him.

Outside, the animals are on the move. He can feel them. He can feel something happening to the sky.

Jesse leaves the water running and returns to his room. He takes Connie's wooden bracelet from the tin, adorns his good wrist. In the den, he gets his keys from Nancy's purse; she has, for a moment, left them unguarded. Then, with the tin, and his keys, and his phone, and the bottle of pain pills he got from the hospital pharmacy, he heads out the door.

The sky is filled with a bright curve of stars. The Milky Way? No, it's too early in the evening; the sun has barely set. What Jesse sees is the Miskwa River, hovering over its earthbound counterpart, that same snaky shape he saw on the wall of the Night House: Hook Bend to the west, downtown to the east. A perfect map. And to the north, somewhere over the Miskwa Swamp, is a round, blue-white glow, like a second moon. A guide. A destination.

Jesse sees. Nancy doesn't. She can't hear a thing until he starts his car, and by the time she runs out onto the lawn, he can barely see her in his rearview. His head is ringing. **Ivy blood spade.** Find her. Find her.

A thousand stars reflect on the river. Scaly backs break the surface of the water and dissolve them. All throughout the county, families pick up their dinner plates and wash them in the sink.

They sit out on their porches. They shoo pigs from their lawn. One pig is struck and killed on the bridge to South Greene. The driver of the car gets out and looks at the mess of blood in his fender. At 403 Eden Circle, Mr. Swink sits and waits with someone from the sheriff's office. Someone suggested Alice may call, but this seems unlikely. No one has found Mrs. Patton's car; it's still out on that back road. No one will find it until tomorrow evening, when a farmer calls it in.

Jesse imagines what it would be like to drive to South Greene and confront Mr. Swink, but he has no idea what he'd get from that. Does he want a father in his life? Would he simply want Mr. Swink to realize he exists? Here I am, he'd say. Look at me.

But Jesse has no plans to go to South Greene.

He goes north, toward that blue glow over the swamp.

He's nearly past Red's house when he spies a deputy jeep on the road behind him. Every turn he takes, it follows, a black bulky shadow with its headlights off, just visible in the dusk. He thinks he's being sneaky. He thinks Jesse will lead him straight to Alice. For a while, Jesse circles around Pinewood, trying to shake him. He passes the Quinns' trailer park, the Confederate flag backlit in their window, and Bittern's Rest, and the Night House and all its history, a wreck of wood and bricks to be cleared.

None of his meandering shakes the jeep, which reappears behind him on a long stretch of back road.

Jesse glares into the rearview mirror. What should he do? He can't keep driving around in circles. He can't go back home. Or, he could go back home, face Nancy, give up, get ferried

back to Greensboro—but the map in the sky and the blue
light over Miskwa, those will probably vanish as easily as they
appeared. Already, it's harder to see the river's twisty shape, its
edges washed out like denim. And that stupid deputy! Does
he see it, too? But why would he? Why would he be following
Jesse if he could follow the map himself?

Ivy blood spade find her find her

Jesse accelerates. Dick the hatchback is instantly skeptical,
its engine squalling, but he keeps on. The car's boxy frame
begins to wobble.

For several miles he maintains his speed—an even eighty.
He passes into a part of the county he's never been to before, a
dark blue blur of swamps and fields and nowhere roads, squat
houses, abandoned tobacco barns. He slows down only to turn
onto a side road, tires sliding and throwing up gravel. Then he
speeds up again, the needle on the odometer climbing. The car
makes his teeth rattle. An acrid stink seeps out from his air
conditioner. It stings his eyes.

Finally, the deputy sends up his sirens, and the jeep is on
his ass immediately, its lights strobing through the thick gray
haze that fills the car. A wall of smoke rolls up his windshield.
He can't breathe, can't stop coughing. In a panic, he brakes and
swerves. Pain shoots up his arm; he can't grip the wheel. The
car bounds off the road into a ditch, catches air, and smashes
through a barbwire fence.

It takes Jesse a moment to realize what has happened. Too
much smoke and heat. He throws open the door and spills out
of the car into a bed of mud and switchgrass, lies there gasping
for air. The air tastes like green weeds, cow manure, burning

rubber. A fire roils under the hood. Connie's tin is in there. Where? Under the seat maybe. He can still get it. He scrambles to the passenger door.

Deputy Sleight comes across the ditch, picking his feet over the barbwire. He has his gun drawn and is screaming. Typical cop stuff. *Down on the ground, hands where I can see them*, et cetera. Jesse calls back hoarsely, "I need to get something out of the car."

"It's on fire, you fucking idiot!" shrieks Sleight.

The dog is a round, red-eyed shadow behind him.

"Just let me get something out!"

The fire leaps up, scorching his face. When he stumbles back, Sleight takes hold of his broken wrist and yanks his arm around. He sees white. The pain knocks the breath out of him. By the time his vision clears, he's on his stomach, Sleight pressing his head into the mud, laughing hysterically.

"So *stupid*, Calloway! Like you ever could get away from me in that limpdick lemon piece of shit."

Jesse clenches his eyes shut, hating Pete Sleight, this hokey fascist, this high school bully turned cop. He imagines melting into the ground, becoming the mud Sleight has his face pressed into, and swallowing the deputy up with him.

Then Dick, loyal in its death throes, explodes its front right tire, bathing them in a gust of searing smoke. A shred of hot rubber whips across Sleight's face. He screams.

Jesse wriggles out from under him and sprints off across a soybean field, running at a crouch, afraid Sleight might start blindly shooting. He's at the trees before he dares to look back—at the grass and the weeds catching fire, at Sleight holding his face, dragging himself away from the flames—and he wants to go back and get the tin, wants it more than anything. But then he discerns a black shape running toward him across the field: the dog, its back orange in the glow of the flames. He nearly laughs. Who would have thought this fat little dog could move so fast?

The dog glides more than runs, as if it has no legs, and suddenly it's not so much funny as terrifying, like it's not a dog at all, but something else. Something made of shadow and tooth and claw, which will devour him if it catches him, and as he turns and flees from it into the woods, through a thicket of ankle-high mud and brambles, he can hear its snarl taking on the tenor of a volcanic roar. Jesse doesn't fall to the temptation of looking back at it; he keeps his eyes straight ahead. But he does wonder: Where the fuck did Pete Sleight even *find* this dog? Did it appear out of the woods? Did the same natural magic that gave rise to Connie's language also create this hellhound? God, he can smell the thing, a rotten egg brimstone reek pluming from its mouth behind him, worse than hog lagoons.

Jesse runs until the trees all turn to pines and the weedy underbrush turns to high grasses and back to underbrush again. He clears a berm. The ground falls away on the other side, which sends him sliding down a soft, loamy slope into a creek. He goes under, blind in the green-black.

When he surfaces again, there's no sign of the dog. The woods are quiet besides his gasping breath, his intermittent splashing.

He floats awhile.

Overhead, the sky still shows him the river's windy shape, but its wonder is gone for him. In the water, his wrist pulses inside its brace, a sharp ache. His grief is sharp, too.

Those pictures, the letters and postcards, his kid-detective notebook, all gone. And for what? To come find this girl, this maniac who tied up Morgan in a bathroom, who shot a woman in cold blood, who scrapped together every piece of his life she could find and studied him and manipulated him and knew what she had to say to draw him back here. He hates her. He hates that she has given him just enough to make him need the rest of it, to make it impossible to turn back, because she knows he won't get enough from Nancy, or Harlan, or the cops, or his teachers, or the people he sleeps with, or his friends in college who are getting tired of him. Only Alice, his sister, can explain. He hates her nearly as much as he hates his own blind trust, and the fact that he is now stewing in a stagnant creek, likely toxic with runoff.

Through this surge of self-pity, he hears a rustling in the pines and jerks upright.

A pig roots around in the pine needles on the opposite bank, munching aimlessly. It looks up at him with its small, crinkly eyes and, for a moment, seems like it's about to speak. *They'll come after you, stupid. Better keep moving.*

Then it turns and ambles into the underbrush, like it could not care what he does either way.

In his American history class last fall, his professor taught a unit on the Great Dismal Swamp and the maroons that used to form there, composed of those who had escaped slavery. The swamp was so deep that whole generations of Black families survived having never seen a white person, having heard only horror stories of what white people had done to their parents, their parents' parents. The farther Jesse goes, the more those lectures pop into his mind, not that he imagines himself fleeing slavery, he doesn't, but that he realizes he never grappled with the idea that you could enter a place so deeply as to disappear into it. The pines stretch on forever, surrounded by a cushion of waist-high grass and weeds. Natural fires have scarred their trunks black at their base, and the sky overhead is tinted brown with swamp gas and filled with dim yellow stars. Early on, he crosses a clearing—a long row of transmission towers running east to west—but beyond that he expects to reach a road or hear traffic at some point, and he never does. There's not a single light from a house or a radio tower. Not even an airplane. Occasionally, he smells the clean wet odor of the river, but he can't see it through the trees.

For hours, he follows the river's map, the blue glow over the swamp. Sometimes, he sees the pig in the brush, though it often disappears, and he keeps moving forward until he sees it again. Sometimes he loses his breath and has to sit on his knees in the mud, listening to the bullfrogs, the whine of mosquitos, the crabs clicking in the grass, some unknown animal slinking by in the bushes. One of these moments of rest leads him to drift off into an uneasy sleep, at which point he feels himself dissolve, like the swamp is absorbing him. Bullfrog, mosquito, crab claw. He is sopped up by the life of every animal and tree, every colony of moss and bacteria, everything that was born and died here, the primordial ocean this place once was and the fossil fuels that will form from its peat and rot, and the settlers who came here, and those seeking freedom who escaped through here, and the developers who will one day fill this place in with dead dirt and gravel. What happened in the

Night House has altered Jesse, dislodged him from time. Too many lives. Too much noise. People weren't meant to feel time all at once.

Did Alice lose her mind this way? Did Connie? Was this how Connie died?

Dissolved, like a drop of blood in water.

The pig's noisy rooting wakes him. He's not sure how much time has passed. His wrist aches and itches, the wet brace chafing his skin. He keeps going.

The waning moon sets. A gray glow appears through the trees to his right, which eats into his map and causes it to fade. By now, though, he's found the river itself, or one of its tributaries. A blue fog hangs over it. A fleet of alligators slides upstream.

alligator, noun: **Iron tooth pistol**

A few yards more, and he finds a shelter, a decrepit shack hidden in a grove of scrub oaks. Jesse steps inside through a doorless entryway, squinting into a dark space about the size of his bedroom. Metal equipment lies strewn about, so old and rust-eaten it's impossible to tell what it was, but Jesse suspects this was once a distillery. He's heard stories about moonshine and prohibition. He's seen *Thunder Road.*

Someone has been here recently. A green army blanket lies on the floor. Evidence of foraging sits in a pile by the wall— wild strawberries, dandelion leaves, jewelweed. There's a candle in the window, some burned-out matches, a small square mirror, which catches Jesse's face just long enough for him to be horrified. He has fully transformed. He has reincarnated as a swamp beast.

He emerges from the shack and finds the pig munching in a clearing, and beyond that a pine grove, which guards the riverbank. He spies movement.

When he draws closer, he finds Alice.

She's wearing loose, dirty clothes that have been subject to the swamp, the edge of her skirt so torn it looks like lace. She's working on something, swatting frizzy tendrils of hair out of her eyes as she knots together a length of vine. The rest of the vine lies coiled in the mud at her bare feet. Poison ivy. Leaves of three, let them be. He remembers that from summer camp. A spotty rash has already broken out on her arms.

She hears him approaching and looks up, wide-eyed.

"Is that you, Jesse?" she says.

He steps closer. The light on the east side of the river has turned from gray to pale pink, casting cool shadows. When Alice grins, her teeth look blue.

"Hello, Rabbit," she says.

She sounds so happy, so relieved—it's touching. He's happy he found her, too. His sister. But what is she working on? Why is his sister handling poison ivy? Here's this assemblage of objects on the bank, two sticks as tall as her hip, upright in the mud—

Oh.

An iris of dark contracts around his vision, Alice gets smaller and smaller, like he's looking up at her from the bottom of a well. "Jesse!" she cries. Big, wild eyes. A handful of poison ivy. She reaches out to catch him, but he's already down.

From the Notebooks of
Katrina Morrow, Summer 1995

July 28

Dream

██ and me in the Night House. We are writing spells in our notebooks, passing them back and forth. We used to call those books our babies, wrapped them in newspaper to keep the pages from bending. In the dream, ██ scribbles on the pages so hard she tears them with her pen, and then she has a tantrum and hurls the book across the room. It's fine, she says. I'm just pregnant. I point to the book and scold her: Well then, is that how you should be treating your baby?

I've honestly got no idea how ██ would treat a real baby.

It's weird—in real life, ██ never went to the Night House with me. Said it was for hicks. But I think she was afraid of it. My grandma always told me it was a place where edges met. Where stuff leaked out. Said there were rules to follow—always go in the way you came out, it was dangerous otherwise. But I did some of my best work in those moldy rooms, alone in the dark, knowing that ██ was too scared to join me.

August 1

Anchor jar

GB's cologne and 6 crushed cockle shells. Fill to the top with stones. Fill in the gaps with malty beer

Now bury four keys at his house—north, south, east, west. Sprinkle blood and salt in the soil

August 16

I am so fucking sick of cicadas.

August 21

Jar for the Lost

3 crushed witchfingers, GB's hair and mine tied around an iron nail, 1 oyster shell, 1 shard of mirror, equal parts soft red wine and cooking oil. Should sigh, like the river at night.

He is still wandering. I need to bring him back to me.

September 4

Went to his Labor Day thing. Looked like a princess. Smelled like gardenias and money. One of those country club hoes asked, And WHO are you? Like I was there to clean up the plates. Bitch, I'm Circe, I said. I am the Pagan Pig QUEEN.

Okay, so I didn't say that. But I thought it, and GB patted my butt in front of all those whispering snakes. I guess that felt good.

Thinking of ███ always. This morning by the river, I saw a six-foot gator with a water moccasin in its mouth. For a minute, the snake flailed and twisted and tried to bite the gator's snout, but in one gulp it got sucked down like a noodle. I like gators. I have always envied their armor. And their teeth.

September 18

██, I wish I could talk to you. Our thirteen-year-old selves would be disgusted with us.

September 20

Dream

██ and me by the river. We're kids again. She's building a huge nest out of branches and car parts. She tells me the car parts come from Mexico, and that she knew Mexico before she was born. It's impossible. She knows about Mexico exactly as much as I know about Mexico. Then she says, It's weird to be working at the auto plant where I know my real dad worked, and I say, But you don't work at an auto plant. You work at a meat processing plant, though you are about to lose that job because you are actually crazy, because you couldn't stand me having someone of my own that wasn't you, and you tried to ruin it, but you only ruined yourself. But I'm not going to let you hound me forever, you crazy bitch. I'm going to marry GB and have a family and live in a nice, clean neighborhood, surrounded by nice, clean things.

I say all these things in the dream that I will never say to ██'s face, and then I realize that the nest she's building isn't a nest at all, but an entryway—this dark, loamy tunnel going straight down into the earth. Is this headed to Mexico? I ask. And she says, Why don't you lean in and find out, Rabbit? in this teasing singsong way. I'm afraid she's going to push me. Then that thing happens where when you think something in a dream is going to happen, so it does. She pushes me hard. Down I go tumbling through the dark like Alice in Wonderland, past the foundation of Daddy's old house, and all our old pets that are buried in the ground there, with tree roots wrapping around their bones. Then there's onion bulbs and tin pots, and the brass buttons of soldiers shining like yellow stars, and the Indian tools and pots and arrowheads, then dragon skulls and fossils. I went down until I hit water or oil or something, and the shock of it woke me up.

I forgot big chunks of this dream. Soon as I woke up I could feel it splitting apart and spilling out of my head. I had this feeling like I had to go over to ████'s place and tell her something important. Only for the life of me I couldn't remember what.

10

Alice has held on to the night she first met Jesse.

It was the same night she had that argument with her father, which had been brewing since he gave her that box containing Katrina's notebooks two years before. He said he'd given it to her so she could have a connection to her mother, but for Alice the act was self-incriminating. It proved he knew about the magic all along. She revisited her memories and reassembled them. Satie. *Gymnopédie No. 1.* Her mother's devastated face. *Music is like a spell.* A literal spell her father cast, which made her mother disappear. Knowing this, Alice would no longer play her harp, and Euel's insistence led to terrible rages. The mayor and his wife showed up for dinner, and there was Alice digging a hole in the backyard with a jar that was intended to sour wine and stall conversation (one part each white vinegar and urine, a healthy wad of phlegm for good measure).

The next day, her father said, "I did not give you those goddamn journals so you could become obsessed with them. If you don't settle down, I'll take them back."

Journals. Like he didn't know what a fucking spell was. He told Alice that she, like her mother, had an overactive imagination. An ungenerous spirit. He said her mother had been bored, self-centered, delusional, spiteful. Alice asked him if that was why he killed her.

"Killed her?" He feigned bewilderment. "*Killed* her? Alice, she abandoned you as soon as I cut her a check. When are you going to admit it's not *me* you're angry at?"

To that, she took a paring knife from the counter and stuck him.

Instantly, she heard the pulse of his blood on her fingers, and when she saw the look on his face, she didn't think that bewilderment was feigned. Bobbie came into the kitchen and screamed. Alice fled upstairs. She grabbed a stash of things she'd been keeping under her bed and escaped out the second-story window. Then she sprinted to the river's edge, to one of Euel's tattered old canoes, which he kept under a tarp by the dock.

It was not an ideal getaway. She had no plan. Not even halfway across the river, the canoe began to leak. Cold water soaked into her jeans. She tightened the straps of her pack to lift it up and keep it dry. Sirens crossed the bridge overhead. She ducked down in the darkness and thought she was as good as caught.

Running away had never occurred to Alice. She'd felt closed off for so long that she had no faith she could thrive independently as an adult. She trusted no one, only her mother. A dead woman. A scavenger and survivor who had given Alice the only guide she had for being in the world as she was. By her mother's intuition, she paddled hard for the north bank and made her way to the Night House.

A place where edges met and stuff leaked out.

It was nearly midnight by the time she found her way there, a window wide open in the kitchen, as if the house had been waiting for her. She climbed on in like the place was hers. But she found it occupied. If they were snakes, those Pinewood boys would have bitten her. She managed to hide from them in the dining room, though moments later, she heard someone else in the house. A different version of that one same boy, stumbling and panicked.

By the end of the night, Sherriff Hupp would catch up with Alice on a suburban street and arrest her. She would wait until they were down at the station to tell her Euel wasn't dead. It appeared that she had slipped the knife in as perfectly and delicately as a surgeon, the blade sliding past his organs without fuss. Alice wondered whether her father even had organs. Maybe the doctors were liars, and they found out at the hospital that he was stuffed with dirt and spores.

Once Alice calmed down, she could concede that her father wasn't *literally* stuffed with dirt and spores. This was what she *felt* someone might find inside of Euel. But at Croatan, everyone was more interested in what was inside of Alice. She was told she demonstrated symptoms across a range of disorders: delusional, antisocial, obsessive-compulsive. The pills they gave her brought her GI track to a halt. She had no ear while taking them, every sound a dull cottony throb. The food in the cafeteria was fatty and salty and gave her heartburn. All the silverware was plastic. Inside, every door was always open— bedroom and bathroom—but the doors leading outside were locked and monitored by orderlies with sharkish smiles who called her *sugar*. Worst of all, she had to sit with a psychiatrist as they ran through the stabbing and the accusation she'd made toward Euel. The psychiatrist didn't believe her about the harp or her mother drowning herself, though she didn't outright say so. Instead, she asked how Alice came to *know* these things were true, and whether there might be alternative explanations for her mother no longer being in her life. The psychiatrist's understanding of events was the same as everyone else's: Her mother left town; she'd wanted to leave town for a long time; she'd been talking to Euel about it.

Well, of course Euel will tell you that, Alice thought. *He's a murderer.*

But if the psychiatrist didn't believe, if *only Alice* believed her mother was dead, then there could be no murder. Likewise, if *only Alice* believed in the magic of her ear, then there was no magic at all. Only a moderately talented harpist with delusions. An alternative explanation is that Alice's mother gave up the custody battle because she knew her daughter would have a better life with Euel: college, an orthodontist, music lessons, an absence of slaughterhouses and hog lagoon stench, every need met. She was always insecure about Euel's money. The psychiatrist asked Alice if these things might explain the look of despair she saw on her mother's face when she played the harp for her that first and only time, or if it was possible the harp had nothing to do with it, that Alice's mother was despairing for reasons an eight-year-old wouldn't have understood. So what if Alice was simply wrong about this whole thing? Her mother dropped out of her life, abandoned her, and that was her choice.

"The shrinks don't know shit," said Kenzie. Kenzie was

Alice's roommate. She was full of advice. Like Alice, she was sixteen, but she had a weary attitude that came from having been at Croatan before. "They know what your parents told them. They'll always take their side. Just figure out what they want you to say and repeat it back to them."

So Alice did. The psychiatrist sat behind a desk, knowing Alice's truth better than Alice herself, prodding for still deeper and more intrusive self-interrogations. Alice used words like *catastrophizing* and *magical thinking* and *transference*. The psychiatrist, to her credit, ceded Alice's right to be angry about her parents' divorce, her father's adultery, and she probably would not have approved of the ultimatum Euel gave her when she got back from Croatan: You can keep your mother's notebooks, so long as you play that harp. But Euel could give all the ultimatums he wanted, could practically hold Alice under house arrest. He hadn't stabbed anyone. *She* had. And it was not even the threat of losing the notebooks that made her do it, but rather the plea for her to see things from her father's point of view.

When are you going to admit it's not me *you're angry at?*

Who else was she angry at? She admitted to the psychiatrist that when she was little, and her mother was fighting for full custody, the house on Eden Circle seemed to her like a fairy tale castle. She didn't hate Bobbie then, this slim, chipper woman who was so eager to be a mother, who baked gingersnaps and smelled like gardenias. It was the first time she realized her own mother was constantly tired and irritable and smelled like cheap hair spray and furniture polish. She resented returning to their house. She didn't want to live in Pinewood. She wanted to live with her father.

"Guilt," "shame," "internalization," said Alice.

"Acknowledgement," "forgiveness," "progress," said the psychiatrist.

Sometimes, in the process of repeating back the psychiatrist's language, Alice began to believe it. Her problem was not Euel's insidiousness, or Bobbie's fragility, or the hollowness of her neighborhood and the people there, or the poisoned world and all its injustice. Alice's problem was Alice, with her crumpled little soul and misplaced rage. The psychiatrist knew it. Her father knew it. Alice knew it.

But at night, staring at the ceiling from her small, crisp-sheeted bed, she knew something else. A miracle had happened. The hair that she kept twisted around her finger, the one she found on her clothes the night of her arrest, was proof. It was *his* hair, a black hair, gently curled.

"Before I came here," Alice whispered to Kenzie, "I met a boy from the future."

"Sounds like a trip," Kenzie said, face down in her pillow.

And Alice would lie there, smelling swampy water and the dust of the Night House.

Jesse wakes to pain in his wrist, his cheek pressed against the scratchy army blanket on the dirt floor of the moonshine shack. Despite his discomfort, he drifts off again and has a dream that he's sitting in the Spartina Square gazebo with Morgan, the two of them wearing the jeans and sweaters from that first time they hooked up, at the live nativity. "I forgive you," Morgan says, smiling at him. "You felt a real connection. You needed to go find her." Even as the dream unfolds, he knows it's only his brain seeking reassurance. When he wakes up again, the sun is high, sending spears of light through gaps in the roof. Fork-tailed birds fly in and out of the window, a cluster of honey-combed nests attached to the ceiling.

He sits up, his mouth like sand, his body trembling and feverish. Alice comes into the shack, moving on tiptoe. She sees him and stops.

"You're awake."

"I'm awake," he says.

She gives him a canister of water, lukewarm with a tinny aftertaste. It sloshes into his stomach and sharpens his hunger, and he recalls the bar food at Willy's, ages ago. He takes two of his pain pills.

"Do you have anything to eat?" he asks.

She nods, gesturing toward the door. At first, it looks like she's gesturing to the land, as if to imply they'll be surviving off foraged mushrooms and dandelion leaves. But then he realizes she has a mango in one hand, a paring knife in the other.

Is that the knife Alice stuck in her father?

"Come join me?" she says.

"I will," he says coolly.

He can't stop looking at that knife.

Alice notices his hesitation, staring at him with her sallow, dark-eyed face. "Was it the sticks? Did they scare you?"

He doesn't answer, but he must've flinched; Alice looks almost apologetic.

"I didn't want to start before you got here and we could talk through our spells. But I was beginning to think you wouldn't come. I was beginning to think I was crazy for even…"

She trails off. A smear of dirt on her chin makes her mouth look crooked.

"Why didn't you tell me who you were from the beginning?" Jesse asks. "Why pretend?"

She blinks, as if puzzled. "I couldn't have told you."

"Because I would've thought you were crazy?"

"Well, yes. You had to see the buried place first." Alice points upward. "The rift? What you saw outside the Night House?"

"Oh," Jesse says. "*That* was the buried place?"

"Part of it, at least. Also, if I told you who I was, you would've known who I was when we met. You didn't know who I was when we met, so I knew I hadn't told you."

He squints, piecing this together. When he figures it out, he laughs, loud enough to startle the swallows out of their nests and make Alice step back in surprise. Eventually, she catches on and laughs, too. For a minute, they float together in inexplicable delirium.

But when that joy subsides, his apprehension returns. As do his questions. Why did you shoot that woman, Alice? Why did you hold Morgan hostage in a bathroom?

"Come join me and we'll talk," Alice says, pointing her paring knife toward the door. "There's a storm coming in this afternoon, so we shouldn't waste time."

"Okay," he says, and she goes out.

He doesn't join her right away. Outside, he relieves himself in the woods and goes to the riverbank, removing his brace to clean it. His wrist is softball-size, his skin purple and green. He rinses the grit from the brace, then removes his shoes and socks and soaks his blistered feet. The slimy river mud feels good.

To his right, Alice has uprooted her sticks and deposited them under the scrub oaks. Not far from there, on the ground a little closer to the head of the path, a movement catches his eye.

At first, he thinks it's a burrowing animal pushing up a mound in the sand. But as he steps closer, a red substance wells up and begins leaking from the mound, pooling into one of Alice's footprints. Jesse brushes the mound with his fingers, and a chunk of it falls away, revealing a shard of glass—a broken jar.

He backs away, worried to have touched it, to have wrecked something Alice made.

She met Jesse in the Night House when she was sixteen, but she hasn't told him what happened after that. Not yet.

When the sheriff interrupted their encounter, she fled north along Deer Church Road. A new frequency whined in her ears, growing louder with each step:

neeeeeeeeeeeeeeeeeeeeeeeeeeeeeeeeeed
neeeeeeeeeeeeeeeeeeeeeeeeeeeeeeeeeed
neeeeeeeeeeeeeeeeeeeeeeeeeeeeeeeeeeeeed

And underneath that, a thumping meter:

He—NEEDS—your—HELP
Your—BRO—ther—NEEDS—your—HELP
Your—BRO—ther—FROM—the—FU—ture—
NEEDS—your—HELP

She couldn't tell where the sound was coming from until

she found the hair attached to her blouse, tickling the side of her neck. It was Jesse's hair—thick, black, lightly curled. She wrapped it tight around her fingertip.

What was she doing? She had known that the Night House was a place where marvelous things happened; her mother had said as much. How could she be running away from it now?

No. She couldn't abandon her brother. She turned right back around.

The sheriff only searched the Night House for a few minutes. Then she got back in her squad car and drove off. Alice could tell, somehow, even from her hiding spot in the pine grove, that the marvelous spell had passed. She was devastated. She called Jesse's name at the kitchen window and could feel that he was gone.

But if she followed the map in her head, the Rosehaven Cemetery was about three miles back south. That was where those boys said they were going. If she couldn't reach Jesse of the future, she would find him in the now.

When he returns to Alice, he finds her in the shade near the shack, sitting by a lunch spread she laid out on a T-shirt—fruit, nuts, bread, beef jerky, plus a package of organic sea salt crackers, goat cheese crisps, beet chips. Even Alice, in all her strangeness, bears the mark of South Greene. She brought a delicate amount of food, and it's all Jesse can do to keep from stuffing himself. He gnaws on dried meat and imagines a cheeseburger, a Chuckwagon Hangover Special.

"Should we move away from the river?" he asks, sitting across from Alice in the grass. "It'd be easy for someone to find us."

"I'll hear if a boat's coming," she tells him. "I haven't heard a single one all morning."

"That's strange, though, isn't it?"

She thinks for a moment, cutting off a piece of her mango. He can't help but watch her closely when she has that knife.

"Maybe something's keeping them away," she says. She looks toward the clearing and the three pigs rooting in the grass, including the fat pale one Jesse saw the night before. "Did you say you followed a pig to get here?"

"When did I say that?"

"You were coming in and out when I was dragging you back to the shelter. You said something about a pig. I thought you were talking about my father, but then I saw there were actual pigs."

Jesse observes the pigs, their blank, endless munching. "Yeah," he says, pointing. "That one, I saw him last night."

Alice cuts another piece of the mango, the juice running down her hand.

"They must be Euel's pigs," she says. "I wonder how they got out. Connie has some verbs that are linked to the pig—to work, to clue in, to solve. Pigs are as smart as dogs. It's weird that we eat them."

Jesse's heart aches at the mention of his mother. The tin and its contents are burned to a crisp in the skeleton of his car. "Yeah, I think I've heard that. About pigs."

"I must've read through that book two hundred times," Alice says. "I still don't *know* the language. That's why it always took me so long to message you. I was going through the glossary over and over, looking for the right word."

"Do you have it with you?" he asks, trying to sound calm and not like he would grab the book and run like a purse snatcher.

"Of course," she says. "Hey—tell me. How does it come to you, the language?"

"What do you mean?"

"Do you hear the words? Do you picture the things themselves?"

"Oh. The things themselves," he says. "They're obvious to me, I don't know why."

She nods, chewing a bit of pulp off her mango pit. "We're like a mirror of each other," she observes. "It's sounds that come to me, little pulses and frequencies. The storm that's coming? It's down at the coast, but I can hear it already. Not the thunder so much, but the electricity hissing, the clouds building. Like bassoons." She tilts her head to the east. Jesse tilts his head, too; he can't hear the hissing or the bassoons. He hears the pigs snorting and munching, the river sloshing onto its banks.

"My mother was the same as me," Alice continues. "She used to bury witch jars, putting them together by sound. A spell for grief, for love, for revenge. That's how I got you here. I buried a jar in the sand. I'd never buried anything in sand before. I thought maybe that'd ruin it." She gestures broadly. "I don't have a shovel out here."

Sand, access. See also: rile, goad.

"But Connie," Alice says. "What Connie could do, what she was trying to do, it was stronger than my mother's jars. This is our legacy, Jesse. Our inheritance. It's like we have two mothers. Connie is my other mother and Katrina's yours."

"Oh," says Jesse.

"You don't think so?"

"I don't know. I didn't know about Katrina until I met you." He pauses to think. Legacy. **Gold thread copper oak.** "What do you think it was for? Burying jars, making this language..."

Alice holds out her hands, as if it's self-evident. "What do you think a spell is?"

"Is that a trick question?" he asks.

"Look." She points at the sky. "Where do you think all this magic comes from? You saw that rift outside the Night House, that opening. There's power crossing over it all the time, seeping out. A spell calls that power to you. It speaks something aloud and then *becomes* it."

Jesse looks up. The sky is bright and normal.

"But how do you know it's magic?" he asks. "Couldn't it be something else?"

Alice lowers her hands into her lap. "Well, fine," she says. "It *could be* something else. But let's just call it what it looks like, all right?" She scratches at her poison ivy rash. "Weren't you ever able to read Connie's last message?"

"I told you I couldn't," he says. "It's too complicated."

In truth, he never had a chance to return to the photos, and Alice, for the first time, seems disappointed. He's stunned at how much the idea of disappointing her bothers him.

Before either of them can speak again, Alice freezes.

"I hear a motor," she says.

Jesse's heart jumps. They throw what remains of their lunch into a bundle and hurry to the shack, Alice grabbing her pack and army blanket, Jesse dusting away their footprints on the path. Then they huddle in the scrub oaks, peering out at the river to see who's approaching. Soon, Jesse himself can hear the motor, and a pontoon boat appears around the bend from the south, piloted by an older man, a suntanned stranger.

He'll see their footprints on the beach.

Jesse locks arms with Alice and presses his face into her shoulder. Alice puts her hand on the crown of his head. "Shh," she says.

The stranger doesn't seem to notice anything, and his boat putters on. Jesse lets out his breath.

"I told you," he says. "We're too close to the river."

"No, we just need to work fast."

He puts his hand over his heart, which pounds helplessly. "What's your plan, Alice?"

She looks at him, stern and ready. "Empty your pockets. We'll see what we have to work with."

Alice had never been to a cemetery at night. She'd assumed, based on stories about Pinewood, that it would be crawling with teenagers, the notorious parties she never went to. But the cemetery was deserted, populated only by shadows and moonlight. The only sounds were the hush and drone of mossy granite, the gnawing of worms underground, distant shouts and laughter. She followed these voices through the graves. Some yards farther, she spied the orange glint of a fire, weak flames burning in the husk of an old pickup.

And there was Jesse Calloway, along with the three Pinewood boys she'd seen in the Night House. The scarecrow-thin Quinn brothers. Jim Harlan, bare-armed in a T-shirt, despite the cold. Jesse and Tooly had worked themselves up into a kind of fever.

They danced in circles around the truck, hooting and howling in a language with no words, like they were speaking in tongues. Alice watched at the edge of the light, hiding behind an oleander bush. The two older boys—men, really—watched, too.

Alice didn't know much about Pinewood men and still doesn't. She assumes they have their own ways of acknowledging the buried place, close as they are to its seams. Back in those woods, though, she was scared. She didn't feel like she was among kin.

"These woods are *mine*," Jesse declared.

"Mine, too!" added Tooly.

They collided hard with each other and fell to the ground. Hysterics. Limbs all tangled, like they were one boy rather than two. Tooly. *Too*-ly. An earned name. Everything his older brother did, he had to do it, too.

Sam, the older brother, watched. Simmered.

"What's he doing?" he asked.

Harlan, who was standing next to Sam, looked up from his phone. Alice couldn't see their faces from where she was hiding, but she could hear the sizzle in their frequencies.

"Nothing," said Harlan.

"Don't let 'im do that."

"Sam, they're just playing."

"Get 'im off my brother, Jim."

The fire in the truck was screaming, the air itchy with smoke. Tooly had Jesse in a headlock, but they were both still laughing, still rolling in the leaves. After a long, hard silence from Sam, Harlan intervened.

"All right, y'all, cut it out."

He pried the boys apart. Tooly yielded, but Jesse flailed in protest. He kicked and clawed and snarled—"Don't *touch* me, Jimmy, I told you!"—and the more Harlan tried to restrain him, the more frenzied his movements became. Jesse twisted his body as if possessed. He screamed loud enough to shake the graves in the cemetery:

"You coward! You stupid cunt coward—!"

Harlan smacked his face. Not hard, but enough to silence him. Jesse looked up with a stunned and furious expression. Then he sank his teeth into Harlan's forearm.

Squelch of skin breaking.

They scrambled to their feet. Harlan stood wide-eyed, clutching his arm. Jesse spat blood and wiped his mouth on his sleeve. Alice didn't know Jim Harlan, but his blood sounded like dirt and dust, like something that had been sitting in one place for a long time.

Your—BRO—ther—NEEDS—your—HELP

Harlan turned to Sam. A pleading look. Sam turned to Jesse. For the first time, Alice could see his face, and it frightened her, the way the firelight washed out his hair and skin to the same golden-orange color, which made him seem faceless. She didn't know then that Sam Quinn would be dead in less time than it would take her to complete her stint at Croatan, or that he would haunt the Night House, and that Tooly would see him there. This she learned from Harry Bishop's memoir notes, which she stole and copied at the library, and from the general Pinewood gossip relayed by Mrs. Patton. Sometime after Croatan, Mrs. Patton even drove her over to the Night House to show her it was all boarded up. She didn't ask questions then. She thought Alice was just a weird little homeschooled girl, playing games.

But none of this was a game to Alice. She would come to think of Sam Quinn as a demon, a ghoulish spirit that required an exorcism. That night in the woods, it was clear from the malice on his face that Sam Quinn had been waiting for an excuse to hurt Jesse. He lunged at him and punched him in the face and, while he was reeling, punched him again and knocked him to the ground. The younger Quinn howled and laughed. He thought they were still playing.

Jim Harlan just stood there.

Jesse has his phone, which died when he went in the creek, his mother's wooden bracelet, one pair of earbuds, one bottle of pain pills, one ballpoint pen, one wallet, which contains a damp five-dollar bill, two condoms, a driver's license, a university ID, a debit card, a library card, and a punch ticket for a free smoothie.

"You didn't bring much," Alice says.

"Well," he stammers, feeling as though he's here to take an exam he didn't study for. "I didn't have much time."

Alice is more prepared. She has the green army blanket, the candle, the square mirror, the paring knife, a half-empty bottle of red wine, a pair of scissors, a small sewing kit, matches, a flashlight, a small glass bowl, plus a collection of precious papers including Connie's lexicon, Kat Morrow's notebooks, and the photos of Connie on the riverbank. Also a cockle shell, olive oil, dried sage, onion skins, vinegar, pig bones, salt, incense, and modeling clay.

"And there are plenty of things out here," Alice says. "Plants and mushrooms, seeds, shells, feathers, whatever we can find."

Jesse gazes across the clearing. **Hawthorn**: to judge. **Cypress**: to regret.

"I don't know," he says. "Maybe we need to do this another time, when we're more prepared."

Alice looks confused. "What are you talking about? There's no other time. What other time would there be?"

"But what are you asking for, Alice? My mother's dead. She's not around to teach us how to do this."

"And the alternative? If I go with you back to town, what's waiting for me there?"

Jesse's heart pounds in his throat. He doesn't want to think about it.

"This world isn't for me," she says. "Do you know what that sounds like, knowing that? Nothing. A great fierce howl of nothing. You hear it, too, even if you don't realize. And you can't live in a world like that, not without help from the other side. Our mothers knew that."

"They're both dead," Jesse points out.

"And you think we'll die, too, is that it?" She laughs. "Time itself opened up to bring us here together. Don't you have any faith?" She begins to gather their inventory and stash it in her bag, moving with unbothered assuredness.

"And you're wrong," she says, tossing him Connie's lexicon. "Your mother can still teach you."

Jesse grips the book in his hand. Again, he considers bolting with it, but this desire is subdued now. While Alice goes off gathering things to add to their inventory, he sits in the grass and runs his fingers over his mother's handwriting, feeling it like braille. How long she must have worked on this, a language that could reach across worlds. **Goat harp**: to con. **Whiskey spit**: to confront. **Iris crown**: to have faith. *Faith.* He wants Alice's faith. He tries to put himself in her mind. If he leaves now, if they're separated, he might never see her again.

When she returns, she has sphagnum moss, a snakeskin, a soiled silk bra, a pile of hemlock flowers and milkweed stalks. Each object vibrates. The bra is filled with electric light, as if carrying the power of the woman who wore it. When he touches the fabric, its energy takes the form of tiny golden threads and leaps off onto his fingers. His hands are filled with sudden warmth. A wondrous feeling surges in him.

"Alice," he says.

She sorts distractedly through her things, placing objects into piles as if ranking them. The piles glow; a patina of spidery light surrounds them.

"Alice," he says again, firmer.

"Yes?" she says, looking up.

"Did you slip me something?"

Her eyes get big as she crouches in front of him. **Cat**: to sneak. **Cat thorn**: to haunt. Little devil. Little ghost. "Why? What do you see?"

The warmth takes over his arms, his chest, his whole torso. The wind picks up. At the edge of the clearing, the trees show off the bright undersides of their leaves. Every leaf is dewy, fresh, jaggedly beautiful. In the sky overhead, dimmed by cumulus clouds, the glittering curve of the river flashes at him.

"I don't know," he says. "Everything's sharper."

"Do you want to look at those photos again?" she asks.

She leads him back to the moonshine shack, where they sit

together in the shade. She lays out each photo on the dirt, one by one. Connie's sentence from all angles. Jesse examines it.

"See anything different?" Alice asks.

"Give me a minute."

Have faith, he thinks, though his faith slips around his heart like a fish. A spell for grief, for love, for revenge. Why was it that when Alice said the word *revenge* she sounded like she could taste it?

"I just don't know," he says. "I can still only see pieces."

He traces his fingers between objects. This sentence is in the shape of a web, with the hammer at its center. **Claw hammer**: reverse, revolve. He senses that's the verb. The bowl of stones— **Stone clay**: advantage; **Candle**: guide. **Salt mud**: cleanse. **Feather** is a question, or that could be **Wing**, which is time. What animal did that skull belong to? **Mouse**: tease. **Mole**: blindfold. **Weasel**: bargain. The buckeyes could be **seed**, a plural, or maybe Connie was getting creative; **Eye** marks a future tense. The way the sentence seems to work, any one thing could be serving more than one purpose, could be combined to create hundreds of meanings. **Mouse wing**: dawdle. **Wax river ash**: abandoned. **Hammer skull:** obsess.

"I don't think this was the first time she did this," Jesse observes. "I think maybe this language is what made her crazy."

Alice crouches behind him. "It only *looks* crazy." He feels her hand on his shoulder. "The intent is there. We just have to understand it."

As soon as she says this, the rain begins, sweeping across the river in gales. They huddle in the shack, but the downpour comes through the ceiling. Alice throws herself over her bag to keep her papers dry. Everything else gets soaked. Jesse sits against the wall under a stream of water, his mother's bracelet tight in his hand. The rain runs down his back, and he can feel the water's starry molecules spiraling against his skin. He shivers.

"What did you give me?" he asks.

Alice gazes up at him, looking hunchbacked as she hugs her bag.

"Only a tiny bit. I thought it'd help you see."

"A bit of what?"

"A kind of fungus. It's local."

"Oh," Jesse says, nodding. "Well, good thing it's local."

A wave of rain slams the shack. Alice raises her voice:

"You could still meet her, you know. Connie. Time doesn't work the same way on the other side."

He laughs. "I thought I'd see her in that house. But the only dead person I knew was Sam Quinn, and I hated that guy."

"I know," Alice says. "I was there."

Reverse, revolve. Did Connie lose control? Was it a mistake that killed her? Or is Alice right: The intention is there; you just have to understand. Maybe Connie dying was no mistake at all. What did Nancy say? *She worried about you constantly. Your safety, your future. She was like that to the end.*

The rain ebbs, then slows to a drizzle. Sunlight peppers in through the holes in the ceiling. The shack fills with steam. Jesse's head gets hot and cloudy, and the sweat on his skin shimmers with tiny curls. Alice checks the contents of her pack: her papers are damp, but readable. Connie's lexicon pages are only wet at the edges.

Jesse sits up.

"Let me see the photos again," he says.

She hands them over, and he holds them by the corners to keep the mud off. A reversal. A rupture—no, a *cataclysm*.

"Two years ago," he says to Alice, "Jim Harlan invited me out on prom night, and the Quinn brothers were there. That was—*the* night, you know?"

Alice nods, her dark pupils large with expectation.

"Sam—he was Jimmy's dealer. He had something—mescaline, he said, but who knows. And Jimmy—he gave me this look like *Don't do it*, so I took it, you know, to spite him, because at that point, if I was within sight of the guy, he was pissing me off." He laughs. "And then—then everything fell to shit. That was the end, really. The end of, you know, *high school*. My life, up to that point."

Alice crouches closer to him. "You went with them to the woods, by the cemetery."

"Yeah. That's where I lost it. I, like, bit Jimmy?" He laughs again. "Just—*chomp*, you know—took a chunk out of his arm. I don't even remember why. And then Sam Quinn beat me up. I end up crawling into Jaelah's backyard, and they're having to pull me out of the hedge, and Red's trying to get my face to stop bleeding, and Spence and Bash, they're just freaking out. Then I'm in the hospital with a broken cheekbone and my face is the size of a fucking pumpkin, and Hupp's on my ass about what I took and who I got it from, and she's lecturing me like it was all my fault. And I guess I thought it was. My friends—I traumatized my friends. I could hardly talk to them after that. And of course, Jimmy cut me off." He glances at Alice. "You know Jimmy was—"

"I know," Alice says. "I put it together."

He shakes his head. "But why am I talking about this? Oh, right, right. I'm trying to remember something. That night fucked me up so much, I can't place things, like, in time."

"What are you trying to remember?"

A warm shiver goes through him. He swipes rainwater out of his eyes. "I'm trying to remember when I heard about Sam Quinn and the sinkhole. When did that happen?"

"That same night," says Alice. "As the sheriff was lecturing you, he was right down the hall, already dying. You don't remember?"

He stares into her blank, open face. Her eyes are huge. "No."

"I saw it happen," she says. "I was there."

Alice has been watching Jesse scry his mother's message. She wants to understand as soon as he does. She believes they are one paper-thin membrane away from being able to beam thoughts into each other's brains. For now, all she knows is that he's nothing like her father; he has all of Connie's cunning, but none of Euel's calculating. Inside, he sounds like bells and cymbals, like feet pounding pavement, like the crackle of fire and maudlin Hollywood orchestras. Her dumb, crafty, beautiful brother.

He says Sam Quinn beat him up, like it was a playground scuffle. But that is not what Alice saw. She saw Sam Quinn's demon heart, small and violent. She saw him climb on top of Jesse and hit him over and over with a rage you save for someone you'd like to wipe from the face of the earth. She saw Tooly Quinn laugh and slap his hand against the ground like this was a wrestling match, and then, when he realized his brother had no intention of stopping until Jesse was dead, he became distressed. "Whoa, whoa," he kept saying. "Take it easy, Sammy."

She saw Jim Harlan do nothing.

But as Alice describes to Jesse what happened, she must reveal that she, too, did nothing. There were three of them and one of her. What could she have done? She planted her fingers in the ground and gripped it like she would fly off into space. Your—BRO—ther—NEEDS—your—HELP. His blood on the ground like a whimper. His choking cough as it dripped down his throat.

Deep below them, the earth moaned and growled, like guts churning.

At first, Alice thought that only she had heard it, but from the way everyone froze, she could tell they all had, too. Sam Quinn lifted his head as if snapping out of a trance. He looked at the others. Their shocked faces. He looked at the blood on his knuckles. In that pause, Jesse squirmed out from under him, staggered to his feet, and fled through the trees. Sam chased him, followed by Tooly, Harlan, Alice.

The sound got louder. All that earth and water moving; all those bugs and tree roots tearing through the dirt, as if the plants and animals were in on it, trembling with the same frequency. She remembers standing in the shadows of trees at the edge of the road, watching Sam and Tooly and Harlan stumble out onto the pavement into the moonlight.

"Th'fuck is that?" Tooly asked. "An earthquake?"

"There he is," said Sam, pointing down the road. He pulled up the back of his shirt and put his hand on the gun in his waistband.

"Wait," Harlan said, grabbing his arm. "Please."

"He'll tell."

"No, he won't, he won't; I promise."

Sam jerked away and shook a finger in Harlan's face.

"What'd I tell you, Jim," he said quietly. "I told you, in sixth grade, if you were gonna be a faggot you at least had to be a man."

Then he took off. Alice edged out from her hiding spot by the road, trying to see Jesse. But she could see only Sam in pursuit.

Your—BRO—ther—

That was when it happened, faster and quieter than you'd think. Alice recalls a swampy smell, the earth shuddering, the snap of the ground and a watery breath gasping out. First Sam was there, and then he wasn't, and where he'd been was a wide, black hole in the middle of the road. He slipped away with barely a scream, as if folded into cotton. And how quiet everything was then! Like even the woods stopped breathing.

Cataclysm. Revolution. **Claw hammer fire mud rabbit.** Literally: sinkhole.

She tried to follow Jesse after that, but he was long gone, and she ended up sitting alone on a curb in a winding suburb, waiting for Hupp to find her, looping and unlooping Jesse's hair around her finger. She'd left Tooly and Harlan to fish Sam out of that hole. She didn't know then how badly he was hurt; in fact, she thought it was funny. Served him right. But when she found out he had died, she got scared. She thought maybe *she'd* done it, that she was meant to be Jesse's protector, that this was what her mother's power had led her to. Now, though? Now her brother has scried Connie's final message. His mother. Swamp witch. Time traveler.

Turns out, the sinkhole was her doing all along.

* * *

In the moonshine shack, Jesse imagines his mother. Not dead, but alive with power, stuck outside time to an excruciating degree. Connie knew what was going to happen, knew that he would one day need that sinkhole. As Nancy said, she kept him with her to the end. She gave up her life to seed a trap that wouldn't spring for fifteen years.

Even knowing this, he's still not satisfied. What if she'd been here instead? What if she hadn't done that spell but had simply stayed? Maybe he wouldn't have been in Pinewood, because his life would've been happier, more complete, with a mother. But then, maybe Connie couldn't see herself as a mother—couldn't see her own future at all. She seeded that sinkhole because she knew it was going to happen. She died because she knew she was going to die.

"What are you thinking?" Alice asks, studying his face.

He doesn't want to tell her.

"I'm thinking," he says, "it makes sense now why Jimmy was so scared of me."

She folds her legs under her chin, contemplating. "Don't you want to settle the score with him? He let you down. He practically asked Sam to do it. I saw his face."

"No." He shakes his head. "That's not true."

"Why are you still defending him? If it were me, I'd want him to be terrified his whole pathetic life, him and Tooly Quinn, everyone in Pinewood, everyone in South Greene. I'd become a ghost and stalk them. I'd scare them to death."

"It wasn't Tooly's fault," Jesse says. "I don't even think it was *Sam's* fault; it's just—there was nothing going on with Tooly. It was a misunderstanding."

"But it shouldn't have *mattered*. What Sam did was evil; I saw it."

Alice states her beliefs with a fierce confidence Jesse could never imagine.

"I didn't come here to make trouble for Jimmy," he says quietly.

"What'd you come here for, then?" she asks. "You must be angry at someone. Otherwise, you wouldn't be here." She leans in close to him, her hair thick with the smell of the swamp. "What kind of trouble do you want to make, Jesse?"

Alice is right that he's angry. At Harlan. At this town. But he's not as angry as she is. Her rage is like an additional person in the moonshine shack, taking shape, becoming solid. It emits heat and makes his wrist throb. As he watches, her rage takes the shape of Connie Calloway, and for a moment, Alice and Connie become indistinguishable, same face, same big dark eyes and toothy grin, and he knows that he *is* meeting his mother, or a bit of her vengeful spirit, at least, passed down through Alice in some incomprehensible way. It scares him. He doesn't know what will happen if he helps her. If he can help her. But if he lets her proceed alone, he can't shake the thought that she'll die just like Connie did. And possibly take half the county out with her.

Ink boat. Help. **Blood river.** Connect. **Iris crown.**

"I want to help you," he tells her. "I'll make whatever helps you."

The storm clouds move inland, sweeping their steam and heat along with them. By the time Jesse and Alice leave the shack, the sky is lavender, and a bluish mist hangs over the water. What a sight they'd be to a boat going by: two thin, bow-backed swamp creatures, so muddy and tattered they look mummified. She hauls her bag over her shoulder; he drags the sodden army blanket with one hand, the bottle of wine in the other. Jesse drinks from the wine and passes it to Alice, who also drinks. They both stare at the strip of muddy bank with determination, then drop their things where they stand.

Once the sticks are back in the ground, they work through the dusk and into the night, building their spells. The mist dissipates. The stars come out to reflect on the river. They make careful choices about how to represent what they want to say. Jesse takes the paring knife, some torn paper, some knotted thread, the cockle shell, Alice's mango pit, and a piece of the army blanket. Alice takes the vinegar, the snakeskin, the soiled bra, the glass bowl, the mirror, the leftover beet chips, a clump of sphagnum moss, hemlock flower, and milkweed fluff. The two of them share the poison ivy, the salt, the clay, the pig bones, and a tangle of briars.

They take turns drinking the rest of the wine. When they're done, Jesse takes the wine bottle.

At some point between the last light of day and the full dark of night, a change takes place on the river. It starts as a glow, small and glinting, like the will-o'-the-wisps Jesse used to hear stories about. Then the air grows brighter and slurries about in streaks of color—blue and violet and pollenous yellow-green. He sees ghosts in it, crisscrossing the water. Then he notices Alice, standing stiffly at the river's edge.

"Boats," she says.

Many boats. He and Alice are working under the stars by now, and the glow on the river is bright enough that they don't need Alice's flashlight. They can see the boats clearly, every watercraft that has come and gone through this channel across time: kayaks, speedboats, pontoon boats, dredgers, paddleboards, and canoes; boats trailing the stink of caught fish and cigar smoke; boats laying mines; boats carrying, searching for, and returning enslaved people to plantations; boats transporting convicts, grifters, soldiers, preachers, cotton, tobacco, barrels of turpentine and tar. They see moonshiners shove off from the bank, their raft loaded down with alcohol disguised inside feed sacks. They see young men and women row up in dories, clothed in ghostly white, baptizing themselves in the shallows. The lines of these craft trace through the water, one line on top of another, on top of another, until the whole river looks like lace.

Jesse and Alice stand next to each other and watch.

After a silence, Alice asks, "What's happening?"

"I'm not sure," he says. "This is like what happened inside the Night House."

Alice starts to tremble. "I'm not scared," she insists, but she looks over her shoulder at their sticks like they might explode. He reaches out and takes her hand, and she relaxes a little in his grip. In the sky, the shape of the river has reappeared in full—a rift so bright it appears crystallized, its stars purple-blue, clustered like fruit seeds—and as he stares into it, the riverbank seems to tip under his feet. He holds on to Alice, and their message radiates out from behind them. The rift in the sky radiates back.

It makes a sound

A howl. A moan. Like a ship's iron hull opening up, air rushing out, water surging in—

whOOOMMwhOOOMMwhOOOMM

What is it saying to them?

Maybe Alice knows—she has that magic ear.

But her attention is elsewhere. Downriver. There, a dim shape heads toward them, its outline fuzzy in the light. The sky's brightness creates an odd effect: distant objects appear flat, pale paper cut-outs. It takes Jesse a while to see that the shape is another boat. Not a ghost, but a real and present boat, puttering toward them. A man shouts at them: "Hey! We see y'all!"

The we is two people: Harlan and his Uncle Laughton.

Alice grabs Jesse's arm. The boat's motor picks up again, distorting the sky's watery reflection. Harlan sits at the bow, Laughton at the stern. The barrels of their rifles poke up behind their shoulders.

"We see y'all!" Laughton shouts again. "Don't move!"

Alice runs to their sticks, arms out, like she's about to sweep the whole tangle into her bag. Jesse screams at her, surprising himself with the force of his voice: "*Don't touch anything.* Just run."

He picks up her bag and shoves it into her arms, but she won't run until he does. Is he thinking he'll stay behind and have a chat, like Laughton will be satisfied with an explanation, like Harlan won't look at him in horror? The rifles make him nervous; it wasn't necessary to bring rifles. Why bring rifles if you don't plan on shooting something?

They flee up the sandy path together, past the moonshine shack, across the clearing to the dense woods on the other side. They move arduously, as if in a dream. The pigs, sensing their alarm, leap out of the grass and scuttle into the dark. Or maybe they see the two men coming up from the river in pursuit.

A shot goes off. A pine branch explodes overhead. Alice

screams and sinks into the underbrush. Jesse dives, too, landing on his fractured wrist.

White flashes. Time skips.

When he opens his eyes again, he's on the ground, curled around his arm. Laughton stands over him, the rifle trained on his ear.

"Stand up," he says. "Slow."

He obeys. Some yards away, Alice is shrieking. He sees her through the pines, beating at Harlan with her bag, but Harlan grabs the bag and wrenches it away and shakes her by the arm. Alice makes eye contact with Jesse, like she thinks he has a plan.

"Get both arms, Jim," Laughton says. "You're making it too easy for her."

"I got it," says Harlan.

He shunts Alice along, placing her beside Jesse. Now they stand as a pair, on display. Harlan shines a small flashlight in their faces.

"Their eyes," he says.

"Jee-sus Lord," says Laughton.

Harlan takes a step back. A purple mark checks his forehead where Alice hit him with the bag, the corner of a buckle or something.

"I almost didn't believe you," says Laughton. "But here we are."

Harlan doesn't reply. Laughton tips the rifle back and forth between Jesse and Alice, then gestures behind him, toward the riverbank.

"Go on," he says. "Back to the boat."

They walk slowly, Laughton pointing his rifle. The air is bright and shimmering. Still, Harlan lights the path with a flashlight. He and Laughton don't see the brightness. Jesse and Alice exchange looks, but every time they do, Laughton sucks his teeth. After the third or fourth time, he snaps at them— "Keep moving"—though they haven't stopped.

When the four of them reach the sticks, they do stop. Harlan shoulders his rifle to check his phone.

"No signal," he says. "I'm trying to call Hupp, but it won't go through."

"Mm-hmm," says Laughton.

Harlan circles the sticks and looks up at his uncle with a lost expression. "Should I take pictures?"

"If you think you should."

Harlan crouches in front of Jesse's assemblage. His horrified look stings. Not that Jesse thought Harlan would understand, but there's no need to act so shocked. Beside him, he can feel Alice rage at the invasiveness of the picture-taking.

"Jimmy," Jesse says quietly, partly to diffuse her. "Don't touch anything."

Harlan looks up as if he's shocked Jesse can still speak. Laughton sucks his teeth again and steps into Jesse's periphery.

"You," he says, pointing the tip of his rifle at Alice. "You're just plain crazy. That's your excuse. But you"—he points to Jesse—"I can't figure it. Something's just wrong with you."

"Uncle Lot," Harlan says. His tone is close to chiding. His uncle turns and frowns. "There's no need to ..."

"Just take your pictures and hush."

Harlan continues, shining his flashlight on each cluster of objects, getting pictures from different angles. Now it truly does feel invasive, Harlan staring with wonder at the freakishness of it all. Jesse closes his eyes. Sparks play behind his eyelids. Then: a touch. Alice slips her hand into his.

"They got bones here," Harlan says.

"*Bones?*" says Laughton loudly. "What kinda bones?"

"Ribs, some teeth. Hog bones, I think."

"Why they got bones in there?"

"I don't know, Uncle Lot."

Alice squeezes Jesse's hand. When he opens his eyes, he sees the Night House. Its peeling wallpaper boxes them in. An alligator slides across the green tile floor of the foyer and pins Jesse with its gaze. Jesse looks at Alice—can she see it, too?—but she's watching Harlan. When Jesse looks back, the gator is gone.

"Oh, shit," Harlan says, pushing back a briar with the edge of his phone.

"What?" says Laughton.

"It's a gun."

"Where? Show me."

Harlan steps back and points into a glass bowl. Laughton approaches, his short neck craned. This is the first Jesse has been made aware of a gun; Alice placed it there without telling him. He looks to her for an explanation, but she seems neither forthcoming nor contrite. Only angry.

"It's under the mud and thorns there," Harlan says. "See it?"

Laughton shoulders his rifle and whips a bandanna out of his pocket. He brushes the mud away.

"You shouldn't touch it," Harlan says. "This is, like, a crime scene."

His uncle ignores him. After a few confounding minutes, he declares, "Smith & Wesson. M1917 revolver. Army issued."

"An antique," observes Harlan.

Laughton shakes his head, as if identifying the gun has not satisfied him. Has only frustrated him further.

"Why?" he says. "Jeee-sus."

"I don't know, Uncle Lot."

"Goddamn it, Jim, I know *you* don't know."

"Jimmy," Jesse says again. "Don't touch anything."

Harlan hangs attentively at his uncle's shoulder. Laughton is still brooding over the gun, as if he's working out how to account for its presence here.

"This is from Dodd's stall," he says after a silence (though there is no real silence, with the sky overhead going **whOOOMMwhOOOMMwhOOOMM**).

"At the flea market?" Harlan says with wonder. "You sure?"

"I remember the girl's daddy coming in and buying it, paid twice what it was worth. Not just guns, though, he'd buy anything—chick crates, broken gi-tars..."

Laughton trails off. The gun disturbs him. It disturbs Jesse, too, though he assumes not for the same reasons. Eventually, Laughton scoops the gun into his hand and removes it from the bowl.

"Why?" He turns to Jesse and Alice. "What does this mean?"

They look at each other. Jesse waits to see what Alice will say.

"Verb," she whispers.

"What?" says Laughton.

"Mud pistol," she says, a little louder. "It's a verb. To hunt."

Laughton blinks at her, the gun hanging in his hand, swaddled in the bandanna.

"What?"

"It's a verb," says Jesse, backing Alice up.

"I will thrash both of y'all if I don't hear something that makes sense. Next thing that comes out your mouth better—"

"All right now," says Harlan. "Let's calm down."

"Don't scold me, Jim. I'll be calm when I'm dead." Laughton holds up the gun. "What does this *mean?*"

Alice tightens her grip on Jesse's hand, each finger hot as a live wire. He'll take her side over Laughton's for sure, but even if he could answer this question, he doesn't know how. What does Laughton *mean* "What does this mean"? Is it somehow significant that a gun he recognizes has ended up on this bank? Does he think that implicates him? A piece of Pinewood floated across the river and returned, and that *means* something, but Jesse doesn't know what.

"It's part of a verb," he says again. "To hunt. We told you."

Laughton's face crackles, livid in the electric blue light. He stows the revolver in his pocket and resumes position with his rifle.

"Don't," Harlan says. "They're high. They're just a couple of kids."

"They ain't kids," Laughton says.

"You said you wouldn't—"

Harlan reaches for his uncle's arm, but Laughton shoves him away. Harlan stumbles backward. Then he looks at Jesse head-on for the first time, and it's not unlike the pleading look Jesse imagines he gave to Sam in the woods that night. *But what can I do?* he thinks. *Your uncle has me at gunpoint. I can't help you.*

Laughton sees it, this eye contact. His nephew's face pinched with doubt.

"What!" he shouts. "What's that look for? This was your idea, Jim, weren't it, coming out here to find 'em?"

Harlan trains his eyes to the ground.

For a moment, Laughton seems almost embarrassed—of Harlan or of his own outburst, Jesse can't tell. He lowers his rifle and turns back to the sticks, gently ushering Harlan aside with a touch to the shoulder.

"All right, fine," he says. "Fine."

He takes a long, weary breath. Then he grabs Alice's stick and wrenches it from the ground. Poison ivy uncoils and breaks. Mud scatters. Laughton javelins the stick into the river with the precision of a former athlete. Then he destroys the other stick, ripping up the spine of Jesse's sentence and throwing it in the water. He jumbles their materials underfoot, crushing the cockle shell, the mirror, wedging the pig bones into the sand, an awkward dance, a gym class shuffle. He doesn't move particularly fast. He treats the whole thing like a job. When all the crushable items are crushed, he begins picking up things and hurling them into the river. There goes the wine bottle, the mango pit, the bra, the snakeskin. Meanwhile, Harlan watches on with his shaggy, conflicted face; neither he nor Jesse holds any illusions that they could stop Laughton, so they let the damage run its course.

But Alice is shaking. Jesse holds her arm to calm her, but he feels her splitting off from him, pulled out, spaghettified. She's on the riverbank, and in South Greene, and in the Night House, and in the woods by the cemetery, watching the truck

burn and watching Jesse get the shit beat out of him. Your—
BRO—ther—NEEDS—your—HELP. No, it's all right. You
did what you could. It'll be fine. Your—BRO—ther—NEEDS—

Either way, time is splitting for them both. Jesse, too, is in the
Night House and in the woods by the cemetery. This moment
next to Alice on the riverbank, like every other moment, will
take forever. Alice will always be raging. Harlan will always
be standing there, doing nothing. Laughton will always be
shaking off the piece of snakeskin stuck to his hand, sending
it delicately into the water, where it floats away. For a long time
after, he stands there catching his breath, a wave sloshing over
his boots.

Then there's the gator.

Jesse doesn't know who sees it first. Maybe he does, maybe
Alice or Harlan. Undoubtedly, Laughton sees it last, its
armored snout and marbly green eyes floating toward him in
the shallows. The gator can see the rift, you can tell from the
way its second eyelids blink against the brightness. A ten-foot
body surfaces. A monster.

Harlan shouts a warning, but it's too late. The gator shoots
from the water, teeth in the air, teeth in the flesh of Laughton's
right calf. Harlan runs toward him. The sky flashes, lighting up
the river: a whole host of gators, thrashing the water to froth.
When Jesse and Alice run for Laughton's boat to escape, they
find it surrounded by tails and teeth.

11

The gator can see the rift, but whether she feels its effect is hard to know. Animals might not understand time the way people do, so who's to say if a gator doesn't experience her life all at once anyway. Every moment, she cracks her egg into a nest of thirty wriggling brothers and sisters, competes for dinner and hiding spaces, chomps down on Laughton's leg, hears the pop of Harlan's rifle and feels a bullet wedge into her snout. She wouldn't be able to explain to anyone what this feels like. Her language breaks down to hungry and satisfied, pain and no pain, bones breaking and blood in the water.

At the hospital, two days before, Hupp interviews Jesse in the conference room, her little golf pencil scratching across her notepad. "Where is Alice Catherine now?" she asks. He doesn't know. That's what he tells her.

The gators thrash in the river, whipping up foam, a haze of fishy gator smell. Laughton curses the one that has his leg. He curses all gators everywhere. Harlan relays instructions to him: fight, twist, kick, go limp. He gets a shot in—*POP.*

Jesse and Alice retreat from the boat, another gator jetting at them from the water. They run up the bank. The gator, having missed them, slinks back to its swarm. Jesse looks over his shoulder to see Harlan dragging his uncle by the armpits, up and away from the water's edge. Jesse sees what's going to happen to them. He reads the headline: MAN LOSES LEG IN GATOR MAULING. Not in the headline: Harlan gives up the duplex in Bittern's Rest to move in with Laughton. Many years from now, Jesse will try to explain Harlan to his future partner and find it impossible: He owned a guitar he never played; he said "fixing to" instead of "going to"; he made Jesse pancakes for breakfast that first time he stayed over at his house; his company jacket smelled like blood. He wasn't easily impressed, but when he liked you, when he gave you his sly look, you felt like he gave you a secret world.

Alice yanks on Jesse's shirtsleeve. "Come on," she says breathlessly, pulling him up the bank. But he's hesitating. He could stay behind and help Harlan. Maybe if he does, Laughton won't lose the leg. But it's already happened: Laughton *does* lose his leg, and Jesse would rather follow Alice, away from the gore on the bank and into the dense, bright woods.

Overhead, the sky splits, the lip of the opening bubbling up like a blister. Inside, the rift is filled to bursting with bright blue stars.

Hupp interviews him in the hospital conference room two days before. He tells her he doesn't know where Alice is, and she shows him the messages on his phone.

"What is this," she says. "Explain."

Two days before? No, he has it wrong. This is a different moment, a future moment, after they find him on that bank. The whole room smells like swamp and body odor. Jesse's wrist is a thick, itchy knot of pain. He's all bug bites and poison ivy rash, and his stomach is cramping. That fungus Alice gave him…

"Translate this for me," Hupp insists, tapping his screen.

He looks at the messages, but he's too shaken to make sense of them. He'll discover later that this shakiness doesn't go away. Something on that riverbank broke his thoughtless, easy ability to read his mother's language. From now on, he'll have to pick through it slowly, tediously, the way Alice did.

"You have the glossary," he tells Hupp. "It'll clear up everything."

Hupp will keep Connie's glossary for two years before she gives it back to him, along with Katrina's notebooks, which contain a version of his mother that is clearer, sharper, more frustrating, than any he has known before. At that point, he and Hupp will have achieved an uneasy truce with each other.

For now, though, Hupp is "bad cop." She tells Jesse he could face jail time for the stunt with the car, property damage, resisting arrest; she could pile it on if he doesn't cooperate.

"I don't think you're nearly as confused as you say about what happened," Hupp says with disdain. "I think you're fighting me. All I ever wanted to do is help you, and you've fought me at every turn. Nothing's changed."

Jesse plays the sullen role he's bound to play in this interview, but he also knows something else: The Marty Hupp sitting across from him has an aggressive cancer—a fact she has shared only with her husband and Nancy. Some years from now, Jesse will come back to town to attend Hupp's funeral, noticing how her three adult children side-eye Nancy, but the husband greets her with stoic respect, as one would a minister or a masseuse. Did they have an agreement, Marty and her husband? It's a mystery Jesse will never solve, and his aunt is right that she deserves her private life, just as he deserves his. Eventually, Nancy will move to Greensboro, where her old friend Minerva is eager to rekindle their unrequited flame from grad school, and where Jesse, while happy for Nancy, must decide whether he wants to live in the same city as her, seeing her out with Minerva at breweries and organic grocery stores, while his own love life spins its wheels.

How can Jesse know all this? How he can be in the swamp with Alice and also in the interview room with Hupp, or spying Nancy and Minerva at a brewery in Greensboro? Regardless of what their spells ultimately said, he and Alice must have split the rift open so wide they're now tumbling through time, through their lives in Miskwa and beyond. Past and future splay before him like a deck of cards. Memories flicking by, one and one and one. He sees himself going home to Nancy, recovering his wits, moving on.

But he can't see Alice anywhere but the riverbank.

"Did you see Alice Catherine get in the water," Hupp asks.

"No," Jesse says. "I lost sight of her."

"When. How."

He shakes his head. "I lost her."

His wrist will ache all year, long after the brace comes off. After that, it twinges before thunderstorms.

* * *

One and one and one.

A plastic Maltese falcon. The burn of whiskey. A cigarette, tucked behind his ear, and a trench coat that almost drags the ground. A potent concoction in a flask that tastes like Skittles. Morgan's whispered dream-voice: *You felt a real connection.*

Six years later, he's sitting with Morgan on the gazebo steps in Spartina Square. It's July, maybe August. The wind coming off the water is hot. Morgan's hair is dyed pink.

"I'm fine if we don't talk about it," she says.

In the woods, the light flattens out what they can see. Shadows turn neon. The shapes of the trees lose their boundaries. Jesse and Alice go deeper into the brush, through switches and briars, but she keeps him from slowing down. She still has hold of his shirtsleeve, tugging him along like a child.

Does she know where she's going?

For a while, she moves like she has a place in mind, but then she stops, scrabbles one way through the underbrush, doubles back, goes the other way, stops again. He hears what he at first thinks is an animal, a whimpering pant, a trapped sound—but it's Alice, breathing ragefully through her teeth.

"Alice," he says. "Wait."

She ignores him, plowing forward. Up ahead, a bulwark of dense growth separates them from a row of pines. Beyond that is the spot where the rift meets the horizon. It's still bulging, filling up with stars so thick it looks like it could burst and spill its contents to the earth. Alice heads for the pines. She shoves the branches of a myrtle tree aside, but an explosion of sharp wings forces her back. Swallows, hundreds of them, burst out, squeaking around them in a cyclone of beaks and scissor tails. Alice yanks Jesse close to her. Jesse covers them both with his arms. The swallows continue to circle them, their beaks and wingtips needling their faces. Then, without cause or warning, they rise and spin off across the trees. In the rift's searing light, the flock disintegrates.

Alice doesn't let go of him. She presses her face into his shirt and screams.

In Spartina Square, Jesse wears the black shirt and tie he wore to Hupp's funeral. Morgan is in town for a family reunion. They sit and watch a little boy of about four run back and forth from the gazebo steps to the edge of the oyster shell parking lot.

"Is he yours?" Jesse asks.

"Ha!" Morgan says. "No, that's my nephew. The reunion was so claustrophobic. Nobody masking. So I said, 'Hey, how 'bout I take Jackson for some park time?' My sister looked at me like I was Gabriel the archangel, descended from heaven." She calls to the boy across the lawn: "Hey, Jack-Attack, how high can you count? Can you go run around that tree *one hundred times*?" and then he's off, panting and red-faced.

"It's the only way we can get him to sleep at night," Morgan says. "Take him out to a field and let him loose."

Jesse is both watching and participating in this future memory. His polyester shirt is hot against his skin; Morgan's perfume smells like citrus. He already has a sense of how this is going to play out, what he's going to say. He doesn't consider saying anything different than he otherwise would.

Why would he? This is the first time he's seen Morgan in person since watching her disappear into Brooke Barnes's house in South Greene. It's awkward as fuck and he can't control that. Conversation comes in short spells with long silences. She offers perfunctory condolences about Hupp. Then she tells him things he already knows from following her socials: She works at a nonprofit; she's dating a Bengali man named Dev; they live together and own a rescue; they're vegetarians. Jesse also knows they're going to get married. Would it come across as combative if he asked whether her parents approve? He recalls that he and Morgan are sitting at the same gazebo where she slid his hand under her sweater during the live nativity eight years before. He can feel his hand there now and blushes.

"Did you get my mix CD?" he asks. "And the card?"

"The what?" she says. "Oh. You sent... oh, yeah, thank you."

The wind tugs wisps of pink hair out of Morgan's ponytail. He watches them, fixated. Is he expecting to see a scar? Does she feel him looking for it? Is that why she says what she says, plainly, without any urgency or fear or defensiveness? "I'm fine if we don't talk about it."

He's in the woods, by the river, in his car, Dick, the old hatchback parked at the waterfront. His head is between Morgan's thighs, but then she sees something pass by the window and screams. Jesse sees a figure under the shadow of an oak tree: a hunched and furious Alice, covered in swamp mud. She's watching them.

Then the four-year-old nephew scuttles across the lawn shrieking, "GIFTS! I'VE GOT GIFTS!" and dumps a handful of objects into Jesse's lap: a buckeye, a crumpled plastic cup, a cigarette butt, a pine needle.

"Whoa," Jesse says. "What amazing stuff."

"I found it on the ground," the nephew says proudly.

"Oh *gross*, Jackson," says Morgan. "You can't drop trash into people's laps." But her nephew is gone, sprinting back to the oak tree.

A quote from the Tao Te Ching, taped to his therapist's office door: *Do you have the patience to wait until your mud settles and the water is clear?*

Hupp has zero patience for any of this witchy mumbo jumbo. She thinks Alice gave Jesse his mother's lexicon that night they first met two years ago. To communicate in secret, Alice worked from her copies, Jesse from the original. She thinks it started as a game and became a shared delusion. Folie à deux. Alice started taking it too seriously. Jesse followed suit.

Hupp thinks the sinkhole that killed Sam Quinn was a freak accident. The Night House was just a house. Connie Calloway was simply crazy. Jesse was drugged. He hallucinated. She's convinced that Alice drowned herself and/or was eaten by alligators. When the swarm dissipates, divers will go out to the river and search the murky bottom.

Jesse has no idea what the rest of the county knows or doesn't know about what happened to him. He doesn't hang around to hear their theories. A year from now, when he comes back to town, he runs into Red Koonce stocking up for his house-sitting party at the grocery store, and Red, after an excitable bit ("Cal-loway! Do mine eyes deceive me, brother?"), invites him out like he has no idea anything happened at all. And sometimes that's how Jesse has to get by day to day: *as if* it never happened. Or *as if* it happened the way Marty Hupp thinks it did.

In the woods, Alice screams, then sucks in her breath to scream again. But Jesse hears someone moving in the brush behind them, and Harlan's voice calls out, "Kid, where'd you go?" He clamps his hand over Alice's mouth.

She sinks her teeth into one of his fingers.

Jesse leaps back, stunned. Alice doesn't scream, but the look she gives him is savage, and this is the first time he feels her rage directed at *him*. What did he do wrong? Hasn't he gone along with her at every turn?

"I know you're out here; quit playing," Harlan shouts into the woods.

Jesse rubs the purple indentations of Alice's teeth. His hands are so filthy he's left a smear of dirt on her face.

"Why did you do that?" he whispers.

"You could for real die out here, Jesse," calls Harlan. "You hear me?"

Alice bares her teeth, as if she would bite him again.

"A shared delusion?" she whispers. "You think it's not real?"

Oh. She can see that?

"No, no, no," he says. "I just have to *act* like it sometimes. Nobody would understand if I—"

"You're on *his* side. After everything. He lies, and you believe him."

He hesitates. Who is she talking about? Then he realizes that she can also see him returning to Miskwa County in a year's time. He'll talk to Mr. Swink in South Greene.

Behind them, a frustrated Harlan tears up a weed with a fleshy crunch, and he tramps back through the brush the way he came. Moments later, the drone of his uncle's johnboat ignites and fades upriver.

Jesse will never speak to Harlan again.

In a fantasy memory, however, they sit down to lunch at the Chuckwagon to hash things out. Jesse orders a Hangover Special. What does Harlan order? Let's say a grilled chicken sandwich. Is it petty to emasculate him with a diet? Jesse is in love again. The relationship is good. Harlan is happy for him.

Harlan then asks him what exactly he was trying to say with the sticks on the riverbank; it doesn't make sense that Harlan would ask that, but so what. It's Jesse's fantasy and he can make Harlan ask for whatever he wants. Jesse says he was asking for several things, some of them untranslatable. Peace and protection for Alice. Closure for himself. **Wool fruit briar**: closure. He wanted for everything in his life to come together and make sense so he could move on like Harlan always wanted. He didn't get that. He got alligators. Maybe when Laughton wrecked everything, that's the message he and Alice ended up sending to the buried place: Please send alligators. The whole thing was maybe a giant miscommunication.

Jesse then asks Harlan if he really did want Sam to attack him that night by the cemetery, if Alice was right when she read his pleading look as a request. Harlan says, "Come on, kid, it's *me*. You think I wanted you to get hurt? After everything?"

Harlan tells him what it was like being friends with someone like Sam Quinn, who would kill for you and despise what you are at the same time. No, it was more complicated than that. Two high school dropouts cruising the same high school hangouts, year after year. Some rules went unsaid. Pinewood is a strange place to be closeted. You can find love there—Sam loved Harlan in his way, just as Laughton did—though it's a difficult kind of love.

"But are you still cruising high school hangouts?" Jesse asks. "Is that how you do it? Your first guy, was that how he did it?"

Harlan's face is cryptic. "You think I singled you out? Like you were a pattern? You showed up at my place. You knew what you wanted."

"You're not answering the question."

"And my question to you is," Harlan says, "where will that get you? You'll never really know, and it'll only hurt you to dig deeper."

Jesse thinks about it. "That's wise, I guess."

"Man, I was always *wise*," says Harlan. "Your ass just never listened."

He laughs. Jesse laughs. This is the most productive conversation they've ever had.

The visit to Euel Swink is not a fantasy memory. That one actually happens. Jesse stands on the front porch in a button-up shirt, khakis, clean tennis shoes. He wants to look nice, wants to seem calm. (Shit, is he about to ask for money? How could that be what he wants, after everything?) In the woods, under the neon blaze of the sky, Alice beams out her fury. She's become a ghost, following him to every corner of Miskwa. **Mud pistol.** Hunt. **Moss thorn hemlock.** Memory sickness. She glares at him on Euel's front porch, but this time, he's the only one who can see her.

"Stop looking at me like that," he says. "You didn't think I'd go talk to him?"

"And what has he got for you?" she snaps. "Why do you need to hear his side?"

Well, here he is to find out. 403 Eden Circle, with its rose-brick facade and white columns. Old plantation vibe. What would it have been like to grow up with Alice in these big rooms filled with country chic furniture and taxidermy, a sunset view of the river from his bedroom window? And the charcuterie board Bobbie Swink brings him! You know it's fancy when there are fruits and meats you've never seen before on the charcuterie board.

"You look so thin," Mrs. Swink observes.

Jesse feels like he hasn't eaten in a year, not since goat cheese and artisan jerky with Alice.

"Eat, please!" she says, smiling.

"Yes, eat," says Euel Swink. "Bobbie's greatest ambition in the world is to fatten up a child."

They're in the sitting room. Mini bar, blue linen sofas, a wall of white shelves—no family pictures, only framed botanical prints and paintings of boats. A gorgeous harp sits in one corner, strings humming with every footstep. Bobbie Swink brings in another plate of food: shortbread cookies, candied figs, hummingbird cake. He would've thought she'd be hostile toward him as Euel's illegitimate child, but any rage she feels she expresses through hosting.

"'Fatten up a child,'" she says. "He says that like I'm the witch from 'Hansel and Gretel.'"

She stands awkwardly for a minute.

"Well, I'll let y'all get to..." she says, and leaves before finishing the sentence.

Get to: know each other. Get to: negotiating. Mr. Swink settles onto the couch across from him, fingers folded around a whiskey glass.

Like Jesse, he's small-framed and wiry. His voice has a similar cadence. Right now, he appears disheveled, his mustache frayed, his curly hair cowlicked.

"Cal-lo-way," he says. He repeats the name, as if testing the music of it. "Jesse Calloway. Glad to see you finally. In person."

Jesse nods with his mouth full.

"I guess I should've reached out sooner. It's been—well—a rough year, as you know."

God, he needs to be careful about how much he eats. He's so nervous! He doesn't feel fully here, like he still has one leg in the woods, like half his body is being bathed in radioactive heat. Ghost Alice watches, seethes.

"A rough year for sure," Jesse says.

Mr. Swink lifts up a hand and says, "But it might help me to know why you're stopping by. If it's money, honestly, I don't mind giving you money for school or..."

No, it's not about money. Money would be nice, but that's not his motivation. He thinks he might've come here to pick apart this man that Alice hated, but Swink has been open and frank, void of bitterness, uncomplicated about his grief. In the months leading up to this meeting, he has told Jesse that he doesn't blame him for anything. He can't imagine Jesse meant for anyone to get hurt; he was simply chasing Alice. And who wouldn't chase Alice? Who wouldn't want to solve that strange girl? Jesse has been on the lookout for Swink's insincerity, but he's instead picked up the vibe of someone like himself, with gestures that remind him of how he interacts with his friends.

Alice's rage thrums. Nancy's voice pops into his head: *I just want you to be careful.*

Maybe he's falling for Swink's charm, but what else can he do? Where else could he get his takes about Alice? He tried to reach out to the woman Alice shot, Mrs. Patton, who recovered and, shortly after, jetted off to Louisiana with her family. Jesse found her online a month ago, posting Bible verses and motivational quotes and pictures of her husband's patisseries. She is #2blessed2Bstressed. When he messaged her, she wrote back saying, *I know who you are and I'm sorry, but please do not contact me again. I do not want to talk about Alice Catherine.*

He only wishes he could make as clean a break.

"I guess," Swink says, rolling ice around in his glass. "Well, I don't reckon you could tell me any more about what happened out there. Besides what you already said."

"Oh," says Jesse. "No, I—"

"Right, right. No, you're wanting that from *me.*" He laughs. "I don't imagine we're fixing to go out in the yard and throw a ball around."

Jesse smiles. "Probably not."

Swink rises, refills at the minibar, and leads Jesse into a vast living room. Bay windows look out on the yard. The river shines pink with evening light. Alice's guesthouse stands silhouetted against it. Swink gets a paper bundle out of a big wooden chest: letters, pictures, old drawings Alice did in third grade, before she was homeschooled.

"I heard about the biting," Jesse says. He touches his finger where, moments ago, Alice's teeth sank in.

"Mmm," says Swink. "That's not why we pulled her out, though. I mean, that didn't help. But she wasn't fitting in. The other kids tormented her. And I couldn't prove it, but I think that damn teacher encouraged it, after the biting episode." He takes a long, contemplative sip of his drink. "Alice always had this intense personality. That's probably where her talent came from, you know, her musical talent. I kept thinking that intensity might wear out over time. Find an outlet. But as soon as I thought things were getting better, she'd go off again. I never learned."

Jesse nods slowly, examining Alice's childhood materials, the many drawings of cats.

"And her mom?" he asks.

"Right, Katrina." Swink directs Jesse to a slim stack of printed emails. Dear Euel. Dear Alice. "She left when Alice was eight. I might've misrepresented—I mean, I suggested to Alice that she left after I cut her a check, and I did. I gave her five thousand to find a place, settle down. She moved to this college town in the mountains. Set up a little store there for homeopathy or…plant therapy or something." He pulls up a website for Jesse on his phone. Here is a photo of an attractive woman at the grand opening, big bushy hair and airy clothes.

Here she is again in the orange light of a salt lamp, surrounded by air plants.

"Of course, Alice has seen all this," Swink says. "But she wouldn't believe it."

Jesse stares at the photos on the website. Katrina's face is rounder and softer than Alice's, but there's no denying this is her mother. Those same huge, dark witchy eyes.

"To be fair," Swink says, holding up his finger, "at this point, we don't know what happened to Katrina. Last few letters I sent got returned. Radio silence ever since. After Connie, after what happened to her—Katrina said she just couldn't find her happiness again. Told me if she stayed here, she thought this place would kill her. And, in the end, in exchange for a little help to move on, she left Alice with me."

As clean a break.

"Hey." Swink pats Jesse's shoulder. "I didn't offer you a drink. You want one?"

"Yes," he says. "Please."

They return to the sitting room. Swink pours Jesse a whiskey. Nice whiskey. Top-shelf. Jesse's therapist in Greensboro has suggested he abstain from drinking. One way to avoid impulsive choices is to avoid those situations where impulsive choices get made. One way to avoid any and all situations is to kill oneself, Jesse thinks, but you can't make jokes like that to therapists.

"Here's a theory," Swink says, settling back on the couch.

"Okay," Jesse says. "Let's hear it."

"I don't think Alice ever actually *wanted* to hurt me. I think the whole stabbing thing was about proving something to herself. That's why I wasn't mad, you see. In her mind, she needed to do something drastic. To *commit*. And when Alice heard your story, she clung to it, and she grafted *you* onto the story she wanted for herself. Connie and Katrina had me in common, that's a fact. Connie died. Katrina must've died, too. She couldn't resist connecting them."

He ruminates, smoothing an errant hair in his mustache. In the pause, Jesse speaks up:

"She told me it was like we had two mothers. Connie and Katrina were both our mothers."

Swink shakes his head. "Jesus. I mean—sorry, sure, all right—I understand. It's not even that crazy. Alice—that poor girl, she reminded me so much of Connie."

"How so?"

Swink has placed the whiskey decanter on the coffee table between them. He refills. "I don't know. Why the hell did I just say that?" He laughs. Another shake of the head. "I'm about to get myself in trouble."

"How did Alice remind you of my mother, Mr. Swink?"

"Euel," Swink says. "You don't have to with the—" He waves a hand. "You know what, kiddo, never mind. Call me what feels comfortable." He rubs his forehead. "Look, I don't know how in the weeds you want me to get with this. You might have a certain way of thinking about your mother. I don't want to mess with that."

"I'm fine with how I think about her. I want to know what you saw in her. Why did you choose her?"

Mr. Swink stares at Jesse, from his sneakered feet to his face. His eyes are an odd color, a dark slate blue. For the first time, they seem troubled.

"Well," he says. "She was young. Sharp. Kind of angry. Always seemed like she knew what she wanted. She didn't let folks in often, so when she did, you felt special. But she kept you guessing, you know. A real challenge." He sips his drink. "That didn't sound right. I don't mean that she was a conquest or—"

"No," Jesse says. "I didn't think—"

"What I *mean* is." He holds a long, whiskey-ish pause. "What I mean is, she was difficult to understand. She and Connie both—she and *Katrina*, I mean. They understood each other—at least, I think they did—but I was always on the outside with those two girls as close as they were. I was jealous of it. And it always felt lonely, me going downriver and—you know, feeling that place, those woods. And I'm not gonna press too hard about what you saw out there, if you saw anything. But I know what it feels like to *feel* like something's there that you can't see or understand. I've felt that. I—maybe—played around with a few things, even. I couldn't help it. With the harp—" He tilts back his head and groans. "That stupid harp. Sure, I had my little rituals with it, when she played, with the dinners, and folks coming over, and the seating arrangements. Everything was always so goddamn *nefarious* to Alice, but I didn't even know if it *worked*; it was superstition, like throwing salt over your shoulder. But I figured, hey, if there *is* something special about my girl's music, if it sways folks' minds, even just a little—can't hurt, right? And Katrina wanted to leave, she *told* me she did. Even if the music nudged her, it didn't put the idea in her head."

Jesse watches Swink carefully, his glass condensing in his hand. When he takes a sip, a little fire ignites on his tongue. The house at 403 Eden Circle is alive, humming, haunted.

"Why'd I choose Connie, though." Swink grins and sweeps out his arms. Whiskey spills on the sofa. "Why'd I choose her! Ha! Why not ask why she chose *me*? She was the one in the driver's seat. She was getting all the perks. But Katrina had someone and she didn't like that, so maybe it didn't have a thing to do with me at all. And let me tell you, I was an easy target back then, barely conscious of what I picked for dinner, much less who I *loved*, and *why*. And I *did* love those girls, those women. Wholly, honestly. I'd have done anything for them. I was *obsessed* with them. You understand what I'm saying, don't you?"

"Of course," says Jesse calmly. "I think that's something I might've inherited from you."

"Oh—ha ha! You think so?"

"I've been in my share of trouble."

"Sincere apologies. My troublesome genes at work."

Swink reaches across the coffee table and clinks Jesse's glass against his own. Jesse feels Alice's ghost rage through the house, her scream in his ears, her teeth chomping down on his finger.

Back in the swamp, he whispers forcefully to her, "Stop being so angry! He's not going to be in my life."

Which is nothing new. It's hard to believe that Swink never suspected Connie's baby was his, or that it never occurred to him that he should reach out and help her. Maybe Katrina stopped him; it could've been around the same time she blacked out Connie's name in all her notebooks. Or maybe Swink had some tenuous deals to consider, and a scandal was bad for business. Or maybe, as is the case with infants, people cease to exist when they're not in Swink's line of sight.

"He's just selfish, Alice. He doesn't see who he hurts because he doesn't think about it."

But Alice won't be consoled. In the kitchen at 403 Eden Circle, a cabinet flies open, and a punch bowl shatters on the floor. Bobbie screams.

Swink, irritated, calls toward the kitchen: "Everything okay? What happened?"

Bobbie laughs and shouts back: "Nothing, nothing!"

Jesse laughs, too. For the first time, Swink gives him a suspicious look, like he's starting to see that Jesse is withholding something.

"Anything else you want me to say, kiddo? I know it's been a year, but I'm still a little, you know—" He shakes the ice in his glass. "Addled."

"No," Jesse says. "I don't think I need anything."

"But you're here!" Swink's laugh is strained. "Here you are. It's super."

Then, after a pause, Jesse says, "Actually, I do have one question."

"Yeah, okay," Swink says tiredly.

"Have you by any chance been seeing Alice around?"

Swink stares at him, blinking. Jesse is starting to think Alice is pretty good at being a ghost. He recalls Tooly's terrified face in Red's living room, the way he stared past Jesse's shoulder at nothing. How Harlan did the same thing in the Night House. That was Alice, then and now, haunting them just like she said she would.

"In the house, you mean?" Swink asks.

"I didn't say in the house, but sure. In the house. Or anywhere, really."

Swink looks unnerved. "Well, like I said, we're a little addled. Regrets, mistakes—that's what they do, isn't it? They chase you around."

He stares morosely into his whiskey glass.

"Hey!" he says, suddenly brightening. "You wouldn't be interested in a harp, would you?"

"The—?" Jesse points toward the sitting room. "The one in there?"

"It's a nice harp. Paid a good bit of money for it."

Jesse goes to the doorway. The harp sits grandly in the sitting room, its strings humming. "I don't think that'll fit in my car."

Swink waves his hand. "I'll have it delivered to your aunt's place. She could learn to play it. Or you could. Or something."

In a week or so, Nancy will go out to get the mail and find the harp on the front porch, wrapped in packing foam. "What the fuck am I supposed to do with this?" she'll call him to ask. From how eager Swink was to get rid of it, they assume the harp must've been playing by itself, but it never gives them any trouble.

This is the only thing Jesse ever takes from his father. Some years later, his partner will end up in the hospital following a bike accident; a series of surprise medical expenses will put them behind on rent. Jesse considers contacting Swink to ask for money that's rightfully his, but he'll come to realize that his pride is too great and his loyalty to Alice too strong. Turns out you can sell a used lever harp online for about nine hundred dollars.

Then Jesse will hear pieces of things from out of Blacknot, about Tarbarrel expanding or about Bobbie filing for divorce and Swink marrying someone else, some young, smart girl who worked for him, and occasionally he and Nancy will talk about it, and he'll wonder how many other half-sibs he's got out there, and Nancy will sip her tea wisely and say, "You're better off without him, sweetheart." A few years after that, Jesse will hear from Nancy that Swink, at seventy-three, had a heart attack and died in bed next to his wife and two small dogs, and this will cause Jesse some concern. He'll get back into running, become more mindful about what he eats—no more greasy diner food, less alcohol, less salt, cake but no ice cream at his niece's second birthday. Really, he won't think much about Swink otherwise, because there was never much to think about to begin with.

Swink's wife has a hard time selling the house.

Everyone knows it's haunted as fuck.

Alice haunts every corner of Miskwa.

In Red Koonce's kitchen.

At the edge of the road on Peach Hill.

On the stairs in the Night House.

At the waterfront under the oak tree, when Jesse is going down on Morgan.

At her father's house.

She hunches her shoulders, bares her teeth, a dirty swamp creature that howls and snarls without making a sound.

For years after Jesse's visit, she terrorizes poor Bobbie, banging doors, flinging things from shelves, shattering dishware. By contrast, Euel is frustratingly hard to scare, though he's clearly exhausted by her efforts. "Morning, Alice," to the mirror, trimming his mustache. "Nice work, honey," to the air, pouring a drink in his office. "You always had a tough time as a person," he says bitterly. "Glad you're having more fun as a ghost."

Meanwhile.

The rift swells with brightness. It splits so wide that a piece of the sky peels away and comes down like a curtain. Jesse, who always sensed that the sky in Miskwa County was closer to the ground than in other places, feels vindicated. Here it comes! It booms over the pines and the scrubby pocosin swamps, shaking birds from the trees. Voles and field mice flee over their feet. A ring of hot wind blasts them with leaves and briars. Alice covers her eyes. Jesse wraps his arm around her shoulders.

Afterward, the woods go dead quiet. He relaxes his grip. Alice takes her hand down from her eyes. Her face is wet with tears. When did she begin crying? He wants to comfort her, but she's looking past him, past the bulwark of underbrush and the pine grove, to the flap of sky that hangs like a veil, breathing lightly, a row of shimmery trees visible behind it. Her rage eases. Across time and space, so do her hauntings.

Mrs. Swink will send Jesse a birthday card and a Christmas card every year with a brand-new fifty-dollar bill, never with any message or explanation besides generic well-wishing and a signing of her full name: Roberta Marian Calhoun Swink. Even after the divorce she sends the cards, until he moves to a new city with his partner and forgets to send her the address.

He feels the weight of each card in his hand, smells each crisp bill.

At college, he treats the crew to diner lunches—chicken-fried steak, mac-and-cheese casserole, stacked chocolate pies. He jokes about having a secret lover who's loaded, but the meals are cheap, and he breaks about even every time. All he wants to do is thank them for being his friends.

Nearly three years after Nancy shakes his shoulders in the dorm parking lot and calls him a survivor, they sit and talk at a coffee shop in Greensboro.

"Before she died, I used to watch you," she's saying. "More and more toward the end, but I didn't mind it. You were an easy baby. So happy and easy."

Jesse sits across from her in his apron, listening. Technically, he's on the clock, but it's a slow day, a dead, dry summer. The coffee shop is nearly empty.

"One time—" Nancy's voice becomes halting. "One time, Con looked me straight in the eye and said, *If I were gone, and you were raising him, would you just tell him that you're his mother?*"

"What did you say?" Jesse asks.

"What do you think I said? I said no, I'd raise you, of course, but I would never be your mother. At the time, I thought she was baiting me. That she was jealous we were so attached. But then, when I found out she'd destroyed all those pictures of the two of you, I realized it was a sincere request. My sister—underneath it all, she had no faith. She never felt like she belonged."

"In Blacknot?"

"In Blacknot." Nancy shrugs. "On this planet."

She still hates talking about these things, and he still feels guilty when he prods her.

"No, that's not fair, she did have faith in something. I looked in her notebooks a couple times—pretty overwhelming. So maybe she really was in tune with it. Some force not of this world."

That night, when he goes back to his apartment, he smokes a vape pen on his porch, counts the beads on Connie's bracelet, one, two, three. Sometimes, the bracelet is a comfort, and sometimes he wishes he could throw it away. His eventual aging and death, even in the timeless space of the buried place, is a distant, hazy obscurity, but the idea that he would carry around this object until he dies makes him feel heavy, as if a tiny black hole sits in his pocket.

Hupp will determine that Alice is dead, that she most likely drowned in the river. But Jesse doesn't see Alice go in the river. He sees her enter the buried place, through that veil of fallen sky.

He follows her part of the way, through the thick brush and into the pines, and she turns around and pins him with a look like she's puzzled by what he's doing. They already know he doesn't come with her, and he doesn't convince her to go back.

"I'm sorry I bit you," she says after a pause.

He laughs. "No worries. Are you still mad?"

"No, not right now." She turns away, a hook of hair stuck to her sweaty cheek. "Maybe a little."

A breeze provokes the stillness, carrying with it the smell of hog farm and river stink and the electric heat of storm clouds, the landscape speaking. It lifts Jesse's hair off his sweaty forehead and teases what's left of Alice's skirt, and it makes the veil of sky breathe in and out. Alice watches the horizon intently.

"What if my mother's in there," she says, uncertain, as if

testing the sound of the idea. She turns to Jesse, but he can only shrug.

"Maybe."

"I know what our father will tell you," Alice says, sharper. "But I still think he killed her, in his way. And if not her, then Connie."

"No," he says slowly. "I think Connie saw a future without her in it."

Alice blinks, still crying. When he reaches toward her, she draws away.

"It's okay, Jesse," she says. "It's okay. I'm not scared. I'm happy. I'm happy that you came out here and found me, and that I get to keep going for the both of us. Maybe your mother's in there, too. And I could tell her all about you. How you helped me, and how brave you were."

"Maybe so," he says. "I hope that's true, Alice."

She turns away from him, toward the veil.

"All right," she says. "I'm going in there to find out. You go back to the river, Jesse, and take care of our mothers' things. I'll keep going."

"When will you come back?" He doesn't see it happening, but he asks anyway.

"I'll keep you in the loop," she says as she picks her way through the brush.

When he returns to the river, the water that was stirred up by the gators is mirror still. He stands on the bank, his body aching, his wrist a knot of throbbing pain. Their destroyed spells lie to one side of him, Alice's bag to the other.

In the sky, the rift is closing up, dimming as it goes. A cool gray twilight sinks over the trees across the river, then over Jesse himself. A boat's motor whines in the distance.

It's time to go home. He'll have his long chat with the sheriff and lose his driver's license for a year and see the therapist in Greensboro and live his life day-to-day as if none of it happened, but he knows it did, it did happen, even if he doesn't remember every little thing, even if all that future time goes with the rift when it closes. Some pieces stick to him here and there, which will result in moments he knows he's lived through before: when he goes out with his friends to get donuts at four AM and tells them his secrets, when he makes them strong drinks as they silently sob on election night, when someone he loves cries at him in exasperation, "Sometimes, I swear, it's like you're not even here!" and he'll realize he's out in the swamp with Alice again. Little surprises him, but he still yearns for surprises as much as he yearns for connection.

Years later, in Spartina Square, Morgan's nephew dumps some trash into his lap, but Jesse doesn't mind. He keeps it. A buckeye, a cup, a cigarette, a pine needle. Each thing links and couples in the palm of his hand, each whispering to the others. Does he hear them? **Buckeye:** Wish. **Vessel:** you. **Ash smoke:** were. **Needle palm:** here. When he closes his fingers around them, they feel charged, imbued with cosmic weight. It makes him think that Alice has learned her way around, that she's kept him in the loop after all.

Acknowledgments

Writing is presumed to be a solitary act, and though it requires copious amounts of work alone, I owe infinite gratitude to many members of my community, without whom this book would not exist. Firstly, thank you to my rockstar agent, Jessica Felleman, and the team at Jennifer Lyons Literary Agency. Jessica, you saw potential in this manuscript's shabby early stages, and you've championed it since with tenacity and grace. Enormous thanks also to my editor, Bradley Englert, who helped me hone this book into the best possible version of itself, and to the entire Orbit team: Tim Holman, Nick Burnham, Elina Savalia, Brit Hvide, Bryn A. McDonald, Emily Stone, Janine Barlow, Rachel Oestreich, Ellen Wright, Kayleigh Webb, Alex Lencicki, Eric Arroyo, and Blue Guess. Astonished thanks to Lisa Marie Pompilio for the exquisite cover art, and to Danny Hertz for his boundless energy pitching this manuscript in the distant wilds of Los Angeles.

Additional thanks go out to Kelly Link and Anthony Varallo for their continued mentorship. To Kendra Fortmeyer and Rachel Cochran, who read earlier versions of this book and saw the glimmers of what it could be. To Maggie Cooper, for her sage advice on querying. To my Quarantine Queens: Charlie, Elise, Kate, and all their glorious cats. To my Saturday Writeshop group—Joanna, Leanna, and Corinna; though we diverge in genres, we're united in the drafting spirit. To all my kind, brilliant, supportive friends around Young Harris and scattered elsewhere, too many to name here; I'm so fortunate to know all of you.

Also, thanks to my family in the Carolinas, especially my parents, who still amaze me with their unconditional love and support.

And lastly, thanks to Goldsboro, NC, hothouse of my adolescence. We were not always on the best terms, you and I, but in the end I can see I've grown from fertile soil.

Meet the Author

Phil Julian

JEN JULIAN's previous publications include a short story collection, *Earthly Delights and Other Apocalypses* (Press 53, 2018), which was the winner of the Press 53 Award for Short Fiction, as well as work in numerous literary journals, most recently a story in *Third Coast* magazine, which received distinction in *The Best American Short Stories 2023*. Jen holds a PhD in English from the University of Missouri and an MFA in fiction from UNC Greensboro. A 2016 Clarion alumna, she has contributed fiction to both the Sewanee Writers' Conference and the Texas Book Festival. These days, Jen lives in the mountains of northern Georgia with her enormous ginger cat and teaches creative writing at Young Harris College.

if you enjoyed
RED RABBIT GHOST
look out for

THE BLACK HUNGER

by

Nicholas Pullen

*A spine-tingling, queer gothic horror debut where
two men are drawn into an otherworldly spiral
and a journey that will end only when they reach
the darkest part of the human soul.*

*John Sackville will soon be dead. Shadows writhe in the corners of
his cell as he mourns the death of his secret lover and as the gnawing
hunger inside him grows impossible to ignore.*

He must write his last testament before it is too late.

The story he tells will take us to the darkest part of the human soul. It is a tale of otherworldly creatures, ancient cults, and a terrifying journey from the stone circles of Scotland to the icy peaks of Tibet.

It is a tale that will take us to the end of the world.

14 April 1921

I do not have long now. I can feel it. It has crept over me so slowly that, at first, I was hardly aware of it, but it's in my flesh now. A burning, tingling feeling, like when I was bitten by a spider as a child. Spreading through my limbs and my body, inexorably and painfully. I am outwardly in good health, despite the wound's grey festering. But I know, and my minders know, that there is no fore-stalling the inevitable result. And I am always hungry.

The asylum is cold and grey; its stone walls seem to emanate a deeper, more lasting cold than the frigid wind and rain outside my barred window. The darkness is absolute, at all hours of the day. I have a private room at least, and do not have to mingle with the other inmates. That is a small mercy. I interact with no one at all, except my minders, and their clumsy attempts to get the truth from me are hardly companionship. I will never know companionship again. Garrett is dead.

I know what it is you want from me. And I will give it to you in my own time, and on my own terms. If this is to be my last testa-ment, then damn your urgency. I do not fully believe you can stop what is coming now, anyway. But I will help you try. I will tell you what happened. You will have your intelligence, but I will tell my story. And Garrett's.

You don't know who Garrett was. Or, rather, you don't know who he was to me. No one did, so far as I can tell. No one even sus-pected until the end: for a decade. I'm astonished at having hidden a best friend, a brother, a lover in plain sight for all those too short years. And now I will never see him again. Now that you know, I find I do not much care what you think. I have days left to live, if I'm lucky, and have no time or patience for your disapproval or the disapproval of God, or the law, or society at large. How can you punish me now? You talk of sin, but not of love. You talk of disgust, but not of beauty. And the love we had for all those years was beautiful. And perhaps it would have been even more beautiful had it been allowed to flourish in the light. God, if He is interested at all in what Garrett and I did when we were alone, now has bigger problems than us.

My name is John Sackville, and I am the only son of the Earl of Dorset. I have no children, and so the line will die with me. I was born in 1888, and I was the only one of my parents' children to reach adulthood. There were three boys and a girl before me, but they had died of various childhood diseases before I was born. By the time I was born, my parents were in their middle forties, and had long since resigned themselves to childlessness. I was an unexpected blessing that they seized upon fiercely, and I was the recipient of their entire affections; of all that was best in them.

I grew up on my father's estate outside Lyme Regis. Most of my father's peers had great, rambling estates and elaborate country mansions full of pompous grandeur. My grandfather let his father's ornate baroque palace go to ruin not long after he inherited it, and moved his family into a small manor house within our gift in the little village of Dalwood, just over the hill from the decaying old mansion. It was a quiet, unpretentious place. Clean and comfortable, and certainly spacious, but without grandiosity or pompous ornament. This was in keeping with my parents' beliefs, for my grandfather had become a secret Quaker, and though my parents kept up the outward formalities of attendance at the Anglican Church, quietly, behind closed doors, they practised a kinder, gentler version of the faith of their fathers. Perhaps this is why they never judged me, even though I suspect, indeed am almost certain, that they knew.

My father had no interest in London, or politics, or society, or anything but managing his estates and raising his family and keeping to his religion. He kept an enormous diary and would spend the mornings beavering away at it in his study. He was also an amateur naturalist, and would go on long walks around the countryside, through the fruit orchards, often with me in tow, spotting birds and pressing flowers. My parents loved their version of God, loved each other, and they loved me, dearly. We could have spent our entire lives in Dalwood and never felt the need to leave.

And it was a pretty place, nestled in a glen, with enormous oak and chestnut trees shading a brook that flowed under a yellow stone bridge. The air was redolent with the smell of fruit from the orchards all around. All the houses, built in the same warm yellow stone, would glow in the late afternoon summer sunshine, and the light would flash and dance through the leaves of the trees in a wind which carried a faint tang of the sea. The packed earth roads would be warm under my bare feet as I skipped across the bridge looking for chestnuts and oddly coloured rocks. By winter candle-light, as frost glazed the ancient windows, my mother would read me stories by the roaring fire in our parlour, and I would doze off to Walter Scott novels and old collections of Arthurian folk tales, my head in my mother's lap. The village had a timelessness, as though nothing had changed there for hundreds of years, and nothing would change for hundreds of years to come. At Christmas I would be allowed a glass of elderberry wine, or golden cider from the local orchards, and we would make Christmas pudding from the fruits of our own trees. My mother would always remember where the coin had been placed, so invariably my portion contained it. Perhaps it was the accumulation of luck that allowed me to pass in polite society all these years. Perhaps it was what led me to Garrett.

We were near the same age, though Garrett was about a year my senior, which made him seem so much older at an age when nine months is an eternity. I first met him when my father engaged him to give me swimming lessons in the river that ran near our home. He had been born the son of one of my father's tenants, a thin, taciturn, black-haired man, with a dusting of a moustache, and a wife he did not seem to care for very much. Garrett and I grew up playing together in the village and in the fields and forests around it, and my father never made the slightest effort to curtail the friendship. Throughout our childhoods we were hardly aware of the class difference between us. That cruel truth would be made plain to us later. In those early days it was hardly more than my gentle mockery of his ponderous, cumbersome West Country accent, which he never lost, in later life, despite everything that happened.

He grew up stocky, with flaming auburn hair and bright blue eyes that would crinkle into his face when he smiled, which he did often. He had dimpled, pudgy cheeks, a thick beard that came to him early, and no discernible resemblance to his father of any kind. By the time we were both fourteen, it was rather obvious. And to hide his shame, Garrett's father would beat him with a belt, imagining all sorts of crimes that deserved such punishment. I found out this secret pain one evening the summer I turned fifteen. We were playing around in the vine-covered, collapsing ruins of my family's old estate, and he broke down in tears and confessed everything his father was doing to torture him. He sat on a low stone wall and he buried his face in his hands, weeping in that choked, broken way some men do, as though they would rather die than be seen to weep. I put my arms around his shoulders, and I kissed him once on the forehead. It seemed the natural thing to do. He looked up at me in shock, and I realised what I had done. But before I could cover my instinctive action with some plausible indifference, he was kissing me. His cheeks were wet with his tears, his lips were dry and cracked and his face rubbed mine raw with its thick, bristly stubble, already grown back from the morning's shave. But I kissed him back with all the passion I could muster from my frail frame.

It took us months to figure out the mechanics of love for men like us. Mostly in the ruins of the old estate where we knew we would never be disturbed. I would take him inside me, and my knees would be covered in red lines from the grass where I knelt. He would take me into his mouth, afterwards, when he was spent, and finish me then. But often I didn't need him to. It was enough to have him inside me. Sometimes, as though he felt guilty, it would be his turn to kneel. And I would do it because I knew he enjoyed it, too. But I was happiest when I was beneath him. And afterwards we would lie naked in the grass in the gathering summer dusk, a blanket discarded beside us, bathed in each other's sweat and with our arms draped around each other. I felt safe. I felt home.

My father had avoided sending me to boarding school as a child, as most children of my class were forced to do. The Empire relies for much of its strength on brutalising children in the system of organised violence and torture that we call the Public School System. The children are torn from their parents' sides, and thrown into a world of cold showers, casual cruelty and crushing loneliness, where they learn the delicate ropes of hierarchy and obedience, when to give, when to take, when to punish and when to accept punishment. They are stripped from love and safety and forged in the crucible of brutal conformity and rote Latin learning into good little psychopaths who can be trusted with the governance of the Empire. He put it off for as long as he could (most children were sent away before they were ten) and I had a succession of wonderful governesses and tutors, but eventually it couldn't be postponed any longer. I cried when my father called me into his study and told me that I had to spend the next four years at Rugby School, far away in Warwickshire. He embraced me, and dried my tears, and told me that I would be home for Christmas, and that all would be well, and that he and my mother would always love me.

"Is there anything I can do that might make it easier, John? Anything at all?" I shook my head and sniffed. "Perhaps you'd like Garrett to come with you? You're allowed one servant, after all. I suspect he would do the job well, and he would remind you of home." He looked at me rather significantly when he said this, and I felt a sinking feeling of discovery. But to this day I do not know if he knew or suspected anything at all, or if I merely imagined it. I suspect the former.

"Yes. I would like that."

I told Garrett that evening as we sat together, dangling our legs over the little stone bridge in the centre of the village. I wanted to hold his hand, as I sometimes did when we were alone in the ruins, but we knew enough even then to know from the fiery sermons of the vicar that we could not do so where we might be seen. I was terrified that, despite everything, he would balk at going so far from the only home we'd ever known, but he only smiled and looked in my eyes, and said:

"I'd go anywhere, sir, so long as it's with you." When he called me sir it was with a quiet, gentle mockery that only I understood, and an ironic knowledge of how things really stood between us. It made my heart sing with the hilarity of it.

And so we went to Rugby. I lived in my rooms, and Garrett lived in the servants' quarters, but he was with me in the evenings. We couldn't do anything untoward. There was no privacy to be had. And Garrett and I learned quickly under the cruel mockery of the other students and the other servants to hide in public whatever intimacy we possessed from our childhoods.

But sometimes Garrett and I could contrive to be alone with one another. And after a while, with his pay Garrett rented a little room above a pub in town from a landlady who didn't ask questions, and I would give him some of my allowance from Father to help with the rent, and we would be alone on Saturdays and Sundays. Sometimes for the whole day, if we were lucky. Garrett would tell me casually about the mockery he faced from the other servants, but after so many beatings from his father it did not faze him in the slightest, and he mocked their pomposity and their crude Essex accents to me as viciously as they mocked him, to my raucous laughter. He was a talented mimic, and had a devastating wit.

I didn't need to study. Mother had already drilled me in Latin and Greek, and I was well ahead of the other boys in my form. And when one day when we were sixteen Garrett expressed an interest in what I was learning, I began to tutor him myself, and smuggled him some textbooks from the lower forms, and before long he proved an astonishingly quick student, to whom languages, ancient and modern, came with uncanny ease. He eventually became a considerable classic in his own right. I admired him more and more as the years went by. I always will.

"If you'd been born with land, you'd be the talk of the school."
I wrapped my arms around his neck and pulled him away from his
Virgil for a kiss. He smiled up at me.

"If I'd been born with land, I'd have been born far away from
you, and I would never have known you at all, sir. There can only be
one Lord of the Manor."

"You don't have to call me that when we're alone." I grinned.

"Don't I … sir?" He grinned again. Then he pushed me away. "I
guess that's just the way of it. God doles out the titles before we're
born, and the rest of us suffer what we must."

"I wish it wasn't this way." This was the first time we had ever
addressed the subject directly.

"Wishing won't make it so, now, will it, sir? We have to live in
the world we've got. And we're happy enough, far as I can see. I
could be in the workhouse, or back on David's farm." He shud-
dered. He had stopped calling his father anything but David a few
years before.

"Still, it's bloody stupid that you are where you are, and we are
where we are. You'd have a brilliant career ahead of you."

"Well, your career will just have to be brilliant enough for the
both of us." He stood up and pushed me against the wall. "As long
as you and I always know the score … sir." His breath was on my
neck, and I was pinned against the coarse oak boards, panting with
anticipation. He whispered in my ear:

"*Pedicabo ego vos et irrumabo*, sir." Then he flipped me around,
and with a quick pull at both of our belts he was in me, and I forgot
all the injustice, the deception, the risk. He was in me, and that
was all that mattered. It's all that ever will. And you can keep your
judgements to yourself.